Tony Bond £3

Penguin Books
To a Dubious Salvation

Etienne Leroux was born in South Africa in 1922. He
studied law at the University of Stellenbosch but decided
to farm in Koffiefontein, where he now owns a 42,000-acre
sheep ranch. After a period in Paris in the 1950s he
returned to South Africa to help found the avant-garde
literary group, the 'Sestigers'. His first novel was published
in 1956 and since then he has continued to write novels.
Seven Days at the Silbersteins, which won the Herzog
Prize in 1964, was the first to be translated into English
from the Afrikaans. Etienne Leroux lives on his ranch with
his artist wife and their three children.

Etienne Leroux

To a Dubious Salvation

a trilogy of fantastical novels

Seven Days at the Silbersteins
and *One for the Devil* was translated from
the Afrikaans by Charles Eglington

The Third Eye was translated from the
Afrikaans by Amy Starke

Penguin Books

Penguin Books Ltd, Harmondsworth, Middlesex, England
Penguin Books Australia Ltd, Ringwood, Victoria, Australia

Seven Days at the Silbersteins first published in South Africa 1962
First published in Great Britain by W. H. Allen 1968
The Third Eye first published in South Africa 1966
First published in Great Britain by W. H. Allen 1969
One for the Devil first published in South Africa 1968
First published in Great Britain by W. H. Allen 1969

This trilogy published in Penguin Books 1972
Seven Days at the Silbersteins copyright © Human & Rousseau
(Pty) Ltd, 1964
The Third Eye copyright © Human & Rousseau (Pty) Ltd, 1968
One for the Devil copyright © Human & Rousseau (Pty) Ltd, 1968

Made and printed in Great Britain by
Hazell Watson & Viney Ltd, Aylesbury, Bucks
Set in Linotype Juliana

Contents

'Mr Leroux writes his books in static scenes; between them he allows his camera to track rapidly and wildly around his location. The influence of the cinema is clear – not the conventional cinema but the cinema of Robbe-Grillet or Godard . . . Mr Leroux will not find an instant audience; his novels are too original for that. They tease, they trouble, they elude. His audience will be the audience that only a good writer can merit, an audience which assembles slowly from far away in ones and twos; while the big book club motor-coaches hurtle down the highway toward oblivion, the rumour spreads that here an addition will be found to the literature of our time' – Graham Greene in LIFE

Seven Days at the Silbersteins

No such farm as Welgevonden exists.
All the characters are imaginary.
The events are improbable.

Contents

For Marianna and Alexander Podlashuc

'We are not alone,' said Jock Silberstein. 'Every day we understand more and more our collective share in the fate of humanity. Solitude is the longing, the pain inherent in contemplating the false image of the individual that is vanishing piecemeal with our new understanding.'

Chapter One

Dance of the Rich

The Van Eedens felt that it was about time for their only son
to marry someone who, in some respects, was worthy of their
standing. The young man had had, thank God, a sophisticated
enough upbringing to realize that love should enter into the
matter only in the last instance. The name Salome was mentioned
and, after frank consideration, she was declared acceptable. An
uncle of the scion in question was chosen to do the necessary
spadework and, where necessary, to be helpful in this delicate
matter of a social contract against the background of unpredictable
human relationships. The name of the uncle was J. J. van Eeden,
a bachelor and boulevardier; the name of the young man,
Henry.

They were now on their way to the Silbersteins where they
would spend a week. J.J. wore a tweed suit with accessories such
as pipe, tobacco, silk handkerchief and cravat. In his immediate
vicinity there was the aroma of pine needles. Henry drove the
Riley with a guilelessness in which it was difficult to distinguish
between luck and skill. The Western Province landscape of vineyards, mountains, trees and cosy little rivers all contributed to the
décor. They soon approached the estate which lay at the top of a
valley.

The entrance gates consisted of two huge pillars painted white,
on either side of which, equally white, painted circular walls
embraced, like two arms, the earthly possessions of the Silbersteins as far as the horizon. The name of the farm was inscribed
on a plaque of stainless steel, the letters of iron, the type Gothic:
Welgevonden. The road to the house was tarred and ran in calculated curves between old Cape-Dutch homesteads on one side
and old Cape-Dutch stables and sheds on the other. The doors

looked like stinkwood, the roofs were freshly thatched and re-paired, the gables curved gradually to rounded tops and were decorated with grape motifs, Ganymedes and cornucopias. The gable of the mansion itself was a poem in curls, undulations and whitewash. There were interesting corners and alleyways that led nowhere, and little ladders of old wood that indicated lofts, and huge cement blocks with crossbeams that formed vine arbours, and heavy wooden doors with heavy bronze handles and orna-mental knockers. There were large palm trees, cypresses, oak trees, loquat trees, peach trees, beeches, rubber trees and walnut trees. There was bougainvillea, cascades of purple and red falling over small walls that appeared suddenly from nowhere and ended suddenly against lanterns of cast iron. There were footpaths that wound their way impassably through overhanging growth, a tennis court festooned with climbers, a roller in the corner, a tattered net, a completely overgrown pagoda, and there were ar-tistic little fountains of irregular shape with gnomes and crazy little walls. The Riley came to a graceful stop and J.J. and Henry got out, feeling slightly lost, as one is all too inclined to feel on arriving suddenly at someone else's homestead – a moment of reflection, of depression, of what am I doing here? where am I going?

An ornamental keyhole plate with a leaf motif gleamed in the late afternoon sun on the front door. 'It looks like a womb' said J.J. He lifted the heavy dragon-shaped knocker and rapped with the appropriate firmness : not, on the one hand, too boisterous nor, on the other, too unassuming – as befitted a man of standing who had been initiated since childhood in the civilized musicality of announcing himself. First the top half of the door opened and a Coloured girl in a starched cap, and a starched white collar that made her narrow, half-oriental little face seem even narrower, looked merrily at the two men who, with proper lack of interest, were blinding themselves in the rays of the setting sun. Then the bottom half of the door opened and they strolled under the bar-oque door-light into a passage where a distinctive interior pano-rama caught their stealthy attention, before they would presently turn right to the drawing room, on the heels of the sideways-dancing little maid. Blue and white tiles stretched the length of the hall to a bay window which let in, through its small, elegant panes, a violet light. Four Persian carpets of finely woven silk with intricate flower patterns, covered the entire floor in squares and oblongs. A Cape armoire of yellow-wood, wooden feathers on the curve at the top, stood against a wall to the right; a convexo-concave wall cupboard to the left; a small sculpture by Epstein on a small table farther down with, on either side, a pair of hide-thong stools of Quaker simplicity.

Everyone stopped talking when the two men entered the draw-ing room – that moment of portentous silence when the most accurate summings-up are made and a delicate balance is sought for the imaginary line between rude indifference and subservient respect. On a corner stool, her arms folded on her lap, sat the ugliest woman Henry had ever seen. A square chin, adorned by a black mole from which a single hair curled, aimed in his direction beneath the visor of two small ebony eyes that watched him and would follow him for the rest of the evening. Beside her stood a slim woman dressed in a black sequined evening gown, her neck white as a swan's, her breasts half-exposed, her eyes alight with intense pleasure as she approached J.J. with outstretched arms and draped herself around his hand.

'J.J.,' she said. 'At long last. Are you tired? Are you thirsty?' From a table nearby she handed him a glass filled with light white wine. 'Someone will show you to your rooms soon. But first a drink. Do you prefer red or white? I've already had too much, but what else is there to do at this time of the evening, when the sun sets and one is overcome with boredom. .. Is this Henry?'

Henry was introduced to Mrs Silberstein. The Alice-in-Won-derland duchess mumbled something from her chair and he was introduced to old Mrs Silberstein. She seized him with both her hands, pulled him nearer and suddenly let him go. 'You are small and thin. I thought you were taller. Runtish little Goy.' 'Mummy, mummy,' said slim Mrs Silberstein, still clinging firmly to J.J. 'Jock ... Henry,' and Jock came forward, six foot four, immacu-late in dinner jacket, his face aglow, his hands broad yet soft as he pressed Henry's sensitively as a pianist. 'Miss Silberstein, Miss

Silberstein,' and two mousy little women bobbed up and down on their chairs to one side in a corner, encircled by bottles, enlivened by light wine which they drank like water from goblets.

'Well,' said Jock. 'Now you have met the whole Silberstein ménage.'

'Except Salome,' said one of the little women and both of them doubled up on their little chairs with exuberant pleasure.

'That's true,' said Jock and put his arm round Henry's shoulder, making him feel like a child being embraced by his father. 'Come and sit with me.' He peered out of the window. 'Is that your car? Beautiful, beautiful.' He dug Henry in the ribs and suddenly fell silent.

J.J. and slim Mrs Silberstein, in a circle of light under a Martinus Smith candelabra, were enjoying the wine and each other's company while the rest, the duchess with prying eyes, and the two drab women with jolly poses, followed every one of Henry's movements and reactions.

'It's a lovely house,' said Henry.

'Bought fifteen years ago from the original owners,' said Jock. 'Spent a hundred thousand rand simply to get the place into shape. Do you like the wine?'

He took up one of the bottles, three-sided, with the name, Welgevonden Riesling, on a triangular label.

'The Welgevonden wines are coming into their own. This same riesling we sold in an ordinary bottle at forty cents, and there was no market for it. Now . . .' he put the bottle down, 'three-sided and at a hundred and fifty cents it sells like hot cakes. It's the psychological approach. Advertisements, advertisements and gimmicks, and then you can bring a place like Welgevonden into its own.' He looked approvingly at Henry. 'I am glad you take an interest in old Cape-Dutch homesteads. So many of the younger people find the places uncomfortable. We try to establish a way of life here – as in the old Cape. A liberal way of life, civilized and stimulating. We have guests every evening, you will see tonight. Every evening of the week. This place is alive. Something, something is alive.' He gestured with his hands. 'Something is alive and as long as there is life, Welgevonden is alive. Nothing is allowed to come to a standstill; there must always be something doing. Listen! Do you hear that?' In the distance Henry heard the drone of a machine. 'It's a big diesel engine that supplies the lights. We get electricity from the city, but it is supplemented by our own installation. Welgevonden must always have something that works. That is the heart of Welgevonden beating. When that engine stops another begins. It empties the swimming pool, purifies the water, and fills it again. When the pump stops, the fans on the ceiling work to circulate the atmosphere. When they stop, the bottling plant in the cellars begins and so it goes on.' He glowed with pleasure. 'You must come round the farm with me tomorrow. The tractors roar, the brewery drones, the trucks growl, the milk cans clatter, the waters murmur, Welgevonden's workmen sing... Wait, listen!' A peacock skirled its death-cry from the direction of the garden. Jock emptied his glass and banged it down hard on the table. Then he fell suddenly into a melancholy silence, his shoulders hunched, his chin on his hand, his elbow on his knees. 'Goy,' said the duchess. 'Oh, shut up, Mother,' said Jock. The two drab Misses Silberstein became more and more intoxicated and giggled musically. J.J. and slim Mrs Silberstein looked calculatingly at each other. Henry toyed with his wine and peered round the room.

He was twenty-seven years of age and already caught in a pattern of behaviour over which he had no control and over which he desired no control. Except for love, he believed in everything: the value of religion, beauty, the influence of nature on the human being, the state, the liberal conscience, the future of humankind, the imperishability of symbols, good order, goodwill, charity, security and man as the perfection of divine creation. It was time for him to marry, have children and perpetuate himself. Lovelessness was replaced by universal compassion; love was selfish. Henry van Eeden was a flawless little robot, deliberately created by the sexual act and properly conditioned. He would be mated with Salome and all he knew about Salome was what J.J. had said about her: she had dark eyes.

Someone touched his arm. It was Jock. 'Sarie will show you your room.' He followed the servant girl down the passage to a room where a copper bed with hangings stood exactly in the centre and where a single wardrobe of Cape Flemish design awaited his clothes. She opened a blind by pulling a small chain which set a catch *à la Provence* in motion. She pushed up the window and the bosky garden obscured the view. She stood in the doorway, swaying, waiting, and when he said nothing she closed the door softly behind her and trotted off to the old Dutch-Cape kitchen.

'A pleasant young man,' said Jock.
'Well brought up,' said slim Mrs Silberstein.
'Slim and elegant,' said the two drab Misses Silberstein.
'Small,' said the duchess. 'Impotent.'
'Seven days,' said J.J. 'That ought to be enough.'
They touched glasses.
'The guests will be here at any moment,' said slim Mrs Silberstein. 'We just have time enough to change.'
She looked longingly at J.J.

The drawing room emptied and then filled again as a horde of servant girls in starched blue dresses and starched collars, their small faces delicate, their mouths toothless, began to put the room in order, polishing, sweeping and then filling it with all sorts of snacks : olives, fruit, chicken, turkey, fish rolls, asparagus, herring, caviar and tinkling glasses.

In his room Henry put on his dinner jacket and lit a cigarette. Outside the light-engine droned with a diesel-throb. He sat erect and stiff in a stinkwood chair, and without any outward sign of emotion watched a bee trying to get through a window pane.

II

A light tap on the door, an announcement that the guests were already assembled and Henry made his way to the transformed drawing room which, blindingly lighted, contained a moving mass of human beings. He appeared in the doorway and everyone fell silent. They looked at the angel-faced young man in his black dinner jacket, a cigarette in his left hand, his right hand at his

side. Everyone was dressed in ordinary clothes : slim Mrs Silberstein in English tweeds and low-heeled shoes, the duchess with a
scarf round her head and a shawl over her shoulders, Jock in a
hacking-jacket, J.J. without a jacket and a silk cravat tucked into
his shirt, the rest of the guests relaxed in casual, everyday clothes.
Then they all resumed their conversations.

The duchess clawed Henry's arm. '_Sefer nashim, Hilkot issure
biah ve-kaleë behemah._' She looked meaningfully at him and disappeared in the crowd.

He heard the name Salome time and time again, but when he
looked up there were usually a number of girls together, all with
dark eyes.

He found himself among a group of men who took him with
them to a small bar in the corner where each poured himself a
stiff tot of brandy (Welgevonden Special). Someone confused
Indian tonic with soda, but they all ascribed the taste to a special
quality peculiar to the estate brandy – stimulating, bittersweet, a
little something about the aftertaste. They snuffed their balloon
glasses.

Henry was introduced to Dr Johns of Bishopscourt, Judge
O'Hara of Bishopscourt, Sir Henry Mandrake of Bishopscourt.
They spoke about water skiing, tuna fishing, cricket and Mar-
garet Armstrong-Jones. Women joined them and were encircled
by their arms. Someone served olives and asparagus; someone else
rissoles; someone else chicken and turkey. Henry danced with an
Italian contessa (six years in the country) who admitted shyly to
him that she had six children. 'How marvellous,' said Henry. 'I
feel like a rabbit,' she said. 'Bloody shmok,' whispered the duchess
in his ear and tickled his cheek with her mole. They forced him
into a discussion on art : Tretchikoff and others. Someone explained to him the symbolism of the orchid on the step, the fresh
drop of water, the tattered ornaments and the cigarette butts. Pleasure was shorter even than the life of a picked flower, the existence
of a drop of water. A drunk, blonde girl pulled Henry back to the
dance floor, teased him with pelvic movements, smeared his collar
with her lipstick, prepared herself (through him) for someone
else, questioned him about Salome and disappeared in the arms

of a pukka-moustache who talked of nothing but fishing, sport and sex.

'*Nebelah*,' hissed the duchess and drifted away into the throng.

One of the drab Misses Silberstein beckoned him to go and sit next to her.

'Salome,' she said, 'likes flowers and the veld. Early in the morning, when the dew is still on the grass, she wanders through the valley in a light dress, like a nymph. She loves animals and sings like a nightingale. She is delicate and furtive as a small wild creature. Speak too loudly to her, and she is gone on the morning wind.'

The other drab Miss Silberstein came sweetly nearer and whispered in his other ear.

'Salome is soft and wonderful. Treat her tenderly, initiate her with love . . .' She stopped suddenly and brought her hand to her mouth. 'Initiate her with understanding in the land of . . .'

Suddenly they began to giggle and, giggling, withdrew into a drab cocoon.

Henry had a habit of tugging his ears; he tugged first one and then the other. But he did it only when deep in thought, as now. He was about to experience an intimation of death – not completely, but merely by way of vague indications. It did not invoke any feeling of fear; he simply began to wonder what it would feel like not to be there any longer. He tried hard, but he himself remained always present; he saw his own corpse, the grave, the distracted family and he had an intimation of time passing. He tried to imagine to himself what it would be like to arrive in heaven. A merciful state of perfect harmony. Then he thought about how disillusioning it must be when, *in extremis*, one closed one's eyes, waited and nothing happened. Both conceptions were difficult, too much for him at the moment, and he turned back to the living, who had become considerably more boisterous.

'Why don't you move round among the people?' asked Jock who had come and sat down beside him, his shoulders as broad as a mountain in his Harris tweed jacket. 'Why don't you drink?' He gave him a glass of brandy. 'Do you know the people?' He pointed to a man declaiming amusing nonsense to an appreciative audience. 'Judge O'Hara is a great friend of mine. He is an outstanding jurist but, alas, a philistine. So are they all, my friends here, good at their professions, and rich as well. Do you think it's a disgrace to be rich? Do you doubt their integrity? Do rich people have no integrity? Life is not as simple at that. I see that you must get rid of certain fixed ideas.' He was somewhat aggressive. 'Come on, tell me – does good family count more than wealth? What do you mean by good family? People who for generations have achieved something for the community? People who jealously protect certain codes of good breeding in their own circle?' His aggressiveness had subsided. 'Do you think us vulgar? I am rich and I am just as proud of my achievement of wealth as you are of your pedigree. That's your first lesson. You must get used to wealth and to the the wealthy.'

'I was thinking about death,' said Henry. 'I have nothing against you and your guests.' He suddenly began to feel the heat and wished he could get rid of his dinner jacket.

They walked together between the whirling couples.

'You look rather unsuitable in your tuxedo,' said Jock, 'but it singles you out, makes you more interesting. I assume you are an individualist.'

'No,' said Henry. 'It was simply a misunderstanding.'

'Who do you want to talk to and what about?' asked Jock. 'About pedigrees, castration, purity and impurity, damage, divorce, primogeniture, feasts, inheritances, the intermarriage of groups belonging to different races, leprosy, marriage, murder, food, the poor, prostitution, the cultivation of beards, slave labour, theft, trustees, religion . . .? You have only to name the subject and I can pick out somebody here who will give you the necessary information, to the best of his ability, which is not trifling, if one takes into consideration the fact that so many people are present here who have been successful in their different vocations. And, mark you, together with that, have gained material rewards for their ability. Or would you prefer an impecunious expert? In that case, perhaps later in the week.' Someone tugged Jock's arm. 'That was a pleasant conversation. We must talk again'; and he left Henry stranded in the middle of the floor where a drunk but sweet-smelling woman of advanced age embraced the young man ardently.

Jock returned, called her aside and whispered something in her ear. She turned back to Henry, linked her arm with his and wandered with him to the window from which they looked into the lighted garden.

'One lives in the land of the living, one mustn't think constantly of death,' she remarked. 'Life is so interesting. Take my husband, for example – that one over there in the corner, the one with a white beard. Sir Henry Mandrake. Sir Henry and I have been all over the world: Hong Kong, Hawaii, Greece, Majorca, Venice and Capri. We have seen all the most beautiful works of art and Sir Henry is a keen collector, although he cannot appreciate the latest abstractions. Sir Henry's life was full and he suffers with his heart. Dr Johns is our family doctor and he has informed me confidentially that Sir Henry must be careful. Death is round the corner, but do you think that Sir Henry goes and sits aside in a corner, like somebody we know, full of death thoughts? Look at him.' Sir Henry had his arm around a slim girl. Her eyes were dark; her skin white as cream; she looked like a madonna. (Was it Salome?) Sir Henry's face was blood-red, the veins on his temples purple and distended; he fought for breath; his eyes were wild; his movements jerky. 'Life and again Life is Sir Henry's attitude. Death, where is thy sting?'

She looked with great solemnity at the young man. Her bone structure was impressive; her lacquered make-up had been fashioned by an expert into a beautiful mask which began slowly to dissolve as she started to cry; first the blue eye shadow, then the rouge on her cheeks, then the powder which began to disintegrate everywhere. 'Oh, the despondency of youth!' She seized his arm. 'Live! Live! Dance and be gay; the whole world awaits you. Live, live, live!' And she buried her face on his chest, while her Junoesque coiffure began slowly to fall apart and small combs, hairpins and clasps fell one by one to the floor with the sound of drops of water.

Henry put his arm round her and looked up into the radiant faces of slim Mrs Silberstein, J.J. and Jock, who waved to him with gay approval across the room from a fireplace with yellow-wood screens.

A little later, when he was again alone in the middle of the room, with another glass of brandy that had been shoved into his hand by a passing guest, someone attracted his attention. It was Judge O'Hara, who was with Dr Johns.

'Jock tells me that you're very much interested in leprosy,' said Dr Johns. 'Isn't that rather morbid?'

'And adultery, murder, impurity, prostitution and theft,' added Judge O'Hara. 'I must admit, that's an unusual interest for some-one of your age.'

'To begin with leprosy,' said Dr Johns, 'I won't bore you with its medical aspects. The chances are very slight that you will ever catch it in this part of Africa, or ever encounter it. It's evidently the psychological-moral aspect that interests you.' He cleared his throat and smoked and drank for a while before he resumed. 'According to Moses Maimonides, it is clearly stated by the old philosophers that leprosy is a punishment for gossipping. The malady begins in the walls of the house. If the transgressor stops his gossip, the object is achieved. If he continues, the disease spreads to his bed and furniture; if that still doesn't scare him off, the disease attacks his clothing and his body. Since leprosy is con-tagious, everyone avoids the individual and the object is achieved, the slanderer is rendered harmless. I think there is tremendous wisdom concealed behind that reasoning.'

'Very interesting,' said Judge O'Hara, and they gazed at the walls of the drawing room, at the impure in little groups, their mouths moving and drawing the disease from the walls to the furniture. They fingered their clothes and it was as if the whole room were filled with lepers. 'The entire world,' said Judge O'Hara, 'the entire world is infected with impurity.'

'Purification is effected by cedarwood, hyssop, scarlet thread and two birds. The reason for this, as given in the Midrashic sayings, is obscure and not altogether acceptable.'

Dr Johns and Judge O'Hara had forgotten about Henry and, continuing their conversation on the subject, they moved towards the bar.

III

It seemed to Henry that something had suddenly happened to the house: the people were still talking, dancing and gabbling, but it was as if some other quality had been added to the noise. It seemed to him like a gramophone beginning to run down. He could not shake off the impression and he stood with his head tilted, listening intently. Then he realized suddenly what had happened. The diesel light-generator had stopped. But almost immediately the quality of the noises changed again and, although there had been a change of pitch, there was life again. In the garden another engine had started up, with a faster beat, with more revolutions to the minute – the pump that had taken over from the generator and was slowly at work emptying the swimming pool, filtering the water and filling the pool again.

The brandy was having an effect on Henry, who found that he was more readily able to join the rich in their dance. He danced with slim Mrs Silberstein and adapted himself to the rhythm that she subtly suggested. She told him about Jock, who did not always understand her and who drove her frantic with his moments of insane jealousy. Henry left the leprous Mrs Silberstein and danced with a madonna of the dark eyes who looked as fresh and pretty as a lily. 'Are you Salome?' he asked, as she gave herself willingly to his arms. She suddenly began to laugh, softly at first, biting her lip repeatedly, then louder and more musically as her feelings overcame her. 'Oh, Henry,' she said, helpless in the grip of her laughter. The next moment he found himself dancing with another dark-eyed maiden who, with strict decorum, and a more restrained rhythm, confined him haughtily to the joys of a more classical measure. He dared not ask *her* and left her in silence when the dance came to a sober end. He danced in succession with dark-eyed female forms, with skins white as milk or brown as old wood, who led him through all the nuances of the dance, who bewitched him with all sorts of movements that stirred his senses, who teased him with an endless combination of personalities, who invited him with becoming immodesty into their erotic heavens. Then he came across J.J., alone this time, while Jock hugged slim Mrs. Silberstein to him like a bear and danced her, protesting, away.

'Which one is Salome, J.J.?' Henry asked him.

J.J. did not quite catch the question, as he was absorbed in following slim Mrs Silberstein with his eyes.

Henry had to repeat the question.

J.J. could not believe his ears. Then he suddenly laughed and prodded Henry in the ribs.

'You're a rare one,' he said. He studied Henry as if seeing him for the first time. 'Why did you put on a dinner jacket? It's a bit conspicuous. This is hardly the time and place for all sorts of eccentricities.'

Slim Mrs Silberstein had succeeded, in a quite remarkable manner, of ridding herself of Jock. She suddenly rested her forehead on his shoulder, pressed her body against his and, to the measure of the music which had imperceptibly increased in tempo, compelled him to spin her round and round, counter-clockwise, until at last their dazzling speed merged them together in the spin. Her hair could be seen waving like a black scarf from the vortex of their movement; the two faces, male and female, were at first recognizable and then became neuter. Round and round, more and more wildly they moved, until the movement decreased and flagged and at the centre of the vortex the poor masculine brute suddenly materialized and came to a standstill, while she herself slowly finished whirling around him, in widening circles, until she reached J.J. who, with perfect timing and to the changed measure, took her in his arms and disappeared, waltzing.

Jock walked stiffly up to Henry and placed his hand on the young man's shoulder.

'She has an obsession about counting things,' he said. 'She cannot weep. She can knot an aiguillette in fifty ways.' He looked anxiously in Henry's face for understanding and then turned his back on him disconsolately.

But Henry had seen the fear in his eyes and was considering it carefully, as was his habit of devoting his undivided attention to every phenomenon. However improbable it might sound, fear, next to love, was one of the emotions he knew least. Anxiety, yes : the feeling that gripped one suddenly without cause, which sprang from deep in the unconscious, which made no sense; that, but not fear, because fear required a danger-object and if one had had a protected upbringing, were free from ambition, surrounded by the security of material possessions, supported by one's common sense, protected by one's God, then one could avoid all danger-objects. It should be added that Henry had no knowledge of war and other forms of violence, had never been threatened by any calamity, had no inkling of the subtle threat of the modern state, did not believe in the devil. Faith and love were almost synonymous; to extol a thing meant also to love it. Henry *believed* in his God and this meant simply that God was there to protect him. To that exent he was accordingly as innocent as a child and shared with a child ignorance of love and the limitation of faith to a restricted : 'I believe.' Henry was going to be mated in marriage with Salome and, as slim Mrs Silbestein had rightly remarked : 'His innocence must be destroyed. How otherwise dare he marry ?' And how otherwise could one be corrupted than by meeting as many people as possible?

Someone barred his way. It was the duchess. He tried first to start a conversation with her about the pleasant party, the charming guests, the Silbersteins' interesting way of life; but she stood squarely in front of him, fast as a rock, her little eyes fixed with implacable hate on him. In the midst of all the unpredictable people she was the only steadfast object, with her feet in *veldskoen* placed wide apart, her rustic face framed appropriately by a milkmaid's head-cloth, her contempt real and consistent. He stopped talking suddenly and felt strangely relieved by her single obsession. Here at least was something uncomplicated and understandable. He noticed that she found some difficulty in finding the apt word, and then it came : '*Schlemiel!*'

Most people had stopped dancing and were moving from group to group to impart to one another the surprising fancies of the moment. Lady Mandrake appeared beside Henry and linked her arm with his. She was rather unsteady on her feet and used him as a prop while she counterpointed the conversation with sympathetic movements. Her mask had in the meantime been restored so that only her eyes and lips moved.

'I have spoken to Sir Henry about you and it would be a pleasure for us if you would come and visit us at Shangrila.' She smiled at the duchess: the mask creased and recomposed itself. 'Sir Henry is interested in young people. Young people are his life. He rejuvenates himself in the company of the young.'

'Ah,' said Sir Henry, who had appeared beside them, without a mask, his face lined and crumpled. He bowed to the duchess: 'Mrs Silberstein.' His bow tie, adorning his shirt front like a butterfly, colourfully matched the colours of his face. 'Ah, Mrs Silberstein, what a pleasant party.' He nodded to Henry and something stirred in his tired, cloudy eyes as he regarded the fresh young man. He pointed his finger and moved it to and fro.

Dr Johns and Judge O'Hara also joined them, white as lepers. 'The young Mrs Silberstein and Mr van Eeden . . .' began Dr Johns slanderously, noticed the duchess, and fell silent.

'Dear guests !' Jock's voice was suddenly heard loudly above the sound of the other voices, and he rapped twice with his knuckles on the old Dutch sixteen-legged stinkwood *achterhuis* table.

The drunken-cultured noise subsided to a cultured, disciplined silence.

IV

'Dear friends,' said Jock, 'it's perhaps already clear to you that we have not assembled tonight merely for sociable reasons, but that we have gathered to celebrate the union of two pleasant young people.'

He smiled in Henry's direction, who was now surrounded by a group of blushing, laughing girls.

'I mean, of course, Salome and Henry.'

Everyone nodded affably at Henry and began clapping softly. Then slim Mrs Silberstein and J. J. joined Henry.

'On occasions like this it is usual to eulogize the good qualities of the couple, but I am not going to do that. I am going to point out to the young couple the qualities of their good friends, who have gathered tonight. But I am not going to specify those qualities, I am simply going to ask them to keep their eyes, hearts and minds open. I shall say only : 'Salome and Henry, look around you and become aware of your friends.'

Everyone smiled whitely at Henry, surrounded by the girls.

Jock tapped again on the table and two servant girls opened the door. There was a slight scuffle and then the two drab Misses Silberstein appeared carrying between them on a tray an enormous cake. They carried it to the sixteen-legged table, on which they placed it carefully and disappeared bashfully into the background. On top of the cake were two figurines, male and female – two faceless little dolls representing Salome and Henry. Impelled by the growing crowd around him, Henry moved to the table where he accepted a silver knife offered him by Jock, and then turned round for the first time to identify his life's partner. He looked at the dark-eyed girls, at the slim Mrs Silberstein, J.J., Lady Mandrake, Sir Henry, and all the others and he waited for his loved one to come forward. But all at once the whole giggling group swarmed around him and in no time at all the cake had been cut into pieces and distributed among friends.

Everyone clapped him on his shoulder to express their affection and he was kissed on cheeks, mouth and temples by lips dexterous with every possible emotion. Then the party was resumed and Henry was left alone holding a piece of cake on which a headless girl had already crumbled to icing sugar.

The party became wilder, because it was nearing its end. Henry was invited to every pukka place by people known and unknown to him, supplied with a list of business houses where he could obtain the best fishing tackle, motor-boats and frogman equipment, given tips about gold-mining stock and horses, and overloaded with addresses in case he should feel disposed for further appointments (with many dark eyes full of promise).

Sir Henry Mandrake urged him to forget his death wish; Dr Johns, his morbid interest in diseases; Judge O'Hara, his obsession with all forms of social deviation; and Jock, his prejudice against the rich. Once, when everything was still in full swing, he paid a short visit to the bathroom and on his return found the drawing room empty. From the garden came the last voices of the departing guests. He was about to leave when he noticed the duchess sitting alone on a chair, her hands folded in her lap, her small dark eyes fixed on him.

'Schnorer!' she said, but she was tired, sleepy, old and vanquished. Her little eyes had become dull and she was on the brink of losing consciousness.

In his room the young man lay exactly in the middle of the double bed, sunk down in foam rubber, in the light from a phallic sconce which, supported by three legs, first hexagonal, then top-shaped, then spiralled, culminated in a bronze candlestick, from where a repitition of the foregoing design was resumed to end with an imitation candle of fake wax, the plastic frame electrically lit. The house was quiet and in the garden the faster engine gushed the last water into the swimming pool. Then suddenly this noise ceased and the quietness of the house spread to the garden.

In the passage someone moved. He heard soft footsteps, the whisper of a dress. He got up and opened the door. Right opposite his room another door was being closed. He saw a girl's leg, the swirl of tweed material, part of an arm. All movement froze suddenly. Invisible, they became aware of each other, the movement remained captive. Then time resumed its passage and the door was softly pulled to. He was about to go back when something further down the passage attracted his attention. Slim Mrs Silberstein had appeared from somewhere in a transparent nylon nightdress and was running up the passage. She might just as well have been naked. At the top of the passage Jock was waiting for her, blue-striped in his pyjamas. His face was crimson and his mouth wide open.

His voice thundered in the silence: 'LILITH!'

The young man smoked a last cigarette and went back to bed.

Suddenly another engine started up – with slower, hypnotic sounds. And on the ceiling, slowly at first and then faster, two gigantic fans turned, forcing the warm air outside through numerous vents.

Chapter Two

Antics of the Artists

Henry awoke at eight o'clock and found himself staring straight into two bronze eyes. On his bedside table someone had placed a coffee urn of ornamented yellow copper. The handles were hinged to the beard-tips of two satanic faces, and the cup, into which he would presently decant his coffee, was as big as a bowl. After he regarded it for quite a while, he turned on the little tap and filled the cup. It was delicious mocha coffee and he drank two cups in rapid succession.

The sounds of all household engines had stopped and the whole of Welgevonden was noisy with productivity. In the distance trucks, heavy machinery and a variety of indeterminable installations that had something to do with the making of wine rumbled. Everywhere, in the house and outside, were the sounds of voices. He decided that it was time to get up and went into the bathroom where two huge black lions' heads jutted over a tiled bath. He pressed the knobs on the lions' snouts and streams of water, hot and cold, gushed from their gaping jaws. In a trice the bath was filled. As he lay drifting around in the water he regarded the white, black and bottle-green colour scheme of the room. When he returned to his bedroom he found that someone had brought in his breakfast. After he had eaten it and dressed, he went outside and met Jock on the verandah – dressed like a farmer in khaki pants, shirt and wearing *veldskoen*.

'Come on,' said Jock. 'I want to show you something of the farm,' and he took him by the arm.

They walked past the house, under pergolas, over little wooden bridges, along little streams of water, between outhouses and then, unexpectedly, again past a wing of the house, up a road where, in the distance against the hill, the noise was localized in a series of buildings where the cellars and wine-farming installations were housed. As they approached, numerous trucks passed, stacked in pyramid-shape with cases of wine and brandy. All the trucks were green, of exactly the same make, and the drivers were all dressed alike in yellow uniforms. The name Welgevonden appeared on every available space. Ahead of him Henry saw an object that gleamed so brightly in the sun that he could not at once identify it: it looked like a broad, white flame flaring up high. After a time he saw that it was a huge steel tank. On the top of the tank was a galvanized iron roof welded by means of silver iron bars to the structure. Beside it, when they were right up against the tank and the metal seemed almost to move with shining, Henry noticed a ladder which led up and up to where a sort of observation platform was suspended in the air.

'This tank is sixty feet high and fifty feet in diameter,' said Jock and he began to climb. 'It's the biggest of its kind in the world.' As they climbed higher and higher the wind began to buffet them and he had to shout loudly over his shoulder. 'We use it for the storing of distilling wine,' he bawled. 'From here it's pumped automatically to the continuous distilling plant.' And still they climbed, while the wind made Jock's shirt flap and every now and then he had to pull his hat more firmly on his head. When they reached the observation platform, they leaned against the rails to get back their breath. The view was not only breathtaking but decidedly alarming.

'Come on,' said Jock, removing his hat and leading Henry to a small bench. Next to it a telescope was mounted and he began fiddling with the screws. 'I use this instrument at night to look at the stars. By day it's useful for watching everything that goes on. I can even see into the rooms of the house.' He smiled and the wind rumpled his hair. 'First of all I'd like you to notice the gables of the house and the outbuildings. There are eight types: early-slanting, concavo-convex, late-slanting, baroque, late-slanting with fishtail top, Flemish, late-slanting with baroque top and scalar.' He had finished focussing the telescope and sat down on the bench again. 'Would you like to look at the gables, or shall we rather find out what's going on in the rooms? The rooms, rather, what? Me first? Perhaps that would bc better, then I can see that everything is properly in focus. The instrument is very sensitive.' He put his one eye to the telescope, keeping the other eye open as was right for a man with experience of such things. He moved the telescope back and forth and fixed it on a certain point. He stared long and attentively at something and then leaned back again, chin on hand, while the head-on wind ruffled his hair.

Henry, too, peered through the telescope, but it was some time before he could identify anything and then he was suddenly aware of J. J.'s face directly before him. The R.A.F. moustache-ends stood out like moving wings on either side as he inhaled and exhaled the morning air deeply. His cheeks were bulbous, his eyes protuberant, his hair falling over his forehead, his chest exposed from under his flowered dressing gown, when a woman's arms moved from behind him around his body. The slim Mrs Silberstein's face appeared above his shoulder, tilted sideways and nestled against his neck.

'Have you any knowledge of witchcraft?' asked Jock.

'No,' said Henry and looked up, while the telescope remained fixed on the little scene, which at once vanished from the range of vision of the naked eye.

'There is so much that you must learn in a very short time,' sighed Jock. 'Or, to put it this way: there are so many things you will have to learn and unlearn. All those things that protect you now. Your ignorance, your innocence, for instance. You simply can't go through life as you are. Life isn't all that simple.' He lit his pipe with difficulty and was about to flick the match in the direction of the open tank when he bethought himself and put it back in the matchbox. 'That state of false grace impedes us all at one stage or another. It's the tragedy of being human that you are forced suddenly one day to become aware of the darkness of human beings and, against your wish – note well – take cognizance of good and evil.'

Henry considered this, lying back on the bench and watching the drifting clouds that looked like small ships sailing straight down towards him.

'I think I can distinguish between good and evil,' he said.

'Then you must be an angel.' Jock clasped his hands behind his head and himself watched the clouds which were now flocking together like an armada. 'Evil, according to your faith, means violation of the divine law; the law is the definitions supported by divine authority. For the angel everything is encompassed by the small word "serviam" – the perfect, all-embracing concept of dependence on the Creator. For man, in accordance with the limitations of his nature, the laws are contained in the Ten Commandments.'

'I know the Ten Commandments,' said Henry. He was already bored by the conversation.

'All the explicit definitions . . . Are you bored?' Jock regarded Henry over his pipe.

'No,' said Henry.

'I thought not,' said Jock. He leaned forward suddenly. 'The trouble is simply . . . how can I put it? The trouble is just that man in his pride cannot always distinguish between self-interest and the Divine plan. You can't wash your hands in innocence; evil is a force that is increasing, not only in scope but also in form. That's why ignorance is so dangerous. Not in regard to a lack of knowledge of good, but the equally heinous sin of lack of knowledge of evil.'

Henry gave no indication of his growing impatience; he concealed it in a well-mannered way. However, he took advantage of a pause to look suddenly through the telescope again. There was no sign of J. J. and slim Mrs Silberstein. He moved the telescope ever so slightly to the right and was in another room. A naked girl was admiring herself in a looking-glass. First she stretched her arms out sideways and peeped over her shoulder, then lowered them and stood motionless. Once she looked directly in Henry's direction and he saw her dark eyes and black hair. She was slim as a caryatid. He wanted to ask Jock if this, perhaps, was Salome, but for reasons of decency dared not; and also because Jock was just finishing a sentence.

'. . . and it's the tragedy of maturity that you must lose your innocence and be ruined rather than live in innocence, that you must learn to know the devil before you may enter the gates of paradise.'

The wind had now become so strong that they decided to leave. Before descending the steps they looked down into the huge tank where a lake of distilling wine surged.

Suddenly Jock spat into it.

'It doesn't matter,' he said, 'alcohol is the best disinfectant there is. But just think of it . . .' He spat again. 'Somebody here and overseas, perhaps in China, Japan, England or America, will drink an infinitesimal quantity of Jock Silberstein's spit.' He looked expectantly at Henry. Henry spat too. Jock slapped him on the shoulder. He roared with laughter and his laughter vanished on the wind. 'Just think of it: the spit of Jock Silberstein and Henry van Eeden spread all over the world! It's a bond between us, isn't it?' They began climbing down, because the wind had become very strong.

They returned this time along a different route. Jock had suddenly lost all interest. 'I'll show you the cellars and the distillery tomorrow,' he said. 'Now I feel like going for a swim.'

They had to go through a pine plantation, where a cool road divided the plantation in two. After a while they turned off and followed a path through pine needles to the house. The sun was entirely obscured and the branches, moving slowly in the wind, let through chinks of blue sky. The carpet of pine needles was cushiony under their tread and a delightful piney fragrance rose from it as their footsteps disturbed it.

'How wonderfully sequestered this is,' said Jock. With raised head he walked with a springy step with which Henry found it difficult to keep up. 'And how rare seclusion is! Your bathroom, an occasional forest, some place difficult of access – only there can you find a refuge. These days one is compelled to live together with one's fellowman.'

All of a sudden they reached the edge of the plantation and crossed a pasture where a few Swiss stud cows were grazing. Mole holes occasionally made them stumble and hampered their walk. They reached a wooden fence and heard the clatter of a horse's hooves. Henry looked up just in time to see the silhouette of horse and rider against the sky: the arched legs, the mane, the silky chestnut hide, a slim, small girl in jodhpurs, a white shirt and a hat under which her dark hair was piled, her small face pressed close against the horse's neck. They seemed for a moment to hover in the air, as if they had been sketched there – then the horse landed on the soft grass, stumbled slightly as the elegant rider straightened up again, and the next moment they disappeared in the direction of the forest.

'Was that Salome?' asked Henry.

Jock looked to where they had last seen a moving speckle.

'It's difficult to say. Possibly it's Salome; possibly it wasn't her. I didn't take much notice.'

This time they were on another road, near the house. A truck raced past and smothered them in dust.

'Did you notice,' said Jock, 'they don't even know who I am. They don't know the boss, because the boss is invisible. Do you think I ought to wear a uniform?' He smiled at Henry. 'Welgevonden is a supermachine and nobody is indispensable. We're a big organism, a superdemocracy that works perfectly. The mere human event has become a clinical conception; being human is an abstraction; we all work together as a team in the laboratory.' He put his hand on Henry's shoulder. 'Welcome to the organism, Henry.'

Henry looked up into the face above him.

'But I feel at home already, Mr Silberstein.'

Jock stopped for a moment and looked attentively at the young man.

'I really think that you are already part of the plan. It's remarkable how quickly the young surrender their individuality.' He resumed his walk. 'Only, you must get rid of your innocence. First you must understand properly the true nature of the devil and original sin. In these days the knowledge of good and evil must be thorough. It's no longer as simple as it used to be; you must learn to forget about concrete images and get used to the abstract form.' They approached the garden and made their way with difficulty through overhanging growths. 'Remember,' said Jock, holding a branch aside so that Henry could go first, 'our

interest is no longer in the individual and the face he presents
to everyone; it's an anonymous humanity as a whole.' Jock struggled to get his large body through the overgrowth. Sometimes
Henry could not see him at all and only heard the crackling behind him. 'External truths are not carried automatically from
one period to another – they have to be found anew in each epoch.
Each time there is a new self and ours is faceless.' A branch broke
and Jock appeared, his face red with exertion; but his voice droned
on uninterruptedly. 'No time is wasted on the *persona* you hold
up to your family, friends and acquaintances. No, my boy. There
are no more illusions. During this past decade we have eaten
of the fruit of knowledge. You, I, Salome, all of us accept the
individual for the sake of convention, but we search behind the
common mask. We ask in a different way: who are we?' He
now walked ahead to the lawn from which they could see one
side of the house. 'The new era has begun. The magnificent individual lies dead on the scrapheap. The carnival is over!' He
pointed to the house. 'The old Welgevonden no longer exists –
the Welgevonden that the Monuments Commission gushes about.
There is a new truth, a faint glimmer of which we are only now
becoming aware. It's just a pity that I sometimes . . .' He was
suddenly silent and shook his head. 'Did you bring your bathing
trunks? Right, go and change. I'll meet you here in five minutes.'

When, after a search, Henry found his room, got into his bathing trunks and went outside, he could not find Jock. After another
search he found the swimming pool. It was of Olympic standard
and the water was a vivid blue. A good many girls, scantily clad
in bikinis, lay sunbathing by the pool-side, in varying shades of
oxidation – from pale bronze to rich copper. He was astonished
to find the Misses Silberstein there; hideous, but come what may,
in bikinis.

He stood for a moment indecisive and felt all eyes turn upon
him. One of that group with brown hair and dark eyes must be
Salome. He felt that the time had come for him to make some
or other approach to his loved one. He decided on the only solution. He looked towards the group of girls and called, suddenly:

'SALOME !' It was as if his voice had hit and been stepped by the faces turned motionlessly towards him, as if he had shouted up against a wall that had made no echo, as if, even, he had never shouted at all. The silence was dreadful, and he stood alone while inside him an unknown emotion trembled on the point of becoming actual. Then, suddenly, one of the girls repeated : 'S-a-l-o-m-e' and 'Salome, Salome, Salome' came the word from mouth to mouth like charming little echoes.

'Where have you been all the time?' asked J. J.

Unabashed, with his bulging belly and his trunks that disappeared into his navel, he lay beside the slim Mrs Silberstein, whose body was as pretty and well--proportioned as the youngest and prettiest of the girls.

'You and Jock,' repeated Mrs Silberstein. 'Where have you been all the time?' She laughed suddenly. 'Did he show you his telescope?' She beckoned to Henry. 'Come and sit here'; and as he sat down beside her . . . 'Did you peep at Salome?'

Presently Jock appeared, an impressive figure, athletic, a cluster of muscles that multiplied with every movement, and from the highest diving board he rose up in the air, jack-knifed, hung motionless, and then shot down into the water, disappeared without a sound.

Luncheon was announced by a slave bell.

A genuine blackamoor struck the bell with a clapper suspended from a rope and with metronomic beat sent seven rings into the midday air.

The guests went towards the house as a group and then dispersed singly or in pairs to the rooms. When the same little manikin (an African from Blantyre without a permit and with sharply filed teeth) beat two cymbals together, producing a vibrant sound of indefinable pitch, they assembled *en masse* in the dining room at a copiously laden table where the slim Mrs Silberstein showed everyone his place and ensured in the process that J. J., freshly and aromatically scented, took his place close beside her.

No grace was said aloud but there was a moment, after food had been served and the plates were overflowingly piled, that a pause occurred when everyone momentarily genuflected to his or her gods, god or nothing.

Slim Mrs Silberstein had placed Jock on one side of Henry, and on his other side a lovely brunette who kept a mistrustful eye on Henry all the time.

'To return to our conversation of this morning,' said Jock as, chewing, he leaned towards Henry and emphasized his words with a silver knife, 'evil, the dreaded *malum,* is every bit as subtle and involved as good, *bonum.*' He chewed his food with strong, white teeth. He was the only one who had not changed for lunch and had stuck to his farm attire. 'According to our Jewish faith, all evil is a negation, but I see it as one of two positive forces diametrically opposed. And I see all misery as the product of ignorance: more than ignorance in regard to negative and positive qualities, but ignorance in regard to equilibrium, the two opposite poles that balance one another.' This time he pointed to Henry with a silver fork (the crest of the former owners of Welgevonden religiously preserved on it). 'Beware of your jealously guarded innocence; your spiritual virginity that you protect like a silly young girl. A blind man is continually stumbling and causes harm, to himself and to others. Ignorance causes damage; innocence is blindness of the spirit.'

He put down his knife and fork and began cleaning his teeth with an ivory toothpick.

'Through knowledge the lion and the lamb will lie down together.'

In spite of his overflowing plate he had eaten frugally, leaving what remained for servants, cats and dogs.

'Don't regard me as a Jew,' said Jock. 'I am a renegade. The final surrender will be you and Salome – humanity without the trimmings of race, absolute anonymity. This grieves old Mrs Silberstein. You have already noticed that she isn't brimming over with enthusiasm?'

'Yes,' said Henry.

'Take no notice of her.'

He lit a cigarette.

'Talking of Salome, why do you keep so aloof from her? I have seen you together very seldom. Is that merely the modern manner of courtship? I must admit it seems to me a bit sterile. And Salome as *shegal* as you could wish her.'

Before everyone rose to have coffee on the verandah Jock urged them to take full advantage of the siesta as the party that evening would demand considerable energy.

II

Henry slept like a log and awoke towards evening with the disturbing thought that he had no idea what sort of party it would be. Putting on his dressing gown he went to J.J.'s room where he found his uncle, pink from his bath, freshly shaved and as cheerful as a cricket.

'Well, well, little Henry,' he said. 'And how is Salome, hmmmmmm?'

'I don't know her at all,' said Henry.

'O-hooo!' said J.J. 'All those philosophical talks! Rather leave them to Jock Silberstein. As far as your uncle is concerned, sonny, there is only way to get to know a woman.' He winked at Henry.

'I really came,' said Henry, 'to find out what sort of party it's going to be.'

J.J. raised his eyebrows, struck a pose of pretty, affected nicety, his knees together, one hand on his side and the other with its index finger in his cheek, and said : 'Artists, sonny.'

Like all very masculine philistines he regarded artists as effeminate, if not homosexual.

Back in his room Henry decided that it would be safest to follow the example set by the guests of the previous evening. As he was knotting a paisley scarf round his neck he heard the light installation throb a few times and then reach the required number of revolutions. He was about to leave when he noticed that on his bedside table, where the coffee urn had stood earlier that day, something had been put that looked like the head of a reindeer, complete with horns and glass eyes. The object was made of rubber and, despite its size, as light as a feather; the reason for this being that it was hollow inside. Henry inspected it from all angles and replaced it on the table. In the meantime it had grown dark outside and he decided that it was time to join the other guests.

When he reached the drawing room it was empty, all the chairs and couches covered with white drapes. He found one of the Coloured maids and asked her where the people were and she signalled him to follow her. She moved with light steps through the hall, round corners, through sun porches and outside; and he found it difficult to keep up with her as he stumbled every so often when they passed through unlighted places. They reached the lawn at last and a surprising scene dazzled Henry's eyes. Around the swimming pool lights of every colour had been placed between trees, shrubs and flowers. On the lawn, changing from colour to colour, there moved objects that looked like animals – a whole park of fauna. As he came nearer he saw that they were men and women: bikinis below, but animal heads where their faces should have been.

As he appeared in the lighted area they suddenly stopped moving and talking and a full range of animal faces turned their snouts and glass eyes towards him: bears, lions, pigs, antelope, lizards, salamanders, frogs, cats and dogs. Then they all began to clap, and an enormous bear said: 'Welcome, Henry. Welcome in our midst.'

A small reindeer in a silver bikini appeared and stood, the lights shining on her, in front of Henry. The silver gleamed and drew his attention to well-covered sacrum, acetabulum, pubis and coccyx. She linked her arm with his and the tiny horns reached hardly to his shoulder. They made a beautiful couple, the two of them, like something from a folk tale: the handsome young prince and his woodland bride.

'Ah,' said the bear Silberstein. 'How lovely. But where are *your* horns?' He did not wait for an answer. 'Move among our guests, you two'; and he embraced a passing cat with slender legs who tried unavailingly to extricate herself.

She walked lightly beside him and her hand lay quietly in his. She followed him closely, as if they were dancing, and he could feel the movement of her body against his. They sank into the grass and, beside the swimming pool, their images were reflected blue in the water. In utter silence they wound their way between the guests and the tableaux of their antics. But what can one say to one's loved one when she is entirely faceless? He drew her more closely to him and found, for the time being, sufficient communication in the physical contact. Even if they were to speak now, their discourse – the chance revelation of the chance personality of the chance moment – would be meagre by comparison with this deeper, bodily union. Therefore they did not speak and Henry and Salome wandered in harmonious silence through the bewitched landscape.

But not for long; presently they were intercepted by two old owls. Two stomachs drooped peacefully over bikinis, old men's knock-knees showed and their legs, untouched by any sun, shone white in the light.

'Ah! Mr van Eeden,' said one. 'You are probably surprised to see us here?' He bowed to the little reindeer then turned again to Henry. 'But we of Bishopscourt are not unacquainted with the arts. Who do you think will buy the paintings done by this young crowd if we do not? It is quite true that we often buy only after the works of art as such have been acknowledged, but we pay in hard enough cash for our lack of foreknowledge.'

A full goblet of champagne disappeared somewhere under his beak and reappeared empty. Two huge owl-eyes stared unmoving at Henry.

'Jock Silberstein says, however, that you are interested in the concept of good and evil. Now I must say, for someone of your age, you have an unexpected' (he emphasized the words) 'and profound interest in humanity and all its ramifications. It does you honour.' A peahen with pretty legs attracted his attention but lost it as she was lifted on to a lion's back. 'There are, however, a few other of Jock's postulates that I want to criticize and I hope you will agree with me.'

Henry nodded and drew Salome closer to him. Nothing is so delectable as concealed caresses in public.

'Jock's description of *malum* as a hardship is consistent with the Christian view,' said the owl. 'Evil is then a *privatio boni*. But when he talks of the two opposite poles (good and evil) that balance one another, he goes astray.'

He moved his head towards the other owl who was following the conversation attentively with saucer-eyes.

'He confuses the concept too,' he continued, 'by thinking too much of evil as something positive. Would a normal person who had knowledge of good and evil be so stupid as to chase after evil for the sake of evil? There is a theory that Satan himself, in his opposition to God, demanded equality with the Creator and even that ordinary mortals should receive their salvation from *him*. He wished to be the only source of good.'

Henry felt Salome move slightly away from him; the glass eyes of the reindeer head were turned towards the other guests. But the owl's voice became louder and held his attention again.

'Evil therefore, remains negative, according to our Christian view, and is *not* the unavertible opposite pole of good. Satan forms no part of a mystical *quadratum*.' He looked at the other owl and, facing each other, they looked like two stuffed creatures in a museum.

It was now clear to Henry that Salome was trying to slide her hand free of his. He struggled against his loved one's withdrawal and kept up the resistance while the melodious voice held another part of his attention captive.

'*Privatio boni*,' the owl declaimed, 'acknowledges the *reality* of evil because it deprives the natural goodness of God's creation of its goodness. There lies the danger of ignorance. Only to that extent is Jock Silberstein correct. For the rest, I am afraid he attributes too many positive attributes to evil, that he regards the devil alone as the source of all evil and even insinuates that it was created by God's dark side.'

The little reindeer suddenly tugged herself free of Henry and moved quickly away among the crowd. He saw her flashing legs, her small body appearing and disappearing among all the others and he tried to follow her, but the owl held his arm in a steely grip. He watched her in despair and saw that, once, she looked back at him as if expecting him to follow her and that, in the process, she walked straight into the arms of a tiger who lifted her up, danced her round and round, and disappeared behind a shrub.

Now the other owl had a grip on him too.

'Then there is the question of innocence and ignorance,' said the other owl. 'In my profession one must use words with care. What does Jock mean by "innocence"?'

One on either side, the two owls had taken possession of Henry. They walked together to a table where there were a few bottles of champagne. Three glasses were touched in a toast, two were emptied under beaks, and the last owl, his voice somewhat muffled by all the feathers, resumed the conversation.

'Innocence in regard to evil means that the individual is not capable of responsibility for the evil in himself. But that's a *contradictio in terminis*, because good is part of Man. The devil is simply the first one who fell. A *priori*, Man is responsible and guilty.' He glanced at the other owl as if expecting opposition and then went on. 'When one speaks, therefore, of an innocent human being, an ignorant human being is actually meant.'

The owl settled himself down on the grass and the other followed his example.

'Suppose that Man has no knowledge of evil; how does that affect his responsibility?' The owl pondered the problem with beak in the air and lowered his beak, in imagination back on the Bench. 'Not at all. Lack of knowledge is no defence. To that extent Jock is right and innocence (actually ignorance) is spiritual blindness; Man is responsible for his deeds.'

It was plain that the two owls were enjoying the discussion. Sometimes their heads were close together, the better to speak and to hear since their voices, behind the masks, were completely insubstantial.

'But,' said the owl, 'ignorance in respect of good is at the same time a cause of evil. To that same extent ignorance of evil means exactly the same. Ignorance does not alter the existence of good or evil. Ignorance of good and evil can accordingly lead to the same thing.'

Henry searched in vain. There were many kinds of antelope, but no reindeer.

'Knowledge of only good means ignorance of evil and can lead to evil. Knowledge of evil alone means ignorance of good and can similarly lead to evil. Knowledge of both good and evil, to be able to distinguish, as Jock says, can possibly lead to salvation. The human being, because of his limited capacity, can distinguish only up to a point. Jock is right there.' The owl turned to Henry. 'Jock's meaning must be: ". . . and it's the tragedy of maturity that you must lose your ignorance and be destroyed knowingly by evil, rather than live in ignorance; that you must first learn to know the devil . . ." '

Henry was sure that he could now see the little reindeer beside the swimming pool; over the owl's shoulders he had at first seen her silver bikini gleam, and then had noticed the supple movement of her legs as she walked slowly towards the swimming pool.

He jumped up swiftly, past the hands that reached out to restrain him.

'Where to now?' asked one of the owls. 'I am only now coming to an interesting point: the difference between a moral and an amoral evil.'

'Perhaps later,' said Henry and walked away rapidly, while the four immobile glass eyes glowed in the electric light behind him.

Slowly the eyes turned to one another and continued to glitter malignly, as the philosophical discussion was genially resumed.

III

Henry was convinced that she was waiting for him: she was wandering round aimlessly and the gleam of her eyes turned frequently towards him. He was already within speaking distance when a woman's hand, softly yet firmly, made him change direction. A cat-head, which tallied grotesquely with slim body and legs, smiled at him – a smile which, like the yellow eyes, never changed.

She grinned: 'I'd like to talk to you, Henry. Let's have a little chat.'

She led him to a seat beside the swimming pool. As they sat

there the water lapped against the sides of the pool and, in the distance, the boisterous voices of the guests sounded.

'I want to talk to you about Salome,' she grinned. 'D'you mind? You won't be annoyed with me?'

'No,' said Henry.

'Salome complains that you pay too little attention to her,' she grinned; a small red tongue showed between fine, small gleaming white teeth. 'She says that whenever she's with you, you carry on all sorts of philosophical conversations with other people and don't make even the slightest attempt to talk to her.'

She moved a slim arm round Henry's shoulder and grinned.

'Look, Henry, there are certain fundamental things between a man and a woman that you mustn't ignore. There's a time and place for everything, and I admit that a man and a woman should share one another's interests, but ... don't you think the moments of tenderness, the little personal talks, the little indications of a personal interest in each other are also important? Surely it's natural, when a young man and a young woman are on the point of ...'

She stopped and grinned.

'Naturally ...' said Henry.

'And then there's the most important aspect of the man–woman relationship. The erotic. It must not be underrated. It's the basic urge, otherwise marriage would be ridiculous, not so?' She stroked his arm and grinned.

'A woman likes to be desired by a man, even if he pretends, on the surface, not to care. But she wants to know, she wants to feel that a man is prepared to renounce all his other interests for the sake of those moments of intimacy which are theirs alone. Listen, it isn't that she expects him to jump into bed with her all the time. Excuse the platitude.' (She grinned.) 'But she wants to feel sure, after all, that those moments of intimacy between man and woman will be strong enough, potentially, to dominate everything else. It's the most personal contact that can ever exist between two people, and everything ... all theories and philosophies become empty words before this reality.'

She grinned and chucked him under his chin with a slim fore-finger and a sharp, red nail.

A donkey's head appeared suddenly between them.

'Yes, yes, yes!' said J.J.'s voice.

His legs and belly appeared whiter than ever under the electric light; his body hair correspondingly darker. He adjusted his head-piece.

'Couldn't you have found anything else for me?'

'It's Jock. He handed out the masks.'

The cat stood up, linked her arm with his, pressed herself against him and looked up into his face, grinning.

The antics around the swimming pool were becoming more abandoned. Someone had turned on a wireless and the artists were improvising dances to kwela music. In his search for the elusive Salome, Henry joined a group engaged in a pompous dis-cussion of the wittiness of Cape Coloured humour. Someone else was giving a rendering of 'Gatiepie van die Gabou' and everyone was following the score with the insight of cognoscenti. When they became aware of Henry they all fell silent and directed their many-coloured eyes at him.

'There's a "gentleman" in our midst,' said one.

It occurred to Henry that he was the only odd man out and he realized suddenly how absurd the countenance of normality was. They had all brought their own wine, a claret-type sold dirt-cheap in big glass demijohns – the trademark of their parties. Looking all round him Henry saw everything except a small rein-deer. An emotion – a combination of anxiety and jealousy – had welled up in him. It was, for him, an unusual combination of feelings, from which he even derived a certain amount of pleasure. He recognized his emotions by the taste they induced; this one, bittersweet, tasted like wild sour figs. The fact of his being near-sighted contributed: everything appeared illusive; sometimes he thought he saw Salome; for a moment he caught sight of her with someone, only to discover that she was a different object. Two pairs of legs in the long grass beside a shrub, the moving legs of a girl and the inert legs of a man, filled him with consuming suspicion; but he discovered nothing as, night-blind, he lost the place and found only grass and coloured lights beside a honeysuckle bush. In the midst of increasing uproariousness he became increasingly excluded. He began gradually to feel that there was something wrong with *his* appearance : the ludicrous little human eyes, the body pointlessly clothed.

'Ah, death thoughts ! Death thoughts ! Death thoughts !' giggled someone cheerfully in his ear; and there she was, the tigress, in the black bikini with long legs on which the blue veins of age had begun to spread their pattern, with the huge fangs and wide-open jaws from which the voice came as if from an amplifier. 'Still melancholy ! Ah, how I wish that you could pluck, with Sir Henry and me, the real fruits of life's joy !' She swept her hand up to the dark heavens. 'Blue oceans, distant shores, exotic palms, tropical flowers, wine, the Mediterranean air, heathen gods, the alabaster statues, the vineyards, music, warm love, dark eyes, the sensual joy of every swooning moment . . .'

She rocked to and fro on the wings of her thoughts and then lowered her hands.

'Sir Henry and I believe in no god; we find your world dull. But we take what is there to be taken . . . Can't you *feel*, can't you *understand*?' She embraced him suddenly from pure exuberance, but her mask was in the way and injured Henry slightly on his ear.

Instantly she was all solicitude. She fetched a handkerchief from somewhere and dabbed at the small wound without any practical result. Then she threw her arms round his neck and her voice changed.

'Most of our friends are dead. There are only old people left now, waiting to die. But here and there, like little pools of light all over the world, there are still a few of us – in villas in Capri, on little islands, on a ship bound for the East, in a gondola on the Grand Canal at fiesta time.'

Suddenly she rested her tiger's head against his forehead and inflicted another wound, while her whisper came, as if from a cave, past his ear.

'Do you know that Sir Henry and I have a death pact ? If illness or an infirmity of age should overtake one of us, so that one of us is unable to keep up with the other, then the other will put an end to it. There are so many ways of leaving this world. It's not really a problem, is it?'

The tigress raised her head again and turned towards the other guests where her tiger-mate, a light silk snake in his arms, but staggering nevertheless, managed with difficulty to reach a marble seat.

'Sir Henry feels at home tonight,' she said. 'Artists are timeless.'

Sir Henry had abandoned the little snake and she rolled off his lap while his arms hung helpless by his sides. A small group approached and clustered anxiously round him, but presently dispersed. In the meantime Sir Henry had risen to his feet and was leaning against the seat. Then, releasing his hold on it, he straightened up slowly and the tiger head, albeit shakily, was held proudly up.

The eyes of the tigress beside Henry were turned on her mate. Behind the mask they were very likely compassionate and wistful, but in the light had the callousness of an animal watching its prey. She waved to Sir Henry, who became aware of her for the first time. New, desperate life seemed to flow into him, and he toiled away with a frisky hobble towards a passing group, among whom an amazonian leopard-girl became the object and prop of his embrace.

Alone again, Henry resumed his search. Sometimes he joined groups of people, partly from inquisitiveness and partly to find a resting place before, once again, pursuing the spectre of his fleeing reindeer among the coloured lights in the haze of his half-blind world. The conversations he heard had one theme only (between witty slander provoked by professional jealousy) — an almost pathological worship of everything coloured or black, an obsession with the purifying effects of poverty, a disgust with order, a surrender to a vital anarchy symbolized in the rough awakening of the black man in the stylized West, a longing for the daring of chaos, the intensity of violence, the excitation of the primitive on the varnished hide of civilization. Within themselves they carried guilt feelings about their own satiated culture, nihilism before the ruins of their crumbled gods; godlessness in the silence of the Great Silence; formlessness at the grave of the departed New Age; uncertainty before the nature of Being. Among the neglected girls with their shabby bikinis and the tough, sinewy legs of the men, among them all in their grotesque animal heads that were their common mask, Henry moved – completely excluded, searching for Salome. It was suddenly decided, at the proposal of someone unknown, to have a midnight swimming party, without clothes – as befitted this universal desire for the beginning. They undressed in the shadows and, without bikinis, looked almost the same. It was as if the white where the bikinis had been had become the common colour of the new bikinis. They rushed to the pool and jumped with abandon into the water which became turbulent under the sudden impact; it spattered against the sides and surged in blue waves above the beams of the dimmed electric lights. The pool was filled with animal heads so that it looked as if a tidal wave had broken over a jungle: a second Deluge, lit by floodlights.

Then the light-engine stopped; and from the shrubbery, coughing, snorting, the new one began. Its drone increased in speed and the water began slowly to sink in the pool. The torsos of the men appeared first, then the breasts of the girls, then their legs with drops of water clinging to them like small diamonds, and finally they stood dry-footed in the empty swimming pool as in a public grave. They had all stopped screaming and laughing and looked at each other in dismay. One by one they struggled up the steps to the poolside where, in the farther shadows, they donned their bikinis. Then, with a hissing sound, high above, a thin jet, like a fountain spray, slowly, unhurriedly began to fill the pool from a dolphin's mouth.

IV

Among the crowd Henry was still searching for Salome; among the half-naked figures he found and lost her and, on reflection, wondered if he really ever had seen, found and lost her.

In the distance beside a sixteen-footed *achterhuis* table Jock had begun to speak. Henry could not hear all he said, but the words 'happy couple' reached him above the noise. Two little duikers in black bikinis brought flowers. Everyone applauded. Something sailed through the air and appeared on the water: patterns of blue and pink, flowers that composed the letters S and H and which, rocked by the rising water, bobbed about for the rest of the chaotic night.

The party dispersed haphazardly.

When Henry reached his room he found an enormous elephant in his bed, dressed in a cotton nightdress with a ruffed neck, its trunk swaying like a pendulum a few inches from the floor. A little later Jock appeared and together they helped the recalcitrant figure up, bore it lurchingly to the room next door, laid it on the bed and pulled the heavy mask off with a great deal of trouble. The small black eyes opened, saw Henry, and expressed a Semitic curse.

Henry lay by the phallic lamp-stand and waited for the footsteps in the passage, the swish of a dress, the creak of a door, the ritual of the captured moment – but nothing happened.

Only that the water-engine stopped, interrupting the heartbeat of Welgevonden, and then restarting it with the life-giving whirr of fans that drove out the stale air for the rest of the night.

Chapter Three

Ballet of the Farmers

When Henry woke up the birds were singing in the trees outside his window. It was one of those mornings in the Western
Province when everything in the environment combined to create
the memory of a sunlit day that would in future continually recur
as 'one sunny morning . . .'

The coffee in the urn had been laced with a dash of Benedictine,
the curtains had been opened and the full enchantment of the
morning filled the room. In the bathroom he made another discovery: he pressed one of the lion's eyes and a fine jet of pine
scent coloured the water green. Beside his clothes khaki trousers
and shirt and a sombrero had been placed conspicuously. Thus
attired, he met Jock who was waiting for him in the garden, his
hands clasped behind his head, his face lifted to the sky, savouring
the pure air in deep inhalations.

'Fine!' he said, looking approvingly at Henry's outfit. 'And now
we can inspect the farming operations further.'

They passed the flaming steel tank without giving it a second
glance. They avoided the heavy trucks patiently and then contemplated three thousand German merino lambs, as plump as
partridges, waiting in pens to be slaughtered. Then they went to
the cellars. First, however, they were intercepted by a guard who
insisted inexorably on an identity card or some alternative form
of identification. This made it necessary for them to go to his little
office, in which a vast photograph of a baobab tree hung on the
wall.

The entire window sill was cluttered up with pot plants that
grew so luxuriantly that they excluded most of the light and
kept the room in perpetual semi-darkness. For lack of identity
cards they had to fill in forms; then the guard rang a certain

number. He treated them with the utmost disdain. While he was waiting for an answer he sat on the edge of the desk and snipped dead blooms from the pot plants with a pair of secateurs. Then suddenly he listened attentively, read out certain particulars from the filled-in forms and replaced the receiver on its cradle. Slowly, cumbrously and carefully he filled in an entrance permit, peered at them from under dark eyebrows and indicated that they could go.

'Doesn't he know you, then?' Henry asked.

'Of course,' said Jock. 'I appointed him myself. But the old boy is very meticulous. He abides strictly by the regulations and allows no exceptions. Unfortunately I forgot my identity card.'

'But why all the permits?'

They were now walking down a passage that looked like a tunnel and their footsteps rang hollowly on the damp walls, the stones of which were mottled with greenish moss.

'To keep unauthorized persons out, of course,' said Jock. 'Every regulation has its original reason. The more complex the system, the more difficult it is to determine the exact reason for each regulation. Regulations eventually become dogmas, truths about which there can be no further argument.'

They turned down a side passage and continually encountered men in white who, with the self-effacing dedication of priests in a temple, contributed to the ritual of fermentation and fulfilment; who, with pipettes, flasks, barometers and other sacred instruments of their office, led the soul of the wine to eventual individuation.

They came to a cellar in which a series of leaguers lay like coffins in the half-light.

'Here is a replica of Spain,' said Jock, with his priest's dedication. 'Here the *mosto* lies fermenting until all the sugar disappears and the *vino de ánada* appears. It takes twelve to eighteen months; and, like the Calvinist soul of man, some are destined to perfection and some to bitter ruin. We have no control over the results of the fermentation; we can only add the *Yeso* to help – and the rest is in the hands of the Creator.'

From there they passed through another narrow passage, greener with moss, of even temperature, soundless except for their footsteps which broke the proper silence, to another cellar.

'And there is the *criadera*,' said Jock. 'The fermentation is complete. This is the nursery where each kind ages in accordance with its nature.'

On some of the vats there were the marks of Palma, on others the single stripe of Raya, the two stripes of Dos Rayas and the cross of Palo Cortado.

'One can put it this way,' said Jock, 'this is heaven. The bitter fruit has been eliminated. Here every soul rests according to the character of its perfection.'

The passage now led right down to one of the largest cellars. Here the vats lay row upon row in three tiers, each, from top to bottom, connected to the other.

'This is the completely integrated wine,' said Jock. 'Each row represents a certain year, on the *solera* system, close to the earth. Here lie the endless combinations of Palma, Raya, Dos Rayas and Cortados. The combination is drawn from the very bottom *soleras*, and then each tier is automatically refilled from the younger tier above. That is the ultimate attainment, the reconciliation of all the components, the centres of balance, the true Self in every case.'

In the light of the cellar Jock looked, despite his farm clothes, like a hierophant expounding the secrets of the mysteries to his adherents.

'In these cellars,' he declaimed, his voice thundering between the walls, 'perhaps something of the same sort happens as happened to the mysteries of Eluesis in the caves, or in the Atys-Cybele mysteries, or to the true believer in the perfect perception of his symbols, or to the artist in his moments of vision, or to the soul of man when in perfection of insight he achieves redemption, understands the *complexio oppositorum* in the *conjunctio oppositorum*, experiences life in God.'

They left the cellar, and in proportion to their ascent, the mystic light in Jock's eyes gave way to the complex light of common day, which changed from moment to moment and from stimulus to stimulus.

They passed a large building where rows of Coloured people were busy. They were all cheerful and merry and the atmosphere now changed from the supernatural to the commonplace. They looked impudently at Jock and Henry with the superior under-standing of human frailty that eliminated all rank and reduced everyone to ordinary humanity: competence in regard to sex, love, the satisfaction of material needs and the power of survival in the rat race that is life. A young Malay girl looked Henry straight in the eye and gave a sudden laugh as he looked away.

But Jock led Henry past them. Next door was a smaller build-ing, dwarfed by two objects that resembled gigantic locomotives; great heaps of coal were stacked on either side of the building. The ovens were open, and Africans, their faces shiny with sweat, were antagonistically filling the smouldering bellies of the colossi.

Jock walked ahead into a little room that was crisscrossed from side to side with copper pipes. He closed a small door behind him and a clinical silence prevailed in the room. He looked at Henry, signalled something with his finger and suddenly opened a cock; a hellish rush of steam obliterated all other sounds in the room. In a corner of the room was an iron hammer. Jock took it up and struck with powerful blows against a piece of steel; the hammer rebounded in lightning protest and the muscles on his arms bulged as he strained to curb the hammer. But there was no sound except that of the steam. Jock jumped up and down in a transport of boisterousness, hurled the hammer away, kicked the walls, beat with his fists against the pipes – and still there was no sound except that of the overwhelming steam which, in a manner pecu-liar to itself, in proportion as they became accustomed to it, created a silence of its own.

Then Jock closed the steam-cock and instantly his voice reached Henry, clear and distinct.

'This is my room of isolation,' he said. 'In this noise the silence is absolute.' He took Henry's arm urgently and drew him nearer, his other hand on the steam-cock, his voice enraptured by the impact of his own special narcotic. 'Do you mind joining in? As soon as I open the cock I want you to shout as loud as you can. Swear, blaspheme, weep as you please – protest at the top of your voice, as at other times you can protest only in your thoughts; bemoan, like Job, your undeserved human fate, because here you are speaking directly to your Creator; nobody else can hear you.' His eyes were white with the shining light of fanaticism. 'Here you're alone as you've never been alone before, but it's not the impotent voice of your thoughts, it's the full, bodily voice screaming at the universe; it's yourself in complete control of your senses; it's you, Job, bellowing the question all over again at the Almighty. It's your right, as a human being, to protest with all the power at your command in the in-between world of silence that isn't silence.'

He opened the steam-cock suddenly, the rush of steam was overwhelming; it deadened all other sounds and was transformed into the new silence born of the single sound. Only Jock's mouth opened and shut; Henry could see the veins swelling on his neck and his powerful chest heaving with the force of his inaudible cries. His eyes were raised to the roof, his arms curved in the air, his whole body shuddered with soundless unburdening. For a while Henry was dumbfounded by this singular confession and then, in the deafening silence, something in himself began to awake – a feeling of utter aloneness, as if he were standing in a desolate landscape, in the solitude of a wilderness, and as if from the isolation within him a primordial cry were surging up – a yearning, an unconstrained protest against helplessness, the lamentation of his desolation, the liberated, quite different expression of his deepest longings, the emptying of his heart itself. He felt a dampness on his cheeks and knew it was from tears; he brushed them away with his hand and in the process discovered that his mouth was open wide. There was a tingling in his throat, his chest, his lungs, and he realized that he had lost all restraint. Only then did he begin to think and analyse the nature of his sighs and protestation; but soon apprehended that ordinary analysis was not apt. Certain words, certain ideas, certain sounds – these, about which he himself was uncertain, he shrieked aloud; only the nucleus of feeling bubbled up, the half-born thoughts came and went and what would appear was incalculable. It was more than an unspoken wish, longing or lamentation, because it had been expressed without the limitations of ordinary expression. It was an entirely free utterance, without the restraints of self-judgment, because he did not know what he was saying. It was the greatest, the most all-embracing communication with the Almighty that he had ever experienced.

Exhausted, intensely lustrated, he gasped for breath and noticed that Jock had raised a finger to his lips. Then the cock was closed and the other silence, which only their breathing broke, supervened. They looked at each other, with the expression of people who have shared an experience but are nevertheless isolated from each other; with the comradeship that comes from complete participation and yet retains an inviolable centre of secretiveness. It was the perfect sodality; and they left the sanctuary in complete silence.

II

They strolled in sunlight back to the house. Every now and then Henry glanced covertly at the big man beside him who strode forward cheerfully and showed openly his joy in the beauty of nature. His shirt was unbuttoned and showed his bare chest. He held his hat in his hand and drew attention with expansive sweeps of his arm to everything that pleased him. His thoughts bubbled over, as if his joy were being translated directly into words. When they reached the middle of a clover meadow, in their short-cut to the house, he suddenly stopped and sank lazily down into a reclining position.

'Let's rest for a bit,' he said to Henry, 'before losing ourselves presently in the crowd.'

Now Henry could observe him closely. He noticed that Jock's eyes were not always the same colour. At present their blue was darker. His whole body, as well as his features, were slightly larger than the normal; which suited his emotions, that exceeded the normal too. He lay on the grass chewing a grass stalk and Henry felt that this moment of rest and leisurely talk was a sign of an equally profound silence that would soon come over Jock.

'Do you remember what I said yesterday?' Jock asked. 'About

the featurelessness of Being?' He turned on his back and looked up at the sky. 'That's because the individual has lost his dramatic image. There are too many people in the world. There is a fundamental indifference to the fate of the individual, there is only compassion for the group, the greater unit.' He now lay flat on his back, disturbed in his thoughts. 'There are no longer any single characters; we are all simply conduits. Do you, for instance, know Salome?'

'That's what I've been trying to discover for a long time,' Henry said. 'I don't know who Salome is. Nobody has told me yet who she is. I've already been searching for her for two days.'

'Exactly,' said Jock. 'Nobody is really interested in the uniqueness of anyone else's character. We are a combination of faces and we understand the futility of getting to know anything about the complex patterns. The true self is total, part of the anonymous multitude. Each of us is simply a conduit carrying the stream of accumulated knowledge. It's an oppressive thought. We no longer have any single image of any sort at all.' He sat up suddenly. 'Henry! Henry! Think of it! Think of the appalling disaster of the individual human being disappearing, the nearer we come to the truth of existence!' He clasped his huge hands and squeezed out his thoughts. 'Do you feel the solitude, the aloneness?' He looked anxiously into the face of the young man beside him, afraid that what he was trying to convey would be lost. 'Do you know what this aloneness and solitude mean?' He took Henry by both shoulders. His words were soft and emphatic. 'It means exactly the opposite. We are not alone. Every day we understand more and more our collective share in the fate of humanity. Solitude is the longing, the pain inherent in contemplating the false image of the individual that is vanishing piecemeal with our new understanding. So we long always for the discarded time when we are born into a new one. Your search for Salome is doomed to failure.'

He stood up suddenly and began to walk, driven by whatever it was that always drove him. He moved so fast that Henry had difficulty in keeping up with him.

The complex of buildings that was Welgevonden loomed up.

'Welgevonden is already a mockery of the past civilization. Reality is with us: the rumbling machinery, our communal efforts, our little parties and the chaos of our thoughts.'

He walked faster and gradually Henry began to fall behind.

'Remember, Henry, we have lost our images. There are no individuals. There is only the caricature of Jock, Salome, all the others and yourself!' Henry could now hear only certain words: 'Salome ... Henry ... Jock... There are no ...' And as Jock disappeared among the trees surrounding his enormous house Henry found himself alone.

Alone, Henry meandered between the walls and through the garden in search of the inhabitants of Welgevonden. He was imbued to confusion with points of view and burdened with so many theories about the essence of being human that everything merged into a multiplicity of patterns in which his own image and those of everyone he knew kept changing, like living cells under a microscope, and expanded and contracted in endless combinations with elastic amorphousness. Even his surroundings were an illusion of this inconstancy : at one moment the building had a certain appearance, the next it was a completely different place. Presently he lost his way altogether. He found himself confronting walls that impinged on other walls which soared up to immense gables of varying design; then, again, he faced gleaming windows of people he did not know. Everywhere there were chimneys of a particular shape that kept changing the appearance of the complicated house : from the rectangular, cubic kind with four small columns at the top, to others with intricate spirals – all of them changing, with something of one and something of another, to an uncoordinated, drunken dream of brick and plaster.

Suddenly the bell rang. Somewhere behind the nightmare walls the little blackamoor was summoning the inhabitants of Welgevonden to table. Henry passed in and out of doors, through rooms still warm from recently departed humanity, where the echo of their conviviality still hung in the air and half-completed movements lived in displaced objects. But the sound was deceptive. It lured him to one change of course after another and led him in sheer desperation to a large door which he opened half-heartedly and behind which he came all of a sudden upon the assembled guests.

There they sat, in the half-light of the room, all the friends and the ever-changing strangers who, as a pattern, were not unknown, on either side of the yards-long stinkwood table on which a white cloth constituted the gleaming base for silver cutlery. The Silbersteins and their friends on either side of the silver: pale silver meat dishes in a dead straight row, dark silver salt and pepper pots, heavy Welgevonden-Huguenot silver forks and spoons and well-worn silver, bone-handled knives, and chunky antique silver serving spoons besides bowls of vegetables, salad, rice, curry, corn on the cob and something steaming hot in spherical silver dishes. They sat there, erect and tense, ready for the great assault on the midday meal, young and old, with fatalistic hedonism, in their epicurean challenge to the sun and the humidity, prepared to submit to gastronomic torture in that climate that enchanted lightly while it castigated bodies and compelled souls towards the one, single, incomprehensible God.

'Henry, you're late,' said J.J., reprimanding his young nephew from a sense of duty. He whispered something jocular to slim Mrs Silberstein who, with a pallid hand, indicated to the future son of the house a place beside her.

Henry looked at the girl next to him. She was certainly the prettiest of them all, and he had observed her before, this one – so refined and well-groomed, such a paragon of refinement and calculated aloofness, with her haughty self-confidence, her perfection of figure, feature and grooming, that he looked in vain for the slightest signs of irregularity, weakness or diffidence to bolster his own self-confidence.

Outside, the delicious morning sun had become a malignant ball of fire that made the air hot as a furnace.

Jock referred to the forthcoming party, and the siesta. This time he defined the nature of the party: their farmer friends; and he smiled at Henry.

As on the previous afternoon, Henry slept like the dead and

woke when the light-engine had already started up. After the adventure of bathing and the discovery that the lion's other eye dispensed a heather-scented essence, he fretted all over again about his clothing for the evening.

There were no strange objects in the room and he concluded, accordingly, that it would not be a fancy-dress ball. He tried to solve the problem while sitting in his underclothes on the edge of his bed, smoking. The first supposition would be that their dress was unpredictable, determined by the caprice of local custom; but, on the other hand, it was nevertheless possible to rationalize and find an appropriate indication from the nature of their occupation. The rich, for instance, were noted for their nonchalant way of dressing; the artists for their unconventional way. But the farmers? The conservatism of an ordinary suit would, perhaps, provide the most acceptable solution; but he was immediately on his guard, because he had only recently learned that life had a logic of its own that was apparently illogical. And yet, on closer scrutiny, there was a simple and acceptable explanation for everything. No, a suit would be too much in the commonplace order of things; casual dress was too irreconcilable with their outlook; anything exotic, like masks and fancy dress, would be too much in conflict with their way of life. But what of ordinary farm clothes, such as he and Jock had worn that morning? From a practical point of view they would be the most reasonable on the occasion of a barbecue; from a subtler motive they would be sufficiently piquant, with that suggestion of self-mockery which everyone reserved for his own calling; in general, it was significant that precisely such clothes had been laid out in his room.

Accordingly, Henry dressed in the khaki shirt and trousers, rolled up his sleeves and betook himself to the party. He went in the direction of voices, opened the door of the drawing room and in the brilliantly lighted room found the guests immaculately attired in dinner jackets and evening dresses. As, at his entrance, the voices died down and everyone stared in mute astonishment at this distinctive object, it suddenly dawned on him: of course! The farmers were the aristocracy of the country.

III

The duchess looked especially formidable, sitting in her chair over yonder, laced-up and buckled in a tight-fitting black evening dress that gleamed with mother-of-pearl buttons. She wore a tiara; she had just drained a glass and was fastidiously nibbling a *sosatie* when she noticed Henry, and immediately stopped eating. The two drab Misses Silberstein, sweetly pink in evening frocks, were acting as hostesses with frolicsome elation; forcing 'another little bit, come, another little bit' on the guests until in the end their small plates were spilling over with sausage, barbecued meat, chestnuts and milk tart. Then there was slim Mrs Silberstein in blue, her hair over one shoulder, her eyes (Henry noticed for the first time) violet. The dark-eyed girls had had their numbers supplemented by blue-eyed farm girls who looked as if they had never been in the sun. The farmers and their wives were inclined to robustness, somewhat stiff of bearing, bolstered by their smart attire, in a manner that tolerated no deviation from their standards. All the same, Henry noticed that the Welgevonden brandy was flowing freely. The wine was hardly touched.

He felt exceedingly uncomfortable in his farm clothes and time and again found eyes, cold and disapproving, fixed on him. A woman remarked in passing: 'Probably one of those artists,' and turned her broad back, stiffened by a corset, contemptuously on him. It was, therefore, with a great measure of relief, which even predominated over his surprise, that he found himself confronting Judge O'Hara and Dr Johns, who, rocking on their heels, cigars in their mouths and glasses in their hands, welcomed him gaily.

'Ah, Henry!' said Dr Johns. 'Still the individualist!'

Over his shoulder Henry could see the grim face of a farmer staring cold-bloodedly at him with grey eyes – the .303 steady on the target.

'Are you surprised to see us here?' asked Judge O'Hara. He blew a solid smoke ring into oblivion. 'If you think about it carefully, at Bishopscourt we live, actually, on small farms, compared with the usual plots. The cultivation of our shrubs, trees and other plants demands the same amount of specialized skill, although perhaps on a smaller scale. Apart from that, some of our best friends are farmers.'

'Where's Salome?' asked Dr Johns.

Henry pointed vaguely in the direction of the dark-eyed girls and suddenly Dr Johns waved amiably across the room.

Judge O'Hara cleared his throat and looked meaningly at Dr Johns. Dr Johns took Henry confidentially by the arm and the three of them moved among the guests, chatting.

'Now, Henry,' said Dr Johns, 'let me admit that both Judge O'Hara and I were upset yesterday evening when you left us so abruptly in the middle of a conversation.' Henry gestured but Dr Johns restrained him. 'Judge O'Hara and I realized at once that some of our arguments might have seemed naïve to you.' He coughed self-consciously.

'With your permission, we'd be glad to put certain aspects more clearly,' said Judge O'Hara. He looked anxiously at Henry and Henry nodded.

'To start with,' said Judge O'Hara, 'I spoke of man's knowledge and choice of good and evil without taking into consideration the matter of free will. Dr Johns pointed out to me that you were very probably a Calvinist, and accepted the Augustinian doctrine of predestination. In that case, I must apologize.' He inclined slightly towards Henry. 'God, in His wisdom, destined some to inherit eternal life through Christ's redemption, while others . . .' He gestured. '*Et hoc dicitur reprobare.*' Judge O'Hara smiled. 'Jock's obsession with knowledge does not apply then, does it?'

Two of the farmers had joined the group and were listening attentively.

'In that respect Jock is a bit of a Thomist,' said Dr Johns. 'But we don't want to hurt anyone's feelings, although Judge O'Hara is inclined to believe that St Thomas's definition of free will should be accepted: God as the primal cause which set everything in motion; man's will as the immediate cause of human action . . .'

Two more farmers had joined the others and looked meaningfully at each other: this sounded like familiar territory.

'But,' Dr Johns continued, 'there is really *one* question we must
put to Henry.' He turned to Henry and the farmers drew nearer,
interested. 'If you accept the postulate, *praescientia meritorum
non est causa vel ratio praedestinationis,* if God willed all . . .'

Judge O'Hara interrupted him with raised hand.

'But both groups accept that, Dr Johns.'

Dr Johns was slightly nonplussed and one of the farmers smiled
broadly; another had just lit a cigarette. They were about to take
sides – as soon as they could understand a word.

'Very well,' said Dr Johns, 'if one pursues the doctrine of the
predominating divine will to the extreme logical conclusion of
the supralapsarians, one can ask oneself: did God plan and
create an evil?'

He was looking straight at Henry now and everyone followed
his example. Above the black suits and white shirt fronts shone
the faces: the hard faces of the farmers and the more mobile
countenances of the savants of Bishopscourt.

There was a long silence and then one of the farmers, his long
face enthroned on his bow tie, answered: 'The answer is in Job.'

Dr Johns thumped him on the shoulder. The man smiled broadly; for the rest of the evening he would defend the doctor.

'Exactly,' said Judge O'Hara. 'What is the answer?'

'The answer is,' said Dr Johns, 'that God is suprarational and
that we, with our limited understanding, cannot comprehend
God's will.'

More farmers had joined them; at first in silence, but now
that the ice had been broken by one of their buddies, ready to
air their opinions.

'That,' said Judge O'Hara, 'is a logical evasion.'

Gradually Henry was being jostled to the periphery until presently he could hear only the voices.

'And yet,' Dr Johns continued, 'Augustine denies that God's
prescience of evil makes evil necessary.'

The farmers' faces swung from side to side as they followed
this theological tennis match.

'That is why I believe in the mystery of free will,' said Judge O'Hara. 'It is through free will that the risk of evil exists and evil is a negation, a negative force. God created only good.'

Henry moved back and farther back as the elegant farmers revealed their love of dispute and drove him, bobbing on the black flood of their evening finery, aside.

'And yet,' said the invisible Dr Johns, 'if free will is dependent on the primal movement of God's will, as Thomas Aquinas says, then free will is limited and exists only as an illusion.'

'That's the mystery,' bellowed Judge O'Hara in reply, since his voice was getting lost in the bee-noise of the two swarms that were forming around the two points of contention.

'Knowledge drives one crazy,' a farmer said calmly and immediately expressed his opinion which was based on belief and not on knowledge.

Suddenly someone next to Henry guffawed: it was Jock, who was observing his contending guests with a big smile.

'Their trouble,' he whispered to Henry, 'is that they see evil as something negative and are too scared to acknowledge a duality in the godhead.' He shrugged and with a gleam in his eye moved forward to join the rumpus.

A woman's hands came from behind him and covered Henry's eyes. 'Guess who,' said Lady Mandrake. 'Did you think it was Salome?' she asked as she removed her hands. She looked at the assembled farmers and they listened to Jock's voice that rose above all the others. 'The believers!' said Lady Mandrake. 'They argue and argue . . . it reeks of the cloisters and one feels the hard benches of Protestant churches.' She glanced round the room and, catching sight of the bar in the corner, linked her arm with Henry's. 'Women on one side and men on one side,' she said as they crossed the no-man's-land to the source.

The marshalling of forces around the argument had, as Lady Mandrake had rightly observed, changed the pattern of the room. On one side the farmers were grouped in an abstraction of black and white, the variety of their faces a surrealistic contrast of eyes, noses, mouths, teeth and eyes. On the other side were their wives, a gradation in full regalia of all the colours of the rainbow, with the glitter of ornaments and a kaleidoscope of features that rose to breathtaking beauty and receded to the grimace of old age.

'Where is Sir Henry?' Lady Mandrake asked suddenly. She had emptied a glass and was looking anxiously round the room. In the farthest corner was a small black blob, the only one in a garland of farmers' daughters. Lady Mandrake sighed with relief and poured herself a second glass. 'Sir Henry and I do not concern ourselves perpetually with all the dreary problems of the modern world. We believe in the richness of all living things, the magical process of growth, change and maturing, the melancholy of a day past and in the process of passing, the warmth born of love for everything that lives.' She looked lovingly at her little black blob, who was never still for a moment but bounced around among the girls like a small rubber ball. She inclined suddenly towards Henry and whispered: 'I want to tell you about a promise I had to make to Sir Henry. Sometimes I weep when I think of his courage, but then again I feel proud.' The tears came readily and she wiped them away with the corner of her handkerchief. 'Sir Henry made me promise that when he is dying the doctors must use no pain-killing drugs. He wishes to be fully conscious of every sensation; to experience life until the very last moment. Isn't that marvellous?'

Lady Mandrake caught sight of her hostess and waved to her with the handkerchief. She kissed Henry lightly on the cheek and went towards Sir Henry, and it was as if the little rubber ball acquired fresh energy: as she drew nearer, it moved up and down, to and fro, faster and faster, with nervous vitality.

Henry noticed that the dark-eyed girl who had sat next to him at dinner was pouring herself a glass of wine. He hastened to help her. He offered her a cigarette and held a lighted match ready. She narrowed her eyes as she lit the cigarette, then tilted her head back and exhaled the smoke.

'Thanks,' she said.

Sometimes they looked obliquely past each other, sometimes into each other's eyes.

'It's a lovely evening,' said Henry, prepared to start a conversation, like a civilized person, about anything impersonal and uncontentious.

She smiled and drew on the cigarette.

Henry looked over her left shoulder and saw the duchess in the middle of the room; she was moving across the floor, in her stiffly elegant gown, with great concentration. She shuffled her feet no more than six inches at a time; one hand hung by her side, the other lay over the pearl necklace on her bosom. From time to time she smiled with gold teeth at the guests, this way and that, with metronomic impartiality. She had just left her chair and was on her way to another part of the room. Her whole bearing was eloquent of determination. She steered her course with dignity among the crowd and then reached her destination : another chair that faced in the direction from which she had come. She gathered up her gown, turned round and sat down slowly, without looking back. She saw Henry and her face tightened. Her eyes remained fixed, motionless, on him.

Henry smiled at the girl who smiled mechanically back. They had in the meantime moved a few paces apart, both still smoking.

He looked over her right shoulder and saw the two drab Misses Silberstein engaged in vigorous argument. Each carried a tray on which a great many cream cakes of various shapes were arranged. First they put down the trays and made signs to each other with their hands; then they took up the trays again and the argument was continued with all manner of head-movements. All of a sudden the argument came to an end and they moved in opposite directions towards the segregated guests.

Henry and the girl had now moved so far apart as to have broken all contact. He saw J. J. and slim Mrs Silberstein moving towards an open door. Mrs Silberstein looked fresh, but J. J. seemed tired and there were rings under his eyes. When Henry looked back to the girl, he found that she had disappeared.

The electric-light engine had stopped and now the swimming pool was being emptied and refilled.

Two of the farmers' daughters joined Henry, plaits over their shoulders, an arm around each other's waist, their feet in ballet positions *sur la demi-pointe*.

'We hear,' said one of them, 'that you and Salome are to get Brutus.'

There was envy in their eyes.

'Is that true?' asked the other.

Henry shrugged and looked out of the window. He did not understand a word of what they were saying.

The Welgevonden garden, illuminated as always, stretched into the night and now, for the first time, he noticed the neon lights beyond. In the far distance, in letters as large as the screen of a drive-in cinema, flowed the streams of red, green and blue: WELGEVONDEN . . . QUALITY . . . WINES; first in a crescent, then in a straight line: WELGEVONDEN . . . QA TY . . . WI ES.

The two farm girls had disappeared but others had taken their place at the small bar. In the background the men were still arguing. Henry was surrounded by girls who smiled at him, moved closer and said shly: 'Congratulations on Brutus.'

The rumour had now spread through the room. Brutus. Brutus. It penetrated to the men, who repeated the name. Brutus. Brutus. One after another they deserted their second love and rejoined their wives, and the room became evenly filled; and Brutus, Brutus came from all directions. The girls' dresses rose and swirled as they turned to one another and whispered Brutus, Brutus. Was it Brutus? Could it be? Was it true? Ask Giepie Ollenwaar.

And there he stood, in the middle of the room, Giepie Ollenwaar, his gold chain across his little paunch, his old-man's legs in their black pipes, his narrow shoulders humped in his jacket, his small chest pigeon-puffed behind his stiff shirt front, his toothless mouth gaping with pure delight – a crow among the charming farm girls who touched and tugged, clutched, prodded and pestered him to come out with the truth.

Only Dr Johns and Judge O'Hara, blissfully sequestered, continued to argue about free will and to examine good and evil.

Suddenly Jock clapped his hands, everyone fell silent and listened to the

'Dear friends, we've come together here . . .

'Dum-dum to celebrate our dear . . .

'Salome . . . Henry . . . Silberstein . . .

'A present fit for Oppenheim . . .'

And then came the moment, as he rapped on the sixteen-legged *achterhuis* table, and the doors swung open, when the dainty Misses Silberstein appeared – bashfully on either side of the enormous head, timidly bound by two cords to the nose-ring, horn-encircled – with the bull. They walked prettily to thunderous applause, whistling and the stamping of feet, while the bull grew more and more immense as, first, the buffalo-neck appeared, then the tremendous muscles that distended with every ponderous tread of the huge hooves, then the strong, round belly that grazed each side of the door, then the bulging haunches and plump, gleaming buttocks under the back, flat as a table – until the room and the people were dwarfed by the full presence of the imperial animal.

BRUTUS! BRUTUS! BRUTUS! shrilled the girls and the farmers stamped a measure on the floor while the boom-boom of their handclaps synchronized into the rhythm of a drumbeat.

This lasted for at least five minutes; silence returned tardily and then became complete so that everyone could regard the animal in wordless transport.

And Henry noticed for the first time that the forequarters of the bull were red and the hindquarters pitch black.

Jock called upon Dries van Schalkwyk, secretary of the Red-Black Ollenwaar Stud Farmers' Society, to say a few words; and he appeared with his cropped head, to exclamations of 'Hey Dries!' Laughing with horse teeth ('Hey, Dries!'), redly sunburned, uneasy in bow tie, silk collar and sash, to introduce to the guests Esteemed Uncle Giepie (applause fortissimo), Mr Silberstein (*forte*), Salome (piano), Henry (pianissimo) and BRUTUS (cacophony!).

'Is there anyone present here tonight who has never heard of Brutus?'

Loud laughter, uproar and 'Me!' bawled a young rustic wit who was playfully thrown down by the men and pounded by the girls.

But seriously: all honour to Uncle Giepie Ollenwaar who (his hands on Brutus's silky hump) had raised this breed to the glory

of all South Africa. This animal, Brutus, bicoloured, magnificent
– this stud bull, true to breed with descendants high in butterfat
. . . Astronomical ! Meat quality . . . super prime ! Consistency
of colour . . . from snout to midriff, from midriff to tail – measure
them, they're precisely equal ! This sire of the red-backs – take
good note – made as a gift to the happy couple Henry and Salome
Silberstein.

Applause. Applause. Applause.

I was there, Uncle Giepie, when Brutus . . . How much was it?
Eight thousand? Ten thousand rand? When he was bid for at the
cattle auction of the firm Veenstra and you refused.

Applause. Appl. Appl.

Quiet now, quiet, quiet – for Dries with the white light in his
eyes and love in his heart, and the madness, the utter insanity
that lives exuberantly in every creative form. Quiet now for
dynamics, for brokenness, for patience, wild dreams, good fortune
and ecstasy. Quiet now for chance, about which there is no reasoning – for uncertainty, doubt, disenchantment, frustration, the
butterfly-flight of creative dreams.

'But let us take a closer look at Brutus, this animal, this . . .'
– a gesture of the hand, since he was deeply moved and lacked
words to describe the breeding of the paragon.

Silence. Equivocal silence. And courageous recovery. As you
will observe, dear friends, the red area and the black area are
exactly the same size and the two colours are divided by a straight
line exactly, take good notice, exactly in the middle of the body.
The black is unblemished black; the red is unblemished red. The
slightest fleck is a disqualification. Not so, Uncle Giepie?

He turned to Uncle Giepie who sat with folded arms on a
shooting-stick, eyes half-closed, nodding his head in careful assent.

And now, friends, I'd like to tell you a little secret !

He suppressed his delight with difficulty, winked at the girls,
rested his hand on Brutus's hump, clapped his hand to his mouth,
frowned and tilted his small, cropped head sideways.

I don't know if Uncle Giepie will shoot me, but . . .

Wait for it . . . Wait for it, while the guffawing gathers volume
and the dresses flutter dazzlingly.

But . . . Brutus has a small blemish. Here (the hand moved from the hump to a place between the ears) here, if you look carefully, you will see a small white spot the size of a tickey.

Now the secret was out; the well-known secret about Brutus; the slight deviation that denied perfection and that made everyone, now unpent, explode into laughter, nudging Uncle Giepie lightly meanwhile.

But friends . . .

Now, seriously, with lightning seriousness, with light and with love . . .

But in this animal, despite the one single imperfection, over and against it, the positive qualities: Brutus's hide, that of the Ollenwaar-breed, characteristic of the red-black, the breeding secret of Uncle Giepie – the hide under the hair is complementarily red and black; black with the red, red with the black. By way of demonstration, appropriate to this occasion, a handsome gesture . . .

A light was brought nearer, a powerful floodlight connected to a lead from a standard lamp, and there on the black shone the letter S in red and, as the light was moved, the letter H in black on the red.

A drumming on the floor : the thunderstorm of enthusiasm that grew and grew.

But friends . . .

and grew and grew and grew

But friends, please, friends !

and grew

Friends ! Not only double-purpose – milk and meat. Please, friends ! But double-purpose meat ! More finely grained where it's red, more roughly grained where it's black.

enthusiasm, enthusiasm

Truly, friends, is there any doubt . . . this breed . . . fat four point six . . . fertility phenomenal . . . feeding habits undiscriminating . . . weight-increase even . . . !

enthusiasm for Uncle Giepie on his shooting-stick, head bowed; enthusiasm for Brutus, stately in the light, placidly chewing the cud, *natura sui generis*, calm . . .

The arm bent, the wristwatch, the finger on the dial – and silence descended in recognition that the end was approaching.

Then there is the last quality, the mystery, for which even Uncle Giepie himself can give no explanation. Length of the vocal chords? Determined deviation of build? Who knows? But Brutus, the Ollenwaar-breed, our beloved red-blacks, the bull that does not bellow. Bellow, yes, but in a pitch above the threshold of our human ear. Is that a fault?

NO!

Is that a deviation to despise?

NO!

Is it a stigma upon the breed?

NO!

Does Uncle Giepie deserve the scorn of jealous breeders?

NO and uproar. NO and uproar again as Hey, Dries! Hey Dries! he fought his way back to his place (Hey, Dries!) through dresses, graceful arms and silken tresses that made him completely invisible.

Boom-boom, the drumbeat and tap-tap, the thud of feet, and speech! speech! for Uncle Giepie, who straightened up slowly, buttressed by two strong young farmers until his limbs had lost the stiffness of the old position and settled into the stiffness of the new one; and the high priest of cattle breeding, stiff with well-deserved money, spastically approached the circle of light before his fantastic beast. The eyes of Brutus, the deep, soft eyes of Brutus directed at the small eyes of his creator, the bond between man and beast, the reciprocal and yet one-sided knowledge, the silent communication and, finally, the beloved figure of the beloved breeder against the background of his beloved bull.

Elfin farm girls *bras croisé*, elfin farm girls *en l'air*, elfin farm girls *en arabesque*, elfin farm girls dancing *la grâce sautée*, elfin farm girls pirouetting, elfin farm girls *sur les pointes*, elfin farm girls *demi-bras*, worshipping.

And then *tableau*.

Uncle Giepie's message:

Dear friends. Once again we have here proof of unsurpassable honesty that cannot be sensed by advance planning in deviate efforts that our policy through proofs established in this creative work of breeding in the form of foreseeable prospects and extension in contrived prospects can be broken down systematically by the calculation of infallible acknowledged powers at our disposal.

He took a sip of water.

A balanced, tangible, living, unsurpassable animal as slight evidence in these determinations quoted on the ground of available abilities as positive and negative coupling and gradual development from the source serves as further proof of sources drawn from creation.

He was silent for a moment.

Then he resumed.

These determinations adduced, our understanding and available abilities balance in aptitudes on a rock-firm background. And I appeal especially to the young. Through proofs established in the work of creation we have an example of visible consequences from positive and negative couplings. And in conclusion I want to praise my host and hostess and, I think I speak for everyone, bring greetings, red-black greetings from the breeders' association. I thank you.

Dresses lifting, dresses swirling. Slim legs white as milk in the light, plaits waving like ribbons. Teeth, eyes and lips shining with ectasy. Up, up and up the dresses until there was a glimpse of panties and then, Heavens! Whoops! down with a clapping of hands.

Photographers, crouch-backed like wolves in dinner jackets, popped up everywhere and hunched, creeping low, with the barrage of their flashbulbs.

One of Uncle Giepie and Brutus past a pure white thigh for *Farmer's News*.

A call for Uncle Nicolaas van Linden, chairman of the Agricultural Union. He was placed beside Uncle Giepie. A call for the father of the future bride, Jock Silberstein. Positioned to the right. A call for Salome Silberstein. Salome! Salome! A movement among the dark-eyed girls but Salome did not come; she was afraid of the bull. A call for Henry – not afraid, surely! and he appeared, wrongly dressed and therefore placed all alone at the back next to Brutus. A call for 'Hey, Dries! Hey, Dries!' and he was genially pushed, laughing wildly, into a kneeling position in the second row. A call for Mrs Gertruida van der Riet of the Women's Agricultural Union; in the second row. Call for Mrs Fransina van Staden, convener of the show committee; in the second row. Call for Abraham Albertse, agricultural extension officer, in the third row, lying on his side. Call for Barend Gouws of the Veld Trust Committee: on his side in the third row. Call for Wynand Harmse of the Vigilance Committee: third row, lying sideways. And the little farm girls? Ah! Wolf-calls for the little farm girls! Spread out, like a grandmother-rug, right in front and back and back went the photographers. Quiet now! Smile, please. Come on! One huge grimace, a detonation and in supernatural light the front-page photograph for *Farmer's News* was born.

Quiet, please, friends! Keep your positions! Another for the official organ of organized agriculture. Serious please.

And in a group – with the black of their suits and the white of their shirts, with the smart simplicity of their formal attire, alternated by the elegance of elaborate feminine finery, brightened by the rainbow of bashful little farm girls, dominated by the tremendous bull, his eyes glowing deeply in the light – they all achieved the required pattern of seriousness. Waiting for the second flash of the big camera, a silence descended on the room; and suddenly, when the lenses had focused the images, and the shutter had been set to an nth of a second, and the living figures had already assumed the rigidity of the photograph, the huge flanks began to move, the chest swelled under pressure from the expanding lungs, the bicoloured hide rippled as thousands of small muscles came into play, the horns tumbled back, the shiny snout pointed up to the ceiling, and Brutus made – with shuddering abandon, supersonic, inaudible – his silent protest to the heights.

From the back of the room, unaware of the silence and the camera's moment of creation, Judge O'Hara spoke: 'Evil came with the fall of the angels. A will was raised against the will of

God. It was a moral wrong. A shock passed through the universe and reverberated through the whole world. Perfection was shattered into thousands of splinters. Lucifer shot like a star through the firmament...'

The light flashed through the whole room. The shutter flicked at a 50th of a second and beyond the reach of human ear the bull's voice bellowed and bellowed and bellowed.

IV

The night, when the new drone took over and the fans waved the invisible dust through the vents, and the drawing room was empty but still warm from the human beings, and the windows were wide open so that the stench of the bull could escape; while the moon came from behind the clouds and the walls of Welgevonden shot their shadows across the lawns, light footsteps sounded in the passage and someone tapped at Henry's door. But, deep in sleep, the small sounds were outside the range of his senses and he heard only the cries of distress of all those voices that had been inaudible during the day.

Fugue on Spiritual Rearmament, Apartheid and Planning

'If you believe in Raphael, the Astrologer, then today is the last day for the good,' said Jock Silberstein when he met Henry next day in the garden. Dew sparkled in the sun; distant voices sounded cheerfully in the morning air. 'How beautiful,' said Jock as they stood on the hill above vineyards ripening in the sun; and 'How can one possibly describe it?' as they saw a single pine tree beside a granite rock with its branches against the blue; the heather in the *vlei*, the arum lilies beside a stream, and the sorrel among the clover. Jock seemed larger this morning: the dynamic ruler on his estate; the golden god of Welgevonden.

'The first four days are designated for the good,' he said 'the fifth and sixth for evil. And on the seventh, the good triumphs again.'

This time they visited the laboratories of the vinery. Henry was introduced to Professor Dreyer of the research department. 'Probably the best wine expert in the country,' whispered Jock. 'It's said that he can determine the type, year and locality of any wine, blindfolded.'

Professor Dreyer was a tall, sombre man, a deacon in his church, a teetotaller, and Henry noticed that when he held the samples up to the light and described the characteristics of each type, his love was confined to natural essentials. When he looked at the wine, the goblet held up at an incline, its colour ennobled by the alchemy of the sun, he was not aware of the gold and amber hues, still less of the romance of love and wine, wine and conversation, the idea of wine, wine and imaginative flights, but of a coloured liquid, perfect of its kind, its beauty distilled to an abstraction. When they left and had greeted all the student assistants (young men with B.S. [Agric.] degrees, crew cuts and a liking for rugby, target shooting and girls); and as they made their way outside between row upon row of test tubes and chemical apparatus, Henry noticed Professor Dreyer with a test tube in his hand, isolated in a private rapture.

'That's the man of the new being,' said Jock. 'Even our awareness of beauty has lost its form.'

'And now I want to show you Welgevonden's showpiece,' Jock said a little later.

He led Henry through a garden in which Dutch tulips divided an inner court symmetrically in two colours: yellow on one side, red on the other. Of exactly the same height, they glowed in the sunlight, a model of aesthetic prescision.

'Do you prefer this kind of beauty?' asked Jock.

Even the outlines of the buildings that bordered the garden courtyard were of an exemplary mathematical pattern.

'Think it over,' said Jock. 'Is the casual arrangement of colours, the haphazardness of growth and decay, the asymmetry of chance in nature really more beautiful?'

They looked around them and suddenly, in a moment of insight. Henry was overcome by a sort of emotional susceptibility to this beauty of contrivance, whereby all the colours and the entire layout became – like wine for Professor Dreyer – a satisfaction in itself.

'Simplicity,' said Jock. 'Perfection. Not a single plant is unhealthy. Years of study have been devoted to the perfect plant.'

They looked to left and to right and the flowers played their vivid red and vivid yellow back at them; calm from left and from right.

'Think of the old man who issues the permits,' said Jock. 'Do you remember him? The one with his room full of wildly trailing plants? We got him in Cape Town. He was caretaker of the garden of a small Catholic church in one of the suburbs. He brought his little garden with him to his office and his plants are destroying him. His mind is like a calculating machine in which the figures have shifted and every calculation has become chaotic.

But his fidelity to rules, his love of permits, his denial of an exception in regard to his boss explain his unconscious urge towards the mathematics of planning. One of these days he'll stop looking after his plants and pruning the dead flowers. Before long he'll throw them all out of the window. He will achieve everything by the completion of forms.'

Jock sat down on a modernistic bench designed in the shape of an hour-glass.

'One of these days we're going to give him a computer,' said Jock. 'A beautiful machine for every kind of calculation. Once he has mastered it, he will find increasing delight in the combinations it can achieve. It gives deep satisfaction in proportion as you progress according to the instructions and discover all sorts of combinations that are completely consistent. There are more combinations than the human brain, with its casual associations, can improvise.'

Jock beat his hands together, a light in his eyes.

'I foresee that the old boy will have hours of pleasure and yet at the same time achieve our calculated aim.'

There were identical veins in every flower around them: light green determined by the commensurate distribution of sap. And the colours were uniformly red and uniformly yellow.

'When one improvises,' said Jock, 'one loses one's grip on the material in the process. We think with the flame of inspiration, but something is lost in the combustion. We must have equilibrium, balance, a little something of the machine in mankind. It's a fantastic adventure.'

He scrutinized Henry carefully but could learn nothing from the utterly negative expression on the young man's face.

They left the garden and entered one of the buildings.

II

The building had been designed by a Cape Town architect whose object had been to retain the spirit of the Cape style in modern factory design. The big hall they now entered and in which the various wines were bottled, was lighted by large old Dutch windows with small panes; the floor was of Batavian stone; the ceiling of yellowwood with heavy crossbeams. Jock pressed a button and all the windows opened; he pressed another and they slid slowly to.

'In this hall,' he said, 'all the red and white wines are bottled.'

Glass conduits protruded from both sides of the walls. They were connected automatically to bottles that lay horizontal on conveyor belts and were then suddenly raised to a vertical position for the moment of contact when, filled exactly to the neck with red and yellow, they disappeared vertically down a tunnel in the wall.

At the side where the white wine was being bottled there was a row of Coloured girls in white; and on the side of the red wine, a row of White girls in brown uniforms. It was not quite clear what they were doing. Their hands moved; they touched the bottles; they manipulated instruments and were very busy doing something, the exact nature of which escaped the notice of the uninformed onlooker. But their hands moved to a specific rhythm – sure and competent – that implied practice.

'Apartheid,' said Jock Silberstein. 'Complete apartheid. In spite of world opinion, it is nearer the spirit of our time than people think. It's an *individual* contribution to the whole; a protection of the underlying identity in order to attain the common purpose.' He smiled cheerfully at Henry. 'I find it poetic.'

It was pleasant to watch the shining, empty bottles. They came sailing like bright ships over the horizon, rose up to heaven and were filled with colour. The glass sparkled in the sunlight from the windows as the last bottles disappeared into the cloistral tunnels.

'How do you get the bottles so clean?' asked Henry.

'That is done in an earlier room,' said Jock. 'Do you want to see it?'

They had to return to a room of steam and chaos. African men in blue uniforms moved in disorder between the cauldrons, where trolley-loads of dirty bottles were dumped into a great aluminium tank. Some of them were tawny-skinned and spoke with the click-clack of the Xhosa; others were darker and their speech rumbled with a musicality of unknown Africa. There was something attractive even in the disorder: the undisciplined trolleys, the apathetic collisions, the white smiles of enjoyment and the complete absence of a sense of time. Ostensibly regimented by the identicality of their uniforms, they moved at the pace of lower wages, with innate carelessness. In this room horsepower mattered.

'They can keep on,' said Jock. 'That's their use. Keep on also with the unnecessary.'

When Jock and Henry appeared they all stopped working and simply stared. The tank got emptier and Jock nudged Henry.

'Do you feel like seeing the hall where the labels are pasted on?' asked Jock. 'It's particularly colourful.'

This hall was in the centre of the building and was circular. All around the wall were little tunnels out of which the bottles came sailing on their various belts. They sailed in cheerful shades of red and gold like the spokes of a wheel, to a central point where, almost touching as they passed one another, they suddenly swerved and began a circular course that spiralled into the sign of Ubu, by turn brought together on the same belt as far as the hub, where a golden bottle and a red bottle gleamed for a moment in nakedness and were then embraced by two iron bands. It was a deft movement that no lover could equal; it lasted for only a second, then the hands opened and nakedness was covered by a Welgevonden label, with all the colours and all the designs around a central theme; the House of Silberstein. Then a small platform moved away and the bottle disappeared below through a tunnel.

'To the various cellars,' said Jock, 'where they are packed and shipped.'

Except for a single white-clad man beside a large machine up on a platform there was nobody in the hall. All the man did was watch and press a certain button now and then.

Jock looked at Henry.

'Do you find this cold and without feeling?' he asked. 'Do you prefer the old methods of pressing grapes and the personal touch?'

'I think it's marvellous,' said Henry. 'I could stand and look for hours on end.'

From his height Jock looked at Henry and yet, despite their

difference in size, their distinctive personalities were conciliatory and each conducted himself with individual strength.

'There is something of this Welgevonden in you,' said Jock. 'The echo you throw back is clear and true.' He set off and held the door open for Henry. 'All you need is the contact with chaos from which order is born.'

Outside all was quiet and they crossed a lawn.

'You must have knowledge and experience fear,' said Jock. 'One cannot exist without the other.'

They left the lawn for ampler spaces where trees and houses dotted the landscape.

'If you learn to know fear,' said Jock, 'then Welgevonden will stiffen your true inner assurance with routine. Then the priestly office of Welgevonden is yours.'

On their way to one of the group of houses they again passed the gardener's little office. They could see him inside, sitting at his desk, the whole surface of which was taken up by a huge cream-coloured calculating machine with handles, knobs and cranks. The gardener sat motionless, squarely in front of the apparatus, staring straight ahead. It was as if he and the machine were regarding each other in silence.

'I see they have already given him the machine,' said Jock. A little farther on: 'It isn't that the machine will purify him; it will only hide the anxiety and uncertainty. It's towards this silence that the whole world is moving: the protection of specialization and order. Naturally, it will be temporary and the explosion will come.' He flung up his hands to indicate the apocalypse.

They were approaching the group of houses and turned right towards a charming cottage, covered with creepers, picturesque among the trees. Jock suddenly stopped.

'Look, Henry. How can I put it?' He hesitated. 'You must experience the purgation of the whole, understand the reconciliation of chaos and order, be reborn through fear and knowledge.' He resumed his walk, went up to the cottage and knocked at the door. They waited awhile and nothing happened. Jock knocked again, harder this time.

'There is a friend of mine in Cape Town,' he said, straightening his tie. 'Julius Johnson, the big manufacturer. He is being hounded by a mad woman who is trying to blow up his factories. She wants to destroy order to make people aware of chaos, and in that way hasten the rebirth.' He took a comb from his pocket, looked into the pane above the door and began combing his hair. 'The poor soul has the wrong end of the stick. Order is necessary for rebirth. Order will always be part of us; it's inseparable from the new nature of things. It lies even at the basis of abstract art and all the experiments of the *avant-garde* in every field. The change will definitely and for sure not come through destruction. It's Welgevonden, philosophers, priests, artists, writers . . .' He had the comb in his mouth and mumbled while he smoothed his eyebrows. 'All these products of Western civilization.' The comb back in his inner pocket, he knocked at the door for a third time. 'Not the antics of the bushbabies beyond our borders. The New Order is more subtle than the unsubtlety of sheer chaos and sheer order.' He stood erect : six feet four, hair red, shoulders squared, lightning in his eyes. 'We need knowledge, faith, fear, trust and courage. We'll show them yet in this republic of ours . . .'

The door opened, a chubby little blue-eyed, black-haired woman appeared and changed him into a big, naughty boy who seized her arm, gave her a crooked kiss on the temple and led her cheerfully into a pleasant little sitting room.

'Mrs Dreyer,' said Jock, his arm around her décolleté shoulder, she herself pressed at an angle against him, their faces beaming from two height levels at Henry; and behind them, through the frills of chintz curtains, the sunlight played on a glass menagerie, on a scene of middle-class furniture, on the warmth of everyday love and sorrow.

Mrs Dreyer wriggled free and indicated (prattling throughout about the weather, the flowers, the house and the living things of daily life) that she would make them tea. She disappeared through a bead curtain into a narrow passage leading to the kitchen, followed by Jock. Henry could hear the sounds of tinkling china and also the softer shuffle of human movement, interrupted by meaningful silences. Alone in the room, caressed into half-sleep by the sunlight, enfolded in the arms of an ornate armchair, his doze was interrupted every so often by Mrs Dreyer bringing in, first, a tray with cups, then a plate of marie biscuits, then small plates and teaspoons and forks. Each time her dress was a little more disordered: the blouse looser and hastily buttoned, the skirt patterned with fresh creases, the bow in her hair fluttering with every movement and finally, not there at all. The more dishevelled, the more cheerful she looked: a little bundle that, like a cotton husk, unrolled in the joyful wind.

And then Jock appeared, jacketless, his hair mussed and his cheeks stained with warm orange smudges. He carried the teapot under its red, knitted cosy.

They drank tea sociably together in the small sitting room while birds sang in the trees. Their talk was restfully empty; simply a pastime and a prelude to what was to follow.

Henry decided to leave and he thanked Mrs Dreyer for 'the nice cup of tea and the hospitality.'

'Salome was here a moment ago,' she said at the door. 'If you hurry, you'll still find her outside.' She was impatient for him to go; she was pink with an aura of romance; her eyes were soft with desire and she projected her own sweet anticipation upon the two young people.

He turned his back on the picture: the cottage, the green front door, the climbers, the hollyhocks, the pleasant little woman, the red-headed giant behind her – on the small domestic scene that was the prelude to what would presently be gay adultery, in the little room behind the window with chintz curtains.

III

Alone, Henry wandered away from the picturesque towards the orderly factory, across fallow land where nature allowed clover, tendrils, weeds and wild flowers to obscure the footpaths – away, away, with his own thoughts that never knew the responsibility of a personal decision; uncomplicated among all the contending claims to his partiality, with an emptiness that was nevertheless rich in its ability to attract the new without classifying it. He still felt the sun upon him, he looked up at the empty blue sky and recognized something of that rarity that was also in himself. He lowered his gaze and saw someone who might be Salome: a girl, hazy in the distance, and she was pretty, although he could not identify her properly, for there was in her movements a harmony, a coordination and a grace that belonged to all the well-formed.

He followed her slowly and drowsily, while the distance between them lessened when she stopped, or turned and (to him faceless) looked towards him, or sometimes, with or without reason, apparently waited for him.

They approached the factory and she walked somewhat faster past the little office where the gardener suddenly pressed oo on his huge machine, looked carefully at the figures and, when she had passed, recklessly followed with 34269 –. He struck the tabulator and, when Henry made his appearance, pulled the lever and got 65731 +. Nonplussed, and yet stimulated by the abstruseness of numerical mysteries, he stared at the machine, cleared it back to oo + and, when Henry, too, had gone past, took up his textbook bible to read more about this god.

The plants obscured the light and in their shadows made it difficult to read the letters. He looked up with eyes from which new interest had expelled old loves. He decided that on the following day he would remove at least half of the foliage by the window ...

And now Salome seemed different to Henry: no longer the nymph of the heather, but slim and rich, the daughter of the ruler of Welgevonden among the white walls and the red and yellow hothouse tulips. Even in the haze of his myopia there was in the waving outlines the after-image of an original pattern. It was Salome, the replica of Jock and slim Mrs Silberstein, the chemical combination of two beings who had together not exactly created a greater perfection than the total of the originals, but something new that, in compound, was perfect of its kind.

Bright red, bright yellow as they followed each other through the garden: first for Salome with full-blooded movements, with the House of Levi reborn in Welgevonden; bright yellow and bright red for Henry, with the satin sheen of pure satinette, for the goy with the silver soul.

The young students, around Professor Dreyer-in-contemplation, the wine in his hand golden tinsel, stiffened like puppets when she entered, the dark-eyed daughter of Silberstein. Then they dropped their test tubes, swarmed around her and explained things to her with the enormous energy of their youth. But she stood next to the professor with the short jacket, the drab tie, the sallow skin and the dull eyes; who – sexless, forgotten by sex, deprived of sex – could see not the gold, not the warmth, not the romance, but only the *purity*.

A little later Henry entered. He saw no Salome, he noticed only the professor whose wife was now joyfully shrieking her fulfilment.

'She went that-a-way,' said one of the students and pointed to the door into the first room.

Through the steam-bath, now, where the African men, their tank empty, their trolleys caught in a knot, just stared and stared, as far as the next room

– where her torso swayed, and her fluttering legs were caressed by the fringe of petticoat, while the door opposite banged shut and the White and Coloured girls' hands struck and struck like cobras at the long rows of red and white that travelled to tunnels and through tunnels

– as far as the kaleidoscopic room of *pataphysique* with the sign of Ubu

– and there was no Salome.

The man in the white coat pressed a button

– and there was no Salome, only the Silberstein estate as Henry moved back into the open air towards the complex of buildings where the blackamoor was stridently announcing the meal

– at the barbecue.

*

Braaivleis in the sunlight, while the Xhosa cook's white cap became unstarched and collapsed like an unsuccessful soufflé. Barbecued meat and beer in the sunlight with slim Mrs Silberstein, her blue dress spread out on the grass, her eyes shaded by a wide-brimmed sunhat, her relaxation soothed to a doze by the non-sensical chaff of paramour van Eeden who, hands behind his head, lay supine and gave *sotto voce* utterance to his love's inspiration.

Grilled meat, blue sky, beer and the lassitude of a sunny mid-day as groups of guests paired off in the sequestered rooms of their whispered conversations. Meat bones, beer cans and lengthened shadows as, pair after pair, they wandered away to cool dark rooms, cool grass beside streams of water, cool arbours of willow branches, while cicadas droned and ladybirds flew from three-leafed clover to four-leafed clover and two of them suddenly dis-covered in this rare state the reason for abandon.

Interludes between the fluting of birds and sudden silences when shy ones took courage from the emptiness, as if they them-selves were not involved. Silence and heat as adepts carried the old game to new discoveries. Heat and silence as slim Mrs Silberstein stretched herself like a cat and ginger moustache bristled and the old roué-eyes grew blind with pleasure. Heat, silence, sunlight while the giant Silberstein found contentment in the arms of the daughter of Man. Sunlight, while the drab pro-fessor discerned new essences in ineffable nuances in the silence of his deserted laboratory. Heat, as the gardener in his small officc, his meal forgotten, tremblingly experienced the vertiginous pos-sibilities of his machine. And silence as Henry, in the seclusion of his bedroom, drifted into the darkness of a deep sleep that trans-ported him to an overpowering nothingness – a nothingness in which Welgevonden lay like a negative, with everything and everyone there, presently to emerge, with consciousness, in full colour.

Something, hidden in the nothingness but already born, lay waiting for the light. There were voices, thoughts and forms in the magical intermediate world which, alone, could understand the prophetic intimation. There were adventures of love and hate and all the ancient emotions awaiting the silver soul of someone like Henry who, himself without a distinctive personality and without philosophies, simply waited and waited endlessly. There was something in steel tanks, and bulls, and wine, and bottling plants, and four-leafed clover mingled with tulips, and lunatics with machines like Frankenstein monsters, and the mystery of good and evil that repeated itself in parody at Bishopscourt, and adultery, and sex, religion and the nascent spirit of a new time. There was a new chaos simmering in the cauldron. There was the strength of a new order and the stimulation of a new resistance ...

But for someone like Henry. And the fugitive Salome.

IV

Henry felt fresh and glowing after his sleep. He lay staring at the gilded ceiling for a time, while his energy mounted. Then he went into the bathroom where he made an interesting discovery. The room seemed twice as large as before. Someone had opened sliding doors and exposed an extension of the room. The new part was a sort of sitting room, furnished with fragile Chippendale chairs around an ottoman covered with towelling material.

First he bathed, in streams of hot and cold water that gushed from the lions' jaws, fragrant with the perfume from their eyes and then he lay on the ottoman while an even stream of regulated air dried him. Presently he went and sat on one of the chairs and found the whole set-up pointless until it occurred to him that this room had been contrived for intimate communication. A small carafe of Welgevonden wine stood on one of the tables, looking deliciously cool and tempting. He drank some of it and felt himself suffused by a mood of gaiety as he pondered the matter of clothes for the evening.

To dress for the anonymous guests... He decided on the neutrality of an ordinary suit, but in the latest fashion : a jacket cut long with raglan shoulders, rather narrow lapel, seventeen-inch trouser legs, wide shirt-collar points, thin tie with Edwardian knot, the two top jacket buttons fastened. He drank some more wine and noticed the sun sinking between the trees before his window.

Later on he came across the servant girl of the previous evening in the passage, but he hardly recognized her. She wore flowers in her hair and was dressed as a Moslem bride. She indicated with a cheerful smile that he should follow her.

The house was empty and he thought: the festivities are probably out of doors; but he found the garden deserted, too, and she led him to a place where he had never been before. At the centre of a circular clearing between the trees he saw what must surely have been the largest rondavel in the world. The windows, all round it like false teeth, gleamed with light and a tremendous commotion of voices and music filled the evening air. He entered and, as in the past dressed differently from the others, prepared himself to challenge them; and encountered the biggest hodgepodge of attire and colour that he could have conceived; colour, also, in regard to skin. There were Indians, Africans, Whites, Chinese, Coloureds and albinos. The various colours fell into noticeable patterns of national costume that gave the overall impression of those coloured cakes which are to be seen at Malay weddings and bazaars. And everyone was friendly enough to burst. People with teeth: false and their own; white ones with rubies; white ones and yellow; white ones, with two dark gaps where the front ones were deliberately missing. Friendship everywhere, grimacing like death: a deathly multiplicity of teeth; lacunae of passion; tombstones of sex, religion and goodwill. People with thick lips, curled like those of voluptuaries; people with thin lips that, smiling, merely emphasized their coldness; people with spit between teeth and lips, guzzling love; people of calculated goodness, come what may; people with teeth shamelessly displayed – an exhibitionism of the heart; schmaltz with gumflesh and teeth triumphantly over the colour bar. The good God is our pal: His teeth grin over the horizon like an immense building. Teeth of love, of understanding, of compassion, of weakness, of iron, of silver fillings, of Dada-paper, of longing. Teeth in the Welgevonden rondavel; of the Republic of South Africa; of Jesus Christ who loves us all. Teeth, teeth, teeth and teeth until everything became tedious and teeth, teeth, teeth until everything dies of frustration because we are seeking COURAGE and STEELY POWER and FAITH and SELF-SACRIFICE and it's more than teeth, teeth, teeth ...

'Perhaps,' said Dr Johns, 'you are surprised to see us here.'

'Us, from Bishopscourt,' said Judge O'Hara, indicating with a gesture the multicoloured crowd. He smiled at Henry. 'But think it over well: are we, of Bishopscourt, not known for our enlightened conscience and liberal thought? Behold the bonds of intellect between the university and the esoteric hill, fine threads of the spirit that stretch across the magical valley.'

'You're joking, Judge,' said Dr Johns to Judge O'Hara.

'A smile,' said Judge O'Hara, 'in these times . . .' and Dr Johns laughed with a full set of teeth, artfully created in the city workshop of his colleague, Dr Koch of Killarney, Bishopscourt.

They were standing on a kind of platform from which they had a full view of the circular room. A dance was in progress, according to which each group began in the pattern of its national costume, kept the differentiated pattern, changed to a chaos of movement, and then ended in complete integration – all hazy to myopic Henry, but in its colourfulness like a painting by Jackson Pollock: its blinding fortuitousness breathtaking.

'This roof of the rondavel,' said Judge O'Hara, tapping an empty glass against his false teeth, 'I mean the woodwork and the thatch, weighs fifty-five tons.'

They looked up at the roof and then down at the crowd which, during another movement, recomposed itself in racial colours. Against the walls were gigantic arrangements of proteas; the music blared from concealed amplifiers.

'A wonderful experience,' said Dr Johns. 'Listen!' Everyone had begun to sing, and as they sang they again moved through the intermediate landscape of transition and a new abstraction was conjured up. 'Listen,' said Dr Johns. 'They're singing the song of Spiritual Rearmament, but everyone is singing it in his own language.'

'That reminds me,' said Judge O'Hara, 'of the ecumenical assembly of Protestant churches that I once attended in Leiden. Everyone sings the hymns in his own language. As Dr Johns says, it's a refreshing experience: one world united in spirit.'

'It reminds one of the Catholic Middle Ages,' said Dr Johns, 'were it not for the sectarian division of the modern age. I mean the,' (while the dancers recomposed the tableau of integration), 'I mean the total absence of nationalism, the unity of culture and faith.'

'Ah,' said Judge O'Hara. 'But what exactly is the basis of uniformity here? Can you tell me that, Dr Johns?'

'Perhaps Mr van Eeden will . . .' said Dr Johns respectfully.

'But first a drink,' said Judge O'Hara.

Their glasses were filled with an estate wine. They looked expectantly at Henry.

The music had stopped suddenly and been followed by delighted applause. Everywhere white teeth gleamed.

Henry shrugged and said : 'It's difficult to explain.'

Judge O'Hara clapped him on the shoulder.

'Superb! Superb! Mr van Eeden. You have put your finger on the nub of the matter. Where and what is the myth that unites them? What is the face of the new Being like?'

They now linked arms with Henry and moved, talking, among the people. Very soon they were stopped by someone who introduced Judge O'Hara to a former Mau Mau leader. Dr. Johns inquired about his religion and after that they spoke about the Nigerian idea of God. Did they recognize a duality in the godhead? Perhaps Mr van Eeden, a particularly well-read young man, could supply the necessary information – but Henry had vanished without trace among the races.

In the midst of all the exuberance, goodwill and love he felt lonely. He longed for Salome and wondered whether he were destined to see her that night. His purposeless meandering attracted Jock Silberstein's attention who, as host, immediately noticed the apocryphal movement among his benevolent guests.

'Henry, Henry; young fellow, young fellow,' he said, placing an arm round Henry's shoulder. He listened to the stuttering sound of his electric-light engine starting up and then, when after a while the sound satisfied him, continued. 'Do you *ever* look for anything? Is it possible that anyone can be so neutral?'

Henry considered the question for a moment, but could find no apt answer.

'It's part of human nature to search,' said Jock as they wandered along. 'Unless, of course, unless you have found and understood the essence. But can one say such a thing at this stage?' He laughed back at his laughing guests. 'Do you already know of the nature of the *bonum* and the *malum*? Have you already experienced dualism?' He shook his head. The room was hot and drops of sweat were forming in his red hair and on his temples. 'Have you as yet a conception of formlessness? Is it possible that you don't have the least interest and are looking for nothing?'

The repetition of the question obliged Henry to answer, for Jock had stopped and trapped Henry with his blue eyes.

'I'm looking,' said Henry, 'I'm looking for Salome, but I have never yet seen her.'

'That's true,' said Jock and nodded his agreement. 'It's true, you're looking for Salome.'

Then he noticed Mrs Dreyer and Professor Dreyer. He bowed as befitted a host, with a touch of the grand seigneur.

Professor Dreyer, grey as ash even in his black dinner suit, as a teetotaller simply an employee without his wine, as a man insignificant in his commonplace drabness, returned his master's bow clumsily while his wife, commonplace in green crêpe de chine, giggled her secret.

'Does it make me a model of evil, my adultery?' asked Jock with a slight shudder as his plump loved one wiggled her last wiggle before also disappearing socially with her ash-grey husband. 'Is evil sanctified by custom?' He pondered his rhetorical question and forgot about Henry who, in any case, had walked on and lost his host in the process; but found before him, like prison bars, the duchess's teeth. Tonight, *noblesse oblige*, she was *laughing*. Her hair was bound in a tight bun at her nape, a silk scarf was clasped with diamonds round her neck, her head was thrown back, her eyes narrowed to slits, and she grimaced her benevolence at the goy, true to the spirit of spiritual rearmament.

'Oh, lovely evening, colourful evening, dancing, ecstatic evening!' It was she, Lady Mandrake, an assertion, but a challenge to her mystification in this world that was strange to her. 'Oh, Henry!' she bewailed her loneliness and nestled her head on his shoulder. 'Oh, Henry!' she sighed, on the barren island in the sea of guests who lapped lovingly against them.

They saw Sir Henry at the other side of the rondavel, but to-night he looked tired, old and neglected. He sat alone on a bench beside an Indian woman in a shimmering sari, but her interest was purely intellectual and restricted to human rights. There he sat, loveless, in a sterile world of group loves.

'Oh, Henry !' sighed Lady Mandrake and led him to a small bar where they were served an estate wine.

An African man from Kenya, dressed to the nines in an imma-culate dinner suit, a hyrax pelt on his head, danced past them. (Dancing had begun again.) He spotted Lady Mandrake, executed a few intricate steps, and sang the refrain : 'Don't point your finger at your neighbour because/your thumb is pointing at you !'

He looked straight into the cold face of a decaying civilization, a museum piece that endured unfeelingly the gaze of tourists, a history book with funny pictures, a piece of furniture in a dusty loft, dust returning to dust.

He danced on and – whoops ! – was acknowledged by a young girl who – whoop-whoops ! – understood the new rhythm.

'Oh, Henry,' said Lady Mandrake; but then her voice grew suddenly firmer : 'Doesn't Sir Henry look exhausted to you? Doesn't he look ill?'

Together they gazed at Sir Henry, who felt their eyes on him, looked hopelessly at the Indian woman, and let his chin sink with tired fatalism on his chest.

Lade Mandrake raised her glass.

'*Hasta la muerte!*' she said and her voice, words and attitude were suddenly ominous.

V

Henry moved on doggedly. With every step, as congener, Oriental and Negro came within his field of vision, the pattern of segrega-tion-integration changed; the colours mingled, as the image froze for the merest fraction of a second, vistas from two points of view lived by repetition.

He was confronted by a little man who, unshaven, out of place and hopelessly lost, was driven on nevertheless by an obsession.

'Where is he?' he asked.

Henry now recognized the gardener.

'Mr Silberstein, where is he?'

The little man looked at the many-coloured people, but without the slightest indication of interest or astonishment. He caught sight of Jock Silberstein in the distance and forged his way between a Negro and a Canadian. He was the only person who was not laughing. His chin jutted forward aggressively, his stubbly beard purposeful, and his mind was withdrawn into the only world that held meaning for him.

A large group had now formed a conga line and moved round and round towards a central point.

'Chook-chook!' they sang. 'The train of happiness. Off to Hallelujah Boulevard.'

Henry also saw the two Misses Silberstein. Never had they been so uninhibited. 'Chook-chook!' they sang and swayed their small bodies.

He found himself standing before a dark-eyed girl and he wondered, in passing, if she were Salome. She was very attractive and talked to him about love. She had already attained the nirvana of spiritual rearmament. Sex, religion, goodwill and unselfishness pulsed through her conversation and her real personality was drowned forever in the sea of universal compassion. A zombie of love, with her white arms and dark eyes, bloodless in the field of her crusade, the banners of leukaemia fluttering above the battle.

'I have compared myself to everyone,' she said. 'I have often felt superior and often inferior. But now . . .'

She indicated the circle of people who filled the room and tugged at them to join in.

'But now I have driven evil out of myself. Repentant, I have asked for forgiveness; I have examined and revealed myself honestly.'

Then she smiled, a smile that did not light up her face, but was merely contrived, that encircled tombstones with red, that solved the contest between good and evil forever by complete withdrawal to the amorphousness of the Great Togetherness.

Dr Johns and Judge O'Hara joined them, their attention caught in passing by the word 'evil', but they were demolished by her hauteur and aloofness – the academy of their world of books, wine and subtlety exposed as the new philistinism, themselves callously revealed as Right and not worth knowing.

Now Henry could move no farther; he was relentlessly drawn along by the stream of spiritual rearmament, compelled into the rhythm of love, spilled into part of the great protoplasm, and squeezed out in a conga line consisting of

> an Indian
> a Canadian
> a Swede
> a Mauritian
> a Swiss
> a Mexican
> a Sierra Leonian
> a Congolese
> a Matadian
> a Swazi
> a Brazilian
> and a Burmese.

The conga line reached the hub and dissolved in a chaos of understanding. He was carried hither and thither by a lyrical abandon in which, to thundering music from the orchestra, the individual was threatened with being trampled painfully underfoot.

Where *did* Jock find all these people?

Boom-boom ! went the drums and someone screamed in Henry's ear : 'Lookin' for a cat in Caux !'

Henry saw a 'gone' ducktail who, quite lost, had turned up at the wrong party.

'Gimmie a chick from Bánáná !' shrieked the ducktail.

He looked from one to another of the crowd, his stovepiped legs quivering like reeds in the wind.

'Glory Hallelujah !' he shouted. 'Dig that rhythm !'

'Ecstasy ! Ecstasy !' fluted the thin voice of Lady Mandrake who, stockstill, hopelessly drunk, was regarding the gaiety un-comprehendingly.

Henry saw the gardener; he had got Jock into a corner.

'Look, sir,' said the gardener urgently, as he scratched a pimple on his ankle, 'a man must have a future.' He gripped one of his overlord's arms like a vice. 'I understand the machine. Give me a chance. I've got a wife and six children. We must live.'

Love tore them apart and Henry and Jock found themselves alone for a moment.

'He lies,' said Jock. 'He has only one grandchild living with them.'

A Liberian tooted a toy trumpet in Henry's ear.

'He wants the job of the man who presses the buttons in the bottling plant,' said Jock.

'Is it difficult to press the buttons?' asked Henry. 'I mean, does it need considerable mathematical calculations?'

'I don't know,' said Jock.

'Make him an assistant,' said Henry. 'He's in any case harmless.'

'With a magnificent uniform,' said Jock. 'Gold and silver and green.'

It was as if they were spitting together into the tank.

Someone rapped on the sixteen-legged table: the chairman announcing speeches. Everyone fell back into panoramic little groups. They listened in silence, although deafening applause frequently interrupted the speaker.

'I'll work hard,' said the gardener. 'The nobility of labour. I'll know no hours.'

Jock tapped him reassuringly on the shoulder.

A former leader of the African National Union was speaking now.

'The truth,' he said, 'was revealed to me by the spirit of spiritual rearmament . . .'

'Day in and day out,' said the gardener. 'In the early hours of the morning . . .'

(Nobody saw Julius Jool, arch-communist, who was observing

everything with contempt. By chance an hermaphrodite, he/she sat like a Morgenthau of the proletariat awaiting the eventual reaction to *his* universal order. He had already done his work and was waiting patiently for the yield of his labour.)

Speeches and applause alternated so rapidly that even continuity was tumbled into disorder by the enthusiasm and words and cheers merged into a cacophony of rowdy togetherness. In the meantime Henry found himself back on the platform, after having met J. J. and slim Mrs Silberstein *en route*. Like Lady Mandrake, they too had appeared somewhat out of place – actually, like two selfish sinners, entirely unproductive.

Now messages were being read from persons with colourful but supremely unknown names; and yet, coming from former heads of office, impressive – messages embellished with the lustre of Hollywood stars, exalted by platitudes from puissant statesmen, and messages rendered respectable by the cowl of a priest, the missionary spirit of a clergyman from Upsida, and the self-sacrifice of a maiden from Vassar who, in her peace mission to Africa, had been chastised somewhere.

It was getting late in peace and Jock Silberstein rapped on the sixteen-legged table, to prove – in the midst of the universe – the importance also of the individual case. It was a great occasion. He himself felt inadequate and had, therefore, delegated the announcement to someone who might perhaps interpret the spirit symbolically.

And the albino came forward: he with his altogether colourless skin, who proved a truth by a freak of nature. And everyone cheered virtuously as the white-eyed, white-haired, white-negro received, for the first time, the esteem to which, according to all arguments, he was entitled.

'Dear friends,' he began, reading from a white foolscap sheet, 'we are here to celebrate the union . . .'

He spoke in a measured voice and looked often at the audience.
'Henry . . .'

And Henry came forward, irradiated by the spotlight, and took up a position against the background of proteas.
'Salome . . .'

Except for the intervention of a deus ex machina, he *would* see his loved one now. And, over there among the saris, evening gowns, cotton dresses and blankets, there was already a stirring . . .

But . . .

It was the gardener who took advantage of the opportunity to rush to the stage, flailing his arms and bumping into important guests : 'Mr Silberstein, I appeal to those present !'

Silence settled on the room, all movement arrested to contrasting pictures of segregation and integration, figurative and non-figurative, to blocs of good and evil, to fragments where good and evil were invisibly entwined, to a mosaic which, with the conga row, turned the circle inward, to the Ubuturd of lifted, living faces.

The gardener became aware of the albino and, rather disgusted, shoved him aside.

This was the albino's great moment: he had the contents of the foolscap sheet by heart; he had waited the whole evening . . . Fury surged up in him; he regarded the contemptuous gesture as a reproach against his colourless skin. He had seen himself tonight as a part of the greater entity; without kindred, without a country, without a language, without tribal gods – to this greater entity he felt that he belonged and, in conflict with the all-embracing, experienced the emotion that lies at the heart of apartheid. And, sanctified by his fury, he now did something that he would never had dared before – conditioned as he had been through the years as an aberration to be either destroyed or ostracized – he raised his hand against colour and struck the gardener back.

A sound of disapproval ran through the room.

Both the gardener and the albino, compelled by the urge to express themselves, struggled forward and, their hands and arms interlocked and straining, checkmated each other.

Then both began to talk simultaneously.

Gardener : All I ask is the right to work and to do . . .

Albino : A memorable moment for Henry and Salome Silberstein . . .

Gardener: To make a contribution with the machine . . .

Albino: We will not point out to them their good qualities, but ask them to take note of their friends . . .

Gardener: And to use that knowledge in the work to which everyone is entitled . . .

Albino: To keep their hearts and minds open . . .

Gardener: To analyse everything with knowledge and with the machine.

Albino: And to become aware of their friends.

The double doors of the rondavel opened and the two drab Misses Silberstein, at the correct moment according to prior calculation, but blissfully unaware of the trouble, entered with the cake. One wore a sari, the other a ceremonial blanket from Tangaland. They smiled and waved to the guests and, carried away by the rapture of the moment, they danced the high-life. They placed the cake merrily on the sixteen-legged table and then did the chook-chook in opposite directions to positions that had been determined well in advance, and from which each curtsied to the dumbfounded guests.

Motionless, in a nimbus of light, they all held their positions, and at that very moment, for the first time in many years, Jock Silberstein's electric-light engine faltered, the lights flickered and, while the swimming pool was being pumped empty, darkness descended.

VI

In the big house the fans suddenly began to turn. The huge propellers whirled the dust on the ceilings. All the lights around the farmstead were out; the moon was behind clouds, solid objects were simply gradations of darkness. The guests stumbled blindly through the gardens to their motor cars, which were parked somewhere in the labyrinths.

And then the horizon was lit by a vivid glow. In the African location, specially built for his workers by Jock Silberstein, one of the churches was burning. As a school and some of the administrative buildings also burst into flame, the garden was illuminated

and the guests found it possible to reach their cars and to depart
as quickly as possible.

Only Julius Jool (by chance also a fire-bug), his alibi established,
his little party just beginning, ran with outstretched arms towards
the light.

Chapter Five

Death of a Pagan

When Henry opened his eyes, he saw first of all that the room was dusky, the gilded patterns on the old-fashioned ceiling (angels, maidens, Pan with his flute) more sharply defined – as if in this sort of light the work of a forgotten artist (from Europe, many years ago) came more into its own. Then he noticed Jock Silberstein with rings of ash under his eyes, his khaki shirt blotched with dark patches of sweat, his legs scratched, his fingernails bent back and discoloured with clotted blood.

'What a godawful night,' he said and took a sip of coffee flavoured with Chartreuse. 'Saracens around the location. Journalists troublesome as flies. Only a third of the workers at the stills and the washing plant. You've never seen such an accumulation of bottles. And Professor Dreyer threatening to resign.'

'Because of Mrs . . . ?' asked Henry carefully.

'He says he can't concentrate in all the din. He says it upsets him. And half his students have gone as volunteers to guard the buildings.'

They could see a column of smoke through the window.

'The fires have been extinguished and everything is quiet, but heaven alone knows – it's a balls-up.' Jock strode to and fro in the room. 'In a few days everything will be back to normal, but the postmortem is still to come. Whose fault is it? Why? What's up? There will be tons of answers – but the *malum* will hover over everything and nobody will be able to lay his finger precisely on a single truth.'

He waved his hands and crisscrossed the room as if, somewhere among the furniture, he would find the truth hidden.

'There's an accumulation of evil and its nature is formless.'

Between the chairs, his large figure like a hunter's in the grass;

and he opened the wardrobe, the entire length of which was occupied by Henry's clothes.

'There's an accumulation of evil, but we have lived too long in the light and have forgotten the colour of darkness.'

He turned and saw Henry, hands behind his head, negative and peaceful in bed.

'Up, boy!' He fumbled in the wardrobe and brought out the previous evening's clothes, creased and crinkled from all the goings-on. 'You must come with me and today I'll show you that truth is, to us, a being and has nothing to do with our moral contemplation of its nature.' He threw the pile on the foot of the bed. 'Truth is because we feel it so. Our churches fight in this relativity.'

He looked around for a shirt.

'The terrain is no-man's land, and in it lies the power of good as well as of evil. Evil is too positive simply to feed on good; it has a dynamic life of its own.'

He noticed that Henry was getting dressed without bathing and without shaving, and appeared dilapidated, like someone who had known better days.

'I'm afraid the balance has been disturbed, Henry,' said Jock and, without turning, chose an unmatching tie. 'The caress of the good, the sheer unassailability of the *summum bonum*, the banner of light beneath which Tom, Dick and Harry fight, cause Satan to be underrated.' He noticed Henry tugging a comb through his hair and suddenly realized that he had not yet put on his shoes. 'There's an accumulation, Henry. An opposing accumulation of evil to which we all contribute the longer we move in the light.'

The light was dim. (Perhaps because of the smoke.) A haziness hung over the whole landscape.

'Our downfall lies in the hubris of our fixed convictions,' said Jock as they walked along. 'And for that reason I pin my hope on someone like you, who does not seek or decide.'

They went straight to the small native village; the column of smoke was a beacon beyond the factory. It was stifling and Henry very soon began to sweat; he noticed that under his suit his body was getting damp and that the dust in his beard was forming into hard cakes. The sun was behind the clouds, but, together with the haziness, they became aware of an inexplicable light that one may see occasionally in a lifetime at an eclipse of the sun. It was an oppressive atmosphere and Henry felt like someone who, in a moment of melancholy, comes to the conclusion that man lives in a hostile world, that all beautiful things are the false face of an unpleasant reality, that life is heartless, that everything is meaningless (or that the meaning is too difficult to understand).

He looked at the dark clouds, yet there were no signs of rain. Jock Silberstein's factory, his entire farm, appeared insignificant. They could turn to ash at any moment. Suddenly there was no work being done. Moss was intruding; dilapidated figures moved ghostlike between the ruins. Order was fragile; it could fall to pieces at any moment. A chaos of violence and bloody destruction could exterminate everything overnight. New orders might take over, again to become, one inane day, the victims of another defalcation. For what do we fight and strive? And Henry, in his rumpled, sweaty suit, deeply unhappy, felt that he himself was decaying with everything else.

They walked past the factory which, solid as ever, definitely sent smoke over the hill; which used the smoke to grow bigger; which rose out of the mist like a Kubla Khan castle. The steel tank was a silver saucer in the air, floating on the clouds. The outbuildings and cottages seemed European in the smoke haze. They went over the hill and descended to the village Jock Silberstein had built for his African workers. The Catholic church, the school and the administrative buildings were charcoal drawings of frameworks – abandoned at a stage which could not be distinguished as construction or demolition. Only the smoke and ash betrayed the stage – and the herded multitude that, with muted voices and purposeless movements, confirmed the destruction. It was as if they were all, after the outburst of the previous night, looking dully and stupidly for the regular pattern which they themselves had broken.

A few Saracens were drawn up in V-formation at the entrance

to the village. A few soldiers with Bren-guns across their knees sat on the armoured vehicles and looked, amused and bored, as a number of piccaninnies with big eyes circled round the armour. A solitary pick-up van containing a single prisoner stood not far away. Behind the bars was Julius Jool: full of self-confidence, basking in the limelight; every now and then giving the Africa-sign with a dramatic gesture. The other agitators and louts who had assaulted the labourers on their way to work had already been removed, but the thin row now winding its way under police protection to the factory was scanty and would only increase later.

And then there were the faces of the assembled: the African faces that looked all alike to the Whites, the lips and eyes that, according to individual experience, looked pleasant, crafty or cruel. The motionless faces that simply stared; that, perfectly passive now, were waiting perhaps for a call to further demon-iac outbursts – or waiting for the order: To work! Or, the next moment, would burst out laughing at someone who tripped over a beam and broke his leg. Or that merely hated. Or that wanted Jock Silberstein's factory and his wife. Or wanted to live in his house. Or wanted to open the faucets on all the wine barrels. Or simply moved with the others when the summons came.

Last night the women had whistled and the *impis* in say pants and with naked torsos had capered. There had been racial mem-ories, reborn in the flames. But whose hand had set fire to the little church where Father Kostelanitz had heard confession with half an ear, while doing drawings? And who had set fire to the school, where Joseph Ukulele had led the hymn? And who had had what grievance against old man Groenewoud, who patiently, day after day, had to explain the dogma of regulations in his office in the administrative building?

'Who? What? Why?' asked Jock.

'There are so many answers,' he said to Henry. 'Just ask the police, the reporters, the politicians and the clergy. Someone trod on someone else's toes and there was a fight. Give them the vote. It's the awakening of the black man. It's a proletariat on the march. The Church moves slowly, but the Church will triumph.

'Is this the face of evil?' asked Jock, pointing to the faces before him. 'Is this the face of evil?' he asked, pointing to himself. 'Is that the face of evil?' and he pointed to a group of inquisitive onlookers who were gathering and watching everything eagerly.

'Not long ago I knew the Devil,' said Jock, 'but now I no longer know what he looks like.'

As they left he said: 'One knew the Devil according to the image he assumed. But as one understood the true being more deeply, the abstract reality, the Devil became anonymous too.' He stopped for a moment. 'But remember, my boy, when the Devil disappears, God disappears also.'

He looked back, and in the distance they could see the smoke-enveloped village. From that distance nothing moved, everything seemed immobile to the naked eye: the people, the Saracens, the black mass, the trees, the houses, the ruins. Only the smoke moved slowly and obscured the sun.

'Jesus, Henry,' said Jock, 'I'm not trying to be funny. Of what use is it to ask questions and to listen to the apologetic explanations every second person gives you? A child is dead. And two policemen. Three women and sixteen African men. Father Kostelanitz was murdered in his church, mutilated and eaten before his bones were burned. Is that done in the name of the Devil? Then it would be understandable, wouldn't it? Then one would know. Then one would be able to fight against something. But even the men of God take sides. And what else can they do, if we have lost our images?'

There was an explosion in the distance: they heard the sound first and then saw the column in the air. The movement of the crowd brought the pattern to life again. Single figures were still static; there was only the column in the air and the billowing crowd. But it was too far to see in which direction they were surging.

The scene appeared to have made no impression on Jock. He looked at the still-expanding column of smoke. 'Look, Henry, there are various images of God. But what does the original look like? We don't know. There is an original behind our images, but it's inaccessible. We learned to know the divine essence through our images.'

Another explosion shook the earth and a second pillar of smoke rose beside the other. It was now clear that the crowd was moving in two directions. There was a shrill whistle. A couple of the Saracens moved.

'We still have images,' said Jock presently. 'We worship them automatically day by day. But they've become trite; images so trite that they've become false, they've lost their meaning, and merely remain to us as an abstraction *for which we must find an image all over again.*'

The noise had subsided. Motionless order had taken over again. The immobile panorama under the smoke columns was becoming part of the landscape, part of the grey light, and somewhere in one of the trees a dove began cooing.

'It's strange,' said Jock. 'We learn to know our images so well that we reject them and penetrate to the deeper reality of the abstraction. And the nearer we get to it, to the impersonal truth, the more we feel ourselves lost.'

His monologue was interrupted by the third and last explosion of the day. The Presbyterian church, too – small and poor under two pepper trees though it was – had made its modest contribution to the dissolution.

'At this stage,' said Jock, turning his head on the disorder, 'at this stage of the formlessness, evil is at its most dangerous and it is so difficult to distinguish. I mean, it does not matter if you cannot always distinguish the good. At the very least it is harmless. But an invisible Satan can become your visible God tomorrow.'

And on their stroll back they found themselves before Professor Dreyer's cottage.

II

Jock knocked at the door and smiled with a wink at Henry, as if he wanted thereby to reduce his illicit love affair to an innocent game. They waited a moment, the door opened and Professor Dreyer himself stood before them. He was wearing the trousers of the previous evening's suit and a sports jacket. He had removed the loose collar of his shirt and only a copper stud held the shirt neck over his Adam's apple. Just like Henry, he looked rather dilapidated, but there was the light of defiance in his eyes and his whole attitude expressed the challenge of someone who, from strength, was making his justifiable objection.

'You may perhaps inquire, Mr Silberstein,' he began formally (a small bantam cockerel before the large figure), 'you may perhaps inquire why I am not at my place of work. But I have reason to be aggrieved. *I have just discovered something . . .*' and he paused for a moment as a bitter smile appeared and he had the pleasure – on this, his day of defiance – of cornering big, rich Jock Silberstein with his lawful grievance. 'There is a reason,' he said, 'and you, as master, because of your position, cannot escape your responsibility.'

Professor Dreyer had a language of his own – a series of esoteric symbols which only his fellow experts could understand. It had the advantage of being accurate, exact and unambiguous. But otherwise he was a child, encumbered by the clichés of everyday speech.

'When I came here, Mr Silberstein,' he continued, 'when my wife and I came here, and I could take pleasure in work for which I have a love, we felt – well-housed as we are in this, your housing scheme, about which we have no complaints, except that the sewage system does not drain as one might wish it to . . . Now, for that I have an explanation, and I think the sanitary inspector would support me. There is a layer of clay under the surface which prevents the water from the septic tank from being dispersed evenly, and thus it rises too quickly to the surface . . .'

He paused for a moment and resisted the lesser grievance which was threatening to dominate the greater: 'Where was I?'

For the second time in this house Henry saw Jock become a big, awkward boy who hid his embarrassment bashfully by standing first on one leg, then on the other, straightening his tie and smoothing his hair.

'Your responsibility, Mr Silberstein,' said Professor Dreyer – his original grievance slowly mastering him again – 'your responsibility in regard to an injustice done me.'

He stopped dramatically and fixed his ash-grey eyes accusingly on the ruling power who, thank God, was before him incarnate, the Master in person – so preferable to the impersonality of an unknown authority, the wrongdoer hidden always in a mist.

(It was odd, seeing Professor Dreyer in this role. Nothing remained of the aloofness with which, in his own world of research, he had at least attained a dignity distinctive to people who, by giving themselves completely to their task, eliminate all paltriness and triumph over their human insignificance. Henry now saw Professor Dreyer without his specialized ability, as on the previous evening at the party, except from nearer. He saw the incompleteness, alas, of the imperfect man, the product of specialization, the brilliance of a technologist which was fortuitously a quality in the make-up of an otherwise commonplace man with a grievance.)

'I was just about –' Professor Dreyer blabbed his jealously guarded secret impulsively – 'to solve the problem of perpetual fermentation.'

(Like all dear lunatics in the field of *perpetuum mobile*.)

'Thugs broke into the laboratory. Your own labourers, Mr Silberstein. And drank everything. DRANK IT! Imagine that! Persons in your service, Mr Silberstein. Your labourers. Do you expect me to sacrifice a life's work to barbarians who were *allowed* to get out of hand? Which you allow, Mr Silberstein, with all your parties – I was there last night – where there is no colourbar?'

Professor Dreyer really had no interest in politics and would have worked even for President Nkrumah, provided he were left alone and given all the necessary facilities. He fixed his eyes, with all the reproach he could muster in ash-grey eyes, on his master, who suddenly began to smile and as suddenly became unsmiling when Professor Dreyer said : 'And may I add in passing that my good wife, Miemie, was raped last night.'

And at that moment Mrs Dreyer appeared in the door, her hair draped over each shoulder, a Brunhilde clad in a red frock that fitted tightly and under which her jolly breasts swelled exuberantly. She threw up her arms theatrically and then lowered them.

'Oh, Jock! Jock!' she whispered, 'God help me. What could I do?'

What followed was confusing. Mrs Dreyer refused to summon the police. Professor Dreyer insisted that Jock Silberstein should redress the wrong and (with a cunning look) perhaps in future provide better amenities in compensation for the inconvenience caused. And after many promises and words of comfort Jock and Henry left the cottage, which was quickly obscured by the smoke-haze.

'It happens every year,' said Jock as they wandered off. 'She is raped every year, when my interest flags. (Was I a little aloof last night?) It's also a kind of defence against Professor Dreyer. From now on it's tea and adultery in the mornings again.' He frowned suddenly. 'But it's the first time *he*'s begun making demands as well.'

Involuntarily they were heading in the direction of the African village, and presently found themselves right next to the mob under the smoke column, before the unmoving black faces that simply stared: old women, young women with a lobola-value, housewives with brats on their napes, men with tribal blankets over their shoulders – everywhere, in all directions, passive and yet prepared for silence or chaos; the unpredictability of life entirely predictable to this strange phenomenon who had appeared like a genie from a column of smoke.

Very likely all sorts of measures were being taken to restore order: houses were being searched for weapons, mischiefmaking elements were being winkled out, temporary premises were being established for the administrative personnel – but from the outside all these activities were invisible. Yet the two multitudes, the onlookers and the involved, on either side of the dividing line of Saracens and police, were waiting with patience and dedication. Each of them seemed absorbed in his own thoughts and, while waiting for leadership, the hours seemed to pass in quiet contemplation. The busiest of all were a group of journalists who, with ubiquitous cameras and idiosyncratic imaginings, were intent on creating for their readers a world – an unreal world, devised according to the requirements of circulation, a world half-known and half-strange, a world in which every word and every event was pregnant with significance, a world faithful to the fantasy of the fourth estate – a world dreary and monotonous, in which sensationalism repeatedly jolted the reader from his mental stupor.

'As a Jew,' said Jock suddenly, 'I feel, perhaps, more readily the unpredictability of a sometimes benign, sometimes callous, sometimes moral, sometimes immoral Old Testament God. That is why I can't accept the dogma of evil as a *privatio boni*.'

He gestured in the direction of the factory and they left the village.

'Imagine regarding evil merely as degrees of negativity! It's no wonder that Satan is so dangerous.' He pointed back over his shoulder. 'Did we see Satan today or did we not see him?' Nothing could divert him from his dominant problem. 'In the Middle Ages he was a real danger; today, we try and shut our minds to him, so that they even want to leave him out of the Catechism. Do you think he was created by Man? He was an angel, created by God. Whether *He* or Man fell because of an individual decision of will, and whether God is responsible for that decision of will – we can talk about that tonight or tomorrow night. But he is here, Henry. The dark side of God in the mantle of light.'

They had now descended the hill and were approaching the factory to, as Jock said, 'determine in one go the dimensions of the damage.'

In the distance something glittered. It moved in and out among the trees and then, as it reached the level ground nearer them, stood out in full colour. It was the gardener in a uniform of gold. It was clear that the fantastic garment had been completed a considerable time before, since the craftsmanship with sewing machine and needle was clearly to be seen in the richly embroidered uniform. And his face! His shining countenance entirely justified the glittering garment.

'Mr Silberstein!' he greeted his master, and nodded genially to Henry.

He no longer had a grievance.

They walked together to the factory, through the tulips, and reached the room without Professor Dreyer. A small group of students were busy playing cards and jumped up hastily when Jock Silberstein entered.

In the washing plant there was only a handful of Africans who could hardly move between the heaped-up bottles. But, as patient as ever, they were busy dumping trolley-load after trolley-load of dirty bottles into the tank. They were all peaceful. And there was no indication that even a quarter of the day's work would be completed. When the company entered, they stopped and looked, and so the last trolley came to a standstill, too.

In the room where the Coloured and White girls were attending to the bottling, everything was going smoothly, except that only an occasional bottle came sailing by on the conveyor belt and, as on an isolated branch-line, only an occasional filled bottle disappeared into the cloistral tunnel.

In the Ubu-room, the fantastic mechanism was turning undisturbed, but there was no pattern. Because of the irregular supply, the iron hands frequently clapped in the air and a crumpled label fluttered to the ground.

In the meantime, the gardener had quickly mounted the platform and taken his place beside the man in the white uniform. At this stage, as an apprentice really, he was not allowed to press buttons. However, he watched everything with great concentration and nodded his head every now and then as, after the nth repetition, he noticed something he understood.

Most of the time nothing happened when the man in white pressed the buttons.

A beam of light had fallen through the old Dutch windows as they were leaving the room. They saw the gardener up there before the machine, encircled by a halo, surrounded by shadows, by chiaroscuro, like a painting by Rembrandt. The sun burned on the gold, the darkness swarmed with colours, his white hands moved as if he were playing an organ. One could even hear the music, if one listened to one's imagination. But nothing happened. The iron hands still clapped and the coloured labels fluttered from light to shade and played with the colours of the gardener's uniform. The Ubu-room had become a cathedral, the machine an altar, movement a ritual in a soundless, formless religious service. And there was dedication, seriousness, complete surrender, and the moment was full of indeterminate significance.

III

Jock and Henry found themselves back in the eclipse. They wandered on aimlessly, to a point where they came to a sudden standstill. The smoke column had now become a mushroom, a simulated atomic explosion that covered the entire horizon, and nothing moved.

All of a sudden Jock began to walk on purposefully, so that Henry was obliged to trot in order to keep up, until they reached the confessional where Jock turned on all the cocks and filled his lungs for the ecstatic cry. But only a feeble hiss trickled from the moist pipes and there was nothing left to them, nothing left.

'It's nearly lunchtime,' said Jock. They walked faster and Jock suddenly stopped at the steel tank. He looked longingly at the platform drifting in the haze. They climbed up to the platform and could see nothing. But now they were above the cloud. It was a dirty cloud that made their eyes water and left them isolated in the heights. The lake of distilling wine was a turbid mixture that heaved up and down. Jock lit his pipe and deliberately threw the match into the tank. Nothing happened and they climbed down slowly to resume their wandering over molehills, through the binary forest, among the Swiss stud cows.

There came the clatter of a horse's hooves and then they saw the elegant rider soar over the hedge, the slim little figure pressed close to the chestnut hide, rider and steed as one in the exuberant leap, which curved to a crescent and then slowly tumbled together on the soft ground. Hoofs and small shoes whirled over the veld, and rider and horse rolled slowly to a stop, with how many broken and mutilated bones? They hastened to the scene. There she lay beside the horse, the dark-eyed girl in interrupted ecstasy. Jock kneeled by her, Henry stood over her and they looked at the black eyes filling with tears. She gradually reorientated herself, and suddenly sat up, running a hand through her hair.

'Did you hurt yourself, Elsie?' asked Jock.

She shook her head, and they were now three as they walked back to Welgevonden for lunch.

There was a small lake, artificially constructed and fed by a stream in which there were trout. Some of the guests had been out on it in boats and were now returning to the house. A little farther on they saw a gleaming white pergola, Corinthian pillars splashed with red flowers, beneath which slim Mrs Silberstein, draped in classical white, stood hand in hand with J.J. And behind them was the blue mountain, the peaks caressed by a creeping smoke cloud which, suddenly driven by the wind, made all outlines delicate and suggestive like a scene from the golden age.

'Where are we lunching today?' Jock asked her.

She told him that she was herself not sure, but that they should wait for the blackamoor's bell.

In the meantime they approached the house. The procession had swelled and the multitude wandered at leisure through the garden and the flowers. Against the background of the day, there was something decadent in their attitude and appearance : their pleasure in the moment, their indifference to the events about which, in any case, they could have done nothing, the trouble and care that they had bestowed on their appearance, so that all the women looked beautiful and the men elegant. (Except Jock and Henry.) It was as if they were now moving about a garden in Florence while the plague raged in the valley, princes and princesses out of Boccaccio who, in the seclusion of their sparkling conversations, surrounded by beautiful things, fed on delectable foods, their thirsts quenched by the most subtle of wines, hoped that the *Flagellum Dei* would pass them by. The procession grew and grew, of lovely young women and lithe young men, under the trees, over the lawns and under the pergolas. As befitted a a good host Jock did not tell them that his whole farm had come to a standstill; as befitted Jock Silberstein's guests, they did not believe for a moment that Welgevonden could be threatened.

When they entered the front hall they stood aside to enable host and hostess to lead the way. They were led from room to room on a search that did not seem in the least like a search. Conversation continued, movements were easy, the rhythm smooth.

But the blackamoor's bell remained silent.

The two Misses Silberstein darted from room to room and rejoined the guests, having achieved nothing. Slim Mrs Silberstein's pretty voice murmured on softly in charming talk. The duchess, a shawl around her shoulders, peered with impatient eyes through every door. Jock Silberstein suppressed his embarrassment with difficulty as, repeatedly, he came across signs of his wealth, but not food. Somewhere among the lively, gaily chattering girls Salome must be, because above the babble one heard her name continually, Salome, Salome. In one room they found cigarettes, salted peanuts, almonds and cashew nuts. They lingered there for a while and together discussed for the first time the events of the previous night – with an indifference which, in any event, was as useless as a serious discussion. In the meantime the nuts disappeared to the last crumb and cigarette smoke billowed up to the ceiling. In one of the hallways they had to pass the marble statue of a pitch black horse. It was Jock's beloved, dead stallion, Saturnus, which had three times won the Metropolitan Handicap. Saturnus in full gallop while the multitude shouted . . . ! They ascended the stairs, appeared on the balcony (there in the distance smoke surged over the hill) and returned to a room with an empty table.

'I'm afraid,' said slim Mrs Silberstein, 'that the Blantyre has also joined the rioters.'

'The cooks, too, then,' said the duchess.

'But surely not the Coloureds,' said one of the guests.

'Thank God for the Coloureds !'

'But the cooks are Xhosas,' said slim Mrs. Silberstein and the guests assumed courteously that, in any case, they were not entitled to luncheon, in view of all the festivities provided by the Silbersteins during recent days.

And so Henry found himself back in his room after Jock had reminded them all of the party that evening and assured them that by that time everything would be under complete control; a prediction which proved true, since the cooks had begun turning up at the kitchen early because the African village, under control of the police, had reached the least interesting aspect of orderliness.

Towards midday Jock Silberstein's factory was in full swing. Professor Dreyer and all the others were at their posts. The section was full of bottles and the iron arms clapped the labels unfalteringly, squarely, in the right place. The man in the white jacket had now taken over the pressing of buttons and the gardener sat in lost dignity beside him, charged with pressing only a single button after the completion of every gross, promoted thus to higher figures, waiting with secret ambition for the day when he might perhaps press the *one* button which would embrace an entire load : and, later perhaps, on a platform of his own in a uniform of the angels, a button that would encompass the whole harvest.

IV

A restless midday sleep, the pillow becoming damp with sweat, the sultriness of the room increasing. All the windows and doors were shut to keep out the smoke. On the horizon the sun's rays filtered through the artificial clouds and hastened the twilight. Henry went into the bathroom and turned on the full battery of taps, sprinkled himself with all the perfumes and stretched out on the ottoman, drinking cool wine as he meditated upon the uniform for the party that night.

The guests, as Jock had remarked earlier, would be mainly intellectuals : journalists, clergymen, original thinkers – in fact everyone who considered that the appellation was appropriate to him but who, with typical modesty, would promptly deny that it was. The secret of dress had thereby been exposed : everyone was free to wear what he wished, because in the world of pure thought garments were an interesting matter of chance. By way of reaction, after the discomfort of a suit without the proper preparatory toilet, Henry dressed in close-fitting black trousers, a baggy silk shirt of Spanish cut, a cummerbund and soft suede shoes – an ensemble that gave him a free and easy feeling, his body glowing from his bath, tingling with a shy but manly cologne, attuned from head to toe to the classical law *mens sana* ...

He located the guests with ease, for they had gathered in one of the big drawing rooms and the hum of their conversation was a clear indication. He opened the door and entered unnoticed, because in this company appearance did not count, only personality, reputation and notoriety.

And, as in the past, he found himself once again a different kind of object. The men were all dressed in black suits, white shirts and silver ties: a silk handkerchief for the sake of appearance, a clean pocket handkerchief for tuberculotics, a pearl tiepin, fine leather shoes for black silk socks. Crystal goblets of Hmmmmmmmm! Welgevonden claret 1944, held in bone-white hands, limply but appreciatively – to be filled repeatedly, because a gentleman can hold his drink.

And the women: tall, slender, dark, with sharp eyes in which there was no response – basiliskian eyes hard with knowledge, that made a thousand observations through a thousand prisms. Sexless, but sexually inclined, model figures from *Vogue* and *Harper's*, long-legged with narrow hips and small breasts that only dwarfs could suckle. Women enmeshed in intellect and sex – burning with *furor uterinus*, but each bearing her own burden of incompatibility. And then, the occasional Lesbian, perhaps the most beautiful of them all – the only ones with unprismatic eyes, the only ones with warmth and love – wasted, alas, on a parody.

In contrast to the farmers, characterized by their more conventional smartness, and their wives, more bedecked, these men and women were united in groups and cerebrated in concert.

There were, however, a few other figures who shared with Henry his difference: Sir Henry and Lady Mandrake; he, smart in an old-fashioned way, in tails; she, in a black evening dress, with her Medusa face and classical simplicity that were timeless. And then there were Judge O'Hara and Dr Johns – two rather slovenly figures in contrast to the impeccability of the intellectuals; images of two wine-drinking classicists deep in the *humanoria*. 'Henry! Henry! Henry!' they welcomed him with elation

to complete the triangle in their abstruse discourse. As they spoke
and, as in the past, involved him in their own opinions in such a
way that, without saying a word, he shared the responsibility for
them, Henry looked over their shoulders and saw Sir Henry and
Lady Mandrake. It was the first time that the two of them stayed
together. Sir Henry moved with difficulty; the smile for the indifferent guests (who did not know him) was a grin, of pain against
willpower, of willpower in conflict with pain, a tragedy of
willpower pitted vainly against pain. He aimed at the girls with
prismatic eyes, waved the magic wand of seductive words, bowed
flirtatiously in an old man's manner with difficulty, went through
a grotesque mime of the *bon viveur*. Lady Mandrake held his arm
and never left him. She, too, smiled at the guests, but it was like
the facial play of a mother giving the tip about the feeble jokes
of her child: laugh now! A mother who duplicated all the gestures of her tiresome child, who sustained the travesty at once
blindly and perceptively. But behind the caricature, in the eyes –
if one looked into them as Henry was now doing – there was the
desolation of steadfast resolution: the other kind of madness, the
quiet kind that gives tranquillity to the eyes of all martyrs, murderers and saints.

'Ah!' said Dr Johns. 'Tonight Henry feels at home among all
the intellectuals.'

Judge O'Hara, too, nudged his arm jovially. They laughed unas-
sumingly and yet winked respectfully at Henry.

'Jock tells me,' said Judge O'Hara, 'that today you discussed the
disappearance of the images of good and evil. I assume that Jock
means by images those pictures that come into one's consciousness
of the indescribable contents that reside in the Collective Unconscious, not so?'

Henry nodded and Judge O'Hara looked significantly at Dr
Johns.

'Can we also conclude,' asked Dr Johns carefully, 'that you and
Jock accept a Taoistic view of dualism, the reconciliation of the
opposites, the *summum bonum* and the devil, as the ultimate
attainment, the realization of the true nature of the divine composition?'

He looked expectantly at Henry, ready for the prepared argument, but Judge O'Hara's enthusiasm brooked no answer.

'And to what extent do you accept Heraclitus' enantiodromia, then? If there is a constant movement of the opposites, can the opposites ever unite? If there is constant movement, can there ever be equilibrium?'

'Perhaps,' said Dr Johns, 'if I may answer for Henry – at certain times when the image of Satan and the image of Christ are equally strong in the conscious mind.'

Henry was saved by Jock Silberstein who, immaculately dressed, put an arm round him and introduced him to the guests. But here was an even greater threat: he was expected, before being accepted, to give an indication of his intellectual readiness.

'The fault lies with us Whites,' said Henry, in answer to a question about the events of the previous night. 'We must learn to get rid of our old, fixed ideas. We must search our own hearts. We must learn to think courageously.'

The silver ties now shone in his direction. Light broke on the prisms and overwhelmed him with many colours. The warmth of their affection was proof that he had found the right key: *mea culpa*.

Later, Jock said to him: 'My guests consider you a worthy consort for Salome,' and he smiled mockingly.

The two drab Misses Silberstein, hands behind their backs, listened with due respect to any conversation in which, by reason of their status as relations of the host, they had fortuitously been ensnared. Of slim Mrs Silberstein and J.J. there was no sign. The duchess had gone to bed early on account of the ailments of old age.

Henry moved from group to group and listened to the exchange of ideas.

'I gather a child was shot dead during the riot,' someone said.

'White or African?' asked one of the journalists, his attention aroused.

'A White child.'

The journalist weighed this information for its news value. The decision was easy.

'What a pity,' he said and held out his glass for more wine.

'It wasn't a White child, it was an albino,' said someone else.

The journalist drank his wine slowly, his eyes now troubled by uncertainty, his subsequent movements a model of indecision. He was a young reporter; it was his first assignment; he was carrying out his instructions meticulously; he knew his newspaper's policy.

At one stage he caught the attention of one of the guests, a social anthropologist, one of the right kind.

'Tell me, doctor, if an albino is born of African parents, could you describe someone like him as an African?'

Henry joined a couple of divines who were discussing an ecumenical conference in New Delhi with enthusiasm. One of them, with the help of an American grant, had attended it. They were ardently seeking formulas and patching dogmas together in the interests of greater unity. Thinking must be cosmic, the churches must be united, the territory must embrace economics, politics and all other aspects. The formula expanded; the clerics were excited about this, their greater field, and the programme began to assume the appearance of a declaration of the principles of an international socialist movement. One of them pleaded for the re-establishment of demonology and the angels, but that was of lesser importance. A new Protestant kingdom was nascent, a spiritual colonization, a UNO of religion to free the world. The poorest would suddenly become strong, it was superior missionary work with all the appearance and adventure – nobody was being isolated any longer in a tiny parish where he had the care of only a few souls. It was Marxism in reverse. Who knew – perhaps, one day, the two extremes would be reconciled here. The poor Republic! And they smiled. The poor Republic that lived in the illusion that the Almighty was well-disposed to it. A single nation did not matter, but all nations; not the individual soul, but souls. One had to learn to think big.

Henry felt lonely among all these mutual acquaintances. He wondered if one of the girls was Salome. He examined them thoroughly and found them all alike. Here, right before his eyes, she was concealed.

But a little later (Dionysus peeped from every bottle) the party began to change. At first there were no discernible indications, but gradually the vine leaves began to move and the muscles of the ecstatic god to flex. The first intimation was the toleration of all opinions; the tyranny of knowledge was gone. The girls became warm; slowly, slowly the Dior-clad bodies untensed, unwound defencelessly. Something was going wrong with the black suits and the silver ties; the exclusive dresses wilted and Welgevonden roared as of old. Then, as if the change had permeated the entire building, slim Mrs Silberstein appeared with J.J. (R.A.F. moustach bristling satanically) at her side; and the duchess, mumbling but full of beans, was squarely and solidly there.

The intellectuals were getting drunker, except for the clergy (*their* inebriation was of a kind peculiar to themselves). Everyone was forgiven everything. There was no debauchery; everyone behaved with perfect correctness: the lapse affected only their thoughts, which became free and knew no dialectical bounds. Things were going literally with a bang – everyone sinning with impunity in an unconstrained run of thought – when Jock came up to Henry and (although it was not necessary) whispered: '*Omne bonum a Deo, omne malum ab homine.*' Then, more loudly: 'Man has assumed the dark side of God. Don't you think that, on the quiet, we oppose good if we are continually obliged to bear the responsibility of evil?' He smiled at his guests, sinning in thought and in speech. 'Because Christ saw good in the sinner, have we not, perhaps, gone too far and clutched at the straw and seen too much good in him?' He touched Henry's shoulder with a heavy hand. 'God wished to restore only the whole, the totality.'

And at that moment it happened.

Sir Henry and Lady Mandrake had moved to the centre of the room, where there was an almost empty space. Drunken conversation tends to carry people in groups to the sidelines, usually leaving at the centre a gap for exhibitionism. Slim Mrs Silberstein and J.J. were, indeed, dancing there alone and pawing each other. But there was lots of room left and Lady Mandrake and Sir Henry had just made for that open space because Sir Henry needed air very urgently. He was evidently on the point of having some kind of seizure, but at this stage it could easily be controlled and arrested by pills. Lady Mandrake held a goblet, bubbling with Welgevonden champagne, into which she now dropped two tablets. She offered it to Sir Henry, but he refused to drink it. She spoke softly but firmly to him. He gazed wildly round the room and found that nobody was taking any notice of him; then he took the goblet and looked vainly round him again. Everyone's eyes were blind with esoteric conversation. He raised the glass to his mouth, drank the champagne and smashed the glass on the floor with a dramatic gesture. One of the girls saw this, drew the attention of her companion to it and they smiled indulgently. For a moment Sir Henry remained standing, erect as a post, his head held high, his eyes fixed on the ceiling of yellowwood beams.

He began to die before he was ready : his mouth open for last wise utterances. For a fleeting moment his spirit triumphed over his body and a thousand thoughts flashed through his mind. It was a lonely drama taking place in only one mind . . .

There are heights that vanish in the clouds, there are visions that make a human being unique. But there is also the power of speech which fails, when nothing functions, when all muscles slacken and contort. And then there is the second phase, when interest flags, when you no longer try, when your tremendous spirit drains away until there is nothing and you, alas, call soundlessly.

Lady Mandrake had seated herself beside him, his head on her lap. His eyes were staring and his mouth opening and closing. Dr Johns came over and felt his pulse, left the room and returned with his bag. But, when he took from it the needle and syringe, she stopped him.

'No,' she said calmly, 'Sir Henry is dying and needs no drugs. It is his wish. He wishes to experience life to the very last moment.' She held the face more tightly against her. 'Sir Henry believes in life. He has lived a full life. This is the end and I cannot deprive him of the end.'

Dr Johns looked around helplessly and did not know what to do. Lady Mandrake could be separated from her dying husband only by force. The intellectuals had drawn nearer and were watching the scene without panic but, like Dr Johns, without the ability to help. The intellectual girls were prepared to help, but they were accustomed to situations in which their help was sought from weakness: the defenceless piccaninny, the persecuted, the needy. Sir Henry in tails (Lady Mandrake his calm and relentless mouthpiece) demanded, as an agnostic and an individualist, the right to die in his own way. The journalists and clergy were used to death in every form. They found this form strange, unnatural, sinful – and antisocial.

Sir Henry's eyes moved from one to another of them. Without accompanying words it is difficult to explain the expression in someone's eyes. Without circumstantial proof, fury, hate, pain, sorrow and suffering cause a similar expression. His eyes at first were wild and then gradually grew dimmer. His mouth moved ineffectually. His hands gripped those of his wife. Then slowly his eyes glazed and finally lost all expression. The mouth stayed as if, at the last moment, he had said something.

Lady Mandrake remained sitting with her husband's head in her lap, her eyes fixed on the people who had formed a circle round her. One of the intellectuals misinterpreted her look – blind with grief, she herself completely withdrawn in silent suffering: and he asked, more loudly than he would otherwise have done: 'Who is he?'

Lady Mandrake looked sharply at him.

'Who is he?' she repeated. 'His name is Sir Henry Mandrake and he was born in Glasgow in 1880. Sir Henry is dead; his spirit is no longer here. His image lingers on only to that extent to which his personality still exists in the memory of his living friends.

'Sir Henry belongs, perhaps, to another period,' continued Lady Mandrake, as if in genial conversation. 'But is that true? Does one ever belong to any particular period? Does one ever know the nature of any particular period? One has only one's memories and they are really so untrustworthy.'

The guests remained where they were and it seemed as if they, like the multitude of the African village, were also held in thrall by a condition of immobile observation and meditation. Some of them thought Lady Mandrake theatrical; others thought her strange.

She looked down at the little man with his head in her lap. He was like a small doll on the floor. There was now no doubt about his age. He was a grotesque little wax figurine about whom, perhaps, in another century, in other cerements, in a different ambience, a highly wrought lyrical poem would have been recited : the lights dim and flickering, a purple cloak around his shoulders, a stately ceremony, a deeply felt ritual, a belief in images. Now, Lady Mandrake sat in the bright light, illuminated by knowledge (worldly and spiritual) and she said :

'I wish you could have seen him when he attended the first performance of *Pelléas and Mélisande* at the Opéra Comique. The gleaming top hat and the white gloves. The lithe body and the exceptional smile. And the time he was in love with Liane de Lancy and everyone was enraptured when the divine couple began dancing, looking into each other's eyes. He was enterprising, Sir Henry. He had his first mint julep in 1895. He climbed the Matterhorn in 1904 – the whole 14,782 feet, and then got drunk afterwards with the Swiss, in the snow. He was an intimate friend of Ellen Terry and Irving. He knew Max Beerbohm in the days before he went to live in Italy. He knew everyone : Diaghilev, Pavlova, Lydia Kyasht and Mordkin. Nijinsky and Karsavina danced in his room. Pavlova successfully resisted his flirtations. Sir Henry was one of the very first to laugh at the work of Cézanne, Gauguin, Van Gogh, Matisse and Picasso. Sir Henry had all the assets : money, appearance, vitality and restlessness in a period when all these things were not considered as evil.'

Lady Mandrake smiled at the stiff little figurine on her lap.

'I wish you could have seen him,' she said, 'the ubiquitous Sir Henry. The young man with the light in his eyes.'

She was suddenly silent, as if it were too difficult to reconcile the figure of her thoughts with the motionless remnant on her lap.

'Sir Henry in a small boat on the great river. From Aswan deep into Nubia. Regarding the yellow sand, the occasional acacias, the herons in the sky, the inhospitable desert. Sir Henry enduring the heat in order to see the temples of Philae. Defying the cold night on the sand, so that he would awake in the first light of dawn before the four sitting figures of Ramses in Abu Simbel. And the temple of Sebua where everybody, one by one, left their tracks: the Nubians, the Egyptians, the Persians, the Greeks, the Romans, the Copts, the Moslems – and then Sir Henry.' She smiled at the intellectuals who stared fixedly at her. 'I wish you could have seen him,' she said. 'But then he was a little older. Sir Henry in the *tabloncillo*, the great amateur *revistero*, the expert on bull-fighting, the *aficionado* drinking sherry from a skinbag and going into raptures about Juan Belmonte. Manuel Granero dead in Madrid and Sir Henry weeping with the crowd. Felix Rodrigues, his sword aloft – and Sir Henry. Sir Henry with the *fiera* in the ring, and in bed. Sir Henry the personal friend of Joselito.'

She stood up suddenly and laid Sir Henry's head carefully on the floor. For a moment she was as silent as the guests, and then she said: 'Sir Henry will be buried tomorrow. There will be no religious service, and no friends.'

All at once the guests began to move, prepared to go home, but Lady Mandrake detained them.

'This is Salome and Henry's party,' she said. 'I know there is something that remains to be concluded and I am sure that Sir Henry, if he were here, would want everything to follow its usual course.'

The guests exchanged looks and then looked at the one respon-sible for making the speech. He found the situation unpleasant but realized that contradiction would mean a longer delay.

He came forward and began: 'Dear friends, we are here . . .'

Towards the end he mentioned the gift: the guests had all con-tributed and the cheque in this envelope would go (he was sure Salome and Henry would unselfishly welcome the gesture) to the dependents of the Africans injured during the riot.

One after the other they now left the room. Only Jock and Henry remained. Jock laid a blanket over the little figure in the middle of the floor and switched off all the lights except one which shone dimly in a corner. He went off to telephone to the undertakers. Lady Mandrake had already left. Henry gave a last look at the half-dark room, at the shapeless little bundle in the big room, at the speck in the vast Welgevonden; and it was as if he still heard a voice – the *curriculum vitae*, the *modus vivendi*:

'Red wine and Gruyère with Lord Beauchamp at the Embassy Club.'

'His ecstasies over Caravaggio and Botticelli.'

'His love of Neapolitan women.'

'On his way to the Dardanelles with Rupert Brooke by his side.'

'In a gondola at fiesta-time.'

Henry closed the door, then opened it again. He looked into the room once more. It was his first contact with death. There lay the small bundle on the floor wrapped in a blanket. No. Sir Henry – *grotesca* – the *capote* around his legs, in the *redondel*.

V

On the way back to his room he passed the hall in which the marble horse pranced in the gloom. Was there a dark rider on the dark horse? Saturnus on his stallion, the forerunner of the plague. Had there been a blue flame on Sir Henry's lips when he died? Saturnus and Aquarius. At the moment there were four planets in Aquarius. Was it a snake that Henry saw in the passage? A bat grazed him as it flew past. The fruit on the bedside table in his room were bad and a fat worm crawled out of an apple. There were poisonous fungi on the bark of the oak outside his window. There were flies on the ceiling. Birds were flying in the dark outside. A wind rushed through the passages of Welgevonden. There was a black cloud in the valley. Crows flew around in pairs. Dogs were going mad. Jock Silberstein's sheep were dying in their pens. Among the people there was deceit, hate, jealousy and immortality. The signs of Forestus Alcmaronius were everywhere. There was a knock on his door, the soft tap of a woman. *In peste Venus pestem provocat!* And Henry lay still in his room while the wind lowed.

In his great house Jock Silberstein wandered restlessly from room to room. Ahasuerus in the gloom.

In the drawing room lay his guest, his brain and medulla spinali collapsed, his kidneys shrunk, his bladder empty, his spleen discoloured, his lungs fixed to the pleura, green blotches on his left cheek. A man of advanced age, with white hair, staring eyes and gaping mouth; his appearance wholly minatory and malevolent.

Chapter Six

Walpurgisnacht

The sky was overcast and mist lay low over the ground. In the distance the mountain seemed to be floating, anchorless, through the heavens. And the weather was such that one chattered with cold if one took off one's jacket, and stifled with heat if one put it on again a moment later. Jock was waiting for him outside, a rather dissipated looking figure in his khaki clothes, and at first they walked without saying anything in an unknown direction.

They stopped by an old well, one of the original ones on Welgevonden. A neglected hand-pump, overgrown with nettles, furred with green mould, stood enthroned in desolation over the well. The handle was raised as if it had recently still been in use and involuntarily Henry thrust it down. A grating sound came from the wreckage and he went on pumping until water came – lukewarm from the depths, full of slime and putrefaction. The water was blue, the colour of plague, but the blue of old blood mixed with fresh blood, reeking of the lymph of decomposed carcasses – the leftovers dumped into the depths after the hunger for meat which follows kaffir-beer and wild dancing has been stilled.

'This well is poisoned,' said Jock. 'Here stands the sinner,' he said mockingly. 'The scapegoat who murdered the Holy Child of Trent, who caused the plague.' He smiled suddenly at Henry. 'But today *you* feel it, not so? *You* people are guilty in the eyes of the world. The black finger from the pit points at you. Welcome to the ranks of the chosen ones,' and he put his arm round Henry's shoulders, his future relative.

They walked on among flies, mosquitoes and midges that pestered them. Frogs were mounted on one another. Decay brushed against them. Blood appeared on their hands.

'It's leucoma dispar,' Jock reassured him. 'The excrement of butterflies that assume the form of the Cross.'

They wandered on as far as one of Welgevonden's remote corners where guests seldom went : as far as small houses with asbestos roofs hidden, among bush, heath, silver-trees and proteas.

'*Accademia d'amore*,' said Jock, and the girls appeared : the white-lipped, dark-eyed daughters of God knows who, in thin black dresses that exposed the white curves of the legs to everyone from every station in life – preferably to the wild passion of simple people, but prepared also for the complicated, for those with guilt feelings who (thanks to Freud) understood and accepted their true nature and masochistically surrendered themselves in suffering to their inescapable weakness.

Jock disappeared into one of the houses. Henry was cornered by a thin, half-clad girl who waited for his inevitable surrender. She took him to the living room and served tea. She took him to the bedroom and washed herself carefully, expecting him to do the same. Bodily purity (Palmolive soap) and tidiness were her fetish. She waited for him (nobility of labour) on the white bed. She waited without respect for persons, as all the others through the centuries had waited, but today clinically, deliberately, understandably – for the stammering prelude, the excuses for the impotence of the beginners, the story of commonplace frustration, for the task like other tasks that would always find a formula to sanctify itself. She, with her white face on the pillow and Henry passively beside her; the youthful alma mater and the negative student. The technique was like all forms of technique : there were rules and methods that seemed difficult at the time, but came automatically with practice. That was her small lesson. She taught it like an instructress in physical training. Some did better. Others less well. Champions were rare. Everyone could develop a certain competence.

*

Dull light on the walls, on the ceiling, on the horizon seen through the open window. The cloud rolling from an inexhaustible spring of cumulus far beyond; the formless doom that filled the world. Where was Jock Silberstein? Where was everyone? And he looked into her eyes, eyes so dark that one could not tell if they were dark blue or dark brown. The pallid child with her unknown soul and unknown thoughts, with her skill born of a specialized ripeness and the rest of her personality a side-issue of this activity in the sport of Venus.

Welgevonden and the rest of the world were full of expertise; the perfect human being was dismantled into the fragments of his earlier composition – pure beauty, pure intellect, pure strength, pure spirit and pure body. Gone for ever was the sense of whole-ness . . . We know too much. The single dissident cell in the organism is quickly at hand to prove the falsity of the troubled whole. We look at each other from specialized corners. We await the ability to find a new synthesis.

What was Henry thinking as the young girl with the pale face and white lips initiated him efficiently and impersonally in her particular secret? Was there a longing for a time about which, perhaps, he had only an atavistic memory, to the security of a discernible pattern of good and evil which, sometimes visibly, sometimes palpably, conducted their eternal duel – while he, entirely aloof now, was merely experiencing the technical aspect of love? Did he realize that one can never go back, that a com-plete transformation was necessary, that new life-giving symbols had to be found for old truths?

All these things perhaps – for one's deepest emotions and longings are incomprehensible (just like one's awakening con-sciousness of the evil that pervades the world, without being able to specify anything in particular) – all these things, perhaps, as she constrained him, even against his will, to ecstasy.

But where was Jock Silberstein?

Henry found him in one of the small buildings in conversation with a little woman who looked exactly like the grandmother in Mazawattee Tea advertisements.

'Ah!' said Jock, 'let me introduce you'; and with a mocking

smile at the young man he introduced Henry to the little old woman. There was a looking glass on the wall next to Henry. The face outside and the face in the looking glass were different faces. One looked younger, the other older; and both were equally unrevealing. Jock's smile vanished, because he was unable to learn anything. The initiation was over, but there was no indication of the fact. Youth had no face. Truth had no form.

The little old woman nodded at Henry. Her silver-rimmed glasses were perched on the tip of her little nose and she gave him a friendly look from soft eyes which, in their shortsightedness, had assumed the vague expression of charming wisdom. She was busy knitting something. It looked like a coat of the brightest green imaginable. In her basket there were balls of wool of many colours: red, silver, yellow and blue. A moment later the door opened and a girl came in. She was wearing one of those starched dresses that hesitate just above the kneecaps, ready to bounce up at the slightest movement. She walked mincingly on high heels up to the old woman and leaned forward to kiss her on the forehead. Her dress bounced up, showing silk stockings, white thighs and white panties edged with fine lace. She sat down beside the little woman, her hands in her lap, and looked with interest in her dark eyes at Henry, who noticed that she was the same girl with whom he had just been.

The little old woman was thanking Jock for something he had done for her husband: the increment had come in handy to him, since they were the only ones who cared for their granddaughter. She was sure her husband would give of his best. His heart and soul were in his work. He practised every day. In spite of his great age, Welgevonden would find that his worth was incalculable. And she knitted and knitted without looking at the needles. Now she was adding another colour.

The girl began talking gaily to Henry. 'I am going to Cape Town next week,' she said. 'There's a big future.' Her ambitions were limitless. 'Perhaps I'll go overseas,' she went on. 'Once you're in Cape Town and meet the right people . . .' She folded her hands over one knee. Her dress shifted up and she pulled it down decorously. She told him that she had a long list of addresses.

'Wealthy men,' she explained. She used the word as if it were a definition of good character.

The little old woman smiled at her granddaughter and went knitting steadily. She was now adding another colour, a bright yellow. In a short while she had knitted at least nine inches.

Henry was obliged to have tea for the second time, made and served by the girl in the flounced petticoat. It was a domestic little scene and she performed her duties like an exemplary child. She was a model of domesticity and the grandmother watched her proudly as the coat grew visibly with new colours.

Somewhere a bell tinkled. The girl frowned and shifted restlessly. The grandmother's eyes directed a wordless order at her. Jock Silberstein stood up suddenly and said good-bye. He and Jock were accompanied outside and good-byes were waved to them from the garden gate. The old woman still had her knitting. She peered shortsightedly over her glasses at the two men, who disappeared behind the shrubs.

'Not long now,' she said to her granddaughter, 'and Jock Silberstein won't be the *boss* of his own property any longer.' She went on knitting, undisturbed, and nodded her head slowly up and down. 'Your grandfather's got one of the most important jobs already. He's got a key position in the Great Machine. They think he don't know, but he do know. He's found out a lot of things already. There's things Jock Silberstein don't know about. One fine day, before he knows where he is, *he* will have to listen to your grandpa's orders.'

And she looked at her granddaughter with dim brown eyes in which the light shone differently – as if it were radioactive. A corn-cricket had come on to the verandah and was scrambling grotesquely towards them. The old woman raised her *bootee* and crushed it slowly to death. The bell tinkled again and she nodded to her granddaughter.

'Madam always rings for me,' the girl complained.

'Think of your grandpa, my child,' said the little woman. 'Keep on and on, work and work. The reward is for the diligent.'

She walked with the girl, who went to her room, changed out

of her dress as well as her bright-coloured petticoat and butterfly panties and stored them all carefully in her wardrobe. Dressed in a flower-patterned dressing gown she kissed her grandmother and ran lightly through the garden to the house in the centre.

The old woman went on knitting peacefully and finished the front of the coat; she pulled out the knitting needles and held it up to the light. In the haziness that surrounded the house the garment glowed with all its colours – glowed with a light of its own, like the light in her eyes.

'Have you ever seen so many corn-crickets?' asked Jock. They were walking through the marsh, their feet squelching in the viscous soil. Presently they came across a dry, grass-covered patch and Jock sat down there; but he was hardly seated when he stood up again. They wandered restlessly. At times, when they went through bush, spiderwebs pulled tautly against them and they beat irritably at an itchiness on their legs and bodies. Henry almost trod on a fat adder: a thick, sluggish, multicoloured reptile that was about to sow beautiful death with a dazzling movement. But Jock killed it with a log. The squashed jaw was splayed open and the fine teeth protruded like fishbones. They came across a dead sheep. Its belly was distended like a balloon, red blood foamed from its mouth, the mud and dung were mashed to a pulp where the animal had its last convulsion. A sour smell pervaded the vicinity. When they were downwind the stench hit them. It was as if all the plants were decaying. A broken tree stump was crumbly inside and insects crawled from it. They reached a grave-yard, ringed by a moss-covered wall, where the crypt had subsided in the soil.

'It belonged to the original owners,' said Jock and Henry noticed the wistfulness in his voice – the yearning to belong, to be able to refer to decayed vaults. He looked suddenly at Henry and in his imagination saw Salome brought to rest by the goy. And at that very moment they heard the clatter of hoofs and in the distance, through the black mist, discerned the small rider on her chestnut horse – a dot in the twilight that soared gracefully over some obstacle and vanished. They waited for something –

for a repetition of the previous day's event, but the hoofbeats continued and died away.

Sometimes it seemed as if they were wandering at night; sometimes as if they were wandering in daylight. At one moment the sun was obscured by cloud; the next it burned above their heads. And below, the germs of thousands of diseases were hatching. Jock's face was contorted – perhaps because of the sticky heat and the difficulty of moving his big body through the marsh. They passed the African village where all was quiet and where the burned-out houses were moist with a black sweat. They went on and climbed the hill. There was a gap in the mist: far below the factories and houses of Welgevonden shimmered in the heat like a mirage. Blue lakes were conjured up by the heat. Drops of sweat trickled down Jock's face. Smoke rose up from somewhere, perhaps where someone was burning something – but it seemed like the human smoke of Mühlhausen and Nordhausen, in honour of God and of Christendom. They reached the room of confession and Jock opened all the steam cocks and bawled his fear. They went to the tulip garden and it seemed to Henry that the two colours had become faded and dreary. Jock, in his wandering, left the footpath and made his destructive way through the flowers; and unexpectedly they came to the room where Professor Dreyer, a test tube in his hand, stood before the window. He was so interested in what he was doing that he did not notice Jock. He radiated joy. Inspiration flashed from the greyness. He stood caged in a supernatural light. The close-cropped heads of his students were bent low over the papers on which they were making symbols. The Africans were singing and the bottles tumbling in an arc into the silver tanks. The hands of the girls were moving more swiftly, and the trains were rushing through the tunnels. In the Ubu-room the iron hands clattered like castanets. And above, on the platform, by the organ-machine, the gardener's uniform glistened; his hands were raised, waiting, waiting for the ultimate, soul-fulfilling moment. Henry and Jock, struck by the appearance of the harmless virtuoso, hesitated, waited – and saw the lightning movement as the stumpy fingers descended and an entire consignment disappeared soundlessly into the cellar.

They left the building and at once became invisible in the black mist on their way back to the Welgevonden homestead. In one of the small camps they were confronted by Brutus: a bull's head loomed up out of the mist, the red forequarters huge in front of them, the black hindquarters invisible. They hesitated for a moment, somewhat fearful, since Brutus now had the freedom of the fields, surrounded by heifers lowing out of sight in the distance. The bull's mouth was open and he pawed the ground with a hoof. But it was soundless on the moist grass. The jaws opened and shut and then the animal vanished as suddenly as it had appeared.

They reached the house and found the guests assembled on the veranda. The atmosphere was depressing, as in a seaside hotel when there is a downpour of rain and friends of the beach all of a sudden find themselves herded together as strangers. Small quarrels threatened; interesting little habits became irritating; light flirtations took on the appearance of something serious. The amusing young man who put his arm round the women was a real threat; the women found their husbands boring, they laughed at the gigolo's silliness. The married men were cast compulsorily for parts they did not like. They tolerated with difficulty the stupidity of various games in which light kisses were stolen behind pieces of furniture; against their will they were obliged to listen to shared secrets; they had to take part clumsily in challenges that were issued back and forth; unwillingly they took part in the childishness that had suddenly manifested itself. The men suffered most, because they were required to improvise, while the women had simply to follow. It was the extrovert's moment: the young commercial traveller who had had his experience in hotel rooms; the junior in a firm who had been taught the ropes by the blonde typist; the rascal with his treasure chest of knowledge about women. And it was the man who had achieved something, who kept his wife by means of money and prestige, who now suddenly, without prestige and without money, was faced with a basic truth. The women looked with rancour at their husbands' protuberant bellies and shook with laughter as the athletic young wastrel did the twist with suggestive quiverings.

There were no corners in which quick-witted conversation or penetrating philosophical insight could make any impression. In the bleak light of the veranda, on the stage with its norm of entertainment value, the women waited, like cows and heifers in the fields, for the young bullocks.

Slim Mrs Silberstein and J. J. were in their element, unashamedly in the lead. Jock Silberstein was nowhere to be seen. The two Misses Silberstein were together in a corner from where, hopeful and giggling, they drew each other's attention to everything that happened. The duchess peered at everything with the cruelty and wisdom of a grandmother. Henry looked at the dark-eyed young girls. He was young and handsome enough not to feel threatened. He sat apart in a corner and watched the antics with uncomplicated interest, wondering which of the sex-kittens was his loved one.

When luncheon was announced and the guests began the formal meal, the spectacle came to an end. The middle-aged and the rejected came into their own. The social structure was restored. The so-recently repudiated had regained their positions of power and tormented their wives alternately with lack of interest, smart remarks and proud silences. The gigolos were relegated to the background – a black mark against them when they appeared in their offices on Monday, their expense accounts curtailed when next they went on missions for their firms.

Jock mentioned that evening's occasion : a witches' Sabbath, smiling as he said it and leaving his guests to think whatever they cared to, free to believe or not to believe – free to give free rein to their imaginations.

II

It was quiet and peaceful in Henry's room. He lay in bed, the blanket pulled up to his chin – safely under the gilded ceiling, surrounded by wealth and fortified by the freedom that Jock Silberstein granted his guests at this dying hour of the day. There were thick walls and a solid door that shut him off completely from everyone : he was alone in his small cell in the immense labyrinth. Something stirred within him. On the blank page cryptic writing was appearing; through a septum osmosis was taking place. It was too soon to say what it signified. He was already beginning to feel the lack of a state of grace that was passing. He was becoming something different – something unavoidable, something that he had hitherto always been able to avoid by means of deliberate ignorance. He realized that the process was taking place, that the clean page was being filled with all sorts of figures, that there was something in him striving to make the figures understandable. It was with longing that he tried to think back to the lost paradise where everything had been insubstantial – the thinness of blue air, the complete meaninglessness of infinitude. Already he was aware of the limitations which, for the first time, confined his perceptions. He mourned the loss of his loneliness. He welcomed the sleep that overcame him and which in future would take the place of his lost paradise. Without knowing it, he was already experiencing the Fall; the loss of grace, the birth of consciousness, the twilight state of realization, the curse of reason.

Outside it was already dark and he had to switch on the light while he dressed. He chose his clothes as if he had no interest in them. He felt dwarfed by the big bathroom as he combed his hair. Everything gleamed. The lions' heads dribbled and formed a green film on the inside of the bath. The fluorescent light over the looking glass made his face seem unnaturally white and threw shadows everywhere – black lines of dissipation, artificial as stage make-up.

In the passage he paused to listen for the familiar hubbub that would give him an indication of the place of assembly, but the house was quiet as a tomb. He acted on the spur of the moment and arrived in the same drawing room where they had assembled on the first evening. All the guests were there, but they were uncommonly subdued. The lights were dim and it was difficult to distinguish faces. Dr Johns and Judge O'Hara appeared on either side of him from the shadows. They immediately began apologizing for their presence.

'Perhaps as a scientist and a jurist it is difficult to account for our presence at this – aah – sort of gathering,' said Dr Johns.

'Well, we reason this way,' said Judge O'Hara. 'One must acquire knowledge of good and evil. Knowledge is an extension of consciousness. It leads to the discovery of the self.'

'Put it this way,' Dr Johns resumed. 'Jock says more is expected of us than the ability to distinguish between Evil and Good; we shall have to accept the risk of the whole: the mystery of the composite. We shall have to make visible the negative and positive aspects in order to find the true centre.'

Judge O'Hara had meanwhile gone to one of the tables and now returned with a tube which he was opening carefully.

'Assume that Jock is right,' he said. 'That the balance has been disturbed, that the neglected shadow is appearing in another aspect, then it is our duty to exorcize it: to make it perceptible, to see and confront it. The shadow and the light must become more apparent.'

He had now succeeded in opening the tube, which was seen to contain a yellow ointment. He offered it first to Dr Johns, who scooped some out with his middle finger.

'All our energy is being squandered,' he said, 'in our hopeless efforts to discriminate, since we misjudge the shadow. We differ from Jock only in his contention that we will have to learn to live with the shadow, that with rebirth the whole must be discerned, that we must be submissive to the creative darkness of God's will – beyond the scope of good and evil.' He suddenly took off his shirt and began smearing his body with the ointment. 'When Satan fell Jahveh parted from his angel. We believe that after the light of Christ will come the darkness of the Antichrist; the resuscitation of Satan before he is damned forever.' He had now finished smearing himself and gave the tube back to Judge O'Hara.

'We believe,' said Judge O'Hara, as he repeated the process and smeared himself thoroughly, 'that it is better to see Satan as the people of the Middle Ages saw him than to be overpowered imperceptibly by him.'

'And, actually, we agree with Jock in many respects,' said Dr

Johns, as he took the tube from Judge O'Hara and handed it to Henry, 'except that we regard evil as a negative force and not as the dark side of the Creator.'

Henry, too, took off his shirt and smeared the last of the ointment on his body. He now also noticed that all the guests were busy doing the same. Even the women. In the distance the duchess looked like the totemistic image of a tribal mother: her small stomach, her sagging breasts and her shrunken body. The dark-eyed girls gambolled like water nymphs. But at that moment no one was interested in anyone else's body. There was an unnatural sort of detachment, of the kind one finds in a nudist camp: a conscious disregard of sex.

'It's difficult to determine the ingredients of this,' said Dr Johns, 'but I suppose there are components of the *Umbelliferae-Conium* present, as well as species of the *Solanum* genus. In fact, some of those compounds the witches used in their concoctions and that are absorbed through the skin. We should feel a certain reaction soon after this.'

Jock joined them. The red hair on his chest glowed in the dimness.

'God is the Great Unconsciousness,' he said. 'There the archetypal images are fighting each other. Heaven and hell lie within us and, farther back, his infinity. The Antichrist is the dark side taking vengeance, transformed by the complexity of our psyche.'

Suddenly the lights dimmed – the shadows increased.

'The struggle between the great powers is within us,' he bellowed. 'We are made in His image.'

And suddenly it was dark.

There was no sound.

For the first time in his life Henry felt the first indications of fear. It lasted only a moment, but it hung over him invisibly and touched him lightly like the brush of a wing.

It was as if Judge O'Hara could see right inside him.

'Remember, Henry,' he said in the dark, 'everything happens inside yourself. If you have anything to fear, you have yourself to fear.'

'But, alas,' came Dr Johns' voice from his left, 'the victims of sin are those most receptive to perversity – the religious no less than the unbelievers – the seekers burdened with a richness of spirit.'

'And that's where Henry's immunity lies,' said Jock from nearby. 'The man who does not seek.'

It was completely quiet in the room. Nobody moved and there was no sound. Henry waited for something to happen, but nothing happened. He thought about all the stories he had heard as a child about witchcraft and he felt the excitement of the strange adventure. Deep inside him something had nevertheless happened, without his being aware of it. The fact that he did not seek was at the same time an indication that he accepted religion too easily and could easily become a prey to inquisitiveness and, in its wake, the temptation of other possibilities and flights of the imagination. But, more even than that – that the secret longing for self-justification might lie hidden in his negativeness – the opposition to God and order, the provocation of satanic adventure – the repetition of the ambition of the fallen angels: I AM against the annihilating authority of God.

And again it was if Judge O'Hara could see right into Henry. 'Pride is the greatest sin of all.'

And now, for the first time, Henry became clearly aware of something. A fear of death now gripped him. For a single moment he was destroyed and experienced another kind of loneliness. He set foot over the portals of a hell within himself. He was in a room that had no echoes. There was no judgement and no salvation. There was total detachment. There were no psychic streams straining against one another. There was only cosmic silence. And, worst of all, perpetual consciousness. It was as if, in the passing moment, he experienced an absolute annihilation in himself: the impossible I AM NOT.

But it lasted for only a fraction of a second, and then came the rescuing ecstasy that lay at the roots of evil. That insight of a moment ago was consumed in the conflagration of the present moment – a feeling that he was floating through the air, over forests and lakes, over the whole world, and then came tingling to rest at the place of coven. The feeling of elation was so joyfully extravagant that he was prepared to offer the already forgotten feeling of solitude as prize money. Little Henry Faustus was going to make a pact with the devil to rid himself of his negativity.

All of a sudden a green light glowed in the room. Black John, completely naked, with a scaly body and a *papier-mâché* tail, long and arrowheaded, swinging freely, stood on a sort of dais and laughed at the guests, an RAF moustache appropriately satanic, raising its wings. The light became brighter and in its circle could be seen a slim, naked female riding a goat: she clutched a horn with one hand and from the other swung a cat by its tail. This caused endless mirth and everyone doubled up with laughter; the screams of the tortured animals were lost in the noise. Then the lights were suddenly dimmed. The guests, little green bundles in the semi-dark, tumbled over one another to reach the central figure. They curtsied mockingly, muttered the heroic appellations 'grand seigneur', 'nostre dieu', 'dominus deus', as they had been instructed and kissed him in the most obscene manner. It was the women in particular who exceeded themselves and displayed considerable perversity. He bit each on her bare arm and they took great pleasure in comparing their, for the moment, completely painless, witches' marks. When the climax was reached the green light was switched off and it stayed dark until utter silence had fallen on the room.

'Singular,' said Judge O'Hara, 'we are at the place of the local coven; I'm tingling inside; I am ready, but I do not *feel* the presence.'

'Perhaps it is too early,' said Dr Johns.

'The real question,' said Judge O'Hara, 'is not whether all things happen, but whether one approves of the happenings – whether one has the will to believe.'

'That's true,' said Dr Johns, 'one must believe in doom like the author of *De Magorum Daemonomania*.'

Another light now glowed in the room: dull red, which created the impression of fires burning in the background.

The figure on the dais was in a sitting position, his masculinity exposed in the red light, his arrow-tail curled around one leg, a horse-tail switch in one hand.

'Ah! The moment for the recital,' whispered Judge O'Hara.

One by one the guests came out of the red darkness – in their semi-nudity hardly recognizable. It seemed to Henry that he kept recognizing someone he had seen at the various parties. The admissions were like an inverted confession: the glorification of sin, the pleasure of perversity. A slim young woman, the light playing upon her figure, a voluptuous display of thighs, breasts and suggestive attitudes, her face raised to the source of light, told how she drove her husband and her lover to impotence with her insane passion. An ordinary little girl, bony and unattractive, described a subtler knot: how, by her own exemplary behaviour, she drove her lover to a realization of his own sins. A blonde girl of angelic appearance, even in her nakedness unattainable as a marble statue, described the conflict in her lover between manliness and femininity, and how she continually drew his attention to the ambivalence that he was doomed never to overcome. They described everything – not as if they were describing evil, but as if they were simply intent on doing good. The voluptuous one wished only to provoke physical satisfaction, the ordinary one wished only to save her sweetheart, the blonde one wished merely to make her lover understand his shortcomings, for his own salvation.

They came one after the other: those who had sinned carnally as well as those who had sinned in thought and word. The meaning of good was completely reversed: ideas of love, purity, truth, freedom and order suddenly became diabolical ideas – sometimes indistinguishable from evil and sometimes, worst of all, quite meaningless, without content, monotonously empty. They came, men and women, old and young, from all walks of life. Artists in their struggle against discipline, journalists in their struggle against truth, the rich in their struggle against wealth, farmers in their struggle against the theory of breeding, idealists in their struggle against tolerance, intellectuals in their struggle against liberal thought. They made their admissions with deep conviction in the name of the good they were destroying; eloquently, before the satanic figure in the red light, they made old truths meaningless; with fierce abandon they reduced all forms of noble striving to senseless trivialities.

Occasionally someone who was not convincing enough, who deviated, perhaps, on meditation and in inverted faith, was immediately lashed by the figure. It was soon apparent that the torture was a form of self-castigation and that deviation was perhaps the most subtle form a confession could take.

Towards the very end the apparition on the throne jumped down and lashed out wildly to left and to right, so that naked figures writhed in pain and rolled around all over the floor. Slowly the light diminished as the madness increased and Black John's sadism was satisfied by the exciting lamentations : 'Mercy! Mercy! Compassion, Master. Mercy!'

Then it became pitch dark and silence descended.

'It's strange,' said Dr Johns. 'I am not particularly susceptible tonight.'

'It's as if,' said Judge O'Hara, '– and I hasten to say it hesitantly – even sin no longer has the – er – impact it once had.'

'Definitely not,' said Dr Johns. 'To be quite truthful, I find it somewhat dreary.'

Now, in its turn, a blue light glowed, like the moon shining on an altar. A priestly figure – toga, hood and paraphernalia – stood with his back to the altar and muttered some or other incantation. In his hand he held a piece of beetroot. He was attired completely in black. A young girl was led in by two other priests. The blue light made her body shine more whitely; her hair fell loose over her shoulders and she moved as if in a trance. And yet there was something familiar about her movements – her entire appearance and bearing. She smiled suddenly, her mouth squarely open, her teeth gleaming in a calculated grin, her head turned sideways towards the invisible people. And now the resemblance was clear : it was a beauty queen on the dais. Her measurements were in accordance with the required standards; everything was faithful to the provocative ritual : the stimulated trance for the benefit of the crowd, the blind ecstasy, the misrepresentation of an undefiled virgin, the illusion of purity in the youthful curves, the parody of innocence and then, as the phantasmagoria was maintained, the collective rape.

Powerless, she was led to the altar; vulnerable, she was laid on it; her hands sank passively to her sides, she waited defencelessly on the ruler.

Suddenly the light was dimmed and a cry of women's voices in unison filled the room.

Then silence fell.

'I am afraid . . .' said Judge O'Hara.

'Perhaps we're getting old,' said Dr Johns.

'Or perhaps,' said Judge O'Hara, 'nature has been affected by tedium.'

This time there were lights of many different colours everywhere. They grew brighter and the rest of the room was revealed: banquet tables all along the walls. Black John already at the head of them and the slim witch with the love-mark on her shoulder by his side.

'Do you know the procedure?' Dr Johns asked Henry.

'The recital,' said Judge O'Hara, 'the sacrifice, the feast and then the . . .'

But he was interrupted by Dr Johns who, very practically, pointed out that they would have to hurry to get decent seats.

The room now looked like the grill room of a smart hotel: the coloured lights dim enough to assist slow imaginations, all the waiters with horns on their heads to illustrate the theme, the wine and food specially contrived to facilitate one of the deadly sins.

Everyone was there; even old Mrs Silberstein, arms akimbo, a shawl over her shoulders for the sake of modesty – like all the other women. Although half-naked, their appearance was thus little different from what it would have been at an ordinary gathering of this sort. The meagre coverings, the dim, coloured lights, the help of shadows, all contributed to civilized revelry. As soon as they found it necessary they could rid themselves of their draperies with a slight movement.

'Strictly speaking,' said Dr Johns as he poured a glass of champagne for Henry, 'this should be a hellish, undrinkable brew. And . . . [as he began feasting on a roast duck] the meal should consist of rotten corpses and rubbish. I allude here to Dr Montague Summers. However, as Dr Charles Williams has justly explained, everything depends on the particular imagination of the individual. Everything happens within ourselves. Those who long for the most delicious food, get it; those who dream of hell find obscenity in their food.'

Judge O'Hara nudged Dr Johns and cautioned silence. Henry had not eaten anything. Indeed, he had said nothing the whole evening. The two old men looked enviously at him. They were recalling a time when they too, were susceptible and could join the fray with ebullience.

'Perhaps we are already immune to the ointment,' said Dr Johns.

'Next time we should perhaps increase the dose,' agreed Judge O'Hara.

Henry himself said nothing. On the table before him he saw the corpse of Sir Henry. Around him he heard the susurration of the demons. In complete isolation he fought the battle.

For the entertainment of the guests there was also a performance in the middle of the floor. The former virgin of the altar did a striptease. 'Take it off' shouted the guests. Few of them knew that she was a married woman with three school-going children. She also performed successfully in various nightclubs.

Champagne flowed merrily. The lights grew imperceptibly dimmer. The last part of the Sabbath was now being mounted, but unnoticed and naturally. It was the final phase – the free association where Satan, the ape of God, strove vainly to become incarnate. Because of his one predominant limitation his impulse grew increasingly greater but, as the lights faded slowly, he had to rely solely on the sterile act. As the noise increased and bits of clothing fell on the floor in the dark, and the succubi and incubi began their riotous festival, he tried time and time again, as he had done over the years, to produce the fruit, himself and by means of his followers. And from revenge – yearning and revenge – he made the act as cruel and unsatisfying as possible; he made his witches writhe, he racked them all with lust and frustration, he made promises of ecstasy that were never fulfilled.

Gradually the dim lights took on all the colours of the rainbow. The free association had begun as a dance to the accompaniment of macabre, progressive jazz in the background. In the beginning it was no different from an ordinary festivity: the couples left their seats one after another and whirled into the first movement of the dance, the younger people improvising energetically; the elder, more slowly in the style familiar to them. Disintegration began according to the well-known formula – the exchange of partners, the suggestive movements, exposure. The single most important contribution to the dissolution was the realization of general approval; in fact, the feeling of unrestrained freedom; abandon free from sanctions, criticism or derision. Black John was in the lead; with a perfect sense of timing he had led them through all the nuances of demoniac liberation. Differently from his Opposite, he limited in the process the rhythm of disintegration to the pace of the middle-aged. Black John possessed his own special monopoly of wisdom – youth is more sympathetic to evil; maturity is the greatest obstacle to sin. The cult of youth was his creation; the sheep that strayed from his flocks was the mature individual. Satan was not represented as the Holy Child, but as the sophisticated connoisseur. He did not seek children, but waited for the end-products.

In the rainbow lights, in the steady dissolution of the dance, past the stage of self-criticism (the most difficult moment) he led them; and then suddenly abandoned each to his own decline. The music quickened, the lights grew dimmer. Apparel flew and succubi and incubi swarmed exuberantly from the shadows. Every coloured light and every mask of shadow was an incitement to creativity. Just like the banquet, the experience was situated in the psyche of the individual. As the naked figures tumbled over one another and sought vainly for contact, the sensation of delicious pain, like birth-pangs, changed to overwhelming mock delight. The middle-aged maiden was suffering the pangs of 'une extrème douleur'; the aloof woman, the brutal pain she secretly desired.' The young nymphs, because of their youth, found their pleasure in frequency, change, the raging speed of the transient feeling. The male found his succubus and took revenge on his wife; the female found her incubus and got her own back on her husband. In league with Satan they took revenge on the imperfections of their companions – the lack of attention, the lack of love, the monotony, the bitchiness, the desperation caused by one, the personality broken by the other, the dreariness of their knowledge of one another.

Tomorrow Black John, after he himself and through everyone else had been through all the acts in vain, and had realized for the nth time that all was in vain – that everything was a mere travesty, that he could never reproduce himself, that his fruit was rotten, that his malignancy was confined to the deed and the perpetrators of the deed – tomorrow he would leave them alone so that they might suffer as he had suffered; leave them with the malevolence that follows frustration: refined maladies of the spirit, obsessions, psychoses – the only children of his intercourse.

In the middle Black John moved like a film star surrounded by his admirers, tormented by his reputation. There were some who wished only, as cruelly as possible, to suffer through him the unholy caress. Everything he did caused endless rapture: lamentations of pleasure accompanied his slightest action. Artificial or natural – the standards of success were inverted: he was the great failure who had turned failure to triumph. But amid all this he looked slightly bored.

'I find it all boring,' said Judge O'Hara and thus affirmed Satan's attitude.

'There's nothing new,' said Dr Johns. 'One can see all this at any party in any club.'

'Et *Verbum Caro factum est*.' Judge O'Hara exorcised a lascivious succubus who was threatening him in the dark with her embrace.

Whether it was the meaning of the words or the Latin that made her recoil no one will ever know.

Active, but entirely uninterested, Black John moved through

the orgy. These days there was a clinical approach to sin that (and he maimed a fragile disciple in passing) weakened the act. His witches' Sabbath happened every day without souls being damned. These days the priests exorcised with a new incantation. Black John's last trump card was –

'I am bored,' said Judge O'Hara.

'Actually, I've lost interest in sex,' said a voice next to Dr Johns, and it was not the judge's.

'The *maleficium* can be served much better on other ground,' said Judge O'Hara, searching vainly in the dark.

'The churches are expanding and the missions are flourishing. There are more sects than ever.'

'When the ordinary Sabbath disappeared the witches' Sabbath disappeared too.'

'Satan is the ape of God.'

'Satan is an ascetic and a freedom fighter,' said Dr Johns, but could see neither his friend nor the speaker.

Like all festivities this one ended in disorder. Friends and companions did not find each other, or found each other, or partly found each other, and vanished in their noisy vehicles that courted death on the roads in the early morning. At least four had fallen in love and continued their embraces with increasing tenderness somewhere outside. In the light of new knowledge nobody could point to the banquet as the moment of loss of his eternal soul. No one knew whether he was destined for hell or for heaven. There was certainly great interest, but few answers, in one or the other direction. Satan had mocked his own witches' Sabbath. Life was exceptionally complex. The churches adapted themselves to people and became equally complex. The shapeless cloud hung over everything. All they knew was that there was a certain tension, a tendency for all kinds of allergies to develop – a kind of obsession about all sorts of things, a feeling that one would explode before long unless something did happen. They raced homeward into the night. Nothing of real importance or significance had happened. There was a sense of disaster, an increasing tension, frenzy mounting – but where was sin?

III

Henry remained behind in the room alone. Here and there on the floor lay a garment – a blouse, a coat, a handkerchief, some unfamiliar object, soft and light as fluff when he took it up and let it fall again. A feeling of longing, nostalgia, sorrow and powerlessness had flowed together, becoming something he could not for the moment identify, but which in future he was to feel increasingly. The fear of a while back had disappeared quickly, but its aftermath continued to exist in this feeling. The sharp pain of fear had been consumed by the subsequent ecstasy and now, after the ecstasy, there was this smouldering fire that would presently grow cold.

Where the altar now stood, he had on the previous evening seen the little bundle. He remembered the events of the day and night, but the events of the previous night, the start of the chain reaction, were stronger in his memory. Then, too, it may have been because he and Sir Henry had the same name. He could not forget the expression on the face : the fury before death.

He walked across the room and stood under the light that still retained the many colours of the final stage. He made a lonesome figure and he was unaware of someone standing in a corner of the room, watching him. There the shadows were darkest and, himself caught in the lights, he could see nothing at all.

So it was that he and the invisible watcher remained in the room for quite a long time.

The image of Sir Henry existed only in the thoughts of Lady Mandrake, he reflected – and in his, as he had seen it through her. The image of time only in the collective train of thought of acquaintances.

Sir Henry's fury had been before the final invisibility because he could find no image of himself.

The pagan had died, thought Henry, without there being an image of the loved or hated sinner. A mere picture had been sketched by Lady Mandrake – but for Sir Henry himself there had been nothing.

Tonight he had felt fear when there was nothing. Fear had vanished when the figure had appeared and the ritual had begun. The aftermath of the fear lived in the realization that everything had been a travesty.

From under the light Henry looked around the room.

It was as if the invisible figure were talking to him.

'And, as far as human beings are concerned, with the destruction of my image they also destroy His image. But in my imagelessness I have more experience than He. I found my antidote to His magic words: *Et Verbum Caro factum est.* In my invisibility my kingdom is already here. In the imagelessness, close to the abstract, my fifth column moves. In the dead images the maggots of my demons teem.'

But there was no invisible figure talking to him.

The watcher in the shadows was a young girl with dark eyes who saw the young man fighting an invisible fight against something. During the course of the week her love for him had increased. At first it had touched her lightly, and had then irritated her. Love had returned, stronger than ever. She gazed now with love and with tear-filled eyes at the young man. He was alive for her now as Sir Henry had been alive for Lady Mandrake. She would fight like a tigress to keep the image intact.

Actually, Henry was very happy. Some people belong to the chosen.

The seventh day at Welgevonden had dawned. In the distance the first light was already showing. It glowed on the horizon; it grew stronger on the plains behind the mountains. The light gathered and broke like a wave over the mountain. The peaks grew big above the shadows in the valleys. The whole landscape on the slopes of the mountain was revealed. The changes now became more gradual, less dramatic. But slowly, hour by hour, the light came and, with it, all the colours.

We all live in a beautiful world. Each of us has a heaven in this landscape that is reborn every day.

But suddenly there was bright daylight. All illusions vanished. The intensity of light, just like the intensity of darkness, brought its own revelation.

In the meantime Henry had gone to bed. The watcher in the dark, too.

In her dreams she also knitted him a cloak of all imaginable colours.

Chapter Seven

The Coming of Salome

When Henry awoke he dressed quickly and hurried outside. Today he had to be alone. He had sought nothing, he had made no demands. Unasked, they had destroyed his paradise. He wandered around the estate and avoided all the places where Jock Silberstein usually waited for him.

At least he had something to be grateful for: that at this moment, on the day of the good, nature with its overflowing sources of beauty offered the escape one preferred: forgetfulness if one desired it, even temporarily; reconciliation, but at the same time the hope that the condition would change because after all, everything was still growing and there was life everywhere; energy and willpower to fight against powers stronger than oneself, as others before one had fought in other circumstances – there was something heroic in this lovely landscape; its beauty was indestructible. In this light, with music in one's ears, at this hour of the morning...

He had known formlessness; silence and fear. With that he would have to live. At some stage or another, unexpectedly in an unguarded moment, it would come again. His innocence was a lack of knowledge; his lack of knowledge a false innocence. He could see now, but he was not satisfied. But the fact that he could see brought a certain measure of certainty, all the same.

Meanwhile, there was a domain of the Silbersteins that he must now inspect. Thus a general surveys the battle area before the fight begins. One must know everything – every square inch of the terrain. And one must learn to know the enemy as well, camouflaged though he was, here before one's very eyes. One must be able to distinguish the colours of his disguise and penetrate his defensive mask. One must develop cunning: one must never,

never venture against this enemy in one's true colours. Cunning was the word, formless as he himself – and one had to draw one's power from something that in these times had also lost its form. There was no contact, no communication with anything one had known. One must cultivate a mistrust of things in which one had believed; but one must have faith, stronger than ever, in an object of power that had still to take shape and that, just like oneself, had to engage the common enemy. *That* one must believe, otherwise there was nothing left.

He reached the houses among the proteas and silver-trees, the scene of his initiation. The girl with the pale face was picking flowers in the garden. Her arms were full of arum lilies, the wind blew her thin dress against her legs. She waved to him and beckoned. The door opened and the grandmother came out. They overwhelmed the young man with their spontaneous welcome. Would he come in for a moment? They had a little present for him. He stood among the heath and the flowers while the girl trotted inside. On the veranda was a rose window, divided into glass panes of many colours. Through it he could see the landscape and he relived in the blue trees, the red hedge, the yellow clouds and the green mountains a period he had already forgotten but which suddenly materialized now – a world of his early youth, ready to conjure up a maiden, a knight, and a dark object around every corner. The colours were bright but simple: there were no gradations. It was like those picture books that one colours in: black for the monster, gold for the knight, blue for her eyes, red for her lips, green for the field to which the offering was brought. And now the girl came out and offered him the gift.

'Salome and I often played together here,' she said.

It was a knitted packet of strong, thick wool, brown as autumn.

The old woman's eyes were friendly – the little mother who understood everything.

'For the future son of Jock Silberstein,' she said, with feudal loyalty.

He left them while the picture was still in character: the little house, the little garden, the grandmother and child – the *good* last memory, the picture on the tea tin. The wind that blew softly against him, blew against them, too, when his back was turned. The girl's dress wafted up and she had nothing on underneath. The grandmother's eyes grew black with a hint of lunacy. The arum lilies were meant for the bordello. The wind blew again and he looked back. They were still standing there, her dress luminous as gossamer in the sun, the flowers in her arms like a bride's bouquet, the little mother gracious by her side. And the wind blew and blew, creating scenes repeatedly of the maiden and the flowers, the slut and the flowers, the mother and the maiden, the witch and the witch's child.

Cunning, as he wandered through the pleasure garden. Cunning, while everything was invisible. Cunning, as shapes became visible and existed in a chimera. Henry, in his wandering, was rid of his blindness, but they had not taught him how to see. It was like someone, born blind, suddenly being able to see – but how did one know that a tree was not a human being? Trust no tree. Do not be surprised if a stick is an adder. It was only a stick lying there and he picked it up, a round plump fig branch that flexed pleasantly round his hand and with which he flicked the grass as he wandered on. He did in fact see a snake: a swift, yellow cobra that slithered through the grass and disappeared, then reappeared unexpectedly on an open patch of ground. Henry crushed it with the fig branch and the copper body writhed in the sun until it suddenly became motionless. It could, of course, have been a mole snake, a harmless, good reptile that exterminated rats and other vermin. The head was never hooded, or had it been? But the creature was dead and nobody would ever know. He lifted the snake with the stick, swung it round and round like a sling and away flew the copper thread through the air.

The parcel in his hand was troublesome. He decided to put the jacket on, and it fitted well. He put his hand in a pocket and felt a piece of paper. He took it out and on it read 83–7569. Was it a telephone number? Or the number of the wool?

'That was a cobra,' said a voice behind him, 'an uncommon Cape cobra. Very fast and extremely poisonous, but nevertheless of interest to the collector. Do you think we shall find it if we look for it?'

Henry saw a small man in plus fours, his eyes hidden under a peaked cap, his skin blanched like that of a city dweller, his presence in the veld slightly incongruous, as in the case of all scientists obliged by the nature of their work to leave their studies.

'You are probably surprised to see me here,' said Dr Johns, 'but I often take a stroll in the early morning, especially after a night like last night. Do you think it possible to find the snake?'

They searched among the heath and in the grass. Dr Johns frequently saw an extremely rare plant: a *vygie*, a flower of the protea family; a small flower in the shape of a miniature bell, rose-coloured and completely hidden among the shrubs. At last they found the cobra, the head crushed, the body broken in two places.

'What a pity,' said Dr Johns and picked up the snake. He held it up to the light, then put it in his pocket. 'And yet, if you really *must* kill a snake, this is one of the most important. It's extremely dangerous and its venom is deadly. On the other hand, again, there's a snake in this district that's innocent and looks exactly like an adder, a creature with the most beautiful colours, and they are completely harmless. I admire your ability to recognize the dangerous kind so swiftly.'

They wandered on.

'A beautiful jacket,' said Dr Johns. 'An unusual colour.'

Henry explained that he had received it as a gift from the old woman and her granddaughter (and he pointed in the direction of the houses in the distance).

'An exemplary girl,' said Dr Johns. 'She's a great friend of Salome. Her parents died early and she lives with her grandmother and grandfather. She is studying sociology through a correspondence college and works in her spare time. Her grandmother is a remarkable woman, she writes tracts for the Zion sects. The grandfather is a little obtuse and unimaginative. You probably remember the incident a few nights ago when he assaulted the albino.'

They were now approaching the African village. There, all was quiet and peaceful. A number of African women greeted them and said 'Morêna'. One of them, witch-like with her shrivelled skin and crafty eyes, shuffled nearer and touched Henry's jacket. She spoke a mixture of Afrikaans and Xhosa : she greeted the man of Salome. She hoped it would go well with him. And that he would have many children. And that the corn would always bear four cobs. And that the rains would come at the right time. She mentioned a gift : Henry received it : a gleaming clay pot, burned black and glazed. She clapped her hands and accepted the money in upturned palms, counted it quickly with palms turned down. Long would he live, the owner of Salome, the prince of Silberstein.

Dr Johns took his leave, telling him that Judge O'Hara felt a little upset after the banquet.

Henry resumed his wandering, but found the earthenware pot difficult to carry properly – he could get no grip on it and one was always afraid that one of the legs would break off if one held on to it. He left the African village and was soon alone in the beautiful veld. Jock Silberstein applied wild-life preservation to his farming and all indigenous plants flourished in the marshes, in the small natural dams and against the hills. The sky was cloudless and each colour stood out in bright gradations. The peacefulness was entirely neutral. Here the conflict of good and evil was completely invisible. The breeze had gone and there was no movement. Even when he brushed against the plants or trod on them, they moved sluggishly and recovered slowly, or remained destroyed in a position of perfect rest.

But then he did observe a movement in the distance : a feminine figure that at one moment was silhouetted against the horizon, and the next moment merged into the landscape. In their leisurely wandering they drew nearer together and he noticed first the outlines, and then the indications of features, but the whole remained indeterminate – her age, her colouring, her claim to beauty. It was a woman, faceless as in dreams, and a composite of all women. If it should be Salome, then this impending meeting was what he had expected : a slow crystallization, the birth of form from amorphousness.

It was such an important moment that he hesitated for a second, slightly disconcerted by the unexpected conclusion to his search; but then he suddenly recognized Lady Mandrake and hastened to meet her.

'Henry,' she said, 'how pleasant to see you here.'

The sunlight was cruel to her and made the mask seem cheap. It baked it and made it unsightly, but in the process heightened its effectiveness. Lady Mandrake herself was so completely hidden that the apertures that were her eyes looked like two small windows from behind which the real person peeped out.

'I have come back to Welgevonden,' she said, 'because Sir Henry spent perhaps his happiest last days here. Sir Henry has ceased to exist and he has gone, but he still has claims to make as long as his body is visible. How would you bury him?'

She stood directly in front of Henry, the woman inside the painted carapace, the two gaps of her eyes fixed urgently upon him.

'Would you have buried him somewhere in the Welgevonden valleys, with a lily in his arms, coffined in imbuia, landmarked by a simple stone of black marble?'

She brought out a miniature copper casket that she had kept under her jacket.

'I had Sir Henry cremated,' she said, 'and now he is everywhere and in any shape.'

It was difficult for Henry to envisage Sir Henry in the tiny copper casket. She could still not decide how to make him utterly invisible. She asked Henry about a suitable place to scatter the ash. They walked together through the veld and looked at a small dam, a dense thicket, a sandhill, but could not decide. And then the wind rose again, it plucked at them and this increasing movement offered the solution. Sir Henry vanished from sight in thousands of particles: he settled on a flower, on the water, in the lake of distilling wine, on the roof of Welgevonden and, in infinitesimal motes, through space on unknown places. There were eighty years of images of Sir Henry now. Sir Henry had himself found no image in Welgevonden that night; Henry saw a series. Lady Mandrake remained with only one: the young aesthete in Paris, in London, in Capri and in Venice – a young man, like the young man before her, and she gave him a gift in memory of Sir Henry: a ring set with a flamboyant stone. She left him with her entirely false image, for Sir Henry was everywhere; he was distributed in the innumerable motes that had vanished in the sunlight.

Towards the factory now, in his jacket, the ring on his finger, the pot in one hand: thinking indolently about everything Judge O'Hara, Jock and the rest had told him during the course of the week. He could remember little of what they had said; so many things had been thrashed out, so much chaos and so much knowledge had been revealed to him – and yet, at the centre there was nevertheless a total, colourless nothingness. *But*, beneath the surface there was a milling and a turbulence, a continual tension of something against something. As long as one knew about it, as long as one was not misled by the colourlessness. Then, too, there was Salome. He had the tingling sensation that anticipation brings with it. This afternoon or tonight he would see her. He was completely committed. With her, against this dangerous neutral background, he would try to find the enemy. He would at least not be alone. And he would experience love, in the wake of fear, which he already knew.

He suddenly felt tired and put the earthenware pot down on the ground. The jacket was hot and he unbuttoned it. He again put his hands into the pockets and found something that he had missed the first time. It was a kind of postcard. On the back was written 83-7569. On the front was a photograph of a naked girl in an erotic position, the familiar pale face puckered in earnest concentration. He looked for a long time at it and had a sudden fright when he heard the thunder of hoofs. A cloud of dust hung in front of the sun. The rumble grew louder and then he saw Brutus at the head of the herd. Behind frisked and capered the heifers, tails askew, hind legs in the air, muzzles against the ground; and ahead of them thundered the bicoloured monster. The sun shone on his hide, his muscles knotted and billowed with each mighty stride. He brushed past Henry, the tips of his horns thrust out on either side like swords. The herd disappeared over the hill, invisible in a dust cloud which itself disappeared. In the subsequent quiet, for a mere instant, Henry felt the intimation of fear. But it, too, disappeared, and he resumed his ramble in the sunny landscape.

At the cottage he was intercepted by Mrs Dreyer. She must have seen him from behind the chintz curtains, because the door opened and she waddled to meet him.

Henry! Henry! What a joyful day! She felt that she must *personally* congratulate him. A pity Professor Dreyer was not there . . . And Salome, like one of her own children! Two *lucky* young people. Ah, love, love, love! Her clothes were too young for her: frills, bows and the sweetest little petticoat. And she was filled with the joys of life. A little silliness at first – sly references to Oh-what-a-wonderful adventure; and then, sentimentally, the little gift, in all simplicity, to an *exemplary* couple. She had wrapped it in brown paper. Henry thanked him and opened it later. It was a small green book 'from Mrs and Professor Dreyer' – *Cruden's Concordance*. The book fitted neatly into the left pocket of his jacket and his hands were still free to carry the clay pot.

He had now reached the factory. As he had come from the opposite direction, he arrived first at the Ubu-room. He at once looked for the gardener and saw him beside the man in white, the two of them before the great machine. But it was the gardener who dominated the entire room. His uniform was indescribable: it was as if all existing colours had been combined to create a new colour. It was truly a uniform for the angels. It shone more brightly than the rays of the sun falling on it. The gardener had sat unmoving all day, a source of continually mounting energy. He had ignored all attempts at communication by the man in white. The girls from the room next door had often come in to look at him, but he was remote as a god on Olympus. His face was cut from marble, his eyes raised to the machine. It was as if he were waiting for an act of creation, everything in him tensed to the extreme, awaiting the final nuance, the monadic step forward, the transition from nothing to something, the formative rebirth from the universal . . . And at the precise moment that Henry entered and observed him, his gnarled fingers descended on the single button allotted to him.

And nothing happened.

It was an ineffable moment. It was the complete surrender to creation and nothing happened. The old man pressed the button and nothing happened.

But he did not believe it. He knew, he was certain: an entire harvest had been encompassed in the process.

Henry walked quickly to the next room. He gave a last look back and saw the old man in shadow. Without light his coat looked grey and the man in white looked more prominent. But it was all an illusion. When the sun shone on the coat again all the colours would burn as if the whole world were involved in the conflagration. Even if the button were a fake – the red and white juices of all the wonderful grapes on Welgevonden, and all the products of the cellars, where the seasons recurred, and all the sunshine and warmth, and the sparkle, and the drunkenness and the exuberant joy, were newly-born in that single movement.

All the girls in the room next door looked up when he entered. Their hands moved automatically, independent of their thoughts, like piston-rods of flesh and blood, while their eyes were fixed on him. He felt bashful of all this attention, of the way in which the girls looked at the future bridegroom: the peculiar combination of resentment, longing and lewd scrutiny. Burdened by the earthenware pot, he forced his way with difficulty along the narrow passage, and kept bumping against thighs and legs. Just before reaching the door he was confronted by two girls. Dark and blue eyes, moving lips, and feminine voices with all sorts of accents, and unfinished sentences interrupted by giggles, brought home to him the fact that room number two also had a present for Salome's fiancé. It was wrapped in green paper. He was expected to open and display it. Caught off guard, he did so. It was a pair of black nylon women's panties, edged with lace, and in front, fastened with pink ribbon, hung a single miniature lock of shining silver. (Suppressed laughter as the bottles sailed past.) This the one girl gave him. Then the other gave him her little gift, in the silence that descended on the prelude to the next moment of surprise. This time it was a bulky bundle of paper of every colour that, layer by layer, he peeled off until at last he reached the kernel: a small box firmly sealed. Surrounded by the coloured paper, attired like a buffoon in his jacket, hemmed in by eager girls, he opened it and brought to light a silver key. And now there was no end to the boisterousness.

Henry regarded the laughing girls. He could withdraw in confusion. He could also participate in their vulgarity. Certain demands were being made of him: it was the fate of the Silberstein heir.

He applied the key to the lock to open it, to satisfy expectations. It was repugnant, but the matter had to be disposed of.

He realized too late that the key would be either too big or too small. Already, as he went through the motions, he heard the roar of the crowd; and then, in the noise, silence came again – the isolation in noise that he had found with Jock in the room of confession – and, on its track, the intimation of fear that disappeared as soon as he left and took all his presents with him to the room where the African men were washing the bottles.

He found a restfulness there, where the tempo was slow and all activity gradually came to a stop. Also, there would be no gifts.

He walked past the stranded trollies and staring faces.

The gift, the clay pot, had already been given – and paid for.

He hesitated for a moment and then decided to visit Professor Dreyer. It seemed as if his arrival were expected. The students crowded round him and shook his hand firmly. But the professor himself was still in his old place – to one side at the window, unsusceptible to noise. This time he held a glass test tube in which he lightly oscillated a green liquid. It moved round the side, a swirl of singular green. Henry went and stood beside him; he had never before seen any colour quite like it. Sometimes it had the colour of the first green leaves of spring; but, when the liquid became still, it changed gradually to the dark green of summer. Perfectly still, without the slightest trace of sediment, the colour darkened and grew in intensity, as if a shadow had fallen on it – it drew something from the darkness and gave the illusion of depth. Then the professor moved the tube again and for a moment there were all the colours of autumn, with the increasing movement also the white of winter and, as the eddy reached its maximum speed and then subsided, the process was repeated from the beginning: the limpid, cheerful green being reborn.

Professor Dreyer became aware for the first time that Henry was standing next to him and saw the interest in the young man's eyes. One of the students whispered something in his ear. He cleared his throat and, on behalf of them all, expressed congratulations. Then he looked around rather helplessly. Not one of them had thought of a present. All of a sudden he remembered the young man's interest. Here he had seen something that had an affinity with his own world. He picked up a piece of cotton-wool from the table, wrapped the tube carefully in it (after having corked it), put it in a little box and handed it over. Now he recognized Henry; all the associations flashed with lightning speed into his mind and he immediately began talking about the sewage system at his house. Talking away, he accompanied Henry to the door. His attitude was one of mock humility towards the future master of Welgevonden. He mentioned all the money that was needed for research. Where would the Silbersteins be without the contribution of that room? Here were the pioneers who were civilizing the country, uncovering secrets, clearing the way to the utopia of the future. The drab little man followed Henry through the door, took tardy farewell, flattered him, commended his interest; tried to manipulate him, to influence him in anticipation.

Through the tulips and then Henry was away from the factory. He found the little box inconvenient to carry. He took out the tube and put it in the top pocket of his jacket. It was slightly too big and protruded – a glass tube in which, with every shake as he walked, the seasons repeated themselves.

How quiet and peaceful Welgevonden looked! The farm of Silberstein. An Afrikaans farm, 'ben trovato' in peace and quiet. Cinnamon-doves cooed in the trees; there was the sound of water in furrows. He laid all his presents on the grass and rested; and after a while moved on. The observation tower glowed in the distance, the manifold roofs of the house took shape one by one. The trees of the wood were motionless and then, suddenly, the pine needles began to sing. In the distance he heard the clatter of hoofs. They beat on the ground with wild speed, a flirtation with death that reached its climax in a tremendous leap – there, against the sky, rose horse and rider; the sound of their contact with the earth was soft and muted and silence fell.

The tracks of the trucks were deep furrows in the road and around a corner they stood in a tight line, yellow and green, beside the peacefully grazing stud cows. The foreman-driver with his retinue, in their neat uniforms, waiting in order of seniority, constituted an inexorable barrier; hefty men with rigid faces, shirt sleeves rolled up above bulging arms, eyes direct as searchlights. Even when offering the gift, subscribed to by the labour union, they looked threatening. It was a miniature of their trucks, meticulously modelled in steel and spray painted. Few words were said, only those strictly necessary, as Henry received the gift, heavy as lead, and then they turned, climbed one by one into their trucks, revved their engines, and roared away, leaving Henry completely invisible in the heat and dust of their sirocco.

Burdened with his load of goodwill, he approached the house with difficulty. Limping and stumbling he chose all the least-known paths in search of the refuge of his room. In a narrow passage, unavoidably, he met the duchess. She stood squarely in his path, her eyes fixed on the coat of many colours, the earthenware pot, the nylon panties, the test tube, the glittering ring, the toy truck and the book in his pocket. And then she smiled, the Yiddishe Mamma.

'*Der meshugeneh . . .*' she said and shook her head.

'Oh, the looney child !' and kissed his cheek.

II

Sleep . . . in this room where his day was divided in two – where now, for the seventh time, he shut himself away from the world in preparation for the night's revelation. But this time he lay awake and took leave slowly of every second that brought him nearer the one, inescapable occasion, where he would have to look them in the face, where he would have to accept the reality of his loved one.

Because, he thought, it was impossible that even love was unreal, invisible.

In his struggle with sleep he thought of God, who posed fear and love as two inseparable requirements.

In his struggle against thoughts that denied him sleep, he constantly discovered new 'truths' that he nevertheless distrusted. When did conscious thoughts stop? When did the primordial images, that crept from prenatal sleep, begin? And when was man nearest the truth of being?

Henry's thoughts were in turbulence and he was altogether unconscious that a restless sleep had overcome him. Even when he awoke and felt the shock of rational perception, he remained under the impression that he had been conscious all the time.

Somewhere in the house the blackamoor rang the bell. This usually happened at midday, but this time it was to announce the important proceedings of the evening. Henry had no doubts, no speculations about the uniform – the seventh evening was the immaculate finale, the urge towards heights peculiar to man, the climax that made all volition acceptable.

First he bathed and opened the battery of taps; he took a delight in regarding the lions' heads spurting exuberantly; he stupefied himself wantonly with all the flavours of all his senses; he splashed in the bath and floated with his head thrown back in the water, his eyes fixed on the gilded ceiling.

There were moments when he felt calm, when he made simple observations and when he felt deeply moved by a corner of beauty in the midst of all the vulgarity.

He drank some of the wine in the carafe. He dressed slowly and knotted his tie with a hint of asymmetry, to foil perfection. He lit a cigarette – and suddenly he was overwhelmed by the thought of what lay before him. Numbness crept through his limbs; but there was a tingling, too. He could not think clearly, and yet he felt capable of great things. He expected no particular revelation, no great truth, but . . . There was a certain rhythm that was completely real, a pace of impulsive acceptance that carried one closer to invisible truth.

Suddenly he became aware of a sound that had penetrated his room. It had begun as something in the background that had now become dominant. If one tried to attribute it to any single object it was inexplicable; but was explicable as soon as one realized that it was the corporate sound of a gathering of people. There was a special rhythm to the shuffling, a certain musicality in voices, a completely amorphous unity of movement that nevertheless gave the impression of an approaching climax, despite the fact that no specific process of intensification could be perceived.

He combed his hair, put drops in his eyes, flicked every speck of dust from his dinner jacket and hid himself behind impeccable neatness. Physically as clean as possible, spiritually armoured as far as possible, he went towards the noise.

In a room, the existence of which he had been unaware, he saw the crowd, dressed like himself. The place was bordered with black curtains, row upon row of small tables were decorated with flowers, covered with snacks, softened by the light of candles. There was a dais with a single table, two chairs, a snowy cake and a gigantic arrangement of palms on either side. Under the dais was an orchestra that played various tunes. They began with 'The Continental.' Then they switched to 'Lullaby of Broadway.' Jock and slim Mrs Silberstein had already taken up their positions in the front of the room. She was wearing a gown of pure gold. Her eyes were shining more brightly than ever: one could disappear in their blue. Jock was big, elegant, and formidable in his dinner jacket: the undoubted ruler Silberstein. Beside him sat J. J., the roué beyond reproach, with all the marks of well-bred dissipation, with the enormous moustache that was not laughable, the only one with bags under his eyes that gave him status. And beside Mrs Silberstein, the duchess, a shawl over her shoulders because of her age, peacefully resigned to the inevitable. And then there were the two Misses Silberstein, two little autumn leaves touched by the first frost.

The orchestra had now begun 'The Way You Look Tonight'; it coincided with Henry's appearance, bright with anxiety in the searchlight directed at the dais.

The guests had already begun to savour the sparkling Cuvée; there were eight hundred of them: judges, advocates, doctors (medical), doctors (academic), respected farmers, artists, intellectuals, selected Coloureds and members of the Welgevonden staff. Only a small group noticed Henry's appearance and clapped softly before taking another drink. The others followed their example without knowing why.

Jock gave Henry a special smile. There was a mocking look in his eyes.

The orchestra had switched to 'Dreaming of a White Christmas.'

In front of the dais there was a mountain of presents. The earthenware pot, the nylon panties, *Cruden's Concordance*, the coat of many colours, the miniature truck, had been added conspicuously to the pile; even a test tube filled with colourless liquid.

Suddenly the orchestra stopped.

The silence called everyone to order.

And then the orchestra broke into 'You'll Never Know.'

Every one of the eight hundred guests rose when Salome arrived.

She appeared at the far end of the room with her retinue, virginal girls with dark eyes.

It was an impressive procession. They approached slowly to the measure of the music.

Henry, too, stood up. In the distance he saw the movement toward the dais. The multitude flocked together and formed part of the procession: it was a mass movement forward.

The one in the middle was she. There was no arresting the movement. It was a kind of ineluctable fate, this movement towards him. Alone, he waited, his eyes narrowed to slits, so that he would see his loved one quickly when she entered his range of vision.

And then he experienced the now-familiar fear; and together with the fear a feeling that must be love.

The procession came nearer and nearer: an enormous, amorphous cloud before his eyes, a wave on the point of breaking, a hesitation before the great blow that would shatter the whole into numerous fragments.

One should simply not look at the multitude. One should not listen to the noise. One should forget about the hall, the candles, the champagne, the pile of gifts, the crowds of people. One must be able to abandon oneself to the whole; await the wave and seize a single drop as it rose above the crest.

Naturally, one must have faith. It was so simple. One must make one's concession to the invisible.

He looked up and saw the crowd burst into his range of vision; saw how the unit disintegrated into all its component parts; how individual figures took shape and became visible.

III

Imagine that you are alone in a big hall. You raise your hands for your loved one. You are dressed in a uniform. You are afraid, but you have faith. You gamble with your faith. In your uniform of the angels you go forward, you raise your hands, and you wait with complete confidence for the image of truth in the wake of love.

The Third Eye

All characters are imaginary.
The story has been knocked together from two works by
Euripides and Sophocles.
The shopping centre, alas, is contemporary.

Contents

Dedicated to Gloria and Hill Altepost

They all drank the toast eagerly.
They drank to the death of tradition and primordial life. There was much gaiety and freedom, and rejoicing without limits.

Chapter One

The Task

Demosthenes H. de Goede, newly promoted to the rank of Captain in the Criminal Investigation Department and recently cured of a speech defect, of robust build and a model of self-sufficiency, the embodiment of everyone's Ideal Man, but with the handsome, serene face of one of mankind's patient servants etched with something of the sorrow born of perpetual subservience to his calling, sat at his breakfast table eating noisily and sniffing through his nose, while his wife, Hope, a nymphomaniac, looked at him with displeasure. His grey suit fitted him a trifle too tightly. She nearly went crazy with boredom every time she saw him relax after one of his frequent jobs, and she suddenly thought: he used to be able to move his ears. She said, 'Move your ears.' He did so, and she no longer found it amusing. 'Oh, Jesus!' she groaned. She wanted to scream with frustration, but thought better of it when she weighed it against his undisputed ability in bed. Everything irritated her: his exercises at night for the sake of his physique, his off-key voice when he tried to sing. Once she ordered him to stop the exercises, and he developed a paunch. She ordered him to resume them and managed to put up with the irritation to her nerves until the paunch disappeared. No demand she made on him was too much; all her nagging and accusations had so far not altered him; the witches' dance she led him could not weaken him.

Hope had curlers in her hair and complexion cream on her face. She felt miserable and could not forgive him for being such a good person: so sensible in his decisions, so adaptable, such a faithful servant to life, forgivable even when he misused his power. She had deceived him time and time again with other men, and had elevated her feeble lies to the level of truths in the face of his credulity. She was powerless before his virtuousness, his itch to serve, his strong urges which satisfied her so delightfully, his capacity for patient struggle, his acceptance of any privation, his inextinguishable courage, his rages that could pass just as easily to gentleness, the unusual complexity behind the tantalizing simplicity.

She looked at him resentfully and longed suddenly for the sophisticated, aesthetic young officer who had been too modest that night at the Police Ball. She could not explain it exactly, but she felt vaguely dissatisfied with her lot, even though her greatest need was satisfied; her longings were based on her own shortcomings, and one sort of satisfaction most likely excluded another. She peered at him across the table like a vampire at an inexhaustible victim of the wrong blood group; or like something that had wandered out of the Middle Ages and did not understand our present day rituals of thaumaturgy. The four children, adopted by the couple after their frequent matings had proved to be fruitless, sat on either side of the table – curly-headed mites of uncertain lineage, with rebellious manners which, at this stage, probably disguised criminal tendencies behind superfluous energy. Two girls and two boys, ugly and vaguely alike. Their father, who had just finished his breakfast and now raised his unmusical voice in a tuneless ditty, good-naturedly suffered being banged by spoons and spattered with food from all directions. Hope's gown hung crookedly on her shoulders, exposing her large breasts. She lit a cigarette and scolded in the direction of the children, while she blew out clouds of smoke. Cold teacups stood on one side of the table and the remains of food congealed on the plates. Captain de Goede looked longingly out of the window where he saw part of the mountain above the house. On the summit was a massive pink cloud being threatened by a small sooty one, dirty-blue in colour like train smoke. It drifted towards the pink cloud and gradually consumed it.

He got up and kissed Hope on her forehead, playfully pressing her breast with his hand. At first she wanted to push his hand away, but involuntarily pressed it closer. He leaned over and kissed his four children in places that were not too sticky, and then Captain Demosthenes de Goede went out the front door. When he had closed the door, he found himself in the small garden of his semi-detached house, right on top of a steep road. He looked at the mint growing next to the hedge and shoved the hose to the middle of the lawn. He closed the garden gate carefully and caught the bus on the street corner. He looked back and decided to buy the other half of the house for the sake of his growing children.

When he got down in the middle of the town and walked to a grey three-storied building, he hesitated in front of a smart Rolls-Royce parked next to the kerb. A haughty chauffeur gazed straight ahead, the Royal Automobile Club emblem shone in the sun and the engine purred almost soundlessly under the hood. The commissionaire of the building said, 'Good morning, Captain de Goede,' and a well-groomed man sitting in the back of the Rolls-Royce immediately glanced up. He and Demosthenes de Goede regarded each other for a few seconds as though struck by the marked similarity in their looks, in spite of the trappings of class distinction, and then the Rolls-Royce drew swiftly away.

Demosthenes H. de Goede climbed the stairs and knocked at a door at the end of the passage. Everything smelled of the civil service, all the paint was a drab civil service colour and everyone sauntered along at a civil service pace. The door was opened by a pretty girl who gave a professional smile and, having received an unexpected pinch, led him to a door where an effeminate young man with a superior air took over as guide. A third door was opened, and Demosthenes de Goede met Brigadier Ornassis E., head of the D-Service, in his remarkable sanctum.

II

'Shall we come to the point at once?' asked Brigadier Ornassis E. 'Thank you, James.' He nodded to the effeminate young man who left the room, closing the door softly behind him.

There was a painting on the wall directly behind his head, and Demosthenes H. de Goede stared fixedly at it.

'Are you interested in pop art?' asked the Brigadier.

'No,' said Demosthenes de Goede.

The Brigadier shrugged his shoulders.

'It's not everyone's cup of tea.'

Hanging on the wall were a few early works of Max Ernst, Mark Rothko and a Jackson Pollock of the middle forties. Picasso's 'Guernica' hung by itself.

'Reproductions,' said the Brigadier. 'You don't think I could afford the originals on a civil servant's salary, do you?'

'I don't really know much about art,' said Demosthenes H. de Goede. In spite of having overcome his speech defect, he spoke very slowly, as though his thoughts emerged with difficulty.

'A man of action,' said the Brigadier. '*Le parfait exemplaire de la vie energique* . . .'

He was a slightly built man with the face of an ascetic who has seen a lot of trouble. The cut of his clothes was impeccable, his hands (now folded in an attitude of meditation) were soft and delicate.

'The ponos rather than the logos.'

His gaze softened as he looked at Demosthenes de Goede with eyes that had acquired their expression of worldly wisdom from personal suffering.

'Are you happily married?' he asked suddenly.

Demosthenes de Goede's face brightened. He immediately took out photographs of the four little savages. For a long time the Brigadier looked with concentration at Hope's face in the background, her ripe figure – the promise of passion that is aroused by blondes. Absentmindedly he listened to Demosthenes de Goede singing the praises of marital bliss while he opened a file and paged through it with his shapely hands.

He said, 'I see you are the man who destroyed the Giant of Welgevonden.'

'Strictly according to regulations,' said Demosthenes de Goede, 'after I had cautioned him three times.'

'The Lesbian Poisoner of Calvinia, the Swine of Dysselsdorp, the Serpent of Muldersvlei, the Blackmailer of Arcadia, the Sweetheart of Kammaland, the Lion of the North, the Bull of Benoni, the Whores of Humansdorp . . .'

'I'm quoting press headlines, of course,' added the Brigadier.

'There were many more,' said Demosthenes de Goede with becoming modesty.

'You've certainly had a full life as a detective,' said the Brigadier as he closed the file.

'It's a fight that never ends,' said Demosthenes de Goede. 'My life is full of hardships, and there is no rest.'

'De Goede melancholikos,' said the Brigadier and pressed a bell.

The effeminate young man appeared with a tray of drinks.

The glasses were repeatedly filled, and De Goede did not hesitate to swallow his brandy in great gulps under the watchful eye of the Brigadier.

'There is no rest,' repeated Demosthenes de Goede. 'It's one job after another. One has to pay to the hilt. You get dog-tired and hardly ever see your wife and children. And I have never asked for any financial reward.' He gestured to the Brigadier to add less water. 'You just have to live from day to day – that's the only way you can take such a wearisome job.'

The D-Service had no jurisdiction over the Criminal Investigation Department and Demosthenes de Goede felt free to talk in front of this little Brigadier whom he could pulverize with one blow. 'In any case, I'll have to retire one of these days,' he said. 'I've got quite a lot of leave due me.'

'There is still one task,' said the Brigadier. 'The C.I.D. has released you to us for it. It will be your last, because after that, for various reasons, you can be of no further use.'

'I'm tired,' said Demosthenes de Goede. He considered the Brigadier's words for a while and asked suddenly, 'Will I be entitled to my pension even if I have not reached retiring age?'

'Certainly you will be entitled to your pension,' answered the Brigadier softly.

They drank awhile in silence.

'Have you ever heard of Boris Gudenov?'

Demosthenes de Goede thought deeply. In his mind he ran over all the half-forgotten bits of knowledge from his police college days, and said, 'The tyrant in Moussorgsky's opera.'

The Brigadier and the effeminate young man, who had all this time been acting as a waiter, both laughed loudly. 'That Godunov is spelled with a *u*; this one is Gudenov and he is a tycoon.'

He was still smiling, but then became serious.

'This will be your next task. To track down Boris Gudenov . . .' He was suddenly lost in thought. 'To bring him to light.'

Demosthenes de Goede put his glass down on the table next to him. He bored his clenched fist into the hollow of his hand, and it looked like a large knout. He sat erect, foursquare, with his eyes fixed on the Brigadier. His head seemed slightly too small for his body, but in spite of that he was still a handsome man : a huge lock-forward type, the South African hero par excellence.

'Perhaps I should first tell you something about the D-Service,' said the Brigadier. He leaned back in his chair and eased his tie. 'There is a great difference between us and the C.I.D. You catch criminals on the grounds of specific crimes committed; your Bible is Gardiner and Lansdowne's *Criminal Law & Procedure*. How can I explain it ? Ours is uncodified. It is vaguer and more undecided. We really deal with spiritual crime.'

The Brigadier lifted his hand to his silver-grey temples and covered his eyes while he concentrated. 'We must protect the community against spiritual crime, against the degeneration of the self, against the subtle onslaught on order, against the alienation of established personifications, against the danger of the disintegration of the symbolic cosmos and the resulting personal disintegration which reveals itself in all sorts of acts of sabotage, in deterioration and the taking over by demoniac and destructive forces. Is that clear ?'

He opened his eyes and glanced sharply at Demosthenes de Goede who had poured himself another drink.

'I am a simple man,' said Demosthenes de Goede. 'I only know what I learned at the police college. There was a captain with us who had a yen for philosophy, but I'm not one for all sorts of complicated fads and fancies.' He took a sip. 'Just give me that Boris Gudenov alone. After I have throttled him for half an hour, there will be no more mystery.'

The Brigadier smiled. 'It's probably the simple man who has the most success – the man with vision, anger and generosity. He is the one who rises as the man of the hour, as the saviour, to restore the psychic balance of the epoch.'

'He interfered with my wife,' said Demosthenes de Goede, sunk in thought. 'The Police Captain, at the Police Ball one night, and I smashed his jaw for him.'

The Brigadier rose and stood in front of the 'Guernica' with his back to the Captain.

'There are some of us who are fated to sacrifice our personal desire for happiness and security. That, alas, is a fact. Some people belong to the community and are expendable. They are not important as individuals; their deeds are objective and impersonal; they are all men rolled into one.'

'I am a simple person,' said Demosthenes de Goede, 'and many of these ideas are beyond me.'

The Brigadier turned round and sat down again. 'They are sometimes burned in the flame of creation.'

'It's a lonely life,' said Demosthenes de Goede, looking into his glass.

'They have to bring the mother of death to light and deprive her of her destructive powers.'

'I curse the day that I was born,' said Demosthenes de Goede, slow tears beginning to roll down his cheeks.

'They must disclose the shadow, exorcise it and make use of the creative power of the darkness. They must subdue the monster and harness its healing power.'

'My mother told me when I was a child that I would endure much for the sake of my fellow men,' said Demosthenes de Goede while his tears flowed freely. 'She said that I was born to all sorts of hardships. I have devoted my life to the C.I.D.'

The Brigadier was disconcerted by the emotion shown by the strong man and gazed at him in fascination, meanwhile changing the subject.

'But to come back to the D-Service. All we have to rely on is the Suppression of Communism Act and certain other regulations, equally vague. Who and what is a communist?' He looked in vain for an answer to Demosthenes de Goede who had taken off his jacket and rolled up the sleeves of his white shirt to expose his hefty arms.

'Let's rather ask : Who is Boris Gudenov?'

Demosthenes de Goede now showed more interest.

'According to available sources, he is a tycoon of uncertain extraction. An immigrant from Poland or Hungary and a ruling shareholder in a large number of companies. He is a sort of Zaharoff, Gulbenkian and Gould rolled into one. He avoids all publicity, but is connected with more charitable institutions than any other person in the country. Oita, his shopping centre in the middle of the town, is not only an architect's dream, but also a model of imaginative organization. You could be born there, live your life to the full and die there without leaving the building complex. *Life* describes it as a model town within a building.'

The Brigadier was satisfied with the response his words aroused, for Demosthenes de Goede's forehead was creased in concentration.

'Name his crime and I will bring him to justice,' said Demosthenes de Goede proudly, after he had struggled a moment in silence to formulate his sentences.

The Brigadier raised his hands and clapped them together. 'My exact words were : "bring to light", Captain.'

He meditated a moment searching like a priest for intelligible comparisons, but found no elucidating examples. He had lived for so long with the Gudenov image himself that he could no longer create any bridgeheads. Nowadays he could only think about aspects of the complicated personality. It was like having to discuss a difficult theory with someone who did not understand the basic principles.

He tried again. The Captain waited patiently.

'Almost nothing happens in this country that Boris Gudenov does not have a hand in. His influence stretches in all directions; his newspapers cover everything from Right to Left; his lackeys vary from rogues to divines; he is like quicksilver, always tantalizingly elusive.'

Demosthenes de Goede once again considered a painting on the wall, this time the 'Guernica'.

For a moment it seemed that the Brigadier was helpless before the simplicity of the Captain's thought processes, and he himself, in a peculiar way, seemed a defender of complexity against crystal-clear simplicity.

'This struggle is like a dream,' said the Brigadier. 'There is nothing that hasn't a double meaning.' His face cleared suddenly. 'And your job is really this : to bring to light everything that is hidden; to disclose the monster; to expose the cobra to the sun . . .' He was forgetting his earlier resolve. 'It is to wander down into the Unknown, the psychic substratum, and to make the Conscious triumph over the Unconscious . . .'

He stopped himself in time. For a few moments they stared at each other, two complementary personalities; one who had to formulate the job, the other to execute it.

Then the Brigadier came to a decision.

'All I want you to do is to find out everything about Boris Gudenov and report it to us. Even the slightest fact is important. Everything he says or does, or what others say he says or does, or whatever you hear or see.'

Demosthenes de Goede nodded in understanding. He smiled suddenly, for he had expected a far more difficult job.

'And if I find enough evidence against him, may I take action?'

The Brigadier raised his delicate hands.

'In Heaven's name, no violence ! You must not carry your revolver or use anything that may cause him serious bodily harm.'

Demosthenes de Goede looked disappointed, but the promises in connection with his retirement and pension made him control his resentment. It would be an easy task.

The Brigadier seemed to read his thoughts. 'It will be the most difficult of all tasks – you are in greater danger than you think. And that is why it will also be your last work, for after that you will be of no further use to us, not even to the C.I.D.'

The Brigadier weighed his next words carefully : 'There is psychological danger attached to it. Your whole personality is at stake. Even you can become possessed . . .'

'I'm not afraid of witchcraft,' said Demosthenes de Goede firmly. 'In 'fifty-nine the Witch of Hillbrow . . .'

The Brigadier sighed and summoned the effeminate young man who appeared with his notebook, ready to write down the rest of the interview verbatim.

'Are you perhaps homosexually inclined?' the Brigadier asked Demosthenes de Goede, and raised his hands when the roar hit his eardrums. 'It's important in the Service,' he said. 'For some reason or other it is more dangerous than heterosexuality.'

He looked at the Captain attentively.

'You will have to change your style of dressing. Your suit is too drab. Your shoes are all wrong.' He carried on a low conversation with the effeminate young man and then said, 'A leather jacket and trousers not wider than fifteen inches. We'll let you have the outfit at cost price. The young lady at the door will fill in the forms for you.' He turned again to the effeminate young man. 'Loafers, perhaps?' and the young man nodded.

'No revolver.'

Demosthenes de Goede's beloved Beretta was taken away from him.

The Brigadier shrugged his shoulders.

'You might perhaps find everything strange at first, but the world of the D-Service is like that of a chameleon. We adapt ourselves to our surroundings; we follow the spirit of the times; we first melt into the background, then we strike.' He sighed and looked extremely unhappy. 'Everything is forgiven the policeman and the detective, but the public can't bear the Service to succeed. They write reams about us in books and newspapers, but our presence in everyday life makes them nervous. They feel that our existence is necessary, but they regard our actions as immoral.' The Brigadier's attention wandered off in renewed meditation. 'Is it because we identify ourselves with them to such an extent that we even adopt their weaknesses?'

Demosthenes de Goede looked anxiously at his Beretta which the effeminate young man was handling clumsily and ordered him to oil it every week to prevent the barrel from rusting.

Suddenly the Brigadier became brusque and businesslike.

'You will be known as H-12. You will report daily. Any questions?'

'What does Boris Gudenov look like?' asked Demosthenes de Goede.

'An intelligent question,' said the Brigadier, opening a drawer and taking out a photograph.

The Captain looked at it and frowned in an attempt to pin down a fleeting memory.

'I've seen him before.'

'This was the only photograph of Boris Gudenov available to the D-Service,' said the Brigadier. He inclined his ear to the effeminate young man who was plucking his sleeve and whispering. He stopped himself in time when, according to Secret Service custom, he was on the point of burning the photograph.

'A remarkable likeness,' said the Brigadier, studying the photograph again and looking at Demosthenes de Goede. He had now regained his former joviality. 'A remarkable case.' His imagination ran away with him again. 'The inevitable struggle: the pursued under the spell of the pursuer; two aspects of the persona; two masks concealing one ego; Ahab and the whale in the turbulent sea of the Unconscious . . .'

Meanwhile he had taken Demosthenes de Goede's hand and was about to bring the interview to an end. 'May it be of some comfort to you that in the dark struggle ahead of you your efforts will be accordingly elevated to the level of heroism, and the part you play will assume the appearance of tragedy.'

Demosthenes de Goede just managed to keep his iron fist from crushing the flabby, almost boneless hand of the Brigadier to a pulp.

Before he left the room, the effeminate young man again whispered something to the Brigadier.

'Don't forget the function tomorrow night,' said the Brigadier, 'to introduce you to the Service. It will be quite informal, because, strictly speaking, we are dealing with an outsider. A minor gathering, perhaps, but still important for the purpose of making you feel one of us.'

In the vestibule the attractive girl accompanied Demosthenes de Goede to the second door and, having received the pinch she was expecting, giggled joyfully.

Then she helped him fill in the form.

III

'You look different,' said Hope as she inspected her husband in his narrow trousers, scarf and leather jacket. 'You look Bohemian.'

On the way to the bedroom he told her about Boris Gudenov.

'Is he rich?' she asked, removing the jacket of her suit. 'Is he young? Is he handsome?' she wanted to know as she dropped her skirt to the floor. Her mind was on Boris Gudenov as they began to make love.

At a certain stage their children came bursting in at the door and, screaming at the top of their voices, charged through the room and out at the other door leading to the lawn. Later on her questions began all over again. Would she get the chance to meet Boris Gudenov? Was he really a criminal? Whom did he look like? When her questions began to arouse even the sluggish suspicions of Demosthenes de Goede, she pulled him closer and made such vehement demands that his half-formed suspicions disappeared in the completion of his regular duty. The children thundered through the room a second time and Demosthenes de Goede, conqueror and martyr, protector of his house, provider of fruitfulness, orphan of the storm, relaxed for the time being next to his lovely sleeping wife.

There was only the break of a dreary Sunday afternoon between him and the tasks that were waiting around the corner. He thought of his mother who had said that his father had begotten him to endure more trouble than any other man. At that same moment, his wife stirred and stretched her limbs slowly while the children, scratched and torn, chased one another through the room again towards the lawn. When she was sleeping peacefully again, he thought of Boris Gudenov and tried to determine the nature of his task. He remembered the words of the Brigadier, and in his mind he challenged the spectre, seeing himself as David matched against Goliath, the Redeemer in the struggle with Satan, the

Crusader on the way to blessedness; and extremely fatigued, he took his Viking wife in his arms as, half-fuddled with sleep, she continued her unceasing demands. The children stampeded back through the bedroom, poor neglected scraps of flotsam reduced to tatters in their vendetta against one another.

The late afternoon melted into dusk, and the pink cloud crept over the mountain – a deep rose-coloured cloud which was destined to be swallowed every evening at the same time by a small sooty one. It was now evening, and the children, ragged and hungry, stumbled through the room to the empty dining-room table. Their Viking mother awoke. She was fresh, and had completely recovered from her tiredness. She seized her giant urgently and hungrily. She endured his weary coupling, motionless and accusing.

'Heavens!' she said. 'It's late, and the children are hungry. Stop it!' She bounced off the bed and dressed quickly. She was filled with longing for the romantic, demoniac, inscrutable Boris Gudenov.

She was a model of correctness as, prim and proper in her suit and blouse, she went to the kitchen to charge the servants with slackness.

IV

The afternoon before the function, Hope went to bemoan her lot to her mother, Madam Ritchie, who was spending the last years of her life in front of a transistor radio in the Welgevonden Foundation. At such an advanced age it was difficult to see any relationship between mother and daughter. The old woman sat like a mummy in a glass case, without any expression on her chalk-white face, and listened to Episode Three Hundred and Fifty of her serial, while the children climbed all over her. They tore her clothes, already strained over her swollen body, they knocked her wig awry and with the slightest touch left blue bruises on her snow-white skin.

'Very soon they are sending him on a mission,' complained Hope. 'They are just making use of him.' She was listening with half an ear to the serial. 'He has to put up with anything for the sake of others.' She seemed to be repeating the pattern of the story. 'His half-brother inherited the family farm. His stepmother persecuted him all the time. He was an illegitimate child. The authorities make him do all the dangerous work.' She rattled off her complaints while she ate cream cakes and slapped half-heartedly at the children. 'He should never have been born. He should never have seen the light of day.'

Her real grievances she kept to herself; she only grumbled about the acceptable injustices in front of the old woman, her senile mother, who, with her moth-eaten brain, could understand only one grievance pattern: the tyranny of authority, the incomprehensible ways of Providence, the cruelty of nurses, the restriction of regulations.

The old woman's mouth suddenly began to move, and she struggled to get the words out, but gave up the attempt. Her mouth remained open, then slowly closed.

Hope crossed her legs; she exposed a thigh through the slit in her green shantung dress and sniffed at a small bottle of *capricci* perfume standing on the table next to her. She put it in her handbag and pulled at her bodice, which was too tight. 'He is very naïve,' she said suddenly. 'But he has the heart of a lion.'

An hour passed while two more serials were dealt with. Then the old woman tried to rise. She could not manage it and sank back into her chair. She lifted her arm with difficulty, pointing to the wardrobe with her hand extended while a crooked finger, stiff with rheumatism, was directed inexorably to the floor.

Hope stood up, rummaged in the top drawer of the wardrobe and took out a small bottle.

Then the old woman spoke for the first time. Her toothless mouth and slack tongue found the word with ease. It lay in her mouth, it came slithering through a soggy marsh of lips, tongue, gums and palate. Underneath the discharge her eyes sparkled.

'*Yohimbin!*'

Hope danced a few ecstatic steps, followed by her children. She embraced the old woman while she kept her eyes tightly closed to shut out the picture of old age.

Demosthenes de Goede walked through the property of the Foundation to the cottage of the legendary Mrs Dreyer, the fortune-teller. He passed the place where he had had the struggle with the half-witted Giant, and he proudly remembered his first triumph; he became sentimental at the stream where he had first kissed Hope. He saw the cottage where, in Mrs Dreyer's imagery, he had found so many truths that were later confirmed. Under an oak tree a silver-grey Rolls-Royce was standing. The chauffeur's eyes were fixed on the upper branches of the tree on which hung bronze flasks, clanging against one another in time to the wind. The doves cooed softly among the leaves.

Demosthenes de Goede looked at the beloved cottage and saw signs everywhere of Mrs Dreyer's success: her windows were decorated with gilt, the door at which he knocked in awe had a border of silver branches. As he waited he saw the doves in flight: the black ones from Thebes that had sailed into the world and the future and had landed in Ammon, Dodona, and now, after so many centuries, here in the oaks of Welgevonden. He knew it was true – it was recorded in the Book of Life there in her sitting room. All her disciples knew it and were conversant with the esoteric wisdom of the Book. There was a whole chapter on the History of the Doves.

The door opened and he walked into the well-loved room. First he put fifty cents on the table (the fee had remained unchanged through the years), then added twenty rand – the wonderful privilege of old clients who received the blessing of the whole truth from her lips. He noticed a thick wad of notes next to his and smiled proudly: every year he saw how her fame spread; every year the increased amount was proof of this. But this exceeded anything he had seen before . . .

A little later the door opened, and a distinguished-looking man came out. A familiar face, thought Demosthenes de Goede before he brushed past him with a friendly greeting.

Mrs Dreyer received him exactly as she had done many times in the past – as though she had never seen him before. Her plump figure was tightly encased in gleaming satin, her eyelids were purest gold, her make-up of the most expensive, her attitude aloof.

She studied the leaves in a Boche teacup.

'Are you related to the previous visitor?' she asked suddenly.

Demosthenes de Goede shook his head.

'Remarkable,' she said, and looked out of the window at one of the black doves that sat seesawing on an oak branch and suddenly began pecking at a bronze flask in front of the bewitched eyes of the chauffeur.

'The end of your hardships will soon come,' she said. 'Were you abroad for fifteen years?'

Demosthenes de Goede shook his head again.

'That's strange,' she said. 'It's extremely puzzling.'

She paid close attention to the tea leaves.

'You will soon be released of your burden.'

But something was worrying her; she was obviously not happy.

'Have you any enemies?' she asked suddenly.

'Yes,' said Demosthenes de Goede.

She pondered over the situation in the teacup carefully, and repeated, 'There is release. That is certain.'

Demosthenes de Goede waited for further revelations, but Mrs Dreyer had apparently lost interest in him. He had never seen her so lovably absentminded as now when, having picked up another cup, she was looking from the one to the other. He left the room quietly so as not to disturb her secret meditations.

He found the rich and important visitor still in the waiting room.

'She told me that I was destined either to die within a short time or to spend the rest of my life in peace and quiet,' said the man.

'One is not supposed to speak about it,' said Demosthenes de Goede.

'I don't follow you.'

'Did she give you a pointer?' asked Demosthenes de Goede. 'One can usually pick up a hint in her voice.'

'Why must one not talk about it?' asked the man.

'It's obvious enough,' said Demosthenes de Goede.

They walked out of the room together.

'I can't remember exactly,' said the man. 'Anyway, the word

"die" is always louder than "quiet." Your voice usually drops when you say "peace".'

'It's the same as two people pulling a wish-bone. You never tell your wish, because if you do it won't come true.'

'Apparently she couldn't decide herself. And it's so easy to prophesy two extremes. Tomorrow you die, or you live.'

They walked up to the Rolls-Royce, and the chauffeur tore himself away from the doves to open the door.

'Her words are usually obscure, but if you weigh them carefully and think about them, you realize later how true her prophecies are,' said Demosthenes de Goede.

'Well, in my case both forecasts couldn't possibly come true,' said the man.

'She foretold rest for me,' said Demosthenes de Goede.

'She foretold rest for me as well, if I did not die,' said the man.

'You needn't worry unnecessarily,' said Demosthenes de Goede. 'She probably means that you will come to the end of your problems, whatever they may be.'

'Perhaps the end of everything is the beginning of happiness,' said the man.

'The end of everything can also be the beginning of death,' said Demosthenes de Goede.

'Happiness can start with death.'

'Rest can mean that the fight is over, and that you can live the rest of your life in peace on earth.'

'Do you think that all one's problems become simpler in time?' asked the man with interest.

'She could have twisted the meaning of the words and meant rest when she said death, and vice versa.'

'But then you are back where you started,' said the man. 'Even if you turn her words round and round, they remain a mystery.'

'That's the Language of the Welgevonden Doves,' said Demosthenes de Goede.

'Release may also mean death in your case,' said the man.

'And rest may mean release in your case,' said Demosthenes de Goede.

The Rolls-Royce rocked over the boundary of Welgevondon at eighty miles an hour.

'My wife and children are still with her mother at Welgevonden,' said Demosthenes de Goede casually.

The man ordered the chauffeur to turn back.

There was great excitement when the children saw the Rolls-Royce. They wrote their names on the doors; they snatched the chauffeur's cap off on the way to town and they pressed the buttons that adjusted the windows. Hope sat between the two men with her eyes fixed primly on the road, but at the turns she took the opportunity of leaning heavily to the one side. When they stopped at the small semi-detached house and the man accompanied them to the door, she shook out her hair in the sunlight and laughed, showing beautiful white teeth.

'What a nice man,' said Hope as the Rolls-Royce edged its way through the narrow little streets and the neighbours all flocked into their gardens. 'Who is he?'

'I forgot to ask his name,' said Demosthenes de Goede.

'We could try to see more of him,' said Hope.

'He looks vaguely familiar,' said Demosthenes de Goede. 'I've seen a photo of him somewhere.'

'He looks like you,' said Hope.

'Obviously a man of good character,' said Demosthenes de Goede.

He drank half a bottle of whisky while he shaved, exercised his abdominal muscles and dressed in the small stuffy bathroom. He cursed all the unpleasant tasks he had to perform, but his heart was really overflowing with love for his fellow men.

In the bedroom his thick fingers had difficulty in hooking Hope's brassière in the third hole. The huge fellow sighed with pleasure as he saw his wife's attractive body tantalizingly disappear by degrees behind transparent nylon. What privilege, he thought, as her evening dress covered the most important parts from the common gaze. And for the first time he felt fit to tackle this unfamiliar task. He drank the rest of the whisky and amused

himself with isometric exercises while he waited for his charming
wife to finish painting her face like a whore from Babylon.

V

After the children had been fed and forced back into the house,
Demosthenes de Goede and Hope locked the door and waited outside. Four enraged little faces peered through the windowpanes
and then one by one twisted with pain as they began to bully
one another – their only answer to boredom, loneliness and frustration. They could see that a little girl's nose had started to bleed,
and one of the boys disappeared suddenly. Soon afterward Hope's
budgie set up an unearthly cry. 'It's because you are so seldom
at home,' said Hope, primping before the windowpane directly in
front of a small strained face. She smoothed her hair against her
cheeks, turning her head to see the effect from the side, in front
of two icy green eyes. 'A mother can't do everything alone.'

It occurred to her that she had left her lipstick in the house, and
she unlocked the door at the same moment as the taxi appeared
and hooted. Demosthenes caught one of the girls, who had slipped
out in the dark, just in time and walked back with her writhing
like a worm over his shoulder. Hope slapped her lightly just
before Demosthenes de Goede closed the door.

'Heavens ! The children drive one mad !'

When they sank into the back seat of the taxi, she said, 'Do
children ever realize the cross of parenthood?'

The lodge of the D-Service was designed by Cliffox, the avant-
garde architect from the town, a contemporary of Carvajal. It
was cylindrical, in the shape of a missile – a phallus pointing to
the sky, a steel cypress among the Lombardies, a stainless suppli-
cation to the heavens. In the park wild buck grazed in the moonlight and under the stars.

Brigadier Ornassis E. welcomed them first, then embraced Hope
– a liberty that was permissible on account of his higher rank and
advanced age.

'Ah ! The *charming* Mrs de Goede,' he said and remembered in time not to shake hands with Demosthenes de Goede. He introduced her to a group of willowy men dressed in the latest evening suits inspired by *Esquire*. Each responded with a charming smile to the cumbersome witticisms of their chief, while making Hope an elegant bow and nodding somewhat patronizingly to Demosthenes de Goede.

Hope had never seen so many good-looking men together before – there was steel in their litheness (no lack of courage here), there was the refinement which, through the years, she had missed so much. She looked at them with the eye of a connoisseur, but found it difficult in this strange setting to determine the measure of actual heterosexuality. She gave her best smile so that her teeth gleamed; false eyelashes partly veiled the light in her eyes and her full lips became soft and vulnerable.

'You must not be misled by their appearance,' said Brigadier Ornassis E. as they walked into the hall where potplants, bamboo mats and abstract drawings on the walls characterized the décor of the evening.

'*Outré*, isn't it?' he said, damning the decorations with a disdainful sweep of his arm. He led them to the main table where Hope took her seat on his right, Demosthenes de Goede on his left, and his effeminate secretary, James, and the rest of his elegant ménage in order of rank. A jazz ensemble was playing folk songs, and from time to time singers gave their renderings in the style of Trini Lopez and Joan Baez.

The Brigadier's eyes twinkled as he looked at Demosthenes de Goede who looked heavy and awkward in such select company. With a slight movement of his hand he summoned a merry blonde whose avoirdupois was visibly winning in the struggle with her tightly fitting evening gown. 'We choose our corps not only for their intelligence, but also for their appearance,' he said. 'For instance, can you imagine anyone looking like Edward G. Robinson in a Secret Service today?' He took Hope's hand and raised it to his lips.

His silver hair suited him. His evening attire was old-fashioned. His superiority was based on personality, experience and the fact that he was the chief. He had reached the age where he knew how to turn even his shortcomings into assets. The fact that he was sometimes dramatic made him dangerous, an enigma to his followers.

Beautiful girls began to serve the wine. They wore their hair in beehives on their heads, their young breasts striving tantalizingly to emerge above their gowns, while their buttocks undulated under their tight skirts as they walked. They had a friendly smile for everyone and made the young men feel important.

'They are also part of the D-Service,' said the Brigadier, clinking glasses with Demosthenes de Goede and Hope. 'We recruit them on Clifton Beach. No special qualifications are necessary except the obvious, because they work on the surface and save us a considerable amount of manpower by doing small jobs that would be a waste of time for the rest of our staff.'

He was in a genial mood and looked approvingly at the blonde who was trying out her only talent on Demosthenes de Goede.

Some of the young men had already started to dance after making a slight bow in the direction of their chief. They shivered and writhed with the girls, finding communication under drooping eyelids with great hollow eyes staring at them from under green make-up. The narrow skirts were alternately creased and stretched by the suggestive and almost invisible movements of the dance – those restrained movements that were more intimate than the Frug gave a deeper, more spiritual satisfaction hinting at a contained, more intense and greater passion.

'We choose our members not only for their intelligence and ability,' repeated Brigadier Ornassis E., 'but also for their physique and general appearance.' He pointed approvingly to his young men busy dancing. 'Our girls test them out like Gnostic women, and immunize them in the process from any outside temptation.'

He lit a cigarette for Hope, stroking her cheek with his little finger. 'There is nothing that the world of Archon can offer that these girls can't do better.' He stole a quick playful kiss from Hope. 'Do you understand?'

Hope was in her element. She unconsciously copied the girls, completely under the spell of the Service. She was captivated by a new idea : a fuller life, sex as a sort of religion, a servitude that had meaning.

'Is this what I have been searching for all my life?' she whispered to the Brigadier.

At once Brigadier Ornassis E. became a wise old guru. His eyes became cunning. 'Are you still thinking of the poetic Captain? Do you find these young men different?' He began to stroke her thigh lightly. 'Are you afraid that intelligence always goes with effeminacy? Do you find the animus within you incomprehensible? Are you constantly misled?'

Meanwhile Demosthenes de Goede had led the blonde on to the dance floor where he whirled like a merry-go-round and lifted her lightly on to his shoulders, his booming laugh obviously unsettling the other couples.

The Brigadier smiled good-naturedly. 'That's one of the reasons we chose him,' he said. His mouth was close to Hope's ear and he playfully bit the lobe. 'He is so utterly a man, so close to nature, so unlike the spirit of the times. And if we find his character so difficult to understand, how much more so will our enemies find it?' He sat back comfortably. 'There is a complexity in simplicity for all those who are themselves complicated. Our greatest champions were always people noted for the simplicity of their faith.'

Hope was not listening. She was now playing the role of the girls of the Service with whom she identified herself. She was entirely integrated into the movement. Her function was suddenly clear to her; she had found a meaning; she had discovered the outlet of self-sacrifice – a counter image of narcissism. The riddle in the looking glass which she saw every day was solved.

Brigadier Ornassis E. raised his hands to his eyes – his delicately perfumed hands.

'There is death in the building,' he said.

He lifted her hand once more to his lips and kissed it lightly.

'And we can't fight it with camp and twee.'

He made a slight gesture and the orchestra stopped at once. They all gathered around the table. The girls brought wine and smiled at everyone, making them feel happy. They examined one another with expert eyes for any deviation from the group norm. From time to time they went to the powder room where they pulled a neckline wider, made an eyelid greener, hitched a dress higher or opened a zipper fastener a little farther.

Brigadier Ornassis E. placed his fingertips together and addressed the group at the table.

'I can perhaps make a cursory reference to our organization,' he said to Demosthenes de Goede who by now had the dishevelled blonde on his lap. 'We have two lines in our organization : the personnel group and the action front.'

He gestured to one of the attractive young men who continued slowly and clearly, but in a somewhat bored fashion.

'The personnel group are the men with ideas : they deal with the image of the Service; they formulate the principles.'

Brigadier Ornassis E. nodded, and another young man completed the elucidation slowly and indolently.

'We,' he said, 'well, we carry out the policy.'

There was appreciative laughter from his group.

'And that,' said Brigadier Ornassis E. to Demosthenes de Goede, 'is also your task.' He pointed to the first young man. 'The specialized personnel group is limited to their function as men of ideas – even if they are of higher rank. It is the action front who have the most opportunities, in spite of the fact that their function is limited to the execution of a task.'

He pointed to himself.

'I am more or less a managing director. Together with the personnel group, I am responsible for the expansion of the Service. Perhaps I am the nearest thing to a tycoon like Boris Gudenov, although such a thing is naturally unthinkable in our organization. We are an incorporate entity, and I am also responsible to the state, and to society, for the results of the Service.'

He motioned to the blonde to stop offering resistance.

'I feel perhaps more attracted to the personnel group, but I don't deny the importance of the action front. In point of fact, I (alas) am a sort of father figure.'

He laughed aggressively and everyone followed suit. Then he raised his hand for silence and nodded approvingly when there was an immediate response.

'Perhaps it would be a good thing if we look at the struggle in this light: Boris Gudenov is the tycoon, the invisible power behind the scenes; Demosthenes de Goede is the one with the Service, the state and the public behind him.'

The maidens of the Service had meanwhile also gathered around the table, and all were listening attentively to Brigadier Ornassis E.

'There is perhaps a certain similarity, apart from appearance, between the two . . .'

Hope opened her eyes wide, and the Brigadier gave her a light but substantial pinch just where her evening gown slid yieldingly over her leg.

'Oh, so you've seen Boris Gudenov before?' He put a cigarette between his lips and beat his men to it with a Ronson lighter. 'Demosthenes de Goede is big and strong; Boris Gudenov is big and strong, but in a different way.' He blew out a cloud of smoke. 'I have often wondered: is there perhaps an affinity between the intellectual and the athlete?' He shook his head and moved his hands uncertainly. 'Are Boris Gudenov and Demosthenes de Goede not both victims of something stronger than themselves? The tycoon in the empire of his own creating becomes trapped by loneliness; the hero becomes isolated by the persistent demands of his work.'

He pointed to Demosthenes de Goede who, thanks to the Brigadier's order, was now comfortably persuading the blonde to yield.

'One cannot regard him as very complicated. He remains preeminently human, in spite of his strength and his ability to endure suffering. Is there not perhaps in him something of all that we see in ourselves? A lyrical hero of Pindar; a tragic figure in spite of the comic side; a stoical patience and a natural inborn wisdom?' One of the girls who approached too close to the Brigadier was adroitly obstructed by Hope.

In the distance was a huddle of waiters in smart uniforms, but with a different sort of elegance from that of the gentlemen of the Service. Like all in their calling, they had become the reflection of the people whom they served but subject to the shortcomings inherent in imitation – the movement without personality, the gesture without meaning. Brigadier Ornassis E. called the head waiter and whispered in his ear.

The girls of the Service, whose job of serving wine had now been taken over by the waiters, sat down on the floor, their skirts spread out like flower petals, their demeanour bashful, their arms ready to receive, one after the other, the young men of the Service who stretched out beside them, their faces raised to Brigadier Ornassis E.

'They say,' continued the Brigadier, 'that we are living in an age of anti-tragedy, of Christian and Marxist metaphysics – the two myths that, in passing, only take note of one aspect of tragedy – in a world that only recognizes victory in the hereafter, in the one case, and in the material world, in the other. But is this true?'

He turned to Hope who had the look of a woman in love who sees even in an unintelligible play of words a play of love; or of those women who have reached an age where they find themselves free of the limitation of a single defined love, where they all become nymphomaniacs, where a lonely nymphomaniac like Hope suddenly feels at one with all women and becomes quiet and submissive, and quietly gives herself in bondage to love.

'Is this true?' asked Brigadier Ornassis E. 'Are there not in man's psyche uncontrollable forces, demoniac apparitions which can drive him to frenzy?'

He now addressed Demosthenes de Goede who was manipulating the blonde like clay and becoming hopelessly involved in her over-eager concessions.

'Is it not true,' asked the Brigadier, 'that we have reached a stage where both the spiritual and the materialistic myths have fallen away and man, without anchor, is capable of experiencing tragedy all over again?' He looked at the personnel division of the D-Service who were following him attentively. 'Have we not again reached a pre-rational stage?'

The Brigadier was lost a moment in thought, while the girls, lulled by his voice and the music, leaned back in the arms of the young men. Then he straightened himself and motioned to the waiters who at once came bursting out of their own frustration

at the swinging doors. They came pouring from the kitchen behind the bamboo mats and abstract drawings, carrying grilled
uterine animals on silver trays, brown shiny suckling pigs with
glassy eyes. Row after row they came, in impeccable evening
attire, past the Brigadier and his followers, through a second door
into the next room.

The Brigadier rose and, with Hope on his arm, led everyone
to the Coronet Room, a conversation piece designed in the neo-
classical style, fitted with air-conditioning and livened up by a
Continental orchestra playing soothing music for the dinner hour.
He sat at the head of the table, his guests on either side, and
waited with bowed head until the waiter had poured a little
Veuve Clicquot (Extra Sec) into a Steuben glass. He studied the
label, allowed the wine to sparkle on his tongue and declared
himself satisfied. Silently he waited for all the glasses to be filled,
then slowly rose. There was a hush, the orchestra ceased playing,
the waiters stood in serried rows and the Brigadier lifted his glass
high and said, 'To the Beloved Maiden !'

The high-spirited young men of the Service sprang promptly
to their feet, and from every side the toast of the evening rang
through the room. 'The *Kore*, the *Kore* !'

Hope found this 'fantastic' and wanted to know what the *Kore*
was. The Brigadier explained that it was the legendary Maiden.
Demosthenes de Goede, slightly fuddled but bursting with energy,
roared that all maidens were doomed to be violated at some stage
or other. The Brigadier nodded and explained that the psychology
was quite correct: the one who was violated was just as im-
plicated, that defloration was a law of nature, that virginity in
itself contained the greatest temptation to dishonour. After that
they fell to on the succulent suckling pigs whose crisp flesh melted
sensually in their mouths – essentially a symbolic violation and
the first step of self-satisfaction in the narrowing circle of self-
indulgence.

When the tender suckling pigs had been dispatched and the
dessert had calmed down the final tempo of the meal, the Brigadier
again rose slowly to deliver the speech of the evening in honour
of his dazed guest.

He referred to the stirring task of one like Demosthenes de Goede who worked, not for himself, but for the community; who sacrificed himself to solve the problem; who without personal consideration placed himself on the altar to represent our collective participation; who in these confused times appeared like an archetypal hero, to give meaning to the anxieties of the ordinary people and the unintelligible visions of our creative spirits.

He enlarged movingly on one such as Hope, the model mother of our era, who often had to forgo domestic happiness; who had, without the help and support of her husband, to bear the responsibility of her liberty; who had to reconcile her solemn right to emancipation with the absence of her husband.

Then Brigadier Ornassis E. became esoteric, philosophical and difficult to follow. With soaring volubility he described the work of Demosthenes H. de Goede as an attempt at the unification of our world with a cosmic world, where each individual had to discover his true nature in all that was hidden, and therefore unintelligible. It was the lover's way, the artist's way, the way of each one of us.

'And in this can we not see the image of our friend Demosthenes de Goede,' asked the Brigadier, 'as a kind of artist of deeds? And can we not see in Boris Gudenov, the hated enemy (because that is how I know him), also the perverted lover? And can I not see all of us in the role of the lover, the artist?'

Everyone in the hall remained silent. Each girl looked tensely from under green eyelids, dedicated and submissive to the Head of the D-Service. The men, reconciled by the very nature of their calling to the mystery of the abstract, were equally silent, their attention as members of personnel and the action front riveted on their leader, the Brigadier, and on the possible implication of his words.

'You,' said the Brigadier to Demosthenes de Goede, 'are going where many of us fear to tread.' Everyone now turned towards Demosthenes de Goede who sat and listened without moving, a frown on his forehead, rather impatient of all this verbosity, but flattered nevertheless by the attention he was receiving. 'You are going, Captain de Goede, not just to make a bare display of strength in the name of the Service, but to free the world from a corrupting monster that has appeared out of the darkness and seized on our understanding; you are going to free man himself.'

He picked up his glass once more. 'You have drunk to the Maiden,' said the Brigadier. 'Gentlemen, I now give you the Hero of the evening.'

There was loud applause when Demosthenes de Goede stood up and made his bow. They crowded around him as he embraced the girls and pulverised the outstretched hands of the corps. Wine flowed freely, and the Brigadier was proud of his gesture when specially imported blood-red *Sang d'Hercule* from Argos was served. It was at this moment that Hope seized the opportunity to take out her little bottle and slip, unnoticed, a few drops into the Brigadier's glass. She waited patiently for the reaction – the strain about the eyes, the quickened breathing, the flush on the face and all the other characteristic symptoms. She saw how the Brigadier cocked his head slightly, as though becoming aware of something deep within him; she noticed the swaying movement of his body, the signs of abandonment evident in word, gesture and the timbre of his voice. She was on the point of offering herself as victim, unwittingly faithful to the role of the *Kore*, when the Brigadier suddenly lifted his hand, bringing the orchestra to a stop, and with restrained slowness moved in the direction of the third room. On the way there he flung his arms tightly around his adjutant, James, and Hope was dismayed to see how the men of the Service, one after the other, abandoned the girls and, together with Demosthenes de Goede, followed the Brigadier arm in arm.

The door opened, and there was a fleeting glimpse of the El Gaucho room with kinetic sculpture by Lye and Schoeffer, a third orchestra giving a rendering on cymbals of the *Poème Symphonique* by Ligeti. The door closed behind them and the girls of the D-Service found seats on the chairs scattered about everywhere in small groups. They took out their knitting and calmly began to knit while they carried on lively suburban conversations. As time passed some of them dozed off while the men in the inner room were busy bringing the initiation orgy to a conclusion.

Hope, bored, wandered back and forth in the hall, and then began to dance by herself in time to the continental orchestra's 'Fools Rush In'. She rotated her hips and pelvis, lost in introspection, her heart breaking in the only tragedy she knew – the tragedy of waste, of lost opportunities, of moments that have passed – a lament, expressed in movement, for the enigma of life; a reverie in dance time on the squandering of life-giving energy, the wasting of precious libido.

Chapter Two

Early History

Boris Gudenov, back from Lydia where he served Omphalia with all his talents and procured handsome dividends for his shareholders.

He had been abroad for fifteen months, but had not managed, in spite of all the funds at his disposal, to overcome the heat, the flies and the loneliness of Africa. Omphalia was a beautiful woman of platinium and tin, her breasts were the mine dumps in the desert, her breath the overpowering fumes of small pubs with the bottles on Victorian shelves; her urges were inflamed by the fierce warmth of early maturing women and her love affairs were the legends in the brochures drawn up by the tourist guides. Contact with her was dangerously infectious, her beautiful eyes were misty with the first signs of optical disease, her nature was adaptable and obliging as the result of a different concept of servitude – a surrender of the heart and not the head. She smelt of *Chanel* and slept on golden beds where she taught him all sorts of perversions: he dressed himself in her highly-coloured garments, while she fancied herself masculine in gold-spattered pants. He had to pay heavily for all those dividends, and to stand up to the jeering of an ebony Pan who peeped through windows and keyholes. Snow-white teeth mocked his claim to virility, so that one day, in a moment of rage, he seized the arrogant youth and like an old-fashioned Bwana flung him out at the door. After that the mighty Boris had to bite the dust, and his reputation became the laugh of the place. He waited in palace anterooms and listened to threats. It was his money, his know-how and his technical skill that saved him, not his manhood. In pulling him down she bore him fair dividends, but the mighty

Gudenov's name had been dragged through the mud. They mocked him further by riding around in Cadillacs that were more ostentatious than his Rolls-Royce.

A rumour circulated that he was impotent.

He could not bring her to an orgasm.

He was an effeminate weakling who tried to buy everything with money.

He was not even a good boxer or an athlete.

There was a stain on the Gudenov name.

They said he had stabbed his best friend in the back.

But worst of all was the rumour that he was a 'fairy'. There were plenty of similar names that he had to live down : Nola, pix, flit, queer, fag, faggot, agfay, fruit, nance, queen and shemale.

On his return Boris Gudenov devotes his attention to the Oechalia Publishing Company and settles his account with Ernest Eurytus.

Without any compunction he had checkmated Eurytus and ruined him utterly : an example of what is often cited in financial circles as legal expungement.

Ernest was the head of a fine business; a little old man with grey hair, proud of his beautiful daughter, Iole, and his son, Iphitus, who at one time had been a friend of Gudenov's. They said that he had known Boris Gudenov as a boy in far-off Poland and had often helped him in times of trouble. He had started with a small shop in the Little Karroo where he had begun by selling blankets and sweets on the ground floor. Betweenwhiles he had made a small fortune from ostrich feathers – that was before the days of cooperative marketing. He spent his spare time reading on the second storey of the rickety shop which he reached by climbing a spiral staircase and from where he could look out over a pepper tree and across to the great Swartberg range in the distance. He collected so many books that the shelves bent under the weight. Later on he established the publishing company in the town and set up his own newspaper. At first he supported the government, but when he became strong enough he launched out on his own.

Iole, the girl who had played with farmers' sons on the banks of the Olifants River, was 'finished' at a liberal university and developed into a beautiful madonna with a social conscience which made her a follower of lofty causes. The colour question, especially, captured her attention, and she devoted her time to the liberation of the intellectual African. The Oechalia press leaned more and more to the Left and the progressives, and the old man who had sold ostrich feathers could vindicate his past and at the same time gain an entrée into a circle which he had always regarded as inaccessible.

Iole and her father had once spent a holiday on the Côte d'Azur in a villa belonging to Boris Gudenov – arranged because of old friendship ties, and because Boris Gudenov had obtained a share in the Oechalia Publishing Company. The last evening there they had met again, after so many years, at a grand ball which Gudenov attended in person, having just returned from one of his business trips. Iole had immediately felt attracted to this handsome, quiet man with his cold, haughty, intellectual aloofness. They danced together the whole evening and drank champagne under the stars on a terrace overlooking the sea. He had kissed her for the first time and had not been able to forget the cool, damp lips of the maiden.

Back in South Africa and true to her upbringing, she had taken part in an act of sabotage in which three Africans and a white woman were accidentally killed. She was acquitted on the technical grounds of non-participation because of some uncertainty in the evidence. The Gudenov press had given a good deal of publicity to the case – mainly because Iole was outstandingly photogenic – without the knowledge or cooperation of Boris Gudenov who was far too exalted a personage to be worried with the local ramifications of his financial network.

It was a heavy blow to the old man who began to see the first signs of disintegration in his affairs. He was particularly cool to Gudenov after that. His son Iphitus, a homosexual poet, had tried to intervene and had made the mistake of justifying his father and playing off his sister's sensitivity to political problems against the heartlessness of capitalism that had claimed his ex-friend as a victim. Boris was furious at the arrogant attitude adopted by the miserable little milksop who had dared to pester him with banalities. When the rot had gone farther with the arrest of Iphitus in Government Avenue by a policeman called Coertzen on a charge of indecent exposure, and the Gudenov press had gone to town over the incident, the old man declared open war on the mighty Gudenov.

He threw everything into the fray when Iphitus shortly afterwards committed suicide. He had nothing left: his affairs were collapsing under him, and he used everything at his disposal to seek revenge. There was certainly no man more hated than Gudenov in the Oechalia press campaign which coincided with Boris' trips to Lydia where his interests were threatened with nationalization.

Boris had returned with hatred in his heart and had wiped out the Oechalia Publishing Company. The government press had praised his take-over and, for the time being, Gudenov had become a hero in the eyes of the conservative section – against his wish, because Gudenov was Gudenov, and his appetite was not restricted to specified dishes.

The old man followed his son, because he found it beyond his powers to return to the hard reality of the Swartberg.

Boris Gudenov 'takes pity' on Iole and engages her as his private secretary to accompany him everywhere, even into his flat above the shopping centre, where Katy, his wife, by this time used to his 'secretaries', waits patiently.

It was difficult to detect any change in Iole after the death of her father and the collapse of his business – as difficult as it had been to see any signs of emotion on her face during the sabotage case in which she was involved. She was slender, dark and very beautiful, almost unbearably so because her beauty was made perfect by the firm contours of youth, and her aloofness made her unapproachable. She was quiet without being timid; her pride only gave offence to her inferiors. It was difficult to explain the part she played in subversive activities: in that respect she was an enigma even to the liberal group who counted her among its members. The fact that sexual perversion and all kinds of depravity were mentioned in connection with the sabotage group was difficult to reconcile with her madonna-like appearance and high ideals.

Everyone had his own ideas about why she placed herself under the protection of the demoniac Gudenov after her father's death. Some said that she was biding her time until she could take a terrible revenge. Others averred that her participation in sabotage and other undermining activities had rendered her entirely amoral, and that she could never return to normal standards again. Some saw in her surrender a romantic image of an old love that after all those years had come into its own; but that was difficult to reconcile with our times, and her age. She spoke so seldom; she was so unassailable; she was such a mysterious contradiction – the modern, highly sophisticated woman, with the cosmetic mask of a virgin: white lips, dark eyes and long hair hanging to her shoulders. The problem grew, because everyone claimed that he knew the real story of the tycoon: the one who chose beautiful girls with intelligence, but of inferior social status, to release him from his loneliness – girls who, in their basic simplicity, had a better understanding of his needs and would not burden him with psychological complications, who were ready to be materially pampered without further demands on the grounds of personal pride, who had enough sophistication to keep him longer than their better bred sisters who looked upon him as a rival, who were willing to sacrifice a small part of their youth as payment, who made no demands on him with regard to extravagant physical achievements, who did not try to 'understand' him, who with whorish intuition refrained from modern matriarchy thereby reaping higher rewards, who made themselves available for the sex urges of the tycoon and submitted to his attempt to find an inner satisfaction through sexual contact. Girls who began as models and typists, and who were now snug in fur coats.

But none of these descriptions could be applied to Iole, and the alternative, true love and pure, had naturally already been analysed, declared unimportant, commercialized and left to duck-tails, pop singers, teen-agers, drunk librettists, computers and their cybernetica.

However mysterious it all was, the fact remained that Boris Gudenov was in possession of Iole, and he brought her in his silver-grey Rolls-Royce to his flat above the Oita shopping centre with its imitation Greek courtyard, marble fountains and bust of Marcus Aurelius – a prison with flowers, a gilded dome, multi-coloured walls, fruit on the table, thermos flasks, private telephones, music disseminated by PM-4 loudspeakers, bells to summon personal servants, mirrors, shaded lights – the whole sterile complexity with which money serves its master.

He brought her to his 'home' where, in other rooms equally luxurious in autumn-coloured décor, his wife, Katy, was also waiting for him.

Katy, Boris Gudenov's wife, hears about her husband's find and remembers with nostalgia the time when he fought for her hand.

No one knew whether Boris Gudenov had really married Katy; however, she was generally accepted as his lawful wife, and she spent her days in the company of her son Hyllus in the gilded cage on the top floor of the Oita shopping centre. Hyllus was a regular little Paul Pry and took great pleasure in keeping his mother supplied with the latest scandal about his father and the girl, Iole. 'And he is old enough to be her father,' said the young Peeping Tom.

That induced her to think back, as she now so often did, with longing to the past when she was a pretty young girl, the love of Max Aucholos, her young bull of a lover. It was in the little village of Riviersonderend where her parents had lived, and she, the cool silken maiden, with shoulder-length locks, used to pick armfuls of arum lilies in the vlei at dusk. Max there in the reeds with the strength of a bull and the cunning of a snake. And then the appearance of Boris, the up-and-coming young shopkeeper, the darling of all the young women in the neighbourhood. The inevitable clash between the two while she looked on, worried but jubilant: the struggle between these two godlike creatures for her cool little hand; the realization that she was desired by two such important figures: the bliss of being desired without having to give anything in return.

She put Hyllus to bed, put out the light and waited for her husband whom she had last seen fifteen months before.

With silent enjoyment she relived her suffering during the years, the days and years of loneliness when her friends commiserated with her – the grass widow waiting patiently for her husband whom she could punish with frigidity when he came . . . (She remembered with resentment his demands, the eternal touching, as though he could turn on her emotions like a tap, as though he had a right to her body, as though her body did not belong to her.)

She was proud of her beauty which, thanks to his wealth, she could pamper with massages, visits to beauty salons, sweet-smelling herbal baths, electromagnetic treatments, professional make-up and all the advantages that beauty culture offered. She sometimes let him see flesh-coloured lace panties, a sun-bronzed thigh, a flash of her breasts, a nude body just before the door closed on his vulgarity. She knew the mighty Boris Gudenov, and he was not so wonderful. She knew him in all his helplessness when she played frigid and, precisely at the right moment, called his bluff. They said Gudenov was impotent, they said he was a monster – and she always defended him. She quoted him, she referred to him with affectionate teasing, she told stories that sparkled with intimacy and good-natured jesting to demonstrate their special relationship.

She switched on the radio and sank into a chair in front of a large window overlooking the city. She had now reached the second half of her memory cycle, her greatest triumph – the death of Neuman Nessos and Boris Gudenov's jealousy.

Boris Gudenov would always wonder what had happened; it would always gnaw at him. Had they slept together? Had they really committed adultery? Had the whole truth been told about their dear friend, accidentally shot by Boris on safari in the Umfolozi ten years before? She had given him the Hemingway short story, 'The Short Happy Life of Francis Macomber', although she knew that Gudenov was an indifferent reader. Whose shadow was silhouetted on the wall of her tent? Why did she still keep the gown on which the bloodstains grew darker each year? It was still hanging in her room, and she unconsciously fingered it when Boris Gudenov spoke to her. She challenged him openly to raise objections. When he explained how the accident had happened, she always remained silent. She did not reproach him; she just looked at him.

The memory cycle was now complete. She began to feel restless and, rising, walked about the room. She wondered what the new 'secretary' looked like, and when there was a knock on the door she opened it herself without bothering to ring for the maid.

Iole greeted her modestly, and Katy instinctively put her hand to her heart.

Dear God, she thought, it could be me, fifteen years ago!

Boris Gudenov receives a report from one of his numerous spies that Brigadier Ornassis E. has begun the campaign against him and that a policeman, Demosthenes de Goede, has been appointed to carry out the task. Boris Gudenov finds Demosthenes de Goede very amusing and cannot work up any resentment against him. But he decides that Demosthenes de Goede must be put out of the way and gives instructions to his legion of paid lackeys to that effect.

He knew from bitter experience that one must never underestimate an enemy, that respect for the capabilities of an opponent (someone like Brigadier Ornassis E.) puts you in a position to use those very capabilities indirectly against him (there is a constant dialogue as you are learning to know your enemy). But what do you do when your enemy comes to you naïve, upright and pure in heart? You are immediately disarmed, for no man is so degenerate (or dares admit that measure of degeneracy in himself) as to destroy deliberately what is good. As strange as innocence and virtue were to the tragic concept of Aristotle, just so strange was it to the world of the tycoon whose kingdom was built on the vanity and moral weakness of man.

Demosthenes de Goede had to be destroyed; but before that could happen, he had to be exposed to the allurements of the secular world of the tycoon. It was like the struggle between the matador and the bull in the corrida: the most dangerous bull was the one that had not been properly bred, that was not *boyante* but chose its own ground and did not worry about the *capa*. Demosthenes de Goede had to reveal a moral weakness, had to be tempted.

It was easier to leave this side of the struggle to underlings. It was not expected that the tycoon should lower himself to that extent. The picadors first went to work before the matador began. Boris Gudenov had once appeared in the same arena as Sidney Franklin and Sir Henry and was immediately singled out as a Diestro and not a Camelo.

He would first get his lackeys to give Demosthenes de Goede a workout and perhaps accomplish his destruction without intervening. If the fight had to continue after that, Boris Gudenov would give it his personal attention – directly and with finesse as behoved a worthy opponent.

*To the question: Who is Boris Gudenov? Brigadier Ornassis E.'s answer that he was a tycoon is perhaps the only fact that can be established with any measure of certainty – although by the very nature of the case it is impossible to say precisely how anyone becomes a tycoon.**

Although the business world and the stock-market were based

* The fact that John Kenneth Galbraith does not mention his name in his well-known dissertation on the big collapse of 1929 cannot be explained.

on a sane, intelligible law like supply and demand, there was still a legend that certain people were influential enough to transcend that law and, by means of supernatural manipulation in their material world, to determine the future of all interested parties. People like Morgan, Raskob, Sachs, Krueg Mitchell, Boris Gudenov and others. Such influence is not always bad, but sometimes does good as on that Black Thursday, October 24, 1929, when Morgan and others managed temporarily to stem the selling panic. It often does harm, as in 1928 when Mitchell prevented the Federal Reserve Bank from raising the rate of interest by one per cent in time to stop the spiralling of inflation.

It was difficult to determine the role played by Boris Gudenov in this connection. He was a financial genius of scarcely eighteen years and already a legend in an age that lent itself to the birth of legends. He was a young shopkeeper in South Africa. One fine day he turned up in America and immediately saw the possibility of mergers by means of which giant cartels were formed by controlling companies. That was of course before there were all sorts of awkward laws and at a time when the mad rush of free enterprise gave rise to those colourful pirates on the ocean of financial undertaking.

The assertion was that the principle known as 'leverage' was first applied by him when, with a small capital, he established a trust company; and on a basis of one-third debentures, one-third preferentials and one-third ordinary shares, each rise in shares (at a time of easy increase) caused his ordinary shares to treble in value because the debentures and preferential shares naturally remained constant in spite of increased portfolio value. He later discovered that ordinary shares could be made to rise still farther by letting the artificially boosted ordinary shares be taken by other trust companies which, in their turn, were also based on the 'leverage' principle. There was a great demand for ordinary shares, and it could be argued that Boris Gudenov was only supplying a demand. When the Senate committee instituted an investigation into his activities they found nothing wrong with his transactions; but looked at in retrospect, after all the anti-trust laws and laws for the protection of the ordinary shareholders, it could be understood that the image of Boris Gudenov, the creator of that particular system, had become ominous, and that he had gained the reputation of being a Caribbean pirate.

It is common knowledge that after the great crash, well-known people had disappeared overnight, and a number had committed suicide, but the House of Gudenov had survived. One aspect of this is easily explained: he had pulled out in time. More important: he had withdrawn at a time when the Harvard economists had seen nothing but rose-coloured clouds over the financial landscape and had regarded the small black cloud as nothing but the defeatist attitude of a few Leftists. A more difficult side of the question was whether Boris Gudenov had at that time, as opposed to the Morgans and the Rockefellers, a clearer insight into the future, and whether his unobtrusive disappearance (no tycoon dared disappear suddenly without affecting the sensitive market) had been due to an occult rather than a pragmatic power of perception – a realization of the seven lean years following the seven fat years – or had he been warned in time by the first abortive measures against inflation?

Today, in spite of laws which regulated commerce in the finest detail, there were new mergers and new tycoons who were particularly concerned about their image. There were memories of menacing unknowns like Zaharoff. And there were others marking time who had the hound's name – the one with the uncontrollable appetite that was pacified with cake by the Sibyl, the one that was silenced with sand by the magic poet.

According to rumours, Boris Gudenov was egocentric, ruthless, cruel to his enemy (and his friend if he became an enemy), covetous, affectionate but selfish to his family, unsympathetic to his wife, fond of women in general, but short-lived in his affections.

Everyone admitted, however, that he was a remarkable person.

Rumours about Boris Gudenov's origin (for the most part possibly apocryphal).

That he came from a *schtetl* in Eastern Europe.

That his great-grandfather was a *Maggid*, blessed with the gift of the third eye.

That his father was one of the thirty-six *Zaddikim* of his time who lived to the glory of God in saintly poverty. The small Boris had had memories of the *tallith* over his father's shoulders. He remembered how, trembling with fear, he had had to open the door when the Angel of Death went by.

As the first generation in a new country such a child often revolts against his background : poverty and the ritual that reminds him of it. He usually finds compensation in the unorthodox, the search for wealth, the striving after power; and he takes delight in the accumulation of knowledge in the cold world of intellectual power, in the avant-garde adventure of sharpened insight, in the ruthlessness of selfish love.

He is often a genius.

To return to Katy where she last stood, facing Iole.

Deep in her heart she felt sorry for this girl who had lost everything : her father, her brother, her public prestige. She made an attempt to chat to the lovely child who was trying to protect herself by remaining silent and, taking her by the hand, led her through the room. Who could deny it? Indirectly Iole was responsible for all the disasters that had befallen her parents' house.

Katy poured tea from a silver pot, and by chance saw herself in the oval looking-glass above the table with the lapis luzuli top. In spite of make-up, her own beauty was becoming harder. Everything about her was a coarse counterfeit of the natural assets of youth; by imitating, she at once became a wrinkled hag, and she feared the answer to the question which she must, in spite of what she knew, put to her mirror.

She turned her back on the glass and directed her attention to the girl. This was the first time that Boris Gudenov had brought anyone into the inner circle of their home. It was *her* sheets that would cover that lovely figure, *her* pillows that would smother the love cry, *her* bed that would heave on the wave of love.

And then she changed her plans. She concentrated again on Gudenov, knowing that nothing would help, that in the complexity of human relations there was no logic. She overcame the arguments of the plural animus, the ex cathedra wisdom of the misleading philosophers within herself, and gained a greater victory than she knew.

She would punish him with unselfish love.

Boris Gudenov receives Iole in his room, and the battle begins.

She appeared in a Wolsey Vanity Fair nightgown, turquoise blue and pink bows, marabou slippers, a ribbon in her hair and dragon's blood on her lips. He saw her in his luxurious room surrounded by the silken walls, silhouetted against shaded lights, to the accompaniment of music from invisible loudspeakers through the V of two bottles of champagne crossed in the ice bucket. The reputation of the mighty Boris Gudenov was at stake since the bitter affair in Lydia and the mockery that nowadays had more punch than before.

It was the first time that he had been alone with her. He was suitably dressed in a smoking jacket of blue velvet, his hair greying at the temples, apparently in perfect control of the situation and at home in his luxurious surroundings, a picture of manliness, refinement and sophistication, exciting to women because of his appearance of aloofness, fascinating to them because he looked capable of cruelty with the possibility of unexpected tenderness in love: Boris Gudenov who had conquered the world, who at this moment of his vulnerability could hold her in thrall.

He came towards her, took her hands in his and went through all the romantic movements that his invisible judges expected of him. Conquered, she surrendered to him, and the exposure began. But somewhere behind the aloofness was hidden a small boy from the *schtetl* who had had to fetch a kosher chicken for his magical dad, who, trembling with fright, had heard the wings of the Angel of Death rustling in the night; and somewhere there was a little girl who had tasted the loneliness of candlelight and romantic homesickness in an attic room beneath the Swartberg; and there was also the murmur of the sea and the lights of the villa on the Côte d'Azur with its lure of a strange decadence; and somewhere something important had gone hopelessly wrong, and something burst with the fierceness of a magnesium flare in confined spaces, spreading fireworks in a dark night of absolute isolation. There was a diamond-hard central core which followed everything with cold eyes, and there was a childlike desire that nothing physical should take place, but that on the wings of sleep Boris Gudenov should be great and strong like the prince of love, and that she should receive him like the princess of desire in the pleasure garden of their dreams.

They were going through the movements on the blade-thin dividing line between salvation and ruin, when the red telephone rang and the moment was lost.

And Boris Gudenov learned that Demosthenes de Goede, shod with loafers, had just begun his campaign.

Chapter Three

The Way to the Shopping Centre

Suburbia. Captain Demosthenes de Goede, dressed like one of the Stray Satan gang, in leather jacket, drain-pipe trousers and loafers, denuded of his Beretta, but formidable enough on account of his powerful physique, was on his way to the centre of the city and the Oita shopping centre where he had a task to perform about which he was not at all clear. But like all practical people he overcame problems by over-simplification, reduced compounds to basic facts, submitted to the single, established data which would couple life's theorem to an irrefutable conclusion.

The human psyche was as much an enigma to him as the concept of eternity; his knowledge of man was based on formulae and character sketches that he had learned in the police college and from literature, and on behaviour patterns that he had observed in life when a given character had reacted to a given situation according to the textbook. In the end, how did one know oneself and one's fellow men? How could the ordinary man enter that world of the unconscious, how could he break through the barrier of nothing?

His task was simple; he had to find out everything about Boris Gudenov; he had to examine the scene of abstract crime and note down every scrap of concrete evidence.

The side streets of the suburb leading to the city through semi-detached houses like his own were so alike that you could easily go astray if you were not an *habitué*. It was already quite dark, and the shadows of the occupants were thrown against the coloured window curtains. Each open window revealed chrome chairs next to a brick fireplace, giving a uniform picture into the lives of the invisible people behind other open windows. Nothing moved; his footsteps resounded loudly on the concrete; every corner of the small gardens, all alike, was silent and empty. Then unexpectedly a figure loomed up, still and motionless – an eternal gnome cast in concrete above a fish pond.

Around the corner, Captain Demosthenes de Goede suddenly saw someone like himself approaching under a street-lamp; a tall gangling fellow with a purposeful shuffle and a ducktail hairdo, a strong chin and quarrelsome eyes – a teenager whose face expressed touchiness. They approached each other slowly with their hands in their pockets clenching a jack-knife and an imaginary Beretta.

They came cautiously, looking each other straight in the eyes: checkmate. Then they passed on: Demosthenes de Goede with enormous arms and a leather jacket straining against his shoulder muscles; the stranger with sectarian comfort written across his broad shoulders: 'Jesus Saves!'

It seemed that the little streets had no end, streets that never wavered but formed, nevertheless, a labyrinth of right angles. The Captain walked on relentlessly, around a block, and then under a corner street-light his way was suddenly blocked by a girl with a mane like a wolf – mousy, stringy hair, puffed up with the help of cheap hairspray – towering above black eyelids and corpse-white lips, all adding up to the teen-age idea of redemption. He wanted to pass her by and pretended not to notice her suggestive movements. Always ready to accept the challenge of any woman, he steeled himself against his inclinations, but she stepped in front of him and said: 'Come on, honey ...' Captain Demosthenes de Goede found this first obstacle in the path of his duty tiresome; not because he found her irresistible, but because she symbolized that desire for chaos that was in him, that wish to be free. She smiled suddenly as though she realized the clash of purpose in his nature and was mocking him. He pushed her aside, turned down the next side street and found himself hopelessly lost in surroundings that should have been familiar to him.

The streets became darker and the buildings, so nondescript by day, suddenly seemed menacing. The mighty Captain de Goede, who did not know fear, now experienced another kind of fear: a longing for his wife and children, a feeling that he would never see them again, that the home to which he had always returned in the past in some mysterious way did not exist any longer, and that he would be alone for the rest of his life. He tried to shake off the presentiment, walking faster, turning back down the street, always to the left like all lost people. Then he heard her voice again, close to him in the darkness, 'Come on, honey . . .' and he caught a glimpse of her wolf hair which, for a moment, gleamed like phosphorus under the street-lamp.

Demosthenes de Goede stopped, squared his shoulders and shook off his fear. He thought of Hope and her words of encouragement after the party when he had had doubts about his mission. She had explained away all his objections: it was the climax of his career, this adventure into a new sphere, this great undertaking which rose above the banality of his previous tasks. Hope had taught him to be unselfish, his Viking wife who was prepared to accept loneliness for the sake of this higher call upon him.

Captain Demosthenes de Goede pulled himself together, and with renewed direction of purpose wandered about the suburb with firm steps, thinking of his lovely wife. Around every corner came the mocking challenge, 'Honey, it's good . . .' but he was deaf to her voice and blind to her animal nature.

When even the tireless Captain began to feel worn out, and his footsteps were no longer so firm, he met the ducktail again on his around-the-block beat and went forward threateningly to meet him. Brusquely he asked him the way to the city. He was examined by two green eyes from which shone the light of obsession, and he received a sermon from one who had found salvation.

'I was like you,' said the reformed ducktail happily. 'I also slept with whores and worshipped the god of alcohol. I also looked in vain for the truth, and in my utmost misery I saw the light.'

They were walking together now, these two in leather jackets and loafers.

'I smoked dagga and puked on the temple of God.'

He indicated a street to the left and one to the right. The houses looked alike, the streets were dark and far removed from the city lights.

'I can dance the Letkajenka, the Watusi, the Surf, the Frug and the Swim,' said the dedicated ducktail proudly. 'I saw Abaddon and returned.

'I think it's to the left,' he said at the next corner.

'I got drunk on kosher wine,' he said as they entered another dark street and looked in vain at the glass windows with the rainbow-coloured curtains.

'I devoted myself to radical Christian ethics,' said the transfigured ducktail when they came to the following corner. 'Christ would have understood the secularization of our time; he would have laughed at the mystery that the old people were so mad over and that drives us to drink and evil.' His green eyes were fixed on the Captain as they turned to the left under a streetlight and moved forward laboriously. 'He stands by Youth. He belongs to this world. Demonology has clay feet. He speaks a new language. His language is not about angels and devils but about housing, the franchise and living space.' The ducktail paused suddenly, exhausted. 'Have you got somewhere to sleep?'

Captain Demosthenes de Goede explained that he only wanted to find the city.

The ducktail of Christ pointed to a bus disappearing around the corner. 'Why don't you take a bus?' he asked.

Transport

Only when Demosthenes de Goede was on the thundering bus closely packed with people hardly two inches apart, isolated in the desert of their own existence, looking straight ahead with discouraged eyes, their faces stark with the sobering realization of something trying to penetrate their confused thoughts, their bodies tensed by an indecision that pinned them to their seats – only when Demosthenes de Goede had become one of them, and, like the rest, saw the conductor coming down the aisle and looked at his clicking clippers, the different coloured tickets, his swaying motion following the rhythm of the bus – only when the figure of A. C. Theron in his municipal khaki jacket, his sleeves bound with leather, his hair long and his shirt collar frayed, his eyes yellow and sick of the same faces, the same routes, and the same memories, stood before him – only when the yellow, gold-filled teeth were bared in a grimace at his tardiness in paying and the dirty nails tapped impatiently against the silver clippers and the nicotine-stained thumb rifled through the tickets – only when the hollow cheeks flushed angrily and the fever-red lips became a thin line at the unpleasant presentiment of 'more trouble' – only then did Captain Demosthenes de Goede realize that the dedicated duck-tail had relieved him of all his cash.

Captain Demosthenes de Goede explained slowly that he would pay back the amount (seven and a half cents) later, but the conductor's professional dignity was at stake. He rang the bell and the bus came to a standstill. Such irregularity he could not countenance. The citizen *manes*, sitting in regimented pairs, lost their characteristic expression of apathy and looked hopefully at the situation boiling up which would provide an exciting topic of conversation and speculation for the next few days.

The Captain and the conductor looked at each other in their different uniforms, and each waited for the other to take the next step which would decide matters one way or another. Municipal authority was binding in the long run, but there were early stages when the poor official had to depend on himself to cope with an uncertain future.

Then the conductor, having looked in vain to the other passengers, tried reeling off a string of swear-words – impressive, but irrelevant. When that did not help, he stammered out the relevant regulations and referred vaguely to sanctions that he did not understand properly. Then, at his wits' end, he presented himself as a champion for the city council. He grabbed Demosthenes de Goede by his arm to pull him out of his seat and received a blow that sent him staggering the length of the bus. He rose slowly and without dignity. Ringing the bell for the bus to proceed, he shouted threats from a safe distance, knowing that time would bring revenge and that all the powers of the city administration would in the end be on his side.

When the bus stopped in the middle of the town and the passengers all disappeared quickly, impelled by whatever urge it was that drove them on, the conductor wondered if it would be worth all the trouble for seven and a half cents .

He came to a decision and rang the bell. The bus thundered on accompanied by the clanging, and the conductor found a peculiar reassurance in the noise. Each docile new passenger who obeyed his orders added salve to his wounds; each response of the diesel motor to his bell pushed the unpleasant memory a little farther away, and he was soon again part of the orderliness that did not brook any liberties. He seemed to give his instructions and click his clippers with greater abandon, to pull out the tickets more smartly and hand them over more threateningly. He had been free for a space, and it was enough to make him appreciate his lack of freedom.

The shopping centre

Captain Demosthenes de Goede stood in the centre of the city in front of the shopping centre, surrounded by people moving to and fro in the fog – a fog that rolled over the vast table-like mountain and threw a shadow over the city and the sea, increasing in the night until it became the gaping maw of Lion's Head, gnawing at the earth with fangs of cloud. The electric lights were polarized by the mirrors of the shopping centre, the moonlight shimmered faintly at one point through the curtain of mist – an alchemistic light like the glimmer of a dying day and an awakening night. Under its surface of tar the Heerengracht snaked its way to the sea, a stream of many memories that carried one's thoughts to oblivion, disappearing unsorted through pitch-black pipes into the bosom of the ocean. A single ambulance screamed its way like a vulture through the streets; foghorns, like owls, hooted their presentiment of approaching disaster; yew trees, imprisoned in railings along the sides of the streets, dreamed their restless dreams in company with the few sleepers. Gudenov's palace was right in the middle of the town. It was brightly lit by a myriad of lights, but the dark patches, where the lights could not reach, were darker than the darkest places in the town.

Captain Demosthenes de Goede was jostled from all sides by the crowds on the sidewalk, but he was too proud to lift a finger. He looked at the weak, negative faces and the double stream moving in opposite directions, and they seemed to be blown by the whims of the wind which came tearing down the street tunnels from all sides. He waylaid a passing paterfamilias and asked him if he knew anything about Boris Gudenov.

The man stopped uncertainly and looked at the vigorous figure in the leather jacket. Somewhat embarrassed, he looked around nervously and found a measure of security in the crowds about him. He decided that the ever-present dangerous situation did not in this case constitute a personal threat to him. Perhaps this was an artist, a representative of the Cape Performing Arts Board, who was promoting a show.

'Boris Gudenov is a ballet dancer,' he said cautiously.

Captain Demosthenes de Goede wrote down this information in his pocket notebook. The man reconsidered his first impression: perhaps this was someone from the Bureau of Consumer Statistics.

'It's a deodorant,' said the man. 'It comes in a plastic bottle with a roll-on cap.'

Captain Demosthenes de Goede wrote it down.

'Boris Gudenov is a writer who won the Nobel Prize,' said the man in despair.

He gave his name and address somewhere in Vredehoek and disappeared in consternation in the opposite direction from which he had come.

Captain Demosthenes de Goede looked at the townspeople searchingly and with suspicion. He saw how they scuttled back and forth as if something were driving them on; he was a solid object in the stream spying on the world. It was a new experience for him to make such general observations, and it was the first time in his life that he was not committed to the solution of a specific crime. He thought it was all a wild-goose chase – as though that was an original thought. He enlarged on this and saw something of himself in everyone: the pattern of his life woven into the larger pattern of continual change. Life is so short, he thought. As a youngster he had told himself: I want to be a king. I want to liberate mankind. I want to win women's hearts. I want to be a pope. I want to be a general on the field of battle. I want to visit foreign places and overcome the lotus existence on tropical islands. There is something that drives me like the wind. House – palace – hut in the prune stones on my plate. Time is running out, time is running out . . . He listened to the music behind the glass doors of the shopping centre; he looked up and saw the Gudenov slogan above the entrance; he stood among the crowds – a huge man, undecided and full of memories, a magnificent creature with a kind heart, ready to serve.

Someone tapped him on the elbow, and the dedicated duck-tail's face peeped over his shoulder.

'I've brought your money back,' he said. 'It was force of habit, but I've won the battle.' He shivered and shook in time to the music issuing from the building, and he pressed the notes into the large hand. 'Why don't you go inside?' He boomps-boompsed from side to side and shook his shoulders in double time while his feet moved at lightning speed. Then he stopped suddenly.

'What is your wife's name?' asked the converted ducktail, still keeping time lightly with his loafers. He looked at the giant and gave him a playful blow in the stomach.

'Hope,' said Captain Demosthenes de Goede, and he thought suddenly of all the young boys that he had, in his police career, brought before the sergeant's desk from the back streets.

The ducktail smiled.

'You have to keep up with the times,' he said. 'You must know the rhythm: the shivers and shakes of our age.' He embraced Demosthenes de Goede, and the latter's face assumed a good-natured expression. 'Get with it!' yelled the ducktail as a wave of music hit them. He controlled himself immediately. His self-discipline was now evident in the absence of rhythmic movement. He became limp and womanly in his submission when it reached his thought level. He pushed his thin wiry arm through the Captain's substantial one and led him unnoticed to the door of the shopping centre.

'One must try to distinguish between reason and mystic revelation,' said the transfigured ducktail. 'We live in this world, don't we?' He looked at the Captain with youthful green eyes under long lashes. 'Order and religion are based on this world; revelation is directed to this earth, isn't that so?' He pressed his wiry body against the sturdy one of Captain Demosthenes de Goede. 'The secular order is the order of the new Christ, isn't it?' He peered cautiously at Captain Demosthenes de Goede who did not understand a word, and was beginning to wriggle out of the embrace.

'Hope is a whore,' said the offended ducktail suddenly, and dodged like lightning as a powerful punch cleft a hole in the air in the direction of the text on his back.

Captain Demosthenes de Goede entered the hall of the shopping centre through which a stream of people moved deliberately, and also, in a way, involuntarily. They seemed to hate the place with its unashamed exploitation, but could not do without it; as though the sort of life which was their lot with its hurry and inconstant values roused a fear of, as well as an incomprehensible necessity for, participation. The Oita of Boris Gudenov, with everything from a needle to an anchor, had, like all institutions born of their own necessity, become a symbol of the decadent mode of life that everyone criticized but no one rejected. There was not one who entered the gate who did not hate the twentieth-century organization : the collective sterile narcissism, the unrequested product that was palmed off by means of psychological persuasion, the condoned dissipation that roused loathing, the way of life that bred anxiety, all the things that you feared but still desired. They were like cuckolds compelled by the complexity of the social structure to be the confidants of their wives' fellow transgressors; like abandoned wives who desired their husband's mistresses, Lesbian fashion. Their degenerate will was the creator of these degenerate times. They were co-architects of Boris Gudenov's shopping centres everywhere in the world.

Captain Demosthenes de Goede entered the shopping centre cautiously and found the reassuring banality of every day : there were floors below and floors above; strings of tinsel festooned in circles among gold papier-mâché decorations; escalators easying the way to the gay well of merchandise; and always music – a discordant cacophony of schmaltz, light opera, pop ballads, hill-billy tunes, atonal jazz, mood music and folk songs – being pounded layer by layer into everyone's head.

It was an orchestra of dissonance and Captain Demosthenes de Goede immediately felt at home. Here he would get the hound Gudenov.

The Code

Brigadier Ornassis E. lay on the triple bed in his flat and looked at Hope restoring her hair and her face in front of the mirror. He saw her from behind and noticed all the marks on her back, the shoulder-straps of her petticoat that were too tight and left red stripes after each movement, the arms that had looked so soft and now appeared muscular, the hair that seemed primitive from neglect before combing and fashionably primitive after punishment with a comb. He took note of her small waist, her relaxed thigh muscles and the breasts enlarged to mountains by snow-white falsies. For some inexplicable reason he began to long for the lithe young men of the D-Service.

He was busy reading to her from a communication on government service paper.

'Boris Gudenov is a ballet dancer,' he read. 'Boris Gudenov is a deodorant. Boris Gudenov won the Nobel Prize.'

The screams of the De Goede children, locked in the room next door, interrupted his words. He waited until a blood-curdling yell prefaced the next silence.

'It's a remarkable code,' he said.

Hope turned and came towards him temptingly, dressed only in her petticoat, her legs longer than usual because of her high Italian spike heels. The Brigadier forced himself not to look at her and studied the interesting code attentively. He felt her sitting next to him on the bed and smelled her exotic perfume. As she had repeatedly done in the past, she offered her services in the battle against Boris Gudenov. She was sure that she could do her part as a woman in this matter.

The Brigadier considered the situation carefully while he stared blindly at the document in his hand which had begun to tremble slightly. As he had had to so many times in his life, he had to make a decision. He suddenly decided in the affirmative, and when she expressed her gratitude in the only way she knew, he realized too late that his timing was faulty.

Some time later in the day the Brigadier, surrounded by his brilliant young men, waited in the gymnasium of the D-Service for the code to be deciphered by the personnel group. He looked particularly smart in a Harris tweed jacket with a matching silk scarf around his neck. The circles under his eyes lent a certain dignity to his striking appearance; his nervous movements displayed that interesting tension so characteristic of him when he was demanding the highest efficiency from his staff.

'Boris Gudenov is a ballet dancer,' repeated a member of the personnel group while the young men of the action front formed a pyramid and maintained the construction with trembling muscles. He looked at a couple of notes that he had jotted down on paper, and continued. 'We all know the effeminate qualities of ballet dancers. Have we perhaps to do with an archetypal image of the anima?'

The Brigadier waited patiently until the excited exchange of words had calmed down and motioned without comment to another young man, while the pyramid collapsed and the action front turned somersaults and landed lightly on their feet.

'Boris Gudenov is a deodorant,' read the young man. 'Perhaps a reference to the magic talisman? Something like the *ephialtion?*'

The Brigadier, lost in thought, looked at the action front who were jumping up on one another's shoulders and slowly building up a human monolith. He waited until the last man, with a mighty spring, reached the top level, and then nodded to the third young man from the personnel division. 'Boris Gudenov is a Nobel Prize winner. It's obviously an attempt by Captain de Goede to test our credulity. It's a word play on Boris Pasternak.'

The totem pole waved from side to side while a further argument followed as to whether that was true to the nature of one like Demosthenes de Goede, but the brilliant young man defended his viewpoint heatedly; in his opinion simple people were especially capable of reaching a height of subtlety in satire which was not commensurate with their intellectual powers – witness the efficacy of their social commentary by means of scatological jokes. The knees of the lowest member of the totem gave way, and the whole bunch collapsed like a house of cards. The Brigadier listened attentively to the argument that followed, and looked at the member of the action front who was carried away on a stretcher. He allowed his young men to discuss the code further while the action group catapulted one another through the air from a spring-board. Now and then he took part in the discussion without airing his opinion. Towards the end of the interview he went and stood on the spring-board himself and was sent through the air with a mighty sweep. The young men looked at their Brigadier with respect as he flew through the air and ended the argument when he was neatly caught by a member of the action front. After that the meeting was adjourned.

The Brigadier was very relieved when he returned to his tastefully furnished room and found that Hope had already left. She had thoughtfully made him some ham sandwiches and had remembered to be lavish with the mustard. Although she had tidied the room, there were signs everywhere of her presence there the night before: a forgotten handkerchief, tissues in the wastepaper basket, cologne in the bathroom, a floral head scarf of pure nylon and, on the table next to his bed where she had obviously forgotten it, a small bottle of some unfamiliar liquid.

Brigadier Ornassis E. sniffed at it and tried to analyse its contents, but that would have been difficult for anyone not conversant with ingredients like miura, puama, lecithin, aronacein and others.

He went to the room next door where the De Goede children had slept on the floor, surrounded by all sorts of games like snakes and ladders, draughts, Chinese checkers and Happy Families. The state of the room was indescribable, and he sincerely pitied Hope: the mother who had to devote her life, day after day, to the young; the tyranny of children who made selfish demands and wore down her creative urge with their never-ending urge to live. Leave them alone for a moment, and they would destroy themselves. That was the tragedy of life, he thought as he went back and poured himself a drink, that children during their dependent years sapped the life of their mothers.

After a couple of drinks he felt cheerful and even ready to forgive the children. Then the doorbell rang and Hope appeared at the front door: a striking image of Woman, in gold, generously endowed beyond the powers of description, surrounded by her tattered children who each made a timely snatch at a ham sandwich before they disappeared with instinctive discipline, like homing pigeons, to the room where snakes and ladders and cards were waiting.

The Brigadier, a man of worldly wisdom, was aware that he was burning the candle at both ends. But he was also aware of the demands of our times on the Service. He was tired, but upright and ready to accept the challenge. He looked at Hope's hot blue eyes fixed on him, and he saw how she had loosened her hair about her shoulders, and how she was taking the customary few steps of a pre-orgastic dance to music that welled up from a deep erotic source and charged her whole being with a life-giving passion that made her radiate with sparkling energy, as if the rising sun was burning inside her.

The heroic struggle often takes place unseen, and in unusual places; and just as on the battlefield, it deserves its troubadours – those specialists in illusion, those winged liars of all time.

Limbo

Boris Gudenov's thoughts, in a flight of reverie, formed a cloud over the cold kernel of his reason. He sat alone at the window of his room while the girl slept. According to legend, he did not know the ecstacy of absolute faith, because his destiny was a particular torment: he was a square peg in a round hole; a hero in an unheroic age, a genius, a throwback: and he stood alone in the pure, almost classic, perfection of his world. They said he was like the sun, that destroyed everything that approached too closely, but caused everything at a distance to grow. He could only achieve his salvation by destruction caused by a woman.

He looked at the girl, sleeping so peacefully, in the knowledge that he could never torture her with true love. He was Boris Gudenov, and Boris Gudenov was impotent, with the impotence of pure reason – the sexless product of the unchained spirit.

The wailing women

'I feel sorry for her,' said Katy, crossing her shapely legs and nodding to the maid to serve the champagne and snacks. 'I pity her,' she repeated to the women of her bridge club who were tasting the snacks and gossiping spitefully, interested in one another's husbands, and in their forties, temporarily winning the battle against age with the help of cosmetics and diet.

'I can see my own bitter life lying ahead of the poor child,' she said, sucking in her cheeks to make the attractive hollows permanent.

A chorus of beautiful, sophisticated women sang their praises of the loving nature of their dear hostess and they speculated about the irony of fate, while they washed down caviar sandwiches with champagne. They bewailed the lot of their large-eyed hostess, the lonely wife in her gilded cage, the arch of solitary nights over the bed of Paradise, the wandering loneliness that tormented her in the empty house. It was a sympathetic chorus of friends, all cold ghosts of former brides who, adulterous in thought and coquettish in deed, wanted to exorcise loneliness from their own middle age.

They consumed the least number of calories in the most pleasant form for the sake of slender hips, and faultlessly decried the fate of their friend who was burdened by lustiness, without an object to love, in tune with the universal discontent of all women, their own organs of love bronze shields in the battle of sexual assertions.

A warning from the Merzeritzer

If in doubt, turn to the right.

If you see a young woman in the arms of an old man, murder follows.

Boris Gudenov looked at Iole, who awoke, opened her eyes and smiled at him.

Sir Henry believed that you could regain strength through young women; that you could regain youth through strong young women.

But Gudenov's mamma wept real tears in the *schtetl* when she lit the candles on Sabbath evenings.

Pallas Athene

Captain Demosthenes de Goede's ears became accustomed with difficulty to the groove music that was piped to all floors from a sound in the basement. It was a ballad of teen-age yearning to the accompaniment of electronic guitars, interpreted by manic-depressive *castrati*.

'It's the sonic limit,' said the dedicated ducktail, anaesthetized by the pulsating rhythm.

Even if the Captain battered him flat, he would be attacking an empty shell. The wiry ducktail had a girl on his arm who wriggled lightly with him in time to the beat.

'This is Minie,' he said, pushing the girl forward.

She looked at him dully with brown eyes that nevertheless sparkled like polished ebony. The beehive on her head glittered with gold threads; the wings of imaginary bees moving at lightning speed in imaginary flights of thought. She smiled, showing strong white teeth, and licked her lips with her tongue until they shone. She was propelled by a further bump, and said, 'Boris Gudenov is sick.'

Bee-Bee-Doo

Bee-Bee-Doo

Captain Demosthenes H. de Goede accepted as his lot that he had to endure the company of teen-agers and descended the escalator with them under the swaying, flimsy decorations – the Queen of Sheba and her train of followers on the way to see Solomon, floating dolls suspended on silver wires from the dome of the shopping centre. A number of clients were frozen in various attitudes on the escalator: some with one foot on the next step, some stiff and straight, others with their head cocked to the golden dome. A floorwalker, dressed in black and accoutred in a snow-white collar, ran an expert eye over them as they landed with a jerk on terra firma and recovered their equilibrium among the crowd.

They were surrounded by the charivari of this particular floor: record bars, discotheques, tea rooms, bargain counters and photo studios. From one of the stalls came the voice of Dylan Thomas reading from *Adventures in the Skin Trade*, directed by a teen-ager behind a counter; from other cubicles came the voice and melody of the day, as determined by public vote and interpreted by the electronic brain of the computer. On the wall there were life-size photographs of Marilyn Monroe, Gina Lollobrigida, Jean Harlow, Kim Novak and others. As far as they could see above the faces of the citizenry stretched a photographic panorama of feminine beauty, an enraptured procession apparently in thrall to Eros, the father-mother of all higher consciousness.

A smallish man, dressed in a white jacket, who had been watching the scene from a table in the corner, tapped on the wood with his baton when he saw that the numbers had grown large enough to warrant his attention. The noise subsided and everyone crowded inquisitively about the man with the shaggy eyebrows who was blowing his nose, clearing his throat and drawing in his breath, letting it whistle through his teeth, as a warming-up exercise before beginning his speech. He first dealt with a couple of advertisements, then welcomed them all on behalf of the shopping centre and introduced himself as the Man Who Knows – the one with his ear tuned in to Hollywood and Vine. He pointed with his baton and had something to say about each portrait as he moved down the line, followed by the crowds – a bit about Jean, Gina and Joan; scraps of scandal, and the names of the films in which they had appeared, while the girl at the records supplied suitable background music. Then he planted himself in front of the biggest portrait of all and, holding his pointer four inches away from two enormous blue eyes, he uttered a single name: Bee-Bee-Doo!

There was an immediate response: they all knew her, the *Filia Mystica*. They remembered all the films they had seen of her and listened tensely to the tragedy that repeated itself every decade: the tragedy of Jean Harlow, Marilyn, Clara Bow and all the others – a tragedy that reached its peak in the life of Bee-Bee-Doo.

The little man dealt with her early years with despatch. She was born thirty years before, to needy parents. When she was a child, her stepfather often beat her, and then comforted her with caresses which led, in her thirteenth year, to incest which she first regarded as normal, but later, when she was grown up, as an unforgivable crime. She went through the usual madness of a teen-age marriage and was divorced a year later. She failed sixth grade. Her name was Luna Cohen, and she was a lonely child, an ugly duckling who would one day emerge as a swan. She first worked as a nude model in Hollywood, under the impression that they were taking art photographs of her. She played small parts as an actress for a company making documentary films. Driven by hunger, she became the mistress of a publicity agent, and in consequence was given better parts. An enterprising young producer made her a star in a Biblical drama, and won fame for them both. After that she earned thirty thousand rand a week.

The little man paused for a moment and looked at the children eating ice cream, and at their parents staring with unchaste thoughts at the portrait of Bee-Bee-Doo. He eased his collar with his forefinger and rested his larynx; he wiped the perspiration from his forehead with a floral handkerchief. He looked small, slight and ugly below Bee-Bee-Doo who was enthroned above him, in all her glory.

She had been married five times: to a writer, an artist, a musician, an athlete and a millionaire, but each marriage had been a failure. They were all older men, and yet she had not found the security that she had searched for so assiduously. She became world famous and won five Oscars, but Bee-Bee-Doo was deeply unhappy. She liked parties, fast cars, reading, music, dancing, riding, swimming, green bedrooms and Persian rugs. She slept naked, and the whole world spied on her with cameras. And yet Bee-Bee-Doo was lonely and often wept over sorrows that were difficult to explain. She was constantly ill and had had trouble with her wisdom teeth. One day she was found dead, a naked goddess, lifeless against a background of apple-green. The whole world mourned, and everyone wanted to know why she had indirectly taken her own life.

The little man felt in his pocket and took out a crumpled scrap of paper from which he began to read with difficulty as soon as he had put on his old-fashioned gold-rimmed spectacles.

'Writers wrote about Bee-Bee-Doo,' he read laboriously. 'A Dutch poet burst into tears when he heard of her death. Everyone asked for the real reason for her death, and they agreed that we were all to blame.' He looked up from the paper, peering over his lenses at the children who had finished eating their ice cream and were now trying to stay their unappeasable appetites with spun sugar. 'It is we, the public, and all the organizations that exploited her as a commercial product and ignored the human being behind the merchandise,' he continued, 'but we can go further than that. We can put the question: Who was Bee-Bee-Doo? Was she a temptress, a whore, an angel of Satan – or was she a beacon, a symbol of love, profane as well as divine?' He took off his glasses, wiped the lenses, tested them against the light and, replacing them, returned to his abstruse script which he began to attack all over again. 'Eros belongs to the universe,' he read. 'The one who creates for man has little control over his or her life and becomes the victim of his or her daemon. You examine yourself and become aware of an inner, endless, mysterious significance. The candlelight flickers, and life becomes impersonal – a burning confluence that you, in your human weakness, cannot tolerate. There is something stretching from heaven right down into the depths of hell.' His voice became fiery, involuntarily inflamed by the significance of words that he could sense but not understand. 'She had seen enough. She had heard the laughter; she had seen the clown on the stage and shared in the absurdity. With her eyes open she had admitted the presence of the unknown, and she had gone forward into the demoniac as well as the good, into that something that could lead one to madness and yet transport one into the heights of ecstasy. She had to accept the risk of her knowledge and had crashed through fear. She was the Akhamoth that spiralled like a whirlwind in darkness and emptiness in search of the light which she had seen and lost. She was the fallen Sophia who could not attain the Pleroma; she was the Holy Ghost of the Earth who could not, without mediation, go farther than the Horos.'

The little man folded the paper slowly and waited a short while for the background music to reach the required mood. Meanwhile he looked at the teen-agers who were sedately putting up with his speech for the sake of the music and at their parents who put up with anything for the sake of their children. In the incomprehensible world in the shadow of the mushroom cloud, anything went; in the blast, purpose was united with wisdom; the glow that came from the bright pillar illuminated a new alliance. In the meantime, they waited patiently until they understood what was at stake, just like Captain Demosthenes de Goede who made careful notes and let his muscles relax until such time as he would be expected to do something dynamic.

The little man seemed much happier. The first stage was past, and the next part he knew by heart. He even allowed himself the liberty of embroidering a little, as his own contribution to her death.

He was telling them about the interment of Bee-Bee-Doo. 'She lay in state at Forest Lawns in the Dylan Thomas room, under a portrait of the poet who died of insult to the brain. She was dressed in white and was laid out on an apple-green ottoman. The service was held in the chapel of the Ecumenical Church of Enlightened Protestants. The coffin cost fifteen thousand rand, and was made of silver and bronze washed with green to suggest oxidation and corruption – the destiny of us all. The Beatles sang "A Hard Day's Night", and the Animals "Hallelujah I Love Her So." '

He now had their undivided attention, and made full use of the opportunity. 'In the Artists' Plot in Forest Lawns, she lies in her grave under a simple black gravestone, designed by Alan Marshall, the creator of the Flamenco 7, the Raven and all those sports cars she loved so much – his final tribute, in tangible form, to a sublime body by God.'

The music became louder and louder and suddenly a voice filled the hall – a pure, agonizing sound, strengthened by 250-watt amplifiers to almost unbearable stereophonic precision. It was the voice of Bee-Bee-Doo and the song that had made her famous.

The little man had stopped talking and looked at his audience who were unconsciously anticipating every note and modulation. And then the teen-agers took over: they had got rid of all the candy, and their supple bodies automatically began to pay a last tribute by performing the steps of the Frug. Bee-Bee-Doo was not dead. Even at her grave, there were loudspeakers built into the headstone which teen-age pilgrims set going by putting five cents into the slot to hear her voice again over Forest Lawns and to indulge in black magic of their necromancy among the graves, and to satisfy their craving for the wisdom of the dead.

Minie and the dedicated ducktail were well to the fore: she, more sedate in her alliance with the goddess of light; he, like quicksilver in his movement, the Hermes of the shopping centre. When the last note died away and everyone came to a standstill, the little man made a final announcement. There were photographs of film stars, taken at the bier of Bee-Bee-Doo, available at fifteen cents each. They could be found at counter number four. Then he withdrew from the proceedings and retired to his corner, where he changed his white coat for his sports jacket. Out of a tin lunch box he took some sandwiches, which he would have to eat in a hurry to be ready for the next show.

Captain Demosthenes de Goede bought a picture of James Dean at the bier of Bee-Bee-Doo and walked over to the little man who was now drinking tea. He found him an indifferent conversationalist and extremely aggressive.

Captain Demosthenes de Goede wanted to know if he had any knowledge of Boris Gudenov.

'He's my employer,' said the little man between gulps of weak, sweet tea.

With difficulty Demosthenes de Goede controlled his temper.

He asked whether he could give him any *information* about Boris Gudenov.

The little man wiped his chin, folded his handkerchief and looked calculatingly at Demosthenes de Goede. He glanced furtively all around, and beckoned. With his hand in the inner pocket of his jacket, he said, 'For five rand I'll give you a photo of Boris Gudenov and Bee-Bee-Doo.'

Demosthenes de Goede paid the five rand and saw the familiar face of a man, neatly dressed in black, erect, stern and aloof, next to an ottoman on which a girl lay stretched, illuminated by seven candles, her face drained of colour by death, but garishly restored to artificial life by the art of the cosmetic department of Haven & Heller, the friendly embalmers.

Code number two

The brilliant young men of Brigadier Ornassis E. were undergoing the usual aptitude tests of the D-Service scheme. Each young man was sunk in concentration, trying to establish the significance-pattern of the questioner before answering the questions.

The questions were simple.

'Are you in love with your father or your mother?'

'Is Boganski, the wrestler, a greater figure in his sphere than e e cummings, the poet, in his?'

'In your leisure time, do you prefer a book or a trowel?'

'Do you find an unattractive woman more interesting than an intelligent man?'

Brigadier Ornassis E. summarily interrupted the test when he read Captain Demosthenes de Goedes' notes which a messenger had handed to him. He found it very effective to break into their set schedule with an unexpected problem.

'A communication from Captain de Goede,' he said. 'Bee-Bee-Doo is the fallen Akhamoth.' He waited a moment. 'Any comments?'

One of his young men made a cautious attempt.

'In that case, one can regard Bee-Bee-Doo as a Barbelo. Is she a Prounikos? Is it her task to deprive the Archons of the light of the spiritual seed through lust?'

Another expanded on this. 'Is she the one who through the ages moves from one body to another by metempsychosis and summons everyone to the earth and the dissemination of the seed?'

Another saw a relationship between her and Hope. He asked, 'Is she the mother of incantation and love philtres?'

A fourth wanted to know: 'Is she the anima figure that becomes united with the Great Silence; is she the culmination of opposites, the chance wisdom that is also wisdom in intention?'

But the Brigadier had already read out the following communication: 'Hope is a whore.' His words came in clear and measured tones, and the young men looked at him cautiously and speechlessly.

Then one from the action front ventured an answer. 'Perhaps that is Captain de Goede's famous – even notorious – ironic style.' He hesitated a moment. 'Hope to be a whore – that is the final irony in the Gudenov world – Beatrice becoming banal, emotion becoming counterfeit, the sin of the Wolf.'

The Brigadier smiled at the young men of the personnel group who were excitedly urging one another on to contradict the Philistine. He lit a cigarette and blew the smoke up towards the gilded roof.

'Of course we all realize that Captain de Goede has only just begun his journey,' he said softly. He was particularly friendly, and made the hasty young man from the action front feel small by his forgiving disposition. He turned towards the young man of the personnel group who had spoken earlier. 'I think in this case we should rather think of the image of Dositheus' Helena, and of Simon Magus' universal mother prostitute.' The young man smiled happily. 'Love philtres and incantations,' mused the Brigadier, 'ought to give us a lead.'

One of the other young men wanted to cap this line of thought by suggesting the Brigadier himself as someone like Simon Magus, the upright man, the one who imagined he had the face of Zeus, but he thought better of it in time.

'If Beatrice, in the words of the great poet, becomes Sophia,' continued the Brigadier, 'then Hope can become Selen or Helen – the Light, the product of inspiration and eternal thoughts ... the reborn woman of Tyre ... the creator of angels and archangels ... the mother of wisdom ...'

The young man of the personnel group was very happy. The Brigadier had confirmed a suspicion. He had noticed the Brigadier's mental inflation, his obsession, the delusions of grandeur, that primordial power without end or beginning that is coupled with the woman who is both whore and wisdom. The Brigadier was in the grip of his archetype.

The Brigadier asked the young man's name and immediately ordered them to continue the tests. The young man answered the questions with ease, for he had suddenly got an insight into the matter – an insight into what was half abstract and half concrete; half personal and half impersonal; into that which wavered between the actual and the symbolic.

Hope was busy serving tea to the hard-working young men of the D-Service. They had just completed the test by which they would be reclassified under the headings of action front and personnel group. As she went from the one to the other, she good-naturedly put up with increasing assaults on her person.

The rose was pulled out of her hair, her blue garter was taken off and thrown about the room, her whole body became black and blue in the boisterous romp. But she was happy. She had divided the last of the powdered cantharides that she had gotten from her dear mother among the many cups. When the Brigadier, driven by unbearable lust and light-headed with delusions of grandeur, claimed the first right, she received from him as forfeit the exact address of Boris Gudenov – something that he had (perhaps on purpose) withheld from Captain Demosthenes de Goede.

Even the young men of the personnel group were excessive in their demands. She accepted the situation with understanding and compassion. There was life in the building – even if it could only last a short while. In the heat of the passion, knowledge attained carnal heights which even the centaurs could not emulate. The interlude between Eros and intellect was unparalleled – decadence was plainly a lack of passion; sterility found its counterpart in mind as well as body.

Tattered and torn, but blissfully happy, Hope reached her terrace house, surrounded by her children. She fed them with left-over food from the day before and then rested her weary body on the big double bed, while she made plans for the great task that lay ahead. She was still unsatisfied; the gnawing hunger could not be stilled; the creative urge was unappeasable and tortured her like Barbarella on the rack; she could have died of rapture, doomed, like all the dying, to die of what caused rapture.

The Brigadier lay alone in his apartment on his triple bed and mused about incidents that sometimes formed a pattern. His body was spent, but his spirit was alert.

Lou-Salome – a friend of Freud, the beloved of Nietzsche and Rilke – Jean Harlow and Bee-Bee-Doo had all died of uremic poisoning. They had wanted to be mistress, mother and madonna, and also slave, silence and the source. They all desired the seed, but there was no outcome. There was only the abortion that mocked the intention. They had developed by-products of urine in the blood, and that had led to cerebral edema, congestion of the brain. The symptoms were dullness of the eyes, headache, and finally, nausea.

Boris told Iole about Bee-Bee-Doo while her dark eyes were fixed on him. He and Bee-Bee-Doo had often gone out together, years ago when she was at the height of her fame. She had been a remarkable person : she could assume a pose for a photograph in the middle of a conversation – her smile remained the same, the movement was carried out, her eyes were in stark communication with the invisible spectators in the lens aperture. Then she would resume the conversation and the warmth, temporarily switched off, was there again.

There was a sort of warmth that emanated from her, a body heat that blended with her perfume and even activated it. Some women had a chemical reaction that was not attractive, but in her case it was otherwise : she was a woman born to love and to excite a man's senses. An evening with her had been full of adventure and usually ended in the green rooms with green curtains surrounded by the ferns, flowers, fishponds and incense of an Arabian pleasure garden. But she had been very fussy : there was never a crease anywhere, or an instant of angry criticism. She appeared with every hair in place and lay almost prudishly on the bed and waited . . .

Suddenly the perspiration began to pour off Boris Gudenov's forehead. He could scarcely speak. He looked into Iole's eyes and willed her to understand what he could not say. That was not Bee-Bee-Doo! That was someone else lying there! It was a Myrrha in myrtle green with eyes shining with love for someone standing behind you. There was an old man waiting behind you. Was it fetishism that made you want to destroy her? It seemed as if she welcomed the blue bruises on her body, the scandal of her flesh.

Iole took him in her arms. There were tears in her eyes, as with a primitive, elemental intuition, she accepted and forgave the sufferings of the tycoon. He and she were one; and she endured the impotent assault on herself in a moment of mystic transcendency. She endured the pain and the vengeance until he became quiet, and calmed by her subconscious perception, found the peaceful centre of the whirlwind.

He told her of Bee-Bee-Doo's end while they were both searching for their lost halves in each other's arms. They found some comfort in the fact that, raised above the purely erotic,

heterosexual love was based on projection – the truth of the apocryphal, that the woman became like the man, that opposites were
reconciled, that the unconscious was united with the conscious. He told her about Bee-Bee-Doo's end, and he seemed to
take a vengeful delight in it. Life had begun to tell on her; each
morning it took longer to restore the ravishment of the night
before. He took a secret pleasure in seeing her less well groomed
than before. After a long night, her breathing was sometimes
jerky, there was white in the corners of her eyes, fine red lines
appeared everywhere as small veins burst almost imperceptibly.
She often became refractory and forgot her words when the
cameras began to roll. Her hair no longer had the required glint.
Vague problems of life were ousted by little problems that went
no farther than arms that were becoming too fat, wrinkles that
could no longer be nourished away, eyes that would no longer
shine without the aid of eyedrops.

All this time Iole held Boris Gudenov in her arms, and as she
listened her heart was filled with sadness at the thought that,
after fulfilment, the projected love of the troubadour died, and
that after a while you did not need your mate anymore. Her heart
wanted to break in the realization of the tragic truth that she
had sensed : that the woman became aware of the man in her,
and the man of the woman in him. While he was talking, the
realization came hazily that he would become lost in wise re-
flections, and that she would drift farther away in the sharp
light of reason which gave her, even at this moment, a premoni-
tion of the inevitable.

On her apple-green bed, Bee-Bee-Doo did not look the same,
Boris Gudenov told her. Even the bed looked different – perhaps
more like those beds in cheap railway hotels, or like the green
back seats of cars under the trees along the main road; or like
the grass growing in the backyards of pubs. Former fans, seeing
her close up, felt superior . . .

Then they found her in bed, naked and dead. Boris Gudenov
wanted to describe her body, the exposed body of Bee-Bee-Doo
without mystery, destroyed by the life she led, but Iole dissuaded
him.

Boris was suddenly as young as she. Across the chastised body she saw Boris in herself, she knew just how he must have felt years ago when he was young and could mock at women and their weakness – when he was strong – and she seemed to feel in herself that urge to live, and saw in herself the young man with the top buttons missing from his shirt, and felt the hot blood that drove him to exuberant living.

She laughed suddenly, and Boris Gudenov was blinded by her youth and beauty. She was the most beautiful girl he had ever seen. And then he laughed too, but he held his hand in front of his mouth as though he wanted to curb his laughter.

They ceased, as though they were newly aware of the tragedy – the tragedy of one who was moving away from the light, and the other who was moving towards it – the tragedy of a temporary meeting, where each borrowed from the other – the tragic interlude of an older man and a younger woman at the paradisal crossroads of similar sensitivity. And while they had laughed a moment before, they were now filled with sadness which at the same time brought them nearer together; and, in the presentiment of inevitable separation, made them realize, ironically enough, the strength of their growing union.

The rules of the game – and feminine mystique

Katy's friends waited patiently for her to open her heart. They sprawled in expensive dresses on chairs designed by interior decorators, knees together and heels at an angle of forty-five degrees to protect the unmentionable garments against the assaults of fashion.

Unselfishly she told them about Boris and all the demands made on him. 'And may I mention that my child and I also suffer under all the obligations that his financial kingdom entails, the work that he does for the public?'

For a woman to remain in the background was not the modern idea. It was anathema, according to their debauched views, and they shook their heads sadly in front of their hostess who from time to time asked for advice without giving all the direct details.

They answered her equally indirectly in the surreptitious game in which you revealed everything in a roundabout way, and counted on getting solutions by circumlocution.

'All I want is love and humaneness,' said Katy. 'The pleasure of ordinary conversations, the joy of a companion who could mend a broken chair, who even comes home drunk now and then, who is home-loving, and for whom you would like to do something. Someone who makes you feel important, and who can appreciate you. Someone who likes people, and whom people like. A normal man with a romantic imagination and a sense of humour. Is that asking too much?'

They took her hand and pressed it reassuringly.

'I'm not referring to Boris, of course,' she added quickly. 'Boris is very good to us, even if we see him so seldom.' They assured her that they understood. No one would pass on a word or an accusation as testimony, but they were all attuned to the invisible image concealed behind their debauched view of life.

'I'm longing,' said Katy, brushing her hair out of her eyes and looking at her friends with large eyes like a young girl, 'for someone who likes to play with children, and who makes you feel safe and reassured. But what can one do? A whole world rests on his shoulders. We are very proud of him, Hyllus and I.'

They nodded in agreement. Katy's masochism was permissible according to the *regula ludi*: Boris was her lifespring, and even if he gave in to all the demands she made of him, she would not welcome the reconciliation. They could not imagine that she would find harmony tolerable; happiness was humdrum compared to the excitement of self-chastisement.

'I hate geniuses who snobbishly leave their stamp on society,' said Katy hotly. 'I hate men who, in the race for power and wealth, forget their obligations in the home.'

Her friends agreed wholeheartedly. Each had her own troubles which vaguely resembled those of the others. They seemed to find a reassurance in the relationship. They prepared themselves to ply Katy with the sort of advice they would themselves like to receive on their own problems: not so much a solution to the problem, but an admission of injustice.

'Jack Gordon was asking after you the other day,' said one, steering the game into its second phase – the problem of how much to allow the absent Jack without jeopardizing their own positions according to the rules.

'Sweet of Jack,' said Katy moving her toes in her spike-heeled shoes in time to thoughts.

'Jack thinks you are irresistible,' said another, and they drew their chairs closer together.

Jack had as many faces as there was need for: he was a mechanic, an Italian gigolo, a presumptuous teen-ager, or anyone that they desired illicitly.

'Jack says you are the prettiest woman he has ever seen,' said another.

They smiled and brushed the hair out of their eyes, happy at the thought of the invisible someone for whom they were the pretty panties, the lace underslips and the bras of finest transparent nylon, that suggested a focus of provocation, beautiful behind the mesh.

They all talked at the same time and chattered excitedly about the one who could not afford speed-boats and Jaguars like their husbands, but knew how to use them. They warbled their longings for their composite, imaginary figure who achieved the impossible by combining youth with maturity, the one who tormented them with the ice-cold phallus of Azazel, the one before whom their soft, helpless, successful husbands became ridiculous eunuchs.

Katy was surrounded by her friends who comforted and supported her; fine women with the last vestiges of youth still in their poses and gestures, with the last traces of beauty that had to be carefully pampered; filled with a longing for the warm rain of love without the burden of fruitfulness. They were constantly in communication with the invisible incubus that had to satisfy them and together with Katy, their hostess, they made such impossible imaginary demands that even the original creator of ornament and cosmetics would have had to have recourse to artificial aid. The successful husbands could argue and reproach as they chose; they could not pacify the cold desire.

The old formula

According to Andro Man of Aberdeen, 1597, you could conjure up your master, the devil, by calling *Benedicte* ! The devil could be exorcised by catching the dog and putting him under your left armpit with your right hand, and filling his mouth with pebbles and saying, *Maikpeblis* !

Chapter Five

The Lion

Something is here, something is next to me, something is following me

The dedicated ducktail and Minie went down the escalator with Captain Demosthenes de Goede to the floor below, where various departments branched out in all directions from a central point. As he looked down from the steps, even the Captain (a pilot in the Korean war) felt dizzy, because there seemed to be no end to the man-made abyss where invisible teen-agers banged drums and twanged strings.

When they reached the bottom, they hesitated a moment, which enabled a smart old gentleman in a snuff-grey suit with a gold watch slapping against his stomach to come up to them from the corner where he had been keeping a secret eye on them. He bowed to the Captain and asked in which direction their interests lay. This was naturally a difficult question to answer immediately, and the old gentleman laughed ho-ho! behind his luxurious grey beard. He accompanied them, his hand lightly on the Captain's arm, and he told them that Gudenov policy was that the client should be left entirely free to do what he liked. 'We have the products,' he said as he cleaned his false teeth with his handkerchief, 'and we are proud of the fact that we can supply all needs.' He put the dentures back and laughed at the Captain, showing snow-white teeth. 'The client is under no obligation, and if he chooses he can spend his whole life wandering about here without buying anything.'

Captain Demosthenes de Goede stopped next to one of the bookstalls. He picked up a *Physique Pictorial* and began to leaf through it casually. While he was looking at a nude cowboy with two revolvers on his bare hips, he nonchalantly asked the old boy, who was just as interested in the picture, 'Do you happen to know Boris Gudenov?'

'Heard a lot about him,' said the old fellow. He turned the pages of the book which was still in the Captain's hand, and showed him another picture of the muscular young man adjusting his belt.

Captain Demosthenes de Goede gave the dedicated ducktail and Minie a telling glance and, casually leafing on until he came to two wrestlers locked in an octopus hold, he asked, 'Do you perhaps know where one can find Boris Gudenov?'

But the old man had taken down an *Amigo* and a *Strong Man* from the rack and was very busy showing the Captain other, more daring, photographs. Demosthenes de Goede repeated his question, and the old fellow took yet another magazine from the rack. 'Look around and you will see his monument,' said the old chap and laughed so boisterously that he had difficulty in keeping his dentures in place. He took the opportunity of polishing them again.

Captain Demosthenes de Goede looked with interest at a *Homophile Zeitschrift* that the old man had pushed into his hand, and fired a quick question, 'When did you last see Boris Gudenov?'

'Never seen him,' said the old fellow who had taken Demosthenes de Goede's arm. 'Of course, Boris Gudenov is the name of a company, but I can't remember ever having seen a photo of the founder Boris Gudenov. There are enough photos of Bee-Bee-Doo, of course,' he said bitterly, 'but none of Boris Gudenov.' He looked thoughtfully at the Captain who was skimming through the magazine and now looking at the illustrations with real interest. He suddenly darted forward and gave the Captain a smart pinch just above the pectoral muscle, looking inquisitively into his face for signs of pain. The only response he got was an expression of dumb amazement, and the old fellow was in ecstasy at these incredible signs of sadomasochism. He began to talk about leather, uniforms, shoes and discipline and found Captain Demosthenes de Goede really interested, until Minie succeeded in pulling him away and the dedicated ducktail, with a blow of his elbow, made the lewd old man curl up with lascivious pain.

'Narcissism is a pathological curse,' said the dedicated ducktail steering the Captain towards the next hall, where six candidates of the shopworkers' union were bringing the nomination battle to a close by all appearing together beneath a fifteen-foot high picture of Bee-Bee-Doo on her deathbed. This was an annual occasion, and part of the Gudenov policy that client and employee must have a glimpse into each other's lives. Underneath the tortured face of the sex queen, all six speakers got a turn to speak for five minutes, and within that space of time to reconcile an image of selfless service with their own personal ambition.

They were rigged out in shop clothes: scrubbed and shaved automatons, built on the neo-middle-class pattern. They waved greetings right and left like boxers entering the ring and gave themselves up to the enthusiastic applause as though there was some special message in the cacophony; they responded to each display of enthusiasm as though the roar of the enormous crowd was a personal tribute to each one of them. They did not see the individual faces, but danced a ritual fire dance in front of the many-headed dragon, searching assiduously amongst the clichés of eloquence for the one magic word that would tame the monster. Six little men compelled to be opportunists; six puppets who would one day dominate the monster, the master. Each smile, each slavish concession, each small obligation in this puppet show was recorded on the debit side of the account that would one day be rendered. Six mannequins with a longing for greatness, warning against the Götterdämmerung that would follow if they were not accepted. Meanwhile they laughed and greeted their audience with a servility which they would one day avenge. Six mannequins, booted and spurred – ready to answer questions from the audience.

All selling was suspended until such time as the speeches should be finished; the plum was the question time, and after that the occasion would be celebrated with snappy service and exaggerated purchasing.

'Are you for or against the four-day week?'

'Are you for or against ecumenical philosophy in trade unionism?'

One of the speakers spied the robust figure of the Captain

right in front, who slowly and clearly formulated his question:
'What is your opinion with regard to Boris G. . . .?'

The one who had to answer the question rose quickly, his face
stern and earnest, his hand on his heart. 'I am proud to say that
I stand firmly behind our celebrated leader, Boris Goodman . . .'
and his voice was lost in the shouts and cheers of the crowd who,
jumping to their feet, totally drowned the repeated calls of the
Captain, 'GUDENOV! GUDENOV!'

After the enthusiasm and the tributes had calmed down and
peace was restored, further questions were allowed. 'What are
your views on centralization?' – But the most important question came from the little man in the white uniform, the one
charged with the image of the late lamented. He was obviously
the darling of the teen-agers. He was a real character and was
still busy chewing his food. He washed it down with a mouthful
of tepid tea, and put his question, 'What are your feelings with
regard to Bee-Bee-Doo?'

His voice was hardly audible in the renewed stamping of the
teen-agers who suddenly showed some interest.

'What do you feel about Bee-Bee-Doo?' the little man repeated his question and, depressed and hostile, listened for the
anticipated superficiality:

Bee-Bee-Doo was . . .

Bee-Bee-Doo was someone whose life testified to the abuse
of love; the tragic, treacherous nature of our life on earth.

The voice of the pop singer, Charles Aznavour, came over the
loudspeakers and repeated the theme. The teen-agers, in blue
jeans and parkas, in beatle boots and desert boots, in duffle coats
and baggy levis, huddled around the invisible central point of
their gathering, gave an orgastic moan. Exhausted heads bowed,
shoulders bent, they began imperceptibly to move, and changing
from their characteristic pose of controlled apathy, they broke
into the quick rhythm of the Frug, the canned formula of their
protest. The dancing ducktail, converted to the Christian neo-
secular There-was-a-God-but-God-is-dead, with Minie at his side,
led Demosthenes de Goede away to the next hall, for the House
of Gudenov was large and there were many rooms.

Someone offered them wine; it was nomination day and every-one was celebrating. The libations that were poured to the accompaniment of bibulous laughter were zealously drunk by Captain D. de Goede, and he felt decidedly better. He could feel the alcohol running through his veins, and he welcomed the cravings of the lion that now mastered him. He looked around for someone with whom he could come to blows (preferably the hound Gudenov), but all that he could see were the crowds milling between counters of perfume for men and women: glass cases full of preparations; Venetian bottles of coloured extracts for armpits, pubic hair and perspiration – anything to banish the odour of passion and energy. There was toothpaste, rinses for ageing hair, pink preparations for dull gums, all the colours of Joseph's coat for eye shadow, spray for wet hair, scar removers, remedies against emotion, remedies for emotion, appetite stimulants, appetite killers, concoctions to conceal and dehumanize served by girls as pretty and as obliging as Brigadier Ornassis E.'s girls of the Service, and he could have roared with undefined rage and desire for action.

He glanced around the room and saw a fellow who looked like a cockatoo: a great fat windbag, dressed like a dandy, surrounded by an adoring crowd of girls who followed him backward and forward through the *parfumerie*. Captain de Goede went to meet him, his notebook ready, his sharpened pencil poised menacingly.

'Oo-la-la,' said the scintillating dandy in an abnormally feminine voice that reduced his beauty chorus to giggles.

Captain Demosthenes de Goede put his question firmly in a clear voice, with the sensitive pride of one who had overcome a speech defect.

'Boris Gudenov,' repeated the cockatoo, studying a cosmetic preparation, 'is an enigma of our times. If there is any truth anywhere, then Boris Gudenov personifies the indecision of our findings. Double meanings and contradictions . . . is that what you want?'

Captain Demosthenes de Goede handled his pencil like a javelin, while the girls came closer, still giggling.

'Who is Boris Gudenov?' repeated the plumed fatso, uncorking the bottle. He smelled it and pulled his nose up. 'Rabbi Uri said that he had four faces: one when he prayed, one when he learned, one when he ate, and one when he received visitors. In which face of Boris Gudenov are you interested, Mr . . . ?'

'Captain Demosthenes de Goede,' said the dedicated ducktail.

'Captain,' said the fat gasbag inclining his head, but his eyes were fixed on the girls. Then he looked at the Captain standing there, awkward and out of place, with the pencil in his hand; but he also saw the powerful muscles, the splendid physique and the primitive simplicity which did not escape the notice of the girls. He put his hand to his side and felt the rolls that were hidden by his silk shirt.

'Or perhaps, Captain, you are interested in that aspect of Boris Gudenov that turns him into a romantic figure. The episodic brush marks on the canvas of his life, for which of us is really interested in problems?' His puffy hands stroked his hair, softly caressing the curls. 'Boris Gudenov is a potentate of an extensive commercial network, a rajah of banking, a colossal corporate body in economic life.' He came and stood close to the Captain, but he had to look up to him, and the rolls of his neck folded over each other. 'He is a friend of princes; he has received *cadeaux d' estime* from kings and he is so powerful that he is even beyond the reach of his friends. But he has a weakness . . .'

The girls were giggling again.

The dandy pressed the Captain lightly on his arm.

'Boris Gudenov is the most hated men because he has all the power and luxury, and he is the closest to everyone because he is also the destruction of all illusions.'

The dandy now teased the Captain with his pose of mock familiarity while he walked all around him as if he could not get enough of the vigorous frame.

'In a world that has become tired of the unattainable, it is fitting that someone like him should be an example of vulnerability among all the splendour and exotic trimmings of his status as a world tycoon.'

The fat man looked at the Captain's uniform and made no

attempt to control his laughter. He seemed to be performing a dance with his unwieldy body which nevertheless achieved spry and mincing movements; a colourful, foppish bird confronting an animal of the veldt. He touched the leather jacket and tugged at the cheap shirt. Then he stood still, shaking his perfumed head.

'Can someone like you grasp that much?' he asked with affected melancholy in which the afterglow of sincerity shone for a second.

The Captain hit him, and received an unexpected karate blow in return that nearly lifted him off his feet. They were both immediately on their guard, instinctively as intellectual and athlete, conscious of the blunder of oversimplification. They hit, chopped and strained at each other without giving way an inch, while the girls were interested spectators. Every hold of the Captain's was answered by a counter-hold which was, in a peculiar way, a perversion of the true hold; each enormous exhibition of strength on the part of the Captain was used against him by leverage action. When he was on the point of losing his self-respect forever, the Captain abandoned himself instinctively to the most primitive hold of all : a furious embrace in which, as though surrendering to love, you squeeze and squeeze your opponent as hard as you can. Perspiration ran off his forehead, he pulled his enemy against him until he hurt himself, and then the dandy gave in, while the girls crowded around and casually switched their alliance.

'A remarkable exhibition,' said someone.

Demosthenes de Goede looked up and saw his friend of the Rolls-Royce, the one who looked vaguely familiar, with a beautiful girl on his left arm, dark, aloof and haughty. He still had his arm around the bruised ribs of his opponent who was panting for breath like an asthmatic. The dark girl came forward and softly loosened his hold. She wiped the sweat from the young man's face with a dainty handkerchief. The man also came between the two and said, 'Rather let him be. It's not important.' The fat dandy allowed a couple of girls to lead him to one of the counters like a conquered hero, where they laved and perfumed him with all the many preparations available. He leaned against the counter and his fat face suddenly creased into a smile under his alert eyes which twinkled in the Captain's direction. Then the smile broadened into an unbridled burst of laughter as he saw how his supporters clustered around the Captain's muscles. He sat down heavily on a chair and fanned himself with his sweet-smelling handkerchief, his fat body shaking with laughter that became more and more uncontrollable, in spite of his pain. Afterwards he was almost doubled up with laughter, and the tears were streaming from his eyes.

'You are most welcome,' said the man to Demosthenes de Goede. 'I hope you enjoy your visit.' He nodded to Demosthenes de Goede while the dark girl joined him again. 'If we can help in any way . . .'

Now the fat man was laughing so loudly that Demosthenes de Goede could hear just about nothing. He tried to think, he tried to rescue himself from this unaccustomed situation, but his helplessness in the circumstances made even his thoughts stupid. He looked at the man, the girl and the laughing windbag and he tried with all the powers of his muscles to think. He felt something pulsating against his temples. He felt his limitations and traced them to something physical, something that had, at times, prevented him as an athlete from achieving those supernatural bursts of effort that time and again gained him the laurel wreath at Olympiads. He followed the impotence to the level of life as he knew it, as a policeman in his terrace house, with the enormous gulf between authority and servant, caste against caste – all the ramparts that separated one class from another, that meant more than money, that was inconceivable and unintelligible. There was nothing behind him but his strength; and in this case his strength had proved nothing. There was another dimension of thought here, a sphere where the heroic appearance and gesture had no significance. Desperately he took refuge in his work and the methods that would enable him to achieve his task; he took out his notebook and held his pencil ready, a puny thing in the great knout of his hand.

'I would appreciate it,' he said formally, mindful of the Brigadier's approach, 'if you could give me information about a person called Boris Gudenov.'

'That's difficult,' said the man. 'Everyone has heard of Boris Gudenov, but what information exactly do you want?' He pressed the girl close to him. 'Are you looking for Boris Gudenov as the dog, the nigredo who suggests misery, suffering and destruction, who lives in the deepest shadows of the soul's melancholy? Are you looking for the sickling and seeking his destruction, or are you looking for the Boris Gudenov who has shattered traditional images, who has given a new symbol to our times and by means of mass culture has shaped man according to mass average?' Captain Demosthenes de Goede considered the answer carefully. He looked around helplessly at the dedicated ducktail and Minie standing next to him, at the girls who were watching him in an admiring flock, and his thoughts seemed to bang up against that blankness that was the best disguise of all. Why was he here? What did he want here? He longed for the sort of world he had known, but which had changed before his very eyes.

The Captain seemed to realize for the first time that he was growing old, for there was something hovering on the threshold of realization to which he could give no words, and of which he had no clear, incisive idea. He suddenly felt alone, and became aware that he was cutting a ludicrous figure. He heard someone laughing. There was a clown in the shadows: it was here, it was there, it followed everywhere. He shook his head as if to shake himself out of a nightmare world. There was something in the confusion that could only be exorcised by tremendous self-discipline. To understand this present world of dreams and fantasy, there must be firm ground under your feet; there must be understanding, otherwise for the rest of your life you would be doomed to emptiness and nothingness; otherwise you would become the victim of the autonomous powers which could reduce you, by means of their devilish arts, to their own nothingness. That was the danger against which the Brigadier had warned him: something had to be brought to light; something had to take on a tangible form so that it could be overcome by might and reason.

Captain Demosthenes de Goede suddenly became calm. Although he knew nothing as yet, he was at least beginning to get an idea of his task and all the dangers attached to it. He listened with heartrending intensity to the amorphous conception churning at the back of his mind.

All at once the dedicated ducktail leaned nearer and whispered in the Captain's ear: 'God is dead. We no longer recognize the Sacred, the Inviolable. There is nothing. There is nothing but our earthly duties and Christian love for everyone and everything.'

The Captain looked at the dedicated ducktail and then at Minie. A light shone in her dark eyes which would help him if he could understand it. There was something in her eyes that he had seen in women just before he overwhelmed them with sexual love, but he could not put his finger on it.

In the distance the trade union candidates had answered their questions unsatisfactorily, and Bee-Bee-Doo's theme song resounded through the building. The Captain listened to the song, and it brought quite another conception, just as formless. Something was at grips with something, and was leading irrevocably to total destruction. There was a light in Minie's eyes, and Captain Demosthenes de Goede was on the point of getting an inspiration that would explain everything. But it just escaped him.

When he looked around again, the man with the familiar face had disappeared, and the whole situation had collapsed. The Captain was back where he had started. But still, there was something to hold on to: something is here, something is next to me, something is following me.

Captain Demosthenes de Goede followed his two companions through the halls of the shopping centre and he was followed in turn by the horde of girls. He was amazed at all the luxury; he was surrounded by people he met every day in the street: mothers with children, fathers and mothers, couples and groups; and then the lone wolf, the one with a beard or long hair, the affected walk of the deviate, the swaying gait of the alcoholic, the meanderings of the drug addict. The situation was normal, as he knew normality, but there was no sign of Boris Gudenov. At times the Captain thought he saw someone he knew: a face, the cut of a coat, a familiar movement; someone like one of his colleagues of the D-Service; faces that turned towards him, but then became unrecognizable because they were only familiar as types.

Here and there he stopped someone and asked about Boris Gudenov.

'Boris Gudenov is the power behind the scenes in every war,' said a young man. 'He sells arms to all, and he thrives on blood, but his day is over.'

'Boris Gudenov is a Russian dictator who wants to rule the world,' said another.

'Boris Gudenov is the socialist ideal that will save the world.'

The Captain stood next to a little girl sitting on the lap of the shopping centre's Santa Claus and whispering her wishes into his ear while he ogled her mother and caressed her little thigh.

'Boris Gudenov is Father Christmas,' said the little girl.

The Captain felt a yearning he could not understand. He was filled with longing for something that these people as devotees accepted mechanically; something that made him feel an outsider. He began to have doubts about himself: doubts about the heroic concept which had always been clear to him; he had to reconcile himself to an idea that was entirely opposed to his way of thinking: that true worthiness was no longer found in the proud sacrifice for a great cause, but in the meek acceptance of little things, for everything was small, there was no longer anything great. He suddenly stood, tired out, keeping his arm without thinking around Minie and his other hand on the dedicated ducktail's shoulder, while he tried with vacant eyes to see some significance in all the tumult.

They made a group on a platform before a portrait of Bee-Bee-Doo which took up a whole side of the wall, a tragic Venus elevated to form a canopy above the ladies' underwear department, on her face an expression of childish amazement, caused by inexpressible suffering, trapped by the camera for all time; an example of womanly allure according to the rules of the game into which she had been forced; swathed in green gauze which accentuated her curves, 35–24–35, with insertions of black velvet to mask three secrets in three places.

Captain Demosthenes de Goede walked slowly through the halls, followed by the girls and accompanied by the two teen-agers. Buying was again in full spate, although the nominations struggle continued in canvassing on the floor, where employees and customers both took part. There was a festive air about the place, but the possibility of violence lay just below the surface. The slightest inflection of the voice or the equivocal word could start an argument or unleash trouble. It was like a boiling river, deep on the one side where the water bubbled up from the un-known depths of the human psyche, and shallow on the other where it formed tepid waves of over-sensitivity and easy offence.

'It's the heat,' someone said.

'It's the drought and the result of the credit squeeze,' said another.

The clerks' collars oppressed them; their shirts were rumpled with sweat.

The Captain saw a man who had too little money to buy the things he wanted. The Captain followed him from hall to hall as he went from one department to the other, his mouth watering when he saw something tempting: a beach jacket, a tie, some special expression of his vanity that was always just beyond his means. He was ready to commit murder from frustration at the destruction of his daydreams, the vision he had conjured up of himself on a crowded beach with that tie around his neck, that Onyx perfume in his vicinity, those cufflinks in his white shirt – the vision in which he was raised above the banality of his everyday existence. He was a potential thief, but the Captain was hindered by his instructions from coming into the open and acting to protect the community.

Captain Demosthenes de Goede, the dedicated ducktail, Minie and the girls went from hall to hall on a search that every moment became emptier. It was like walking in circles on the hot sand of a desert surrounded by mirages, which they immediately recognized as mirages.

The dedicated ducktail suddenly had an inspiration.

'Who are you looking for?' he asked Demosthenes de Goede.

'I am looking for the hound,' said the Captain, and the clown laughed in the distance.

At once the song of Bee-Bee-Doo became louder, for they had reached the next hall, and everyone was listening to the little man in the white jacket who was continuing his endless lectures.

'She was very beautiful, but she had her troubles,' he said.

'She was very sensitive, and could feel at once if the people in the room were well disposed towards her.'

He swallowed his lukewarm tea and looked calculatingly at his audience.

'They made her a symbol of feminine attraction; she allowed herself to be moulded like clay, she lay bare for the sake of the image of the tragic Venus, but she was unhappy.'

His thoughts became weak, like his tea, but he was encouraged by the message that was repeated over and over again. 'She often doubted her own talents because she realized that the role had been created for her. She never wore underclothes. Her clothes were transparent. One night at a party she danced on the drums in her green frock – and then stripped.'

The little man swallowed his tepid tea, cleared his throat and spat into his handkerchief.

'She followed her men like a lamb, and endured their assaults.'

He completed the first half of his speech which would be continued in the next hall. Meanwhile he sold photographs of Bee-Bee-Doo which were not in the least pornographic. One could see nothing improper: just her face, portions of her breasts, thighs and a smile aimed impersonally at everyone. Shiny photographs of the feminine figure as something to be scorned; glossy prints that were boring rather than a temptation.

Bee-Bee-Doo's song resounded through the hall as Demosthenes de Goede tried to find Boris Gudenov. He went from hall to hall while the subtleties of her voice escaped him. He was a large man, blessed with strength and firmness of purpose, and as a police champion for the community, he was adjusted to obvious decadence: the Sahara of the soul, blasphemy, the crime against the order. But his impotence and anger increased because he could find nothing but tedium, boredom, barrenness and sometimes a specific crime that violated a principle but against which he could do nothing, on instructions from Brigadier Ornassis E. He was filled with anger, like a lion that could not see his enemy. And, because he was a man of action, his anger grew with each frustration and piled up against the mysterious Boris Gudenov who was the personification of it all.

Captain Demosthenes de Goede was ready for action against the enemy. The enemy was here, there, everywhere. His wrath was switched on, his muscles bulged, he arrested the man who had stolen a bottle of *Signature* men's cologne – but let him go at once when he remembered his instructions. He shouted his fury and frustration to the gilded dome of the shopping centre and moved farther down, floor after floor, to the bottom, to the source of sound and trouble, of everything that he did not understand – because something is here, something is next to me, something is following me.

Report

Brigadier Ornassis E. had had an outstandingly good night's rest, and looked at his brilliant young men from both departments with clear eyes, which immediately put them all on their guard.

'Has anyone seen Mrs de Goede?' he asked.

No one could give any information, and the Brigadier tapped on his desk with his pencil. He ordered one of the young men to turn the record player down a trifle.

'Who are they?' he asked.

'David and Marianne Damour,' said a young man of the personnel group.

'I don't like it,' said the Brigadier. 'Too little social comment.' The record was changed for one of Nick Taylor's.

A couple of girls from the Service went and sat on the floor on either side of the Brigadier and leaned their heads against his knees. The Brigadier rubbed their heads absentmindedly, and assumed an expectant attitude.

One of the men rose.

'Two members of the action front and one from the personnel group followed the Captain. He was involved in a fight which he brought to a successful conclusion. He held a short conversation with Boris Gudenov. He was beginning to take an interest in Bee-Bee-Doo, but was showing signs of increasing tension.'

The Brigadier lifted his face to the light.

Another young man stood up (the one from the personnel group who showed exceptional promise).

'We think Captain de Goede has moved beyond the sphere of conscious emotional perception and is experiencing the first indications of primordial awareness.'

'Of course,' said the Brigadier impatiently, trying to free his hand which had become entangled in the intricacies of a beehive hairdo. Tears of pain welled up in the girl's eyes, but she smiled bravely, as behoved a member of the Service, when the Brigadier freed his hand with an impatient tug and held out his glass for a few drops of Rémy-Martin Cognac.

'The question is, naturally,' said the young man with exceptional ambition, 'whether the Captain, as an ordinary soul, is capable of taking in the significance of his archetypes.'

The Brigadier gave a cruel snigger which doomed the ambitious young man, to the great delight of the others, to the action front for the rest of his career. He had a good deal of trouble in freeing his left hand in spite of a couple of impatient tugs which he made as unostentatiously as possible. He frowned as a faint scream came to his ears, and the girls of the D-Service exchanged significant glances. The sunny beach at Clifton would be waiting for Maureen Jones.

'Are you perhaps under the impression that it was our intention that someone like the Captain should interpret his own visions?' asked the Brigadier impatiently, his left hand motionless and hopelessly entangled in the loveliest golden hair in the Service.

The young man sat down, dismayed, and the Brigadier allowed

a few more drops of Rémy-Martin in the glass held in his free hand.

'What worries me most,' said the Brigadier, while the tension grew and the young men of the Service with the greatest effort kept their eyes turned away from his left hand, 'is that Boris Gudenov is slipping farther and farther out of our reach.' He allowed a brilliant young man to fill up his glass; and then the Brigadier did something that demonstrated his greatness and raised him above all other brigadiers of the lesser services. He jerked the shining hair on Maureen's tortured head so that she screamed like a kitten, and he looked straight at the brilliant young men who, smartly erect, were waiting for him to speak.

'Someone,' said the Brigadier, 'is unravelling Boris Gudenov's images and enabling him to find his own identity in the confusion.'

'It's that girl Iole,' said a young man of the action front who rose slowly, walked up to the Brigadier and with a lightning movement let a golden lock fall beneath his penknife's slash while he filled his chief's glass to overflowing.

'Exactly,' said the Brigadier and looked with astonishment at the young man who, in spite of all the tests, had been so strangely misplaced. 'One can only hope that, like most women, she will refuse to return the projected past.'

The Brigadier put his shapely palms together and brooded absent-mindedly. It was a sign to the young men that the greatest danger was past, and they filled their own glasses and began to talk to one another.

After three more glasses the Brigadier again asked if anyone had seen Hope de Goede. All affirmed their ignorance, and the Brigadier shrugged his shoulders.

'The shopping centre need not necessarily be a fatal example in the ordinary sense,' he said after a while. 'It is we who see devilish apparitions in things because we can't reconcile ourselves to the side of our psyche that we constantly fear.' He appealed to his young men. 'And Captain de Goede is supposed to be without fear, isn't he? Was I not justified in my choice?'

They all hastened to reassure him.

'Boris Gudenov shall not win!' bellowed the Brigadier suddenly.

Again he was in a particularly difficult mood, and the young men felt their way uncertainly, trying to restore the peace.

'We dare not risk any form of desecration,' said the Brigadier.

The clever young man from the action front came forward. 'There is always Bee-Bee-Doo,' he comforted his chief.

The Brigadier shook his head. His better judgement confirmed the surmise: everyone was open to the secular ideas of the hound Gudenov.

He listened to the record player.

'Johnny Congos and Keith Blundell,' explained a young man of the personnel group.

The Brigadier hummed a folk tune and drank his cognac. 'Have you ever wondered who Bee-Bee-Doo really was?'

'The one who through the ages moved from one body to another by metempsychosis and called all to the sowing of the seed,' repeated a young man of the personnel group.

The Brigadier waved an impatient hand. 'I mean, who was she with regard to Boris Gudenov?'

A young man looked at his notes. 'His paramour ...?' he ventured.

Brigadier Ornassis E. held his head in his hands and waged a silent battle until he had regained his calm.

'May the All-Wise preserve us,' he muttered, and took a sip of Rémy-Martin. He looked at Maureen Jones who sat next to him with bowed head, an expelled nun in secular clothes, with a small patch of white skin revealed on the top of her head; the thought of Clifton, muscular young men, photographs in the Sunday papers, dances, writers and their bacchanalia, sports cars, yachting adventures, the lotus existence beneath the slopes of the mountain, the bitter enjoyment of a beautiful body and the malaise of youth a shocking contrast to the deeper and worthier demands of the Service. She wept silently for the Paradise lost forever: the desire of all beautiful girls to give themselves up, unnoticed and in silence, to exalted and worthy ideals.

The Brigadier wanted to stroke her head, but had second

thoughts. Better, perhaps, that she should wage her battle alone, in silence, and doing penance.

'No,' said the Brigadier to the young man. 'With regard to the part that they have to play towards one another: the Prounikos and the sick king; the slut and the impotent man. It has come to my notice that there are certain fools in our Service who do not grasp the significance of Bee-Bee-Doo in the shopping centre . . .'

Even the young men from the action front seemed surprised.

'There are even some who expect Captain Demosthenes de Goede to give us in his search a detailed portrait of the tycoon . . .'

A few members of the personnel group began to laugh, cautiously at first, then more loudly as soon as they saw that the Brigadier was smiling himself.

'And,' said the Brigadier, 'that some, perhaps from the action front, quite possibly even a couple from the personnel group, expect form and cohesion . . .'

The Brigadier was all smiles, and the young men realized that the danger was past.

'There is nothing logical,' said the Brigadier ponderously, 'and there is nothing that is unlogically logical. In the Gudenov world everything is uncohesive and amorphous. It is the snare of someone like Boris Gudenov, and it is our duty, as members of the Service, to search and to see if there are not perhaps traces, in the secular chaos, of a metaphysical significance, or whatever it is.'

The Brigadier drained his glass of Rémy-Martin, and did not protest when someone offered to refill it.

'Our danger,' said the Brigadier, 'lies in the fact that Boris Gudenov, the creator of everything secular, will detect a pattern, something that will raise his existential chaos to a form, a materialistic myth, which will lure us, with our involuntary urge for uniformity, to compliancy.'

He looked approvingly at his young men who were diligently taking notes. Then he allowed them to ask questions. There was only one question, and that came from one of his ablest young men in the personnel group.

'Where does Boris Gudenov sleep?'

The Brigadier looked from one young man to the other; it was clear that they had been halted before those annoying problems that often look unimportant, but are indeed important because members of the Service are expected to know everything.

Another young man came forward respectfully.

'A newsletter from the Academy. We hear that you have been proposed as the secretary of the *ad hoc* commission to study degeneration.' The young man handed the newsletter to the Brigadier. 'May I, on behalf of the members of the Service, offer you our hearty congratulations?'

There was loud applause from the rest of the personnel.

The Brigadier acknowledged the applause with a slight nod and looked at his portrait with the caption: 'Snappy dolls in the Academy will have to look sharp to keep ahead when Brigadier Ornassis E. (photo above) tackles his new job with the devil's own energy.'

The Brigadier was still a faculty member; he hoped later to become a full member. He also cherished the anticipation of an Academy award on the grounds of his work in the sphere of degeneration.

The meeting ended and everyone sang folk tunes until the Brigadier became sleepy and made signs to one of the young men to lead him to his room.

On the way to the door he said, 'One must guard against rowdiness.'

The young men grasped at once that it was an anti-correc for the corrective laxity that they were sometimes allowed, to alleviate the discipline of their thought and way of life.

At the bedroom door the Brigadier asked, 'Where is Hope?' He stopped the young man who was going to reassure him.

'I think Hope is dead,' said the Brigadier. 'I've got a hunch. It follows me everywhere. It's p-r-e-m-o-n-i-t-i-o-n.'

The young man poured him a nightcap of Rémy-Martin Cognac. The Brigadier was reluctant to sleep. He wandered around the room and made a confidant of the young man (the clever one from the action front).

'They once asked Borges what death was,' said the Brigadier, 'and Borges said : "Death is a city." '

He looked at the young man in vain. He had not really earned promotion and did not understand a thing. But the Brigadier saw that the young man was well-built – a young Apollo.

'Hope is dead,' said the Brigadier, and motioned to the young man not to leave.

The zonah

Hope, surrounded by her four children, was on her way to Gudenov's palace. In her mind's eye she saw Oita with its golden domes among the daffodils; she saw herself as the chosen vessel that would relieve the Archon from the light; she had come from the higher cosmos into this banal world, the spirit of woman, from far and wide. She had dressed herself as she imagined the pneumatological beings of the air : in shining white; her four children, descendants of Cain, promoted in pale blue to the lineage of Seth. They fought furiously against the frills and furbelows in which their mother had confined them; they were repeatedly impelled with slaps in the bizarre procession through the city's tarred streets in broad daylight. It was an extraordinary procession that drew the attention of everyone as it passed the terrace houses, while the neighbours peered through the windows or leaned over their garden gates. She moved on with dignity, her long dress dragging on the asphalt, her hair streaming in the wind and her bright blue eyes seeing only visions of salvation.

In her hand she held a vial of gold with a stopper of lapis lazuli to suit the occasion. The precious liquid was the last Hope would ever receive from her beloved mother, for she had recently died behind the glass walls of Welgevonden, comforted in her last hours by the background music for *From Crystal with Love*. It was the strongest excitant of all, originating from faraway Mexico: DAMIAN.

It was a long journey, but she managed it with greater ease than her husband, Captain Demosthenes de Goede. She found the correct entrance immediately, moved through passages filled with antique furniture and opened one door after another without knocking. She saw a group of women drinking tea together who gave piercing shrieks as they perceived her over their teacups; she saw a large dining hall with silver candelabra, a reception room, and bedroom with silken hangings; she moved from room to room among the costly pieces collected from all parts of the world until she reached the last door. She opened it and saw the handsome man with a girl in his arms, his eyes blind with fear.

Beloved enemy

Boris Gudenov and Iole walked through the large room with an unhampered view over the city. After the hubbub of the shopping centre, from which they had just returned, it was quiet and secluded here in his bedroom. He told her about Bee-Bee-Doo's last years, and how they went together one day for a swim in a lake next to a wood. Waterweeds clutched at her legs, but it was really her desire for death that he had to fight. Later when they lay exhausted beneath a tree, he tried to talk to her and to understand something about it. But they might just as well have been on different banks. Nothing made sense to him; everything that had been complicated at first had now disappeared in the simple fact of disintegration, which had been carried so far that the original causes could no longer be discerned, nor were they of any further importance. There was probably nothing that made one feel more alone and helpless than when someone was reconciled to his own destruction and waited with apathy for the end.

'And yet she wanted to take me with her,' he told Iole. 'All her life she jeered at me, but at that moment she wanted to wipe me out as well as herself.'

Boris Gudenov stood with his back to the window, right in front of Iole of the dark eyes.

'But what did she want to tell me? What did she want from me, and what was it she wanted to do for me?'

He was a handsome man, very attractive to women until they learned to know him. He was years and aeons older than Iole who at this fleeting moment was nearer to him than any woman had ever been.

'But I unmasked her at the last moment,' said Boris Gudenov. 'She was a character out of the *Ladies' Home Journal*. She was as empty as those cookies and tarts in the shiny advertisements. She was completely under my spell. Bee-Bee-Doo was nothing. I took over her image and made use of it. Bee-Bee-Doo was the creation of Boris Gudenov, and nothing more. She was the sick image of teen-age desire, she was the girl who died on the pillion of a motorcycle, she was the shadow who echoes their songs. When she died, I let myself be photographed with her like all the others.'

It was difficult to say how much Iole understood when she took Boris Gudenov in her arms. In spite of the relatively short duration of their relationship, which they both now looked upon as temporary, they were in other respects perfectly adjusted. Iole had a mystic message, born of love, which she would reshape within a few years into definite opinions; Boris Gudenov was filled with sadness when he realized that he had made use of her in the same way that he had all his life made use of everyone and everything.

But now there was something – something that was following him, that was always with him, that would allow him no rest. Boris Gudenov as tycoon was – perhaps more than anyone else – conscious of order and design based on economic, biological and psychic laws. His pragmatic judgement had never failed him in the past. But he suddenly had a desire, such as never before, for something from the time of his grandfather, the *Maggid*, hidden in the mists of his youth.

He looked over Iole's shoulder while her warm breasts pressed against him. The abstract design on the curtains was part of the décor. Then, suddenly, patterns began to form in the design : a mocking face, Pan with an indescribably evil countenance. He could feel himself being overcome by fear, and enduring the fear as long as he could, he seemed to welcome the moment of madness, until the discipline of his will forced the plurality of forms and shadows back into the abstracts which served as decoration alone.

Iole's head rested on Boris Gudenov's shoulder. There was a look of inexpressible happiness on her face.

Boris Gudenov pulled himself together. His empire and all that it had brought with it had raised him above the cares of ordinary people. He was not as lonely as other tycoons, nor did he have a phobia for invisibility, such as Kirsch, Huntington and others who had tried to buy immortality. He took a pride in all the work he had achieved; the dark, unfamiliar part of his psyche was a world that had to be overcome. Even the fear of a moment ago was something that he could control; the desire that rose in him was only a passing fancy for those things of his youth that were now strange to him; whatever it was that was following him, that would not leave him in peace, was something he had to bring to light, something to which he must give a name.

Iole stroked his hair and rubbed her cheek against his.

Boris Gudenov was a name with magic powers. He could make those mysterious things come to heel; the searchlight of his reason could blind those psychic monsters.

While he was drawing Iole closer to him and caressing her, lost in thought, he saw his room in front of him with a sudden clarity: the arrivé effects he had suffered architects to contrive under the impression that they had a true conception of luxury. He looked at the walls hung with costly tapestries, the many adornments: the altarpieces, the credenzas, the suits of armour, the ikons. He looked down at Iole and saw the sweet retarded smile of love. As he looked up, he perceived how the door slowly opened and a woman's figure appeared between the altarpieces, surrounded by four children, a q'desjáh in white, a vision from the days of the kings, with grotesque make-up that was like blasphemy in contrast to the innocence of the woman in his arms. It was a cabalistic vision standing in front of him: it was Ashtoreth with the vial of love in her hand. Petrified, he looked at her, and he seemed to relive the fear-patterns of his youth, for he saw, in the shadows behind, the image of Azazel and, farther back, the demon woman Lilith.

The mighty Gudenov strained his powers of reason to the utmost to exorcise the apparition. He looked around: there hung the constellation of Shemhazai, upside down, in the bright light. He concentrated with all the remarkable power available to him, then looked before him again, freed by his will-power from the chimera, and saw the zonah, painted like a whore and surrounded by her urchins. He was free from the spectres of his imagination, but now up against a reality more grotesque.

Hope approached uncertainly, while her four children, overwhelmed by the luxury around them, clutched at her dress in terror. The world she had created for herself collapsed, the terrace house was back: forgotten now was the Brigadier and the lofty influence of his organization; without her husband Hope was now a woman alone, with a purpose that she no longer understood properly and which had suddenly become banal and meaningless. The light in the room seemed to worry her; she passed her hand over her forehead and looked around helplessly. What had she wanted to say? Why was she here? The old masters on the walls glinted and overwhelmed her; the period furniture offered no refuge; she did not know what to do, where to stand or where to sit – when to sit, or what to do with her children. The four, who in other circumstances would have immediately begun their demolition tactics, coped more easily with the strange situation. They looked hesitantly around, jostled each other and released her. Four little figures in cheap blue moved in four different directions. They tested the small tables, the chairs, and touched the ornaments; they pulled their dirty little fingernails through the paint of Raphael, Titian and Botticelli; a Houdon bust shattered into fragments on the floor.

Hope stood under a chandelier. She tried to stop her children and stumbled over a 1777 fire iron, designed by the Comte d'Artois; her soft behind landed against a Marie Antoinette marble fireplace, smuggled out of the Bagatelle; the Viking hair refused to remain styled and cascaded over her eyes and shoulders. Pathetically she brought out her last weapon against this man whom she had recognized, but who now suddenly looked strange and different. She swayed her hips provocatively as she approached in her long dragging dress. Half way, she realized that in this setting, in front of that lovely girl with her proud air, she looked a fool. With each step she felt more ridiculous without knowing exactly what was wrong. She hesitated, but went bravely on, trying in vain to weep. It would have been easier if she could have raised some tears, but something far back in the past had deprived her of the ability to weep. She was now in front of the unreachable couple and was conscious of the crushing contrast between her shiny dress and the expensive, simple material that suited Iole's self-assurance so perfectly. While her children messed up a Giorgione, she proffered the vial, handing over, as a gift, her only weapon.

Boris Gudenov received it with elegance, and in his eyes (free now from the fear with which he tormented himself) there was a trace of understanding and sadness. But only for a moment, because immediately the tycoon's ability to handle an awkward situation asserted itself.

He took her by the arm, led her to a chair covered in Beauvais tapestry and allowed her to sit down clumsily. A hidden bell had already summoned his valet who now received low-voiced instructions. He rounded the children up deftly and led them away to the adjoining room. Boris Gudenov, still holding the vial, bridged the momentary gap of embarrassment with small talk until his chauffeur appeared with the children who already had hold of his cap and were skipping elatedly around him. Boris Gudenov first asked Hope for her address, but then anticipated her answer by suddenly remembering the street and the number of their terrace house. At the door he gave the chauffeur instructions to take the whole family – good friends of his – for a little drive first, in the direction of Chapman's Peak, maybe – wherever they wanted to go. When they had all been led away and the door had closed behind them, he returned to Iole and suddenly realized that the vial was still in his hand.

He drew the stopper out and smelled it. Then he looked at Iole who was worshipping him with her dark eyes. He saw her lithe and beautiful, full of promise for all the years that lay ahead; her body supple and young, ready to surrender to the onslaughts of love. He smelled the vial again and walked over to the cocktail cabinet where he poured out a glass of wine for each of them. As he was bending forward, he saw himself in the mirror, and examined his reflection thoughtfully. He went over each little wrinkle, each line of destiny that had developed with his financial empire, each scar of the Fates through the years. Over his shoulder he could see Iole in the glass, and he again saw the vision of the old man and the young woman – Salome in Elia's shadow. He made a quick decision and divided the contents of the vial between the two glasses.

At first, he experienced a feeling of sadness as he went towards Iole, his beloved. As a tycoon he had often been obliged to make difficult decisions. He was used to weighing up the facts against one another and often tipped the scale with a shred of presentiment that was not based on reason. For that moment he had always been in the hands of something autonomous, something that he allowed to take possession of him, something from the depths of his psyche. From that possession, from that surrender, he often received the answer. But it was a risk that someone like him had to take all his life. Only afterwards, when everything had become clear, did others follow him.

He went to Iole and, looking into her eyes, offered her the glass. All that he saw was love, surrender and trust. She had made herself utterly submissive as the vessel for the sacred transformation. While they drank, he kept his eyes fixed on her, and then took her in his arms. As she pressed softly against him, he thought of all the possibilities that he had willingly and wittingly set in motion : the inhuman urges, the animal sex rages, the unbridled passions. It was a calculated risk, true to the nature of someone like Boris Gudenov who had built his empire with human souls as well as tangible material. But there was also the promise; fruition, reshaping, redemption.

It was perhaps the biggest risk he had taken in his whole career, for he had also staked his weakness, the sickness in himself that had become a symbol of decline. It was the fate of one such as he that the demands made on him became greater and greater, that the true disclosure was only granted to the one who took that risk.

He pressed Iole closer to him, as though he wanted to protect her as well as himself against the inevitable. Then the perspiration began to bead on his forehead as, surrounded by his *objets d'art*, enveloped in his creation, the shopping centre, he became caught up in the struggle from which he would not emerge unscathed.

Iole lay alone in the room. She lay on a Bukhara rug under a Velasquez. The marble eyes of Pan, sculpted by Francesco Laurana, were blind to her suffering. Her young body, tensed like a bow, weltered blood – stained in the grip of the lion that had overcome her and her invisible lover. Invisible – for the room was empty. There was no sign of the older man of wisdom. She was surrounded by Fra Angelico, Fra Filippo Lippi and Piero della Francesca – an Annunciation, a Madonna and Child, and a Crucifixion – the relics of a bygone Renaissance.

The gift

Katy, surrounded by her friends, told them the story of Neuman Nessos and his death at the hand of Boris Gudenov. She sent Hyllus to fetch the gown, and she exhibited it. She held it against the light to show the bloodstains that like memories had become more firmly fixed with the years and had taken on fresh nuances. It was the will of Providence, it was Tyche, stronger than all of us, it was the inevitable that destroyed everything and changed our whole future. She told it movingly and wept with her friends who were also victims in their own lives of the unfathomable.

They wept over the gown, touching the material and their own memories. Tragedy lay hidden in something like a gown, a handkerchief, or an almost perished garment. Somewhere in a drawer or a wardrobe there lay, or was hanging, a memento of a moment that the wailing women recalled with misty eyes. They romanticized while they felt the gown with long fingers; and they wept a little as they compared the inurement of their advancing years with the unrecognizable wonderful soft world in the distant past, protected by the hymen.

They hastened to give their hostess advice. She must be protected: against the weakness of a man who was ageing and losing his contact with reality; against the impersonal world of contemplation; against someone who had forgotten what the true desires of a woman were. They burdened her with suggestions, until Katy herself, with sudden insight, thought of the significant gesture. She would send the gown to Boris Gudenov. It would be a gesture of forgiveness; it would be his last chance to rehabilitate himself for his own sake.

The idea was greeted with great enthusiasm. But the gown must be sent without stains; it must be a new beginning, an opportunity for transformation, a new garment for metamorphosis, a significant transfiguration where everything out of the past must contribute to the transformation. A serving maid was summoned, sent away, and she returned with a highly volatile but extremely effective stain remover. The women all gathered around Katy and helped her with the symbolic task until the mantle shone like new, and the stains had vanished forever in the evaporation of the fumes. Then Hyllus was called to hand it over to his father with a message from his mother. No! Without the message, because if Boris Gudenov could not himself understand, if he could not himself see the significance, the message would be meaningless.

They gave young Hyllus charge of the mantle and sent him to search for his father in one of the rooms of Oita, where he was most probably busy working with his typist.

'But remember to knock first,' said Katy while her friends gasped.

For the first time the chorus was silent before the courage of their hostess. And then, after the silence, their voices soft and appreciative laved her with their profound homage.

Presentation

Young Hyllus had no need to look for his father, because he knew exactly where the strange, fascinating game had taken place. He opened the door without knocking, and looked at the girl lying on the Eastern rug in a small bundle under a large painting, as though utterly spent. He approached cautiously, and then seemed to sense the presence of other children in the room. He looked around but saw nothing. He looked again at the soft woman at his feet. He bent down and touched her. Her skin was damp, her eyes closed.

He put the mantle to one side on the floor, and went and lay next to her. He curled up against her, his young body against hers, and he felt how her arms folded around him while her eyes were still shut. He stayed like that, as he had seen his father, the old man, do, and fell asleep.

When he awoke, he picked up the parcel and sauntered out of the room, down the passage until he reached the sanctum of his father, Boris Gudenov – the glass room that now looked totally different. He found his father illuminated by seven candles burning on his desk and surrounded by all his books. He handed over the mantle and stood back a little to observe the reactions and to get further information to carry to his mother.

Boris Gudenov looked at his son with unseeing eyes. He held the gown in his hand and looked at it equally blindly. Then he smiled suddenly and gave Hyllus a fleeting kiss on his forehead. A moment later he thought about it, and put the mantle on. He waited until Hyllus had left the room and shut the glass door, which locked automatically, behind him. He sat down again.

He gave a final wave to his son – such a typical product of his mother. He leaned with his elbow on the desk and inspected his young offspring, then promptly forgot him as he moved his arm three inches from the open flame.

He thought of all the years past, and saw himself as a young boy in the market-place of that distant village he had never seen since, and which through the years had grown in his imagination into a place that did not exist. At which stage did the market, the pedlars, the old men with their long beards and the candlelit evenings disappear? He remembered, too, that early time when he was young and strong, and slept in the haystacks with the gay young girls. They could count as many stars as they liked, for the urge of the young lion in him was endless. What was it that filled one with higher ambition? At exactly what stage did he perceive his strange capabilities? Why had he sacrificed everything for all those tasks that had elevated him above other people?

He looked at the seven candles burning softly, and smelled the volatile vapours rising from the ridiculous cloak. It no longer mattered to him if, to some people, he was the hound, the symbol of evil; or if he was the genius who represented the spirit of the age, and who satisfied all their needs by means of his shopping centre. He felt a nostalgia for the past, yet did not want it back. He felt sick and tired and finished. He was Boris Gudenov, and he was the shell that had to produce the pearl.

Life thrummed through him. Each minute he felt more strongly the demoniacal powers that could waft him away in their flight, although he knew that ecstasy was of as short a duration as intoxication and moments of inspiration. The little human desire that was left could no longer be accepted as such, because it had to become part of the great current; it had to be woven into something that fitted into the inescapable pattern, the sound of the piccolo in the great orchestra.

The candles flared as they had done in the room of his childhood: with crooked and unpredictable flames.

Perhaps your whole life is one great participation. Just like Bee-Bee-Doo who also slept with young men in haystacks – a small-town slut plucked by the greater powers out of her little place and shaped, like you yourself, to fit into the still-fluid pattern that was being formed out of the dark, unrecognizable past.

He longed to have the simplicity of his enemy, Demosthenes de Goede, who would eventually also go to his ruin against the higher powers; he hated his own perceptiveness that made everything insipid and robbed him of his conceit and pride.

He longed for a state of madness when he would be helpless in the grip of primitive forces; he preferred even the fear of darkness; he wished that he could become the victim of that ominous something that was following him, that was always next to him.

He thought of Iole, and his thoughts shuttled back and forth, and nothing seemed to make sense any longer. In spite of what had happened, Iole was all at once the unfathomable silence, the globe, the mist, the still white moon, the golden eyes, the sweet fragrance of holiness, the fire and the passion, something that flamed, and everything in contrast, and she came like the moon across the plains and over the mountains and trees, and through the silver light between the eastern hills . . .

She came, Iole, for a moment only, at the cross-roads. And it did not matter any longer whether he had lost or won. He thought with longing of all those things that formed a hopeless part of his desires and suddenly saw the sleeve of his cloak catch fire, set alight by the seven white candles of his almost forgotten past.

Chapter Six

The Black Wolf

Lupus Niger – putrifactio, mortificatio, separatio & furens

Captain Demosthenes de Goede heard the bells of the orchestra as the Kallman Choir was singing 'Peter Gunn'. A blonde, a brunette, a redhead and a woman with chestnut hair found words to fit the strange music that accompanied the procession. They came through the hall, the bearers, who with a swaying movement, continually changed the picture before the eyes filled with the fear of death. There was a scent of *Onyx* around the bier; there was a silk tie hiding the face. No one moved in the hall; the counters formed one solid image after the other before the frightened eyes. Above them was the golden dome, flaming like the sun; with each swaying movement the rococo decorations loomed up from the walls. It was an exodus in time to music, which was irresistible to the dedicated ducktail. With Minie next to him, he immediately found the dance step that would make procession acceptable to the watching teen-agers as well.

The stark eyes saw one picture after another: the counters scintillating with goods; a hundred hostile eyes, fixed on him; dancing teen-agers with churning bodies crossing and recrossing his field of vision; papier-mâché dolls on the walls; stairs spiralling up to the dome; a circle of faces anxiously watching for his death; and straight in front of him the reflection in a glass of the rope on which he had hung. It was the last exodus of the dying thief as the procession went past Captain Demosthenes de Goede. He had managed to steal his life as well, right in front of the eyes of the law. The bottle of *Onyx* cologne fell out of his hands and drenched his clothes; the tie was pulled over his face to cover the staring eyes; the odour of sanctity rose up against the death-mask of Bee-Bee-Doo, enlarged a hundred times, above the exit through which the procession disappeared.

The voice of the little man in white came through the hall; he was reading aloud from a letter that Bee-Bee-Doo had written before her death to Molly Muggeridge, the chatterbox: 'Do you remember me? I am Bee-Bee-Doo . . .'

He pointed his stick at the giant-size photo of Bee-Bee-Doo laid out in her copper coffin in the Chamber of Remembrance, dressed in white like a moon goddess, her limbs soft and round, as massaged by Haven and Heller. Her eyes were closed; she seemed to be lying in a copper bath, the paint still wet on her face, her skin damp with all the lotions; the sunlight seemed to have been caught at the window and swallowed up in the structure of death.

The little man put his stick down and resumed his speech. 'She drank from the cup of fornication,' he said. He looked at all those who had gathered around him and struggled to get his message across to them. He rubbed his moustache and swallowed some lukewarm tea. Angrily he turned on the crowd.

'She had to mill around in filth because we were sick. She had to watch her own downfall . . .' He could scarcely find words. He looked straight at Captain Demosthenes de Goede.

'The struggle of every one of us is revealed in the sickness of the queen. She died like a moon bitch. You had to break her to get at the precious contents.'

He pointed to the Gudenov dome.

'The Queen is dead, long live the King !' he jeered.

He spat contemptuously in the direction of everyone, while his anger flared up, and it took a couple of people to subdue him. There were a few chaotic moments until the little man suddenly calmed down and turned his back on them all. Then he fought loose and picked up his stick. He smoothed the creases from his uniform and moved to the next portrait.

'Out of the chaos, darkness and weakness, comes a new light,' he said, looking up, and his eyes softened with love for the invisible Bee-Bee-Doo covered with flowers in her copper coffin. 'There is a certain Power, and an unfathomable Silence. It comes from above and from below, and in the meeting lies our salvation . . .'

Captain Demosthenes de Goede moved blindly through the shopping centre with the dedicated ducktail and Minie at his side and the herd of adoring girls at his heels. The anger that was piling up in him at everything that was invisible and obscure was evident from the mighty muscles bulging inside his shirt-sleeves, and the veins swelling on his forehead. He looked like Michelangelo's 'Moses', and his eyes, like the eyes of the statue, were hewn from marble.

They moved lower and lower down the shopping centre to where the lights were dimmer and the atmosphere stranger. He forced his way through the increasing crowds who blocked his path in the search that became more and more hopeless. Now and then the ducktail twanged his guitar and accompanied their strides with the hit beat of the moment; under her teen-age hairdo, Minie's eyes were vacant, with the vacancy of one who understood the secrets of the times. He thought about his mighty past and all the tasks he had performed in the police force, while the dedicated ducktail plucked his base strings to the tune of 'Peter Gunn': wit against wit, might against might, order against chaos, where the final outcome was visible in clear relief. He longed for the majestic path of suffering in his past; he longed for shining steel that could draw warm blood; for the simplicity of torturing effort; and for the sharp dividing line of danger, where the choice between dying a noble death and living a noble life was the only option. For one moment the Captain wanted to give in to despair and the catatonic state of vacillation, but at the last moment the surge of purifying anger rose in him, and he resumed his search with renewed energy for the mysterious confusion that was Gudenov.

They found the little man in white, exhausted, in the last stages of his job to which he had given a meaning. He was brewing tea in a little copper dish, abandoned and alone under a huge photograph of Bee-Bee-Doo's grave with its single flower-bedecked stone covering her in the artists' plot, while her body melted away in a bath of posthumous corruption. They looked at him concentrating silently above the flame: a small alchemist filled with the spirit of the anthropos; a little man in the uniform of the shopping centre who had, with his own eyes, seen putrefaction and mortification, who was filled with the melancholy of the one who understood, who had become part of the drama of death and suffering, and who waited in vain for rebirth.

He looked up at the Captain, at the mighty Demosthenes de Goede who now stood in front of him, and in the chaos still remained an impotent part of the chaos. He looked longingly up at the Captain. He wanted to see in him someone who understood, like the sun who drove away the darkness, like the setting sun who united with his moon-goddess so that after their mutual death, he could appear again, bright and strong on the horizon with the promise of glorious, rapturous life.

He bent despondently over his brew as the dedicated ducktail's laugh rang through the room and raised a faint echo from the clown in the distance. It was the triumph of the hound, the black wolf. There was no fructification.

The flame burnt under the pot, throwing raven shadows on his face, and reached a fierce heat that threatened any minute to blow everything up. The little man patiently attended to his job, for he was old and had learned the patience of age. He believed that with each repetition something new was created: there were no two souls alike, no two creatures, two plants, two experiences, two misfortunes. One day – one day the sign would appear: crystals like stars on the surface, a mauve light that would glow fluorescently in the dark, a purity that would drive away the darkness and would bathe the whole world in radiance, as an elixir of life, like the sun.

He did not look at the Captain again. There was always tomorrow. Tomorrow he would explain the image of Bee-Bee-Doo all over again, as he did every day of every month of every year – and he would recount the story with devotion and conviction and honesty and candour, even though the result would be disillusionment and loneliness. For he believed in his wares – in Bee-Bee-Doo who had become his own. He believed in the same way that his forefathers had believed in their religion. He would hold the matrix up before them all until fruition took place – perhaps with one of the teen-agers, perhaps with someone who was free from the overpowering conceit. And then ... His face beamed in the light of the flame.

But meanwhile, he must live. He brewed his tea and added something that he had bought from one of the druggists of the shopping centre. He beckoned to the teen-agers lurking in the shadows, and offered them each a sip, right in front of the Captain, who would have arrested the lot if he had understood. They came with their cups in an excited group and received the tea spiced with Purple Heart which they hoped would spur the pale-eyed girls on to love. They each paid him one rand per cup until the copper pot was empty, and then the little man packed up his belongings in his trunk, took off his white coat, put his glasses in his inner pocket, tucked his trousers into his socks and walked with his thermos flask and his baggage to the basement to find his bicycle which would take him to the hole in the city where little men with little jobs made their home.

The numbers in the basement of the shopping centre seemed to be increasing. The Captain, moving from hall to hall, thought that the whole world, as he knew it, seemed to be meeting here. An intense feeling of melancholy came over the man of action. He had to pronounce judgement on himself, because he was himself part of secular humanity. The hound was an apparition in a nightmare; it lived in the supernatural. (He listened to Bee-Bee-Doo's song which pursued him and roused evasive memories.) But in spite of the invisible, half-familiar ideas that haunted him, there were only the tangible, existential things that repeatedly confronted him. He was overcome by a feeling of ineffable sadness, the by-product of an undefined sin, and there was no solution to be found in the rational, humanistic ideas of the shopping centre. He began to have doubts about everything he had achieved in the past, while he wandered around aimlessly; he began to doubt his own powers, and worst of all, the mystery of the enigmatical, unknown power that had always enabled him to rise above the usual and achieve the unusual. He felt like an athlete who had lost his sense of timing, like a champion whose throne had begun to totter, and who could not understand what was going on.

Something was dead. Something had died at some stage or other, and there was nothing left. Captain Demosthenes de Goede had his roots in a heroic tradition; he could fight against mythological monsters; his enemy was discernible against a Gothic background. But in Boris Gudenov's shopping centre, as dangerous and as powerful as any primordial spectre, he was as impotent as the victims of Medusa.

Something within you is being destroyed; you look at the dangerous object, and you become part of the apostasy that turns you to stone by means of an inescapable, autogenous logic.

If he could only find the hound, the black wolf! He looked around him and saw all the bizarre phenomena which masked the demoniac, but everything was immediately traced back to the humanitarian ethics of the situation, which explained away and justified anything. A feeling of dread took possession of him; he looked all around and became conscious of a Hell that consisted only of alienation, an inability to compromise with the clearly perceptible, with yourself and with those nearest you. And the hound was somewhere, hidden in the commonplace – safer and more inaccessible than in any other hiding place.

The nomination campaign was over, but the bitterness remained; the successful candidates of the trade union bowed their way through the shopping centre. Their faces glowed like lighted beacons; they listened happily to grievances and carefully toned down their promises. They disappeared into corners where urgent conversations were held and a new hierarchy came into being. Rogues and scoundrels also came into their own in the democratic acquiescence.

There were numerous conference rooms in the shopping centre where politicians, businessmen, technologists and officials held their conferences. Bills and regulations were drawn up while individual rights died easily. There were pharmacies everywhere where procreation could be prevented, remorse stilled and temporary rejuvenation be bought. Somewhere a great clock struck the passing quarter hours. Girls in mini-dresses were doomed to walk forever because they found it impossible to sit. There were tables full of beads and violently coloured garments in a boutique where young men with hair hanging on their shoulders dreamed up far-fetched ensembles for the women. In one of the halls, in a purple light, a girl on a stage was doing a strip-tease in front of the invisible eyes of the men in the dark. Her garments were strewn all around, you could count her ribs, her feminine secrets were exposed to a roll of drums, and she looked small and confused in the anticlimax of revelation without mystery. In a room next door there was a meeting of right-wingers who thought of all possible precautions to counteract degeneration from the left and, dressed like crows in conservative black, tried to establish, by means of censorship, the dividing line between what was permissible and what was not. There were advertisements on the walls, gambling halls, op art and pop art, roulette tables, showrooms for cars that hit the ton, artificial flowers, field glasses, photometers, antiques, pottery, wigs, cigarette holders, ballpoint pens, fruit, vegetables, cheese, buttons, artificial nails, pets, tours, flags, herbs, copper goods, racquets, golf clubs, knives, guns, toys, purgatives, antacid tablets, beer, wine, brandy, books, brooches, diamonds, pearls, batik work, curling pins, crash helmets, windscreen wipers, ball bearings, sculpture, paint, wallpaper, ear-rings, newspapers, flowers, ferns, must, Christmas trees, men's suits, ties, riding breeches, garden chairs, umbrellas, tents, underpants, pliers, scissors, taps, bidets, soap, barometers, theatre tickets, writing paper, bush shirts, grey geraniums, red wild chestnut, Jerusalem flowers, mountain lilies, sinks, refrigerators, ammonia, flypaper, sandpaper, sugar, silk stockings and siphunculata under glass.

Captain Demosthenes de Goede, a mighty athlete, surrounded by the flock of girls, accompanied by the dedicated ducktail and Minie, walked slowly through everything that Boris Gudenov offered humanity. Years ago he had tracked down the Swine of Dysselsdorp, and his wanderings had taken him through the drab hills of the Little Karroo, in the scorching heat, between succulents, past the one-man school with the turrets, next to the aloes and prickly pears and the yellow bush with a snake in its branches, through fields of oxalis, clover and cock ostriches, the sky blue above the Lombardy poplars, and under the yellow flowers of the thorn trees and the snow teeth of their thorns, by water furrows and stinging nettles, finch nests, crassulae, euphorbias and succulents, back to De Rust and Meirings Poort, past the church and the garage, up to the old watermill where the Swine, exhausted and hungry, cornered in the kloof in the shadow of the mountain, with grimacing mouth and as tough as a badger, came to his end; but lived on in a Little Karroo legend, related in the feeble flickering of candles and the moth-filled light of Miller lamps.

But the black hound was invisible under the scalloped cornice and in the gallop of the ducktail's guitar.

Boris Gudenov was everywhere, but he was like a great mountain that was too massive to be seen; he loomed over the shopping centre, he was the shopping centre, he was the sick body in which the viruses reigned supreme. Captain Demosthenes de Goede stood towering in the centre of things and watched it all. The Gudenov current could not be held back. He closed his eyes and listened to the noise, the atonality that never ceased, the strepitoso of the Gudenov orchestra. He opened his eyes and saw the swarming, milling, whirling top of people. He saw Gudenov goods on the counters stretching into infinity. He felt the chaos that was continuously kept in motion of some enormous source of energy in which he himself, with his simplicity of heart and thought, became a part of the discarded past. He listened to Bee-Bee-Doo's song which plucked at his heart-strings and became part of the bickering that mocked ritual. He felt the enormous pull of the Gudenov power that was trying to draw him into the stream, the iron grip of the invisible hand. He felt the anxiety and the fear that came from nowhere, that was vested in no single object, that had no form, image or dimension. Something was robbing him of his senses and he did not know what it was. He looked at the marriage of two idiots taking place in front of him, and he heard the clown laughing.

In Boris Gudenov's shopping centre there was a branch of the civic administration that permitted authorized officials to solemnize marriages. In one of the rooms set apart for this special purpose, a magistrate was considering an application to marry, made by two idiots. Both applicants were in possession of a birth certificate; neither was impotent; neither was certified as abnormal by a medical practitioner. But . . .

Her eyes crossed; her shoulders faced each other; she had nipples but no breasts; she had a mentality hardly above that of an animal; her sex organs functioned with an efficacy that would have roused the jealousy of a sex queen. She was incredibly ugly; she walked in fits and starts; she jerked like an old Ford car; her wasted body was draped in a floral dress; her deformed hands were accoutred to the elbow with snow-white gloves on which she had spent her entire dowry; her crooked mouth drooled with unearthly happiness; her fossilized teeth showed in a wide death's head grin.

Her husband, an idiot with a perfect body, testified his moronic benevolence towards the whole world and his bride by a smile that was never switched off. They only touched on the fringe of reality; they were demanding what was proper, decent and respectable. She looked like a witch; he looked like Apollo; and their marriage was solemnized in front of hundreds of people from the shopping centre.

Everyone laughed at and cried over the grotesque couple. The teen-agers hummed Bee-Bee-Doo's song softly and swung the rhythm lightly as they watched yet another spectacle from the 'gone' world.

When they had to sign the forms and register, neither could do so.

'The . . . papers . . . are . . . important,' she said to him, and he smiled in reply.

The magistrate told them to go to a small table where they had to make a mark: an involuntary sign, a *teth* or *tav* as determined by the Unseen Elect. The laughing idiot put his hand over hers, and with spasmodic movements they pushed the pen over the paper until a mark appeared – born from the depths of their combined psyches – an ancient sign that predicted life or death for the two of them.

This travesty was too much for the Captain. Something broke inside him, and he was prepared to hit everyone and everything to pieces; he would fight the whole shopping centre indiscriminately, without regard to persons, and in the total destruction would also destroy the invisible hound.

Then the dedicated ducktail spoke up.

'God is dead,' he said. 'It's man who counts. There is no right or wrong except in relation to context.' The ducktail twanged the guitar as though he could hear the truth in the instrument. 'The question is whether those two love each other. You must reserve your judgement until you have the picture.'

The Captain turned on the ducktail. He saw the two in front of him: Minie hanging on to her dedicated companion who was all the time improvising on his instrument like a calypso singer.

The Captain's broad hands suddenly shot out and grabbed the young man; he shook him backward and forward so that the guitar skidded away on the floor. There was something in violence that brought a momentary certainty – even if he had to answer to Brigadier Ornassis E. later on. He lifted the dedicated ducktail with one hand and shook him like a dog; he shoved him under his left arm and with his right hand stuffed his mouth with tinsel lying about everywhere on the tables. He throttled him until Minie pulled his arm, and he walked with him through the hall to the outside door. The daylight made the ducktail blink. At first he attempted to struggle, but he was completely vanquished. Then he began to plead and tried to bring the Captain to his senses, until the latter suddenly let him go, turned his back on him, and with dangerous calm surveyed the whole scene in the shopping centre.

Demosthenes de Goede began to move slowly through the hall, shattering a fashion dummy or an ornament at every step with a mighty sweep of the hand. The women screamed and the men tried to protect them, but gave way before the demented eyes of the tall figure. Captain Demosthenes de Goede was fighting against the entire shopping centre. He was in the grip of a power that had mastered his ego. He was fighting against things that he could not see and could not understand, but he fought. By doing so he was attempting to give a shape to all those invisible things. As he sowed havoc, he saw the red, the yellow and black faces of Satan. He smashed the faces. The pretty girl in front of him was the daughter of Cenchreis, who made a travesty of love while her mother was on a pilgrimage – and he hit her out of his field of vision. He was halted by three giant figures, huge clumsy wrestlers, who were private detectives and had to keep order in the shopping centre. Captain Demosthenes de Goede tackled them. He hit out with his fist at their primitive faces, at their grinning stupidity, brainlessness and primitiveness, reliving his fight with Adam Kadmon Silberstein – and then he was rid of them. He fought against twisters, deceivers, traitors and all who were strained with the sickness of the times, and the floor began to look like a battlefield. His fists were blood-stained, and he found relief in the chaos that he had created. He looked at the scene of wretchedness, and slowly turned back to the door where the dedicated ducktail was being revived by Minie, but he took no notice of them. He left the shopping centre and, looking at the sunlit activities in the street, he saw a silver-grey Rolls-Royce slowly moving along a side street.

Suddenly light dawned. There was the man who looked like him! The hound was someone like himself. His bewildered mind saw logic in it : his estranged thinking now recognized the figure that he could not find. He ran up the street before he realized the futility of his action. He suddenly became calm, and his mind now worked with a cunning that lent purpose to his conduct. He got into a car and connected the wires under the dashboard. He started the motor and followed the Rolls-Royce which was disappearing around a bend in the distance. His police training now stood him in good stead. He kept the right distance, not too close, not too far behind. He could see the driver's cap, and also the figure of a woman in the back seat. He now had Boris Gudenov and one of his trollops in his field of vision. He could feel his anger piling up as he thought of all the scorn and mockery he had had to endure while his enemy was all the time watching him like an insect. The moment of revenge had come. Captain

Demosthenes de Goede was ready to stake his whole future. There was one price that no one would pay for life. There were moments in one's life when you had to think for yourself and accept the results of your actions. It would not be a blind onslaught as it had been a while back; he now had the enemy in his sight. It would be his offering to mankind.

As he followed the Rolls-Royce out of the town along the marine drive, past the fishing harbour, beneath the slopes of the mountain where the forest had burned away so that only black stumps showed through the grass and heather, he thought of his wife and children and experienced anew that feeling of anxiety and sadness that he had had at the beginning – a feeling that they were forever beyond his reach. As the two cars approached the Chapman's Peak bend, high above the blue ocean, he realized in his present state of megalomania that that would be one of the sacrifices he would have to make in this task – his greatest, the destruction of Boris Gudenov and all those invisible forces that were ravaging the world. There was a moment of truth as he brought the car up to the Rolls-Royce which, reflecting the sun, was turning the corner at the highest point of the precipice, sheer above the sea. Then at the precise, calculated moment he shot forward and hit the other car. He did not even look around when he heard the screaming of the tyres; he drove on slowly while the little side wall broke, and the screams rose above the glorious scenery. He was not positive, but he thought he could even hear the crash in the ocean below, the dull noise of the blue water which, as always, was ready to receive the refuse from the land.

He drove on slowly to the first beach. Some time later, he returned to the scene, where sensation-seekers had already collected for the enjoyment of experiencing the violent death of someone else. The police had halted the traffic; there, where the crowd was at its densest, the bodies were lying in wait for the ambulance which could be heard approaching in the distance, its siren echoing off the slopes of the mountain. Captain Demosthenes de Goede, in perfect control of himself, stood watching the scene. He moved in among the people, but kept putting off the moment when he would have to look at his defeated enemy. He heard the women chattering.

'There is nothing left of the car. They had to pull them up with ropes. It was the most terrible sight I have ever seen. I'll never sleep tonight.'

An old woman standing next to Demosthenes de Goede took him for someone who had just arrived on the scene.

'She was still alive,' she told him. 'Even the last moment before she died, she was thinking of her husband. She called his name over and over.' The old woman imitated her in a falsetto voice. 'She called "Boris! Boris! Boris!"' She pulled at Demosthenes de Goede's shirt-sleeve. 'Isn't it terrible?'

The Captain decided to go nearer. From years in the police service, he had become hardened to inescapable human suffering. There was no sense in waiting any longer: he would look at his enemy, and then report back to Brigadier Ornassis E. He pushed his way through the sensation-seekers, and forged his way right up to where the remains were lying.

He first saw the chauffeur's cap, and then the man himself. Then he looked at the woman and the four children, and at first he did not seem to understand. He looked for fully a minute before it penetrated, and then he gave a scream that was drowned by the sirens of the ambulance appearing around the corner. But when the sirens stopped, there was no sound from the Captain. His mouth remained open, and his vocal chords were tensed together, but there was complete silence. The bystanders gaped at him curiously and nudged each other, while someone giggled nervously in the sudden hush.

Two men came and took the Captain by his arms. To their surprise, the two members of the action front had no trouble in bringing the huge Captain to their car. They sat on either side of him, and only kept their hands on his arms to prevent him from doing something rash.

Retraite

Brigadier Ornassis E., surrounded by his silent young men of the personnel group and the action front, sat listening to the stuttering Captain who stood before him. They found difficulty in understanding the words, but after a while they got used to it and were able to put some meaning to them.

Captain Demosthenes de Goede was reciting all the tasks that he had achieved, one after the other. They all listened attentively to the account given in ragged words.

'The Lesbian Poisoner of Calvinia,' came with difficulty.

'The Swine of Dysselsdorp ...'

'The Serpent of Muldersvlei ...'

'The Blackmailer of Arcadia ...'

'The Sweetheart of Kammaland ...'

'The Lion of the North ...'

'The Bull of Benoni ...'

'The Whores of Humansdorp ...'

Then the Captain stopped suddenly. He seemed to be struggling with his memory, and his tongue seemed to be entangled when it came to the next sentence. The Brigadier leaned forward to hear better. After a moment's struggle, the words came. 'The Hound of ...' but he could not find the next word. 'Shopping centre' lay quite beyond the capabilities of his stammering tongue.

There was no stopping the Captain; he kept on talking, although most of the sentences was quite unintelligible. He was trying to give an account of his life in the service of humanity; he told it calmly, and his narrative seemed to have no end.

The Brigadier turned to one of the young men of the personnel department, and said that he was worried about the Captain's unnatural calm. It was an extremely dangerous symptom pointing to an explosive condition. He interrupted the Captain's report, and the latter listened very submissively. He confirmed all the tasks the Captain had performed; on behalf of everyone, he expressed his thanks for his unselfish service and the sacrifices that had been necessary. He became more and more eloquent as he gained control of the situation. 'We must remember that disintegration is not the fault of the individual, but the fate over which we have no control.'

He smoothed his hair with his hand, and nodded to his young men to relax.

'After a full life,' said the Brigadier, leaning forward sympathetically and looking the Captain straight in the eye, 'after a full life everyone comes to the cross-roads, where he has to decide what to do with the rest of his life. Should he find release from the moment of tragedy (everyone's lot at some time or other) in self-destruction, or should he look for reassurance in life which is often incomprehensible but which always remains a task and a challenge?' Brigadier Ornassis E. seemed to have a sudden brainwave, and he looked quickly at his young men of the personnel group to see if they were ready to grasp this special refinement:

'Must not one accept torment as perhaps the greatest of all tasks? Is there not perhaps a thirteenth task, not on the record, that everyone ventures upon alone, this time for his own sake? Does true greatness perhaps not lie in the victory about which no one hears? Is the acceptance of life as it is, even if it is without the help and understanding of the supernatural, not a triumph in itself?'

The Brigadier had now even forgotten the Captain.

'Is the patient acceptance of bare existence such as belongs to the least of humans, not perhaps the greatest victory? Is it a crime against yourself to become part of the times and to be content with the shoddy existence of humanity?'

The men of the personnel department looked up strangely at the Brigadier who, as so often in the past, was in a mysterious way going over to the enemy. But they knew from bitter experience that the Brigadier always knew best.

'We shall find our salvation in joining our love with the mere fact of our existence,' said the Brigadier. 'Boris Gudenov is not our enemy. It was just a cunning game of the invisible enemy which the Captain revealed to us.'

At once he became short and businesslike.

'There has been a change of policy. It must be accepted as such. Traditional images must be destroyed. The Service must be modernized. There is a radically new approach supported by the best brains. The image of Boris Gudenov must be reconstructed. That is an order to the personnel department; it is the duty of the action front to execute it.'

And now he turned again to the Captain.

'I think the Captain has the courage to choose life rather than release through death. The D-Service has the honour, Captain, to invite you to spend the rest of your days in the Welgevonden Foundation. Thanks to the vision of Jock Silberstein, a progressive Jew, you will be able to find peace and quiet on the property that he has put at the disposal of the community.'

Captain Demosthenes H. de Goede was driven in a brand-new Cadillac, belonging to the D-Service, to the Welgevonden Institute where a cottage was prepared for his special use. This was where he had met Hope, where he had performed his first task, where Mrs Dreyer would predict peace for the rest of his life.

He was perfectly happy when he saw the familiar scenes. The glass house flashed an exuberant welcome in the sun. It was here that he had overcome the Giant, Adam Kadmon Silberstein, and destroyed the last traces of primordial phenomena.

For the rest of his life he would enjoy the ephemeral design and be free of the curse of suffering, love, grief and creation.

Chapter Seven

The Third Eye

Burn, tycoon, burn!

When Katy and her friends heard the screams, they ran to the room, but their way was blocked by the plate glass door that was locked on the inside. Through the glass they saw the terrible suffering of the great man who totally ignored the observers – the crowds who banged the glass in vain and milled around helplessly. The hostess and her companions, rejuvenated by synthetic estrogen, their love-life infinitely prolonged, looked at this form of suffering in bewilderment and incomprehension. He was not someone like them; there had always been something like the glass between them; his attention had always been focused on himself alone; he had never really been part of the community; there had always been that contradiction in his make-up; he had his own places of refuge; he was a sort of aristocrat; snobbish, actually; he understood women in a way that was completely unacceptable to them.

Katy's friends led her away to spare her further suffering. They took her to her room while she deplored her own part in the disaster that had befallen their house. They comforted her by referring to her own blameless life, an example of self-sacrifice and good intentions. Could she help it if she could not foresee the results of her innocent gesture?

While she wept on one shoulder after another and, with a slight movement, let her hair fall loose on her shoulders, while her face contorted with a grief that immediately commands attention from all women and help from all men, while she leaned fragilely on her companion's shoulder, she asked them to keep the gesture secret, for the whole world would read guilt into the innocence of her deed. Silence would protect her, silence would expunge the shame.

They could no longer look at such suffering. They comforted her on the way to her room, where she sank down on the bed with a sob of sorrow. Nothing had any meaning for her now: her marriage bed that would always be empty; her house; the mockery of wealth that could no longer offer any comfort. What was left to her except death, because was she not really dead?

They hastened to make her abandon that idea.

She lay pale on the bed; a small womanly figure, tortured beyond the limits of human endurance.

They watched over her the whole night. Over their fragile, vulnerable – no, wounded friend.

They pointed out that a new life lay ahead of her, in which she would have to play the role of the man; in which she would be able to serve the community by means of the infinite variety of this source of power.

They talked to her until she ceased weeping; in her hour of sorrow they showed her things that she had not understood in the past; by a kind of dialectic process they managed in her suffering to break up those personifications that had so confused her in the past; they created a bridge; by means of the shock of what had happened, they made her become aware of the psychic processes as they understood them; they made her see the light in the glow of the burning tycoon.

The left eye

Iole also heard the cry from where she was lying under the art treasures, a sacrificial victim, destroyed and bleeding. Something was struggling with itself: a feeling that everything was in a state of reconstruction; that in destruction there was also victory. She herself was the refractor. She had received the original light, which was fading, and she had doused it in her feminine fluid. She had damped down the scorching heat with her moisture. She had enabled her invisible lover to die. While she listened to the cries in the distance, she was already beginning to feel the satisfying regeneration after weakness and impotence. It felt as though she, a young woman, with infinite wisdom became aware of a deeper significance within herself, a greater truth; You are I; I am you; on earth and in heaven; for all time – I on your left hand, you on my right – and we float through the night and the stars to meet the day – and the two halves become one – and the sun suddenly shines brightly over this barren landscape with rays that are blinding to the eyes – and there are flowers growing in the wilderness, and the whole desert is alive with colours that stretch over the plains like an Arabian carpet, right up to the slopes of the Swartberg – and we raise a song of praise to the All-Knowing Forefather – and something new is born in us that is both man and woman, enfolding everything doublefold – and suddenly the clown has stopped laughing, for sorrow is truth, and the whole world is singing the song . . .

of which Bee-Bee-Doo's song was only a tormenting intimation, and whose refrain was unconsciously repeated in the teen-agers' noise that had the dissonance of an unformed sigh

and it lived in the computer that calculated the song and could not destroy the truth even in its monstrous product – for in the banality of the present lay the mutilated truth of the past

and tragedy is relieved of the tragic by the certainty of rebirth – and Iole listened in the triumph of her one and only love to the cries of her invisible lover who was finding release in the burning flame above Oita.

There was something that burned more fiercely that the fiery garment; there was something that caused more pain than scorched flesh; there was a greater agony than self-chastisement. It was the numinosity of the images that came from deep and far. He could forgive those figures behind the glass; their guilt or innocence was no longer important. Even the irony of their vengeance faded before the deeper vision. He thought of everything he had achieved and all the tasks he had performed which were beyond the ordinary man. But he eschewed reproach and natural self-pity, which at that moment lost their hold on him. Even in the agonizing pain he could discern the protection of a deeper insensitivity. Something greater than human reactions spoke within him; a greater knowledge intensified his isolation. The struggling body, the screams and the signs of external torment were not a true reflection of the calm within. He saw his ghastly reflection in the mirror, but something raised him above the earthly and the material. The flame flickered and he was free no longer, an exalted loneliness came over him, everything became impersonal, and something spoke within him.

He saw the menorah on the prayer standard, he saw the four pillars of the holy ark and the wise old men reading from the sacred books. Whatever it was that had blocked the memories of the far past had disappeared in the flames. He was aware of his soul; he felt the presence of the *Shekinah*. There was a gold chain binding him to his far endless past. The mantle of the Baal-Shem, who could understand the Wise Name, gave meaning to the flames that were burning it; the seven candles, that had set it alight, united him with Hermes Trismegistus in the consuming flame. And he saw his mother, her embroidered shawl about her shoulders, who had wept that Sabbath evening when she had lit the candles and could see an image of the future in the far away *schtetl*.

Boris Gudenov burned in the form of a cross, with his arms outstretched on either side. He burned in front of young Hyllus who peered from behind the glass door, and in all the spectacles of the evening had seen things that would haunt him for the rest of his life, although there would be nothing in his education to help him to give them meaning.

Meanwhile his father, the tycoon, burned behind the glass until there was nothing recognizable left. And the millions and all the dreadful responsibilities connected with them became the heritage of himself and his beloved mother who would use the wealth for worthy causes, social services and art exhibitions, and everything that was looked upon with favour by the state, the community and the world of science.

The Brigadier's eyes

Brigadier Ornassis E. sat on the topmost floor of the Oita shopping centre and meditated, surrounded by his young men of the D-Service, while he listened to a built-in automatic organ playing

'The End of a Perfect Day'. The girls had already filled the glasses, and they all waited for the Brigadier to propose the toast as soon as he had completed his reverie. The room was filled, not only with the staff of the Service, but also with many teen-agers, officials from the shopping centre, clients and relatives of the tycoon. As soon as the last notes died away, with tremolo effects, the Brigadier stood up. He closed a book of new verse by the great poet and put it down on the table next to him. 'The gods are great and lonely in the night, and hang like yellow fruit on the trees,' he quoted softly to his young men of the personnel service who formed a tight phalanx around him. He let his hands rest on two broad shoulders, and bowed his head.

'But I peer down in the small shaft of this sunlight . . .'

He was dressed in the black clothes of a business executive, his tie was silver grey with a cultured pearl pin. He surveyed his audience thoughtfully, then raised his eyes to a chandelier with thousands of crystals that glittered in the light.

'Tonight,' he said, 'I am paying tribute to Boris Gudenov, beloved ex-enemy, unhonoured prophet, salt of the earth.' He waited until the applause died down, then took a sip from the glass in his hand. 'But, my friends, I want you to see him, not as he was at the end, dying in weakness and estrangement, but as the man he was.' He looked at Katy, her lady friends, and at Hyllus, the Peeping Tom. 'And I wish to express my sincere sympathy to the family who must now spend the rest of their lives without the great man, but who, thanks to circumstances, were spared the last moments of deterioration.' He nodded in the direction of the family (unknown uncles, cousins and relatives from Mezeritz, Podolia, Bratzlaf and Videbsk).

'Allow me to confess that our Service, with the help of the celebrated Captain Demosthenes de Goede, set itself the task of destroying what we in our ignorance did not realize was the truth.' He took out his handkerchief and sniffed delicately at the perfume. 'And my friends, in order to bring the truth to light for us, Captain Demosthenes de Goede had to sacrifice his own family – perhaps the greatest sacrifice that can be asked of anyone.' He put his handkerchief away. 'Just as Boris Gudenov's family, in a reverse manner, had to make their sacrifices.'

He waited a moment and looked at the crowd. What he now had to say was a difficult idea to grasp. 'There were two forces, my friends, concerned in the struggle. There was Bee-Bee-Doo . . .' As soon as a few began to clap, especially the man in white, the young men of the D-Service silenced them, and the pretty girls from Clifton placed their fingers coyly on their lips to guarantee silence. 'There was Bee-Bee-Doo,' repeated the Brigadier, 'a vulgar relic of the primitive, someone who really should have been in a sanatorium. There was the ritual and mystery that for us ordinary folk became a source of doubt and suspicion. And I am glad to say that many of our spiritual leaders understand.' He nodded to a couple of bishops who smiled and nodded back. 'Dare I mention that even the wife of our beloved Captain, with the ironic name of Hope, also played an unfortunate part in the confusion of ideas? Was it divine vengeance that she had to become the victim because of her complicity?' He looked expectantly at the young men of the personnel division, who with loud No's immediately fell in with the Brigadier's new image. He smiled. 'I am glad to see that all of you, as ordinary people, have immediately appreciated the truth.' He smiled at the teenagers who, mystified, retained their mask of aloofness. 'No. She was the victim of an illness, nymphomania, for which, we hope, a cure will be found one of these days.' He smiled at the doctors, who laughed in reply. 'Dare I admit that I was also a victim? That with the arrogance of the Demiurge I saw myself as a companion?' Only a few young men of his Service laughed at the Brigadier's slip of referring at this stage to an idea like the Demiurge.

The Brigadier had emptied his glass and held it out for one of the young men of the action front to refill.

He laughed at the audience, who laughed back.

'May I mention someone by name who gave us the true picture, a former assistant of Boris Gudenov, who had to accept chastisement patiently, and who, with typical neighbourly love, carried no vengeance in his heart? May I mention someone known as the ducktail?'

There was much laughter as the ducktail, beloved by all, came forward, and strummed the Watusi on his guitar until the teen-agers automatically went through the movements, while the Brigadier looked on good-naturedly and made use of the oppor-tunity to refill his glass.

'Can there be a greater triumph,' asked the Brigadier, 'than the realization that God is dead, and that man, freed from tradi-tional bondage, can build his life purely on Christian morality?'

He faced the audience squarely.

'Is this gathering not an indication of greater understanding, greater freedom, and neighbourly love?

'That was the message of Boris Gudenov, my friends,' said the Brigadier with deep conviction. 'And both the Captain and our beloved tycoon had to end their separate careers to demon-strate this truth.'

He suddenly stood up.

'The Captain, a man like us, misled as I myself was in the heroic tradition, had to go through the valley of the shadow of death and be reconciled with the secular truth. Dare we judge him if he became a victim of this particular situation; should we not rather admire him as he experiences his greatest triumph when he accepts this world and, in the progressive Welgevonden, becomes absorbed in the new world? As people with an under-standing of the new symbols that get a new value through reality and existentialism, dare we judge Boris Gudenov when at the last moment, as a result of physical suffering, he accepted the primitive significance that is completely a mockery of his en-lightened bulwark, the shopping centre?'

The Brigadier had now reached the end of his speech, and he smiled at the girls of the Service who were prepared to receive the men on purely humanistic grounds – sex as sex, love as love, truth as truth as everyone saw it at that moment.

There was new life in the Service.

The Brigadier smiled.

There was a new picture, and he raised his glass. They all drank the toast eagerly. Goodwill and neighbourly love had sim-plified life, so that everyone could understand. They drank to the death of tradition and primordial life. There was much gaiety and freedom, and rejoicing without limits.

Death was no longer in the building, and the Brigadier was satisfied to sit down in the Renaissance chair while they all joined in the revels, and organ music from invisible sources interpreted the new truth with a clash of sound.

One for the Devil

Contents

Dedicated to John Kannemeyer

Qui?

'Therefore the tragic figure of our time is perhaps
he who takes guilt upon himself to make valid for
ourselves our hate or sorrow,' said Dr Johns.

(In a Foundation like Welgevonden all characters are
imaginary and all events probable. Everyone who
recognizes himself in any of the characters belongs
on Welgevonden.)

Ubi?

Ubi?

The lawn stretched between clumps of trees and shrubs that appeared here and there like islands: an artificial green sea on which its creator wandered with his wife, the 'slim' Mrs Silberstein, and his setter. It was a beautiful, restless animal, nourished on concentrates and cod liver oil to black and white Spanish pride – skin soft as silk, eyes dark and moistly shining, free from ophthalmia, ears flapping and tail waving: a useless end-product that lent grace to an aimless stroll. Sometimes it appeared against the hillside, a patch of light on the green; then it vanished into the darkness of a branch, a tree stump, a shadow.

Seen from that corner of the estate, Welgevonden was still in its renaissance and the Silbersteins could have been Medicis, the two of them, if one could imagine them cloaked, if one could change the language they spoke and if, at that moment, there had not been a fault in her voice as she called 'Fido!'

Eighteen years past one's full flowering brought a toughness of sinews where formerly there had been suppleness and slimness; robbed the voice of its music and, at a certain pitch, caused flexibility to fail, so that there was a crack in the call 'Fido! Fido!' What had once been, perhaps, an interesting banality became simply commonplace because, alas, the Medicis have long been dead.

And for him, too, eighteen years in which to become stocky; eighteen years to hunch those broad shoulders, to bleach the blue of the eyes, to deprive rough, youthful masculinity of its youthfulness and begin gnawing already at masculinity itself, so that perhaps one day there would remain only roughness to remind one – of what, exactly? A roughness in his voice, therefore, as he added it to hers, and his 'Fido! Fido!' had the desired effect, since the dog now appeared on the crest of the hill, sharply outlined against the horizon.

They hestitated for a moment and looked with admiration tempered by wistfulness at the silhouette: the pointing attitude, nose raised, tail motionless; restrained concentration which, in the silence before movement, was charged with more movement than movement itself, a state of tension just this side of completion that left something to the imagination – a picture of Timomachus that surprised one in the transient moment. And then, suddenly, the forepaw was raised and the animal stiffened into the catatonic posture characteristic of its breed.

'What would he be seeing?' asked Jock Silberstein.

'Are there still partridges?' said 'slim' Mrs Silberstein.

Hand in hand they hurried up the hillside, past the dog, and then looked somewhat myopically back and forth across the lawn. Years ago they would not have been as breathless as they were now and there would have been something brisk in their movements. They looked up: in the distance a thousand diamonds glittered in the air as the leaves of poplar trees moved. Then they caught sight of the plastic swan, inflated, dun coloured, blown by the wind from the fountain, over shrubs, through the hollows, to a point close by exactly in the middle of the lawn; neatly in position, swollen and discoloured, its arched neck still endlessly on the move.

'Just imagine,' said 'slim' Mrs Silberstein.

'I was always under the impression that they went by *scent*,' said Jock Silberstein.

It was something they could tell their friends. 'Slim' Mrs Silberstein stroked the dog, which at once relaxed, nosed her and then dashed off in the direction of the fountain. It was something they would always remember: an anecdote that would be often aired about the setter and the plastic swan; that would remain with them always, a piece of *kitsch* on the mantelshelf of their memories.

At the foot of the Welgevonden mountain the trout lake was fed by small streams that began somewhere among the peaks and wet heather. To prevent erosion, Jock Silberstein many years ago had twenty Italian prisoners of war build retaining walls with overflows in the middle, to allow so many cusecs to flow off after the dams, which were to keep back the sludge, became full. This was during the Second World War and these men had had to be kept occupied, preferably in some artistic way. The result of months of activity reflected their state of mind : each cement retaining wall had been fashioned on the outside in the form of a tragic mask, with the overflows sculpted in the shape of dripping mouths. This left the impression of a series of huge gargoyle waterspouts, all down the mountainside to the lake. Thereafter the same motif had been repeated on the overflows, from where a single stream tumbled down the hill, across the Welgevonden lawns to the fountain. The fountain, itself almost a lake, was smothered under the water lilies, surrounded by marble statues and populated by plastic swans. It served in reality as a camouflaged reservoir for all the water installations connected with the farm's activities, but it had always been the policy at Welgevonden to conceal the functional behind an aesthetic façade.

With the passage of time, moss had covered the masks and given them a many-coloured patina, so that they gave the impression of having been fashioned centuries ago – like statues that one would expect to come across against the slopes of Mediterranean mountains. Mostly the little rippling streams flowed peacefully, and then the masks dribbled clear, red, mountain water; but when it had just rained, as now, each one spurted a froth-laden red stream into the air.

During the day the sun gleamed on the masks and they shivered in hazy mirages; at dusk they grimaced sombrely and roused in one feelings of approaching doom; at night one was aware of the masks, although they could not be seen. With the years they had become much weathered and had not been repaired : here a nose had been broken off, there was a harelip through which the water seeped. But there were so many buildings and coppices on Welgevonden that it was sometimes days or months before one noticed the masks for the first time. After that, one could not forget them.

On this sunny afternoon after the rain a setter in a crazy mood was dashing to and fro across the grass. In the distance his master and mistress could be seen. He had just pointed out to them a plastic swan that had been blown from the fountain. Now he reached the fountain itself and something caught his attention.

Quid?

Quid?

'There's something at the fountain,' said Jock Silberstein when the dog became motionless for the second time. 'Slim' Mrs Silberstein raised her hand to her mouth. 'The fountain ...' she said and turned her face towards the maze of buildings far below, as if in the labyrinths of Welgevonden she would find assurance.

'It's most likely a plastic swan,' said Jock Silberstein, uneasy with the knowledge that patterns repeat themselves, that each event tends to recur in its own image.

For a moment they remained thus, outwardly still: the tableau of a dog in a graceful, suggestive line pointing to the invisible something in the fountain, and of an intermediary in the form of a divided man with his arms stretched out on either side, to connect the tense dog with an evasive woman. The tension reached a climax, collapsed and disintegrated in the leisurely movement of the woman who moved away and down, to the rounded gables, the flaming walls, the innumerable windows and the complex courtyards that offered protection against a dangerous simplicity. The wind played lightly with her modish dress, it dissolved the severity of *haute couture* to the frivolity of a Botticelli gown, it creased and waved around her in graceful flight. Middle-aged Mrs Silberstein became more youthful with increasing distance; she became attenuated by distance to the slim Mrs Silberstein of eighteen years ago.

'It's a plastic swan,' repeated Jock Silberstein and then turned to the dog which remained motionless in a waiting position. Before him the fountain moved in a continuous eddy as the water under the water-lily leaves poured away perpetually through cement pipes at the bottom. The swan's doubles – white, dun grey and inflated – bobbed around directionlessly. In the distance the waters spurted, the masks stuck out their red tongues, the sun gleamed against the grotesque faces. Jock pushed his hat back and wiped the sweat from his forehead. He stared across the estate: the factory in the distance, the house there below, the moving speck that must be his wife. Then he stroked the dog which by its own compulsion was still faithfully immobile.

'What is it, Fido? What's up, old man?'

His attention was attracted to something that was drifting on the stream towards the fountain: something that moved shapelessly through the water, that dipped and vanished, and then appeared among the swans, imitating their directionlessness, and then suddenly got caught in a piece of flotsam and, slowly, began to move around and around, counterclockwise. Around and around it revolved, sometimes visible, sometimes unseen, around and around like a minute hand moving in the reverse direction. A greyish object – but what was it? And now that his master was also aware of it, the dog relaxed, as if its part in the game were complete.

In the meantime Jock Silberstein had removed his hat and held it in front of his eyes to shade them from the sun; he peered from the shadow of the brim and as his eyes became accustomed to the movement, adjusted themselves to the movement, the object became recognizable. Jock Silberstein's head moved around and around as he followed the rotation, with every completed revolution his horror grew, his emotions swung visibly from horror, shock, incredulity, realization, grief, back to horror. He was powerless with his head following all the motions and gradually his movements became autonomous. He stood there like a big doll with a built-in mechanism. And then tears began slowly to trickle from his eyes. His mouth opened and closed and he wept soundlessly, caught up in the never-ending circle. After a while he began involuntarily to make small sounds, like a mute trying to speak; later the sounds became louder but were still wordless and inhuman; eventually he gave himself over completely to his grief and stumbled into the water with a cry that cut through the midday air and vanished without echo.

Cur?

Cur?

He walked across the expanse of lawn with the dripping objects in his arms. His movements seemed to be purposeless; and his strength was superhuman as he simply walked on and on past the buildings, through the windows of which they looked at him, in the panes of which he saw himself. All impressions came simultaneously and incoherently. He stumbled on and suddenly saw all their images disintegrate in the various mirrors. They looked out at him from the mirrors ... They looked at him through binoculars ... The mirrors splintered in a thousand pieces and the images shattered with them. The windows were the viewfinders on their cameras, through which they peered. They aimed at one another and now they dissected him as he walked on purposelessly across the lawn with his burden.

Then he was alone again, a gigantic figure in the measureless landscape.

At a certain moment he appeared to have found his direction. He arrived at the factory and the cellars. He entered through the big gateway and descended, level after level below the ground, to the innermost sanctuary where the *finos* had been aged. Carefully, he laid the corpse on a table. Here were and had been all the things that encompassed his great love, where everything had come to an end and been reborn. Here was the entire significant, incomprehensible cycle. Here everything was present, lifeless and yet alive. He could no longer distinguish between beginning and end. He felt old, and like an old man could no longer come to a conclusion.

This is my whole life, all my achievements and all my disappointments. I can think no further and for the rest of my time on earth I shall be petrified at this point. What is true? What is not true? What has happened? Why did it all happen? Why does it end or begin here?

At a certain stage he walked to and fro in the cellar. The electric light burned from a single, naked globe. Outside, perhaps, dusk had already begun to fall. He walked to and fro and then he went and stood by the object on the table. He looked closely at the face, as if he had never seen it before. He fingered the hair, at times, and tried to arrange it, but it was wet and clammy and unmanageable. Small things attracted his attention: the shape of the nose, the lips, the eyebrows, two small marks on the throat, the tips of the fingers. A drop of blood had congealed on the skin. He looked at its colour. Sometimes certain articles of the clothing caught his attention and he wondered where and when he had bought them. He recalled the time when he had given this and that as a little gift, and how the few moments of real pleasure had left a warm feeling deep inside him.

There was blood on the lips and between the teeth. A strong feeling of alarm overpowered him and he walked quickly away through the passages, outside, to the steam room where the copper pipes intertwined on the walls like serpents. He opened the steam cock and waited until the sound of steam eliminated all sound and then he began to bellow. It lasted longer than usual: he shouted the questions at the noisy silence, but received no answer and felt no release. This, too, had had to happen: that the room of confession should lose its healing power. When he went outside the sun had already set and a red glow played malignantly on the spurting masks against the mountain.

He walked slowly and resolutely back to the cellars, to the innermost chamber where the object lay on the table. To one side in a corner was a heavy club and he picked it up.

Precisely at sunset the sounds began, the noise of copper and earthenware being broken: the liberating destruction, the safeguard against evil in all its forms, the forgotten ritual of a Jew of Tripoli, the noise *sub magiae fugiendae praetextu*, the assault on death in oneself.

And outside the door, attracted by the noise, there listened

Detective-Sergeant Demosthenes H. de Goede. He looked rather like Jacques Tati in his part as a postman. He was utterly incapable of formulating a single sentence.

'Pittttt-Pittttt ...' he stammered. 'Brrrrr ... Psssst. Mmmmmmm ... ffffffft !'

Quis?

Chapter One

The Interment

'The technical sequence of the unravelling of the heptagonal problem is very strict, according to Quintilian,' Dr Johns said to Detective-Sergeant Demosthenes H. de Goede. 'Who? What? Where? With whom? Why? With what? and When?'

He increased his pace in order to join the funeral procession more closely and stumbled in the process.

'So let us begin with *Quis?*'

The white ring-wall of Welgevonden's cemetery shone in the distance; the wheels of the undertaker's black Cadillac gouged holes in the grass, they churned up the black peat, they rocked the glassed hearse with the colourful wreaths up and down like a ship and forced the pallbearers out of line. The faces of those in the procession were white against the black of their clothes – a uniform white and black which would only later, outside the context of the procession, become recognizable as individuals who, according to Dr Johns, would have to be considered one by one. It was a protective moment: nothing dared interrupt the procession – even if the unknown Who? were to beat his breast and acknowledge his deed. It was a moment of rest which everyone shared with the deceased object in the hearse.

The service was taken by the Reverend Williams in the intersectarian chapel sequestered in a corner of Welgevonden. Against the wall were copper plaques which indicated the names of those who, before interment, had undergone the diversity of rituals intersectarially. Reverend Williams had, in this instance, taken the service because the denomination had been doubtful: the deceased had not been connected to any faith, the choice had fallen on a genial Protestant sect, the oration had been a model of free rhetoric, unconstrained by dogma. It was a lyrical sermon by the intense pastor in his neat little black suit: a genial summary of an unknown life hovering, like all of us, between salvation and the clutch of evil. The deceased had been loved (and everyone present, guilty and innocent, knew how guilty or innocent the love relationship) ... A young girl in the flush of her life, *l'inconnue* brought low when so much lay ahead of her ...

Of Lila, the deceased daughter of the deceased whore with the white face.

'Inspect them one by one,' Dr Johns said to Detective-Sergeant Demosthenes H. de Goede, 'but confine your impressions to the superficial.' The hearse began its winding route as the hill grew steeper, all along the contours, to prevent undue wear to the gearbox. 'Don't get to know them too well; stop short at the edge of consciousness.' The hearse followed the contour line and with its first turn, inadvertently formed a sombre question mark: the loop above, then the stem, and right at the bottom the dot, where the giant, a little behind it, was finding pleasure in the procession. 'The deeper you scratch,' said Dr Johns, 'the deeper you go into the mists.'

The sun had disappeared behind the clouds, everything had dimmed to the greyness that gave the right tone to a funeral procession – a grey file which, with the second contour, had a moment ago lost its question mark and made the line disconnected.

'For your purpose the superficial truth is the most important,' said Dr Johns, 'because the deed was born at that level.'

And now the black Cadillac began to circle around the circular white wall, around and around, to give the procession cohesion, to satisfy the feeling for rhythm of the grey director with his sable hat, until the multitude had been compelled into *his* cycle and everything had come to a stop around the *Dingaankraal* where the former inhabitants of Welgevonden had been laid heterogeneously to rest: for there were the unknown, crumbled graves with slate headstones of God knew who, *and* the angels of the Léfèbres, *and* the star of Juda isolated in its own *Bet Chayyim*, *and* Lila's open waiting grave. Green raffia simulated a lawn between the clay, limestone and black peat. (The soil there was extremely unsuitable for cultivation.) Bars with copper knobs lent an air of stylish swank, the raked gravel ensured neatness, whitewashed bricks bordered the footpaths, artificial flowers perpetuated their illusion in indestructible plastic. The doors of the hearse were opened, they swung open and the imbuia coffin, handsome with proteas, slid soundlessly out into the waiting hands of the bearers who bent double to receive the weight of wood and copper that encased slight Lila. For a moment they hesitated, determining sunrise and coffin direction, and then, at a hint from the man in the top hat and frock coat, they found sequence and direction and laid the coffin gratefully, swaying, on the canvas strips over the gaping grave.

It grew darker, drizzle clouds clustered in the distance, there was a cloud over Heuningberg, Reverend Williams lifted up his eyes unto the cumulus and asked, 'From whence cometh my help . . . ?'

An unknown bystander found his thoughts wandering; he did not feel in the least involved in the proceedings. He went through all the motions and all the requirements of the ritual, but he was actually more conscious of himself and his own feelings. I am moved, he thought, but is it I who am moved? The heat is damp and sticky. Someone is weeping. I look at the people and wonder what they are feeling. That one, for instance, with his eyes closed and an expression of dedication on his face. Is he thinking of the same things as I am, or is he listening to Reverend Williams?

'I knew Lila well,' said Dr Johns to Detective-Sergeant Demosthenes H. de Goede, and his voice sounded so loud that a number of people looked up.

There were few family around the grave except for an uncle from Welkom who had come over specially for the occasion, and an aunt with silver-blonde hair dressed in black, in the finest silk stockings and with the prettiest ankles, and an uncle from the Karroo, with a rugged face, and a fat girl who wept and wept, ceaselessly, until her face looked like a little sow's.

'Lila was loved by all,' said Dr Johns more softly.

Lila was a bitch who came to bed like a virgin, every time

(thought someone else). There she lies, defenceless, and who can say that she was defenceless. Or ... (he bit his knuckles) was I really the first? He looked around him and found everyone unworthy. Pure, undefiled Lila ... his memories began all over again, differently, and he embalmed her in his heart.

Detective-Sergeant Demosthenes H. de Goede had a question clear and ready in his thoughts. He wished to put it to Dr Johns and struggled in silence against his impediment of speech. As soon as he had a sentence clear, as soon as his thoughts were clear, everything would appear clear and distinct. The process of thought was simply the conversion of clear thinking into speech. He turned to Dr Johns.

'Pssssst !' he said. 'Pttttt ... ttttt ...'

Dr Johns held his head nearer to listen, while a hymn was begun. He said something which was inaudible in the noise. His eyes followed the drizzle which was falling and appeared to be coming nearer.

Somebody should speak on behalf of the family, but the uncle from Welkom, the aunt and the farmer from the Karroo, felt like strangers. They had come from three remote corners, attracted by an obscure family sentiment, encouraged by that incomprehensible compulsion of conscience which caused relations to appear at funerals like spectres, thereafter never to be seen or heard of again. They were simply there with questioning eyes, searching the faces around them, as if there they would find certainty about their own origin. And then, if perhaps they met someone who was of the family, they would nod their heads up and down; but the anxious, searching eyes would not change.

Then Reverend Williams began to speak on behalf of them all. It was an eloquent, persuasive flow of words, his facts based on fleeting observations and a prior chat here and there. In the little chapel Lila had been the subject for a text; here he had to depict her finally as someone who had existed, for the benefit of those who had known her better than himself. While he spoke, he looked at the faces around him, expressionless faces that gave no sign of his blunders. He depicted her as an orphan, an attractive, pretty, exemplary girl who had been loved by everyone, who had grown up among them, who had charmed everyone, who had died a violent death at the hands of a sadist who (God help him) would have to account before the Judgment Seat.

'But let us forget all these unpleasant things and remember her as we all knew her . . .'

The rain was coming nearer, softly, glancing over the heather to release him. He followed the blur with his eyes as he spoke. Heavens, he had never seen her, he did not know what she looked like, he knew only the two dates : the beginning and the end.

He ended his sermon with thanks to all those present. 'Some have come far. As far as Welkom in the Orange Free State.' (And the unknown uncle dropped his head.) He thought of her late mother with whom she would now be reunited and he left them inadvertently with the thought of the whore in heaven – the white-faced girl of eighteen years ago who had died in the extra-marital birth of Lila.

The first drops now began to fall, imperceptibly at first, soft and soothing. The coffin sank with rocking movements. The mourners pressed forward and glanced over each other's shoulders. The little bowl of rose petals was handed around by the man in the top hat. Someone began to sob on hearing the words 'unto dust shalt thou return . . .' Many hands seized the petals and sent them fluttering down into the darkness.

And nobody cried harder than Madam Ritchie and her two daughters, Hope and Prudence. They were entitled to weep. They had the right to feel broken, because none had defamed Lila more than the three of them. The tears cascaded down the cheeks of the stout woman, who was buttressed on either side by her eighteen-year-old daughters (pretty, blonde-haired girls with plaits and Viking eyes). At this last moment they gave Lila a tremendous farewell, while the rain increased. They were three lamenting women from a Greek drama : a classical symbol on the stage of the hill, against the grey sky.

Just before they dispersed they made room unwillingly for the Giant, the dot at the end of the procession when it was a question mark. He had just reached the place, he regarded the scene, forced his way through the people, grabbed the last rose petals in his big hand and let them fall one by one, watching each petal attentively until it vanished into the shadows. A last petal, damp from the rain, still stuck to his hand; he removed it carefully, shook it and let it fall meticulously into the depth.

When the rain began to fall harder, and everyone hurried back to the buildings of Welgevonden, with Jock and 'slim' Mrs Silberstein in the lead, Dr Johns turned to Detective-Sergeant Demosthenes H. de Goede and said : 'Remember the technical heptameter. If you are unable to abide by the sequence, then confine yourself at least to the requirements : the person, the fact, the place, the means, the motive, the manner and the time.'

That night it rained so hard in the mountains that all the streams overflowed their banks and consequently cut Welgevonden off completely from the outside world. Throughout the night the masks bellowed as the waters rushed through their mouths. For days on end they dominated the landscape of Welgevonden – because they had found their voices.

Chapter Two

Through the Eye of the Leopard

(Image of light and shadow, of leaves moving, of waters, of human figures, of flickerings in the dark; images that come and go without rational connection. Partly nature, partly thought process, partly feeling. Sub-human perceptions from deep in the unconscious: the differentiated I peering over the partition and repeatedly sinking back into formless primordialism. Levels of thought-energy that sink through all the layers of consciousness to the charcoal, past that, deeper and farther back where everything is amorphous and then, recklessly, to take the form-creating step, to shoot through all the layers to the top and to explode with all-embracing perception in the consciousness. A synthesis of opposites, a mystical experience, indescribable, a moment of hesitation between the divine and the demoniac, and then a grandiose, incommunicable experience ... released from the talons of hell, the feeling of unity experienced in the heavenly unification.

The eye of the leopard through which the imbecile and saints and poets and writers look; the mutation, the mental defect, the divergent gene that has the same effects as mescaline, LSD and psyliciben, that unlocks the portals and makes the perceptions big and intense, that brings inner freedom. What difference that the unlocking is banal: the authenticity and the quality of the feeling is beyond the stigma of the means. In the face of this experience there is no difference in the stature of the individual; and the idiot, the feebleminded, can experience the eternal – he, too.)

To be one with the leaves all around, above, everywhere, moving; with the sunshine and the light in gradations of all colours that glittered on all imaginable forms; and which filled you con-

tinually with that ecstasy which you experienced many years
ago as a young child and which still continued to live in poignant
memories when you contemplated a mountain, a forest, a stream
of water, an aspect of nature that had left its imprint on that
first, wonderful, magical day many years ago.

Images and impressions of Welgevonden that came and went.
Was there ever a dark-eyed mother whom you saw, felt and
heard and of whom you were a part? Was it only later that you
heard the name Salome, or had it been with you from the beginning? Was she part of that paradise, or did you go and fetch her
where images welled up from the inexhaustible spring? And that
big man who followed you continually with his tormenting eyes,
where did he come from? And how do you reach him, the one
who wakens love in you but whom you can never find?

Those were all questions and problems that only half troubled
you as you floated on the stream of consciousness, as you looked
into the green shadows cast by arum lilies, as you hid in tunnels
of blue winds, as you slept coolly in caves of paper flowers, as you
climbed the ladders of autumn-coloured vines against white walls.
In your idiot-brain there was something that isolated this paradise forever; you knew only the fear of intruders, of someone
who removed you inopportunely, of those who disturbed the
overpowering peace, rest and ecstasy with meaningless words
and incomprehensible tasks. But, even though they took you
away, you carried the paradise invisibly with you – and, close
beside it, the intimation of chaos; you took them with you to the
room with cloud-grey walls (when the key grated in the door);
everywhere, you knew two worlds of experience and they could
not exclude you. You were much bigger than they; you could
break down the door, if you wished; you could, if you wished,
destroy everything and everyone: just as you wished to destroy
that apparition who came with anxiety, when that spectre appeared at the window between the waving curtains, with her
glowing eyes (her black eyes) that looked at you and you fought
against her exhausting embrace until at last you submitted as
you were emptied, and lay powerless while she grew warm and
soft with satisfaction. She bit you with her sharp teeth, her breath

smelled of blood, her body trembled against yours, she groaned from the depths in the darkness.

You recovered more slowly than she; as your strength returned you wished to destroy her, as soon as you rid yourself of your loneliness — but then it was too late; by then she had already gone, and you fumbled in vain in the dark and tore the pillow to tatters until rapture again predominated and you felt one with everything, and you sank down into unknown worlds where, suddenly, arum lilies and moonflowers swayed before your eyes, and little trumpet flowers with purple throats sounded small, thin notes against the pale blue air.

You washed yourself in the water that burbled on its way to the fountain. (It chatted over the stones; round, enticing sounds that came from everywhere.) You wedged your feet on either side of the masks, pressed your body against their mouths and strained against the stream. The talking water splashed off your body, arched over your shoulders and soared against the sun. Then you were purified of taint.

But tonight, in your room, you longed again for black chaos and peeped at the window with the waving curtains. You were filled with trepidation, but waited nevertheless for the phosphorescent glow. You were used to it, for as long as you could remember. She would always be there; you had always the same intentions and you were always just too late. It had been thus all your life, and so it would always be in that system of shocking contrasts.

Today the world was wet. Your tracks lay deep in the earth. You wandered over the virginal grass and despoiled the earth. The whole world was fresh and full of sunshine. You felt free and your head swam when you saw the open landscape.

Then you saw the two of them. They darkened the landscape. You stooped and cupped black, muddy soil in your hands; you pressed it into a round, yielding ball of clay. (It awoke memories in you; it lived tremblingly in your hands.) Then you hurled it with all your strength at the intruders.

The clay disintegrated in the air and disappeared on the grass.

But no matter: the feeling of frustration was temporary; there were moonflowers waiting; there was a wall to climb. There was the dark cave of red, brown and purple flowers. There was no end to that ecstasy. You rose above everybody. You were part of the paradise. You would crush them like ants. You raised your hands in the air; already you had wings. You flew; you flew so high that you could no longer even hear them. Your enormous hands could exterminate them; but there were so many things you had to do; there was so much to attract you, there was so much music in the water that already you had forgotten about them.

Chapter Three

To Look Down into a Drained Pool . . .

The clod disintegrated in the air and fell in a spray of sand and lumps of mud on the grass. Dr Johns pointed his finger in admonition in the direction of the thrower and smiled at Detective-Sergeant Demosthenes H. de Goede.

'Adam Kadmon Silberstein!' he called, and the Giant stood still. They saw at first only his cumbersome back, the shirt that clung in wrinkles to the sweaty, wet body, the figure camouflaged by the shrubs. They could see from his posture that he was listening: from the slight tenseness, from the way in which the shoulders were drawn askew and became a sensitive organ that moved light to and fro.

'Adam Kadmon Silberstein!' Dr Johns repeated, and the Giant turned around and laughed at them.

It came as a shocking contrast: from behind he was a grotesque colossus of eight feet four inches, a monstrous deviation from the normal, something one associated with the circus, or the sports field, or a spectacle from a film dreamed up in Los Angeles – but now, from the front, one saw a boy of eighteen who, guilty and abashed, laughed with long, sharp teeth – a serrated set of adolescent teeth.

'Ossians, dentes candide . . .' said Dr Johns. He beckoned to the giant, who came forward a few paces reluctantly and then stopped again.

He had red hair, blue eyes and a pale complexion. Whereas, in a dwarf, one was struck by the old face in the body of a child, here the effect was the opposite: the young face in the monstrous body. His movements were clumsy, like those of someone not able to coordinate the use of his limbs properly, but his strength was disturbing. In his right hand he held a large piece of a log which he jerked nervously up and down with his left hand until it broke in two with a cracking sound. The next moment he jerked at the other, shorter piece until it, too, crumbled after a short while in his mighty left hand. His eyes were never still; he looked around him often, and as often his attention was distracted by something else – the setter running across the grass ('Fido ! Fido !'), or something that crackled in the bushes. When the piece of log had been crumbled to powder and nothing of it was left, he sought with restless hands for something to do. When Dr Johns walked nearer and took him by the arm, he reacted like a naughty child and slapped the outstretched arm rudely away – the awkward gesture of a child, but with uncontrolled force behind it. Dr Johns gave him a handful of sugar candy and the stuffed all into his mouth. As he ate, his cheeks distended, he looked at the Detective-Sergeant with sly eyes and an expression of mischievous naughtiness.

'Pssssttt ... fffffft ...' came Demosthenes H. de Goede's stuttering attempt to make contact, and the giant suddenly doubled up in the madness of a hysterical fit of laughter, his mouth wide open so that the candy spattered out, and his body swayed to and fro, his eyes bulging. The next moment he ran away; but after a short distance came to a stop again. He looked back and there was no aftermath of his fit of laughter. He simply looked at them with his empty eyes and then he seemed to be looking for something, for someone, to join him in his lonely world.

The dog attracted his attention and the two of them disappeared quickly towards the fountain and the noisy masks against the mountainside.

'A lamentable case,' said Dr Johns as they wandered on towards the Welgevonden homestead. 'His mother was a lovely woman, Salome, Jock Silberstein's daughter. He came to the light like a tiger and lacerated her. She pampered him for seven days before she died. An infant of fifteen pounds is not yet a monster.'

He looked at the house among the trees, at the gables that rose like a village above the branches.

'You should have seen the farm then. It was a wonderful place. The Silbersteins lived like princes.'

They approached the swimming pool.

'She died before she had had the *mikvah*,' said Dr Johns.

The swimming pool was empty.

'But the *chevra kaddisha* washed, prepared and clothed her properly in a pure white *kittel*. Salome with the dark eyes. She was a legendary beauty. Do those words mean anything to you?'

The cement was dry and crumbling. Cracks made black lines between the whitewashed sides. The swimming pool had been built to Olympic specifications but, empty as it now was, it looked like a meaningless excavation. Weeds and nettles grew on the bottom; there was the excrement of humans and animals in one corner; silt was building up against the farthest side. After the rain everything was moist and fermenting in the subsequent heat. The sour smell of active decomposition assailed them.

'How can I describe her to you?' said Dr Johns as they sat down on the edge of the pool, their ankles thudding against the brittle plaster. 'Intelligent, full of love and compassion for husband. The perfect wife who, apparently, gave up everything for the mystical togetherness, yet nevertheless held something back: the mystery in which the godlike and the earthly were woven together. We all desired her with longing and pride because we knew that the longing and desire of nobody else would be satisfied. Perhaps she was a figment of our imagination, and their togetherness the romantic dream of all of us. But was it a dream?'

Dr Johns' age was unknown. He looked like a small baboon on the edge of the empty swimming pool; a shrunken piece of facile wisdom that created and destroyed illusions; full of energy resulting from correct diet and exercise, a wiry example of pertinacity, an eloquent example of an old body that with sustained effort might still, after perhaps its eightieth year, one fierce, sweating night, make a virgin fall pregnant, to prove the pathos of human diligence.

'She was married to a Christian, Henry van Eeden,' said Dr Johns. 'The van Eedens had the prestige, the Silbersteins the money. It was an ideal conjunction and a triumph for the calculating machine. But then she gave birth to a mentally deficient giant.'

The man beside him began to stutter.

(Detective-Sergeant Demosthenes H. de Goede was the product of one of the best police colleges in the country. He had done particularly well in all his examinations. In spite of his speech impediment he passed *cum laude* and, also physically, came up to standard by, for instance, running the mile in just over four minutes. He was an excellent pistol shot. He knew Gardener's Law of Evidence by rote.)

'And Henry van Eeden is one of the best read and most intelligent people I know,' said Dr Johns. 'Do you know the basic facts about heredity?'

A cloud obscured the sun and passed on, but the pool remained empty. One could not imagine that it had ever been full of water; one could not believe in a time when people had swam and gambolled in it with those idiot sounds which denoted pleasure.

'In the moronic child, heredity plays an important part,' said Dr Johns, 'but in the case of imbeciles and idiots the intelligence quotient of the parents is unimportant. In Adam Kadmon the aberrant gene probably developed by means of a new mutation in the germ cell of one of the parents. It happens once in fifty thousand cases, and nobody is to blame. It's a comfort to Jock Silberstein : there is no stain on the forebears; the true seed of tragedy is present here, because there can be no blame.'

In a corner of the swimming pool the nettles moved without visible agent. It could have been a snake, a rat or some big insect. The leaves seemed to have a life of their own. Demosthenes H. de Goede threw a stone in that direction. He had aimed well, because the stone fell in the middle of the plant. Immediately the movement stopped, but the crown of the plant had been knocked off.

'Is it possible that the idiot-giant could have committed the murder?' asked Dr Johns.

Detective-Sergeant Demosthenes H. de Goede struggled to answer.

'Usually there are also visible deviations in the physical composition of the idiot child,' said Dr Johns. 'But Adam Kadmon is superficially normal, like a moron; only his I.Q. is that of an idiot. The fact that he is a giant has nothing to do with his backwardness.'

Dr Johns' face was finely wrinkled. His little eyes flickered between the folds, his bald pate gleamed in the sun. 'Is Adam Kadmon a Klinefelter case? Was Lila raped before she was murdered? The Klinefelter's genitals have not developed normally. If we had the answers to those two questions we would have progressed far.'

Detective-Sergeant Demosthenes H. de Goede took out his notebook and made notes in it. His handwriting was particularly neat, as if in compensation for his speech defect. The form of the entries in his notebook was a calligraphic work of art. He sighed and returned the book to his jacket pocket.

'Adam Kadmon is a hypophysical giant,' said Dr Johns. 'No retrogressive gene is present here. Everything is a product of the mucous gland of the brain and is not hereditary. They usually grow weaker with increasing age. He will probably not grow older than twenty years.'

They heard something and looked down. Suddenly the pool began to fill before their eyes. In the past there had been a pump that alternately emptied and refilled the pool; pressure had apparently cleared a blockage and after many years the water bubbled in again.

Dr Johns had stopped talking and he and Detective-Sergeant Demosthenes H. de Goede stared fascinated at the rising water, their eyes held by the deluge scene of thousands of little creatures that appeared from among the weeds and drifted, wriggling, about. A single weed drifted to the surface. It was the broken-off crown of the stinging nettle spiralling up towards the sunlight. Presently they had to lift their feet, so fast did the water rise. When the pool was full, the water stopped rising: the pumping system was in working order again; after so many hours the pool would be emptied and then, most likely, refilled.

From a clump of trees a group of children came running over the lawn, as if they had been in telepathic communication with the pool. They all wore bathing suits and tumbled one by one into the water. There was shrieking, horseplay and noise. The water splashed over the sides and insects and excrement littered the adjoining grass. The entire world shuddered and lived with the clamour and hooting of the children.

Dr Johns and Detective-Sergeant Demosthenes H. de Goede stood for a moment looking at them until they were overcome by that deep boredom which assails everyone who watches children in a swimming pool; then, depressed, they walked away and down to the Welgevonden homestead.

'Adam Kadmon will have to be investigated,' said Dr Johns. 'And Lila will have to be disinterred.'

Chapter Four

The *Apikoros*

It was he who appeared there before them: the *Mayofis* Jew who sought to accommodate himself in the Diaspora by means of a social and spiritual flirtation, who had built his pathetic castle to assure himself of a home there, who shone with geniality and, through his unlimited love, went farther astray.

'Jock Silberstein, our host,' said Dr Johns and stretched out his arms as if to embrace them both, draw them nearer and reconcile them in one single, important endeavour. 'Detective-Sergeant Demosthenes H. de Goede, charged with the investigation.'

Detective-Sergeant Demosthenes H. de Goede stuttered his expressions of goodwill with clear-sounding, meaningless vowels and consonants and received a firm handshake that he avenged with all the power at his disposal.

(Demosthenes H. de Goede had been not only a good athlete in the conventional sense at the police college, but was known for being able to lift a billiard cue from the floor with his index and middle fingers.)

They were directly in front of the door of the Silbersteins' house: the gables arched on either side, the Bacchus-figures poured their over-abundance of fruit and wine motionlessly in hard whitewash.

'Have you seen Adam Kadmon?' asked Jock Silberstein and he peered over their shoulders towards the lawn that vanished expansively in the distance.

'We have just seen him,' said Dr Johns. 'He has probably gone to swim in the stream by the masks and has taken his daily ablution.'

'Is the stream not too strong?' asked Jock Silberstein anxiously.

The rumble of the water could be heard clearly.

'He is strong,' said Dr Johns.

And to each of them came the vision of the giant figure against the stream.

'This morning he took my hand,' said Jock Silberstein, 'and he asked after Lila. He does not realize that she is dead.'

'He loved Lila very much,' said Dr Johns and looked meaningly at Demosthenes H. de Goede.

'He came to me,' said Jock Silberstein, 'without my having done anything. He did not pull away. He came to me of his own volition and took my hand. And then he asked after Lila.' He too, looked at Demosthenes H. de Goede and explained: 'He loved her and does not realize that she is dead. This morning he came to me and took my hand and asked: "Where is Lila?"'

It was as if the waters, after the incessant rain of the previous day, were murmuring everywhere all over Welgevonden.

'He is strong,' said Jock Silberstein. 'The stream will not easily carry him away. He takes hold on either side of the masks and then he lets the water wash over him.'

'Tremendous muscles,' said Dr Johns.

'The strength of a lion,' said Jock Silberstein. 'And a loving, tender heart. He would not harm a person or an animal.' He prepared to leave but decided otherwise. 'The strong are as meek as lambs. They understand their own strength.' His face brightened. 'They don't have to prove themselves.'

They all remained quiet for a moment.

'Lila loved him,' said Jock Silberstein. 'They were part of Welgevonden. The whole family. Her great-grandmother and father, her mother and her ...' He smiled suddenly. 'She could have been my child, d'you know, Dr Johns?'

'And mine,' said Dr Johns.

They seemed to have forgotten about Demosthenes H. de Goede. The Welgevonden of eighteen years ago was being lived again, but at that time Demosthenes H. de Goede was still at school.

'Her mother was a remarkable girl,' said Dr Johns. 'It's strange that she died at exactly the same age as her daughter. Both were eighteen years old. If you could imagine a hereafter, then they would meet each other as equals. Two girls of eighteen.'

'A mother and daughter of the same age with the same appearance and the same past,' said Jock Silberstein. 'Just imagine !'

'A mutual echo,' said Dr Johns.

'A sort of repetition,' said Jock Silberstein.

They looked past each other in opposite directions and fell into a peaceful silence. Dr Johns' eyes were lost among the neglected trees that checkmated one another before the house, where, like giants, they were destroying one another; Jock Silberstein peered intently across the lawn towards the distant masks.

'Well,' he said suddenly, 'I think I'll wander off to the fountain. Perhaps I'll find Adam Kadmon there.' He turned to Detective-Sergeant Demosthenes H. de Goede. 'Enjoy your stay.'

Demosthenes H. de Goede raised his hat gallantly and bowed to his host. He and Dr Johns walked silently up to the enormous front door of the enormous house.

'Actually, an unbelieving Jew,' said Dr Johns. 'But every so often he does something to establish a connection. And sometimes it's the most unexpected and odd things: the making of a *shema*, for instance,' and he pointed to a metal container built into the right of the front door. He lifted the ornamental knocker and rapped three times with a musical rhythm. 'A lewd romantic with a longing to both sides. Is that not perhaps the true nature of the puritan?'

Footsteps sounded in the passage. Dr Johns rapped on the metal container. 'The first two paragraphs of the *shema* written, rolled up and built in by himself. Perhaps soon after he had slept one night with Lila. It wasn't here a month ago.'

The door opened and a Malay maid peeped out. She smiled when she saw Dr Johns. She had two pure white false front teeth, disproportionately big in comparison with the others, with a small ruby added on the starboard side.

'Because a relationship between a married man and an unmarried woman was not considered as adultery,' said Dr Johns, and smiled back.

They waited in the front hall while the maid went in search of their hostess and sat on two of a row of chairs that filled the whole hall. Everywhere there were pieces of furniture and old chests, polished and shiny with rubbing, pushed together and arranged in unlivable order, as in the inner rooms of the Koopmans de Wet Museum. They looked through the door and saw the garden through which they had recently passed: the flowers overcrowded by weeds, the trees full of dead branches as, unpruned, they throttled one another – all in complete contrast to the neat lawn in the distance. And then their attention returned to the room in which they sat waiting, to the stairs at the bottom end of the passage, the dark rails, the huge furniture, the antiques that were now entirely part of the past. Here, in spite of everything, there was no dilapidation. The dissolution was overpolished, the disintegration arrested by varnish and lacquer.

'I wish you could have seen the place eighteen years ago,' said Dr Johns. 'But that was before the Silbersteins gave the place to the Foundation.'

Detective-Sergeant Demosthenes H. de Goede at once stuttered a question.

'After the birth of the Giant,' said Dr Johns, 'Jock Silberstein gave the greater part of the house and all the lands to the Foundation, and kept back the front part of the house for himself and his wife. I'll show you the rest of the house later; they occupy the front rooms.'

He pointed to the furniture.

'That's why the place is so chockablock. And three-quarters of the other antiques are decaying in storerooms.' He looked at his watch. 'I wonder what's keeping her.' He sighed and stretched himself out in the chair. 'The Silbersteins lived in the whole place themselves in the old days. Forty, fifty guests at a time was nothing unusual. The place crawled with people and roared with voices. The entire farm was a model of activity – a factory with and without walls.'

He looked up when he heard the servant girl coming. 'And

then he gave it to the Foundation and everything changed.'

They stood up and followed the servant down another passage to a big room on the right.

On the way Dr Johns asked Detective-Sergeant Demosthenes H. de Goede for his opinion on why Jock Silberstein had given everything to the Foundation. He answered his own question when he found himself dissatisfied with the reasons as he interpreted them from the stuttering sounds.

'They could have accepted the death of Salome and the birth of the Giant without doing that. They could have accepted the double disaster as part of life : the up and down . . . What happens when, suddenly, after a time, a whole way of life ceases to exist? You accept it that way. It just ceases.' The servant opened the double doors of the room. 'Or did Jock Silberstein perhaps, like a realist, destroy everything to ensure permanence?'

And now, as the servant girl disappeared soundlessly, they confronted a huge hall that had once upon a time been a magnificent place of assembly, but had now become a warehouse for all those things that one collects over the years and does not have the heart to get rid of.

There were a few valuable pieces that survived the rubbish and would come into their own in different circumstances, but they now became indistinguishable among the involuntary baroque. Then there were other pieces that derived their value from memories and from all the unpredictable love of human beings, but that now showed their intrinsic worthlessness under the glare of objectivity. There was actually something pathetic about that untidy room. And precisely in that lay the triumph of ordinary small things : that everything became ordinary and that the hideous, gilded nude girl with a clock in her navel could stand in equality with a seventeenth-century escritoire.

At the far end, against the wall, they observed 'slim' Mrs Silberstein before an oval mirror in which she was studying herself. They saw her inspect herself from all angles as they approached : from below, above, the sides and over her shoulder. As they drew nearer, unseen, and stood by her, she used a hand mirror as well. They even saw their own images in the looking

glass: slim and elegant in the mirror-illusion. But – in her abandonment, in the blindness of her liturgy – she was unaware of
them.

And then she began her exercises at leisure: a dance for the
sake of rhythm and her figure. The *apache* Mrs Silberstein with
the guttersnipe expression on her face and blue circles painted
around her eyes. The dance of the menopause in a heat of its
own that scorched her cheeks.

'Mrs Silberstein,' said Dr Johns, and she dropped the hand
mirror, which splintered on the floor.

She changed before their eyes; she turned around and became
stout and square in front, and slim and elegant behind.

'Demosthenes H. de Goede, the Detective-Sergeant charged
with the investigation – Mrs Silberstein,' said Dr Johns and
bowed away his embarrassment impartially between them.

Mrs Silberstein recovered swiftly and regained her calm.

'Seven years' bad luck,' she said and pointed to the shattered
pieces of the hand mirror that Demosthenes de Goede was gallantly scratching together. 'Put them there,' she said vaguely
and looked at him with interest.

'Detective-Sergeant Demosthenes H. de Goede,' Dr Johns repeated, 'here in connection with the death of Lila.'

'What a tragic happening!' said 'slim' Mrs Silberstein and
sank down gracefully in one of the Louis XV chairs. 'So pretty
and young, and yet . . .' She smiled charmingly at Dr Johns.
'Could one expect anything else after the sort of life she led?'

Demosthenes H. de Goede remained standing uncertainly
with the glass splinters in his hand. '*There!*' she said and admired his broad shoulders as he arranged the splinters in a neat
little heap on one of the tables. 'And what is your impression,
Mr de Goede?'

'The Detective-Sergeant is simply still getting acquainted with
all the people,' said Dr Johns, who also had found himself a seat.
'Welgevonden is surrounded by water and the criminal is cornered. Your use of the word "tragic" is entirely correct.' He nodded
to Detective-Sergeant Demosthenes H. de Goede who was staring
irresolutely at the collection of chairs. 'The misdemeanour has

been committed, the ordained deed has been done. The tragic unity is present. Somewhere the mark of the immutable personality of the miscreant has been made. Detective-Sergeant de Goede represents order, the ethical view of life of us all.' He smiled at Demosthenes H. de Goede who, at the moment, was busy flicking the remaining, finer chips from his hands with a silk handkerchief. 'It's a transgression against God and the community, we have lost our innocence, Paradise is threatened and we demand retaliation through Detective-Sergeant de Goede, so that we may retain Paradise.'

'Slim' Mrs Silberstein pressed one of the knobs on the wall and waited until the servant girl appeared with a trolley of drinks. Both she and Dr Johns drank wine. Detective-Sergeant Demosthenes H. de Goede preferred brandy and water with, yes, a little ice.

'They all slept with the little bitch,' said 'slim' Mrs Silberstein. 'Is her body softer because she is young? Does she appear different? Does she feel different just because she is young?' She looked at Dr Johns who acknowledged his implied complicity proudly, with a rueful inclination of the head. 'She had little intelligence,' said 'slim' Mrs Silberstein impatiently, 'and almost no personality. A proper little milksop.' Her eyes shone fervently and it was easy to imagine the unattractiveness of age gone, and to believe the colourful cosmetics in the dim light. The consort of Ashmodai was still ardent enough to inspire amulets and incantations. Her mood distorted her face, like the masks, and Detective-Sergeant Demosthenes H. de Goede showed his willingness purposelessly to satisfy her slightest whim.

'Everything is so confused,' said 'slim' Mrs Silberstein, suddenly calm. 'What can we do with all this furniture?'

She looked around helplessly.

'That Nederburg baroque wall cupboard, for instance – it's blocking the view through the window . . .'

Detective-Sergeant Demosthenes H. de Goede, with a mighty movement of his shoulders, arms and hands, moved the heavy cupboard to the left, and the valuable porcelain inside broke with a tinkle.

'And the curvilinear Meerlust yellow-wood cupboard ...' said 'slim' Mrs Silberstein as she sank back deeper in the chair and her whole body followed the next muscular movement that shifted the empty cupboard three feet to the right and let in a small patch of sunlight and landscape; because now they could see the lawn in the distance and hear more clearly the noise of the waters rushing through the invisible masks.

'Speaking of the personality of the murderer,' said Dr Johns, 'I read somewhere that the I.Q. of murderers is exceptionally low. It has been determined in certain institutions that the average is only seventy-one – about the same as a smart moron.' He looked meaningly at Detective-Sergeant Desmosthenes H. de Goede who, somewhat out of breath, stood beside the cupboard. 'But that is, of course, not so in *all* cases. It hangs together with the fact that the murderer generally has not enough intelligence to foresee the consequences of his or her deed.'

'In that case our poor Adam Kadmon is probably first on the list,' said 'slim' Mrs Silberstein, but she said it in such a way as to suggest that she attached little value to it. Her attention was rather on Detective-Sergeant Demosthenes H. de Goede, who had in the meantime quietened down. 'You no doubt took a considerable part in athletics and displays of strength, Mr de Goede?'

Detective-Sergeant Demosthenes H. de Goede had, among other things, been a wrestling champion as well, and in his spare time at college taken a course of Charles Atlas, according to which muscle-building was achieved by means of spiritual concentration and contramuscular tension. Via Dr Johns he received enthusiastic permission from 'slim' Mrs Silberstein to explain by way of demonstration, and for a start he removed his jacket and then his shirt carefully. The clothing was put neatly on the window seat and the tie hung over a chair. He was tanned a handsome brown and his muscles moved supply together at the slightest movement of his arms and body. He put his right fist in the palm of his left hand, strained all his powers, pushed, and the next moment the muscles moved beneath his skin as if they were charged with electricity. His entire torso quivered in merciless tension, which increased together with the breathless admiration of 'slim' Mrs Silberstein. Waves of muscle careered across his arms, collided with one another, swelled to bursting and vanished immediately as he relaxed.

'With a woman the pattern of murder is naturally different,' said Dr Johns. 'She sets about things more systematically. Her methods are indirect. The chances of her being caught are fewer. Everything points to greater intelligence and, therefore, greater danger.'

Detective-Sergeant Demosthenes H. de Goede was now pushing with shorter intervals and there was a noticeable rhythm in the way in which the tormented muscles collided with one another.

'It's interesting,' Dr Johns continued, 'that it is said of Euripides' *Hippolytus* that the tragic hero is not an individual, but man. The cosmic power is impersonal, the interplay of good and evil is outside the control of the individual, the whole community is the victim, the question of blame is secondary.'

'Slim' Mrs Silberstein, gripped by the muscle-play, began to hum 'The Blue Danube', and Demosthenes H. de Goede, ready as usual, adapted himself to the rhythm of her accompaniment, so that his muscles swelled, collided and relaxed to triple time and in so doing surpassed the theory of the famed Atlas by crowning his dogma of concentration with musicology.

'As Philip Vellacott puts it in the foreward to his translation,' said Dr Johns, 'at the stage when evil achieved the upper hand, it was already beyond the control of the human being. Something subhuman, superhuman, something impersonal, was involved . . .'

'Slim' Mrs Silberstein was now sharing Detective-Sergeant Demosthenes H. de Goede's athletic ecstasy in a way that he naturally did not understand. (Our police colleges endorse with monasticism the celibate dedication to State and God respectively.)

'Something like the Fatum, the Moira, Fate,' said Dr Johns.

Detective-Sergeant Demosthenes H. de Goede now (at the insistence of 'slim' Mrs Silberstein) removed his vest, too, folded it up, put it away and exposed the whole of his torso on which the vertical and horizontal muscles of his stomach revealed another landscape and a jollier rhythm.

'The Giant,' said Dr Johns, 'fits in so perfectly as an unfeeling implement of the supralogical that one should be inclined to detect a clue here, too.'

Detective-Sergeant Demosthenes H. de Goede was now busy manipulating his central abdominal band. It was an impressive exhibition and within the power of only the greatest masters of the cult. First of all he took a deep breath, and then a deeper one, forced out his lungs in the top part of his chest, retracted his stomach to nothing and then to a cavity, and strained as hard as he could. A single, vertical muscle appeared: a phallic symbol which made 'slim' Mrs Silberstein share orgiastically in his triumph.

'Our only expedient,' said Dr Johns, 'is to conceal ourselves, and, like Henry Silberstein-van Eeden – Mrs Silberstein's son-in-law,' he explained to Detective-Sergeant Demosthenes H. de Goede, who had suddenly lifted himself on his hands, his feet in the air, 'our only expedient is to cultivate, like Henry Silberstein-van-Eeden, astuteness. It is fatal to try and be heroic. We must accept Christian humility, turn the other cheek, protect ourselves with benevolence and make ourselves invisible by means of meekness.'

Detective-Sergeant Demosthenes H. de Goede was surpassing himself. Not only was he standing on his hands, but he was balancing himself on the ten slim pillars of his fingers.

'Slim' Mrs Silberstein had suspended all refinement, dropped all pretence of polish and crouched on her knees, like a little girl, before Detective-Sergeant Demosthenes H. de Goede who, achieving the impossible on an elegant index finger, withdrew nine of the little pillars.

'Only a heroic lunatic,' said Dr Johns desperately, 'would destroy himself against the rock and refuse to capitulate. We must adapt ourselves to the spirit of the times.'

'Slim' Mrs Silberstein had just tickled Detective-Sergeant Demosthenes H. de Goede under his arms. She lay beside him on the floor, her eyes close to his face, which grew redder and redder with exertion as he tried to keep vertical and at the same time to resist the teasing of his risorial muscles. Suddenly he collapsed; their laughter rang through the room and they tumbled together in a heap in front of Dr Johns who, silently and with interest now, watched the rudimentary seduction. But then, all of a sudden, 'slim' Mrs Silberstein straightened up, pushed her dress indolently back over garter, thigh and silk stocking, and ran her fingers through her hair.

'The poor Giant,' said 'slim' Mrs Silberstein. 'The poor scapegoat. One for the Lord and one for Azazel.'

'I merely mentioned his name,' said Dr Johns in self-defence, 'to exemplify an impersonal implement in the hand of an impersonal fate.'

She stood up sluggishly and went to the looking-glass, which lied flatteringly. She brought her face nearer to it as if searching for the answer to the riddle. Then she lightly touched herself under her eyes, on her temples and on her neck. Her face again became distorted, like the dripping masks that were noisy in the distance, but even that was reflected untruthfully as youthful melancholy; and in the background, like a bronze god in the looking glass, which clothed him in kingly garments, Demosthenes H. de Goede was carefully putting on, first, his vest, and then his shirt, tie and jacket.

'It could be any one of us,' said Dr Johns. 'I admit that. Not one of us is invisible enough to escape the attention of evil.'

He and Detective-Sergeant Demosthenes H. de Goede left the room in silence, after being dismissed by 'slim' Mrs Silberstein with a slight movement of her head. Her back was turned squarely on them; her eyes, beautified by the looking glass, were fixed motionlessly on herself.

Chapter Five

The Residents: Madam, Hope and Prudence Ritchie

'Beyond this door,' Dr Johns said to Detective-Sergeant Demosthenes H. de Goede as they reached the end of a narrow passage, 'the Foundation takes over. I trust that you'll immediately notice the difference.'

They were now beside the house but were still surrounded by buildings connected to the original house by walls and passages. There were signs of the old bachelor quarters but it was difficult, without help, to single out the originals. The Department of Public Works had, in characteristic fashion, succeeded in obliterating all forms of style by means of extensions and additions. Here and there the Monuments Commission had put up its bronze plaques to identify, for a grateful posterity, the authentic: a handsomely shaped arch beam here, a ringwall there. The green bronze plaques (they were innumerable in that maze) indicated Old Cape architectonic oases in the official wilderness; it was an adventure for the cognoscente to have his supposition confirmed by the dogma of a plaque on a stone arch, an abutment or a cellar dome.

It was, for instance, by no means impossible that Dr Johns had mistaken a plaque of the Monuments Commission for the *shema* beside the front door. It was, however, unlikely, since Detective-Sergeant Demosthenes H. de Goede had as one of his optional courses, 'General Improvement,' under *capita selecta*, made a study of 'Religions of the World,' and would immediately have pointed out the mistake to Dr Johns.

'Have you noticed,' asked Dr Johns, 'that Jock Silberstein defended the Giant and that 'slim' Mrs Silberstein stood kindheartedly aloof? All attention is directed at Adam Kadmon, the stupid colossus. We are all moving in the shadow of the Giant.'

They walked on in a vain attempt to see the house in perspective. Walls, rooms and outbuildings of all kinds turned them back time and time again to an inner circle of buildings.

'Do you know the legend of the Giants in mythology?' Dr Johns asked suddenly.

Detective-Sergeant Demosthenes H. de Goede stuttered his knowledge.

'Exactly,' said Dr Johns. 'The Giant Typhon resulted from the intercourse of Earth and Tartarus.'

Unexpectedly they found a gate; they were once again on the rolling lawns that surrounded the house, and from where they stood they could understand better the nature of the alterations and additions. Here the Foundation had taken over completely and built on to such an extent that the architectural style of Public Works, freed from the Old Cape Dutch burden, had at last triumphed. There were brown doors and windows everywhere, covered with six or seven layers of paint to keep secret the material; dull, heavy and solid, one was reminded of station buildings or those brick-coloured constructions on experimental farms. The trees before the windows were rare and indigenous and grew about half an inch a year to throw, after more than three hundred years, a proud shadow. The flowers in the beds were utterly regimented – but in a different manner to that of the old days at Welgevonden. There was no longer a mathematical cheerfulness; the sickly grew sicklier beside the strong that grew stronger, both under the vigilant eyes of botanists who specialized in both directions and found decay as fascinating as growth.

'I was actually thinking of the origin of the Giants who fought the gods,' said Dr Johns as, in their wandering, they looked at the rows of rooms and at the faces through the windows, hanging disembodied over desks.

'I was thinking of Gaea who encouraged her son, Cronus, to kill her husband, Uranus, while he was enjoying her.'

They had now reached another lawn where Detective-Sergeant Demosthenes H. de Goede was confronted with Public Works in the guise of regeneration, under the influence of young architects who had travelled considerably abroad.

'Cronus emasculated his father with his left hand and threw his manhood into the sea,' said Dr Johns. 'The style of the sixties,' he explained in regard to the buildings that grimaced at them with hundreds of windows.

The new buildings looked like an American suburban paradise. The walls were of various colours, the steel frames chosen from the rich uniformity of a well-known catalogue; each room faced the other squarely and the occupants, separated by large glass windows and patches of grass, lived outwardly and for one another.

'Cronus emasculated his father with a sickle,' said Dr Johns, 'but his blood impregnated his mother and she gave birth to the Giants. To the Giants and to the Erinyes that will persecute until the end of time.'

The residents looked at one another through the windows, through the panes that like the lenses of cameras and binoculars were aimed from one side to the other.

'And then the struggle between the Olympian gods and the Giants originated,' said Dr Johns. 'But like the Titans, the Giants, too, were doomed to destruction.'

Behind a window sat a woman with many coloured curlers in her hair. Her hair was pulled tightly against her skull and fastened with orange, yellow, blue, green and purple clips. She was in earnest conversation with a similar sort of woman. Suddenly they looked up, saw Dr Johns and smiled with false teeth that gleamed through the glass.

Dr Johns waved to them and was greeted with an increasing number of porcelain chips.

'But the most interesting of all is,' said Dr Johns, 'that the Giants were actually primitive early spirits, and that they could only be destroyed by a magical plant. The plant that Hercules found in Erebus. Hercules who saves us from erotic nightmares: from the Giant Porphyrion who wished to rape Hera, from the Giant Pallas who wished to dishonour his own daughter, Pallas Athena.'

Each apartment had a different colour-mark of distinction and they stopped now before variations of blue. They went nearer and the resident approached them from behind a glass door.

'From revenge,' said Dr Johns, 'Gaea slept with Tartarus and gave birth to the greatest Giant ever born, your monster Typhon. But he, too, was doomed to destruction.'

The door opened and Dr Johns said: 'Allow me to introduce you, Madam Ritchie, to Detective-Sergeant Demosthenes H. de Goede.'

A large woman filled the door-frame, raised her fat arms in a gesture of greeting, and stood aside for them to enter. Her head was a network of curlers and her face red and puffy, like that of a woman who had just come from under a hairdresser's dryer. She touched her hair and then regarded Demosthenes H. de Goede with friendly little eyes that, superficially, shone with pleasant acknowledgement but which if one were attentive to the hidden glint behind the glance, held him for a moment in cold-blooded calculation and classified him according to her own Almanac.

'A pleasure, Mr de Goede,' she said and by means of the single word 'Mister,' allowed him – unknowingly – into the inner circle. Had it been otherwise, she would have held him at a distance by repetition of the title 'Detective-Sergeant.'

(Detective-Sergeant Demosthenes H. de Goede's father was a farmer. During his final term at the police college, the ladies of the Sunrise Nurses' Hostel voted the Sergeant the most attractive cadet of the year, on the occasion of their Invitation Ball.)

He bent over her hand and thus gave her the opportunity of sending the mother-sign to her two daughters, Hope and Prudence, who were waiting in the background, in the no-man's-land of the passage.

Two appealing girls: the one athletic and strong of tooth; the other lissome and full-breasted. Their fair hair, at this stage with the gleam of youthful growth, was combed to gleaming wavecrests. Their lips were white, their skins bronzed by sunlight in their glass rooms.

Detective-Sergeant Demosthenes H. de Goede bowed to them with a smiling grimace that held a world of meaning for his

fellows in age. They grinned back and contact on the time level
had been made.

'I have just explained to Detective-Sergeant Demosthenes H.
de Goede something about the true nature of the mythological
Giants,' said Dr Johns. 'The nightmare from the Unconscious,
the terrifying primordial images that can be exorcized only by
means of the magical plant and the intervention of the hero.'

Madam Ritchie indicated that they should be seated and nodded
encouragingly at Dr Johns, noticing with approval that her two
daughters had taken their places side by side and were coquet-
tishly ignoring the Detective-Sergeant.

'The erotic nature of the Giants is, of course, not unknown,'
said Dr Johns, flattered by the attention suddenly accorded him.
'For instance, it is not for nothing that the name of the leader
of the Giants, Ephialtes, means *incubus* in Latin.' He was a little
disturbed that there was no reaction. 'The one who violates,' he
translated freely and leaned back satisfied by the expected giggle.

He stroked his bald pate and looked archly at the girls.

'The one who violates,' he repeated with the pleasure in a
platitude of a very old man who has long since forgotten the
true nature of titillating vulgarity.

The tittering subsided and there was silence in the room as
each waited for the other to make the next move. It was Hope
who turned on a small transistor radio and gradually began to
move her legs to the rhythm of the hit tune, 'Peter Gunn'. She
was followed by Prudence who rose suddenly and, rooted in the
subsoil of the tune, pensively did a few twist movements. The
volume was turned up, the music overwhelmed and isolated
everyone in the room.

Madam Ritchie looked at her daughters and genuine tears
came to her eyes. 'Poor Lila,' she said. 'What a horrible way to
die.' She brought out a silk hankie but did not use it. 'Even if
people did spread whatever rumours about her, even if she wasn't
as pure as one would wish one's children to be' – and she glanced
at her dancing daughters – 'even if she did sin in the flesh, even
so it was a cruel retribution and she did not deserve it.' She
flapped the handkerchief to and fro, as if to the rhythm of the

music, and as if, too, she were cooling her tears and could not bring herself to the point of removing those signs of her grief. 'We all feel threatened, I myself, Hope, Prudence and every girl around here.' Her voice grew more intense and the flow of tears diminished, subsided and ceased in a single, large drop that hung on her eyelash. 'The evildoer is in our midst! He's on the loose! The monster is among us . . .'

The dresses of the Viking daughters swayed as they jerked into the beat-rhythm. They spun round and round and waggled their whirling behinds at Demosthenes H. de Goede.

'It doesn't matter *who* hears me!' Madame Ritchie raised her voice above the sound of the surrealistic 'Peter Gunn'. 'Even if he is the son of the king. Justice must be done!'

She removed the last tear in a becoming manner with the silk hankie: she dried it and reduced it to a damp little spot on the silk. 'We must hide nothing,' she said. 'We must always be prepared to give the facts,' and the sound as she blew her nose was loud above the blare of trumpets.

Then the music ended and Hope and Prudence took up their positions on either side of Detective-Sergeant Demosthenes H. de Goede; and Madam Ritchie folded the handkerchief still smaller, wiped the perspiration from her brow, rolled the handkerchief in the palms of her hands and spirited it between dress and breast where it was pressed damp and firm to strengthen her afresh for the next virtuoso performance.

It was quiet again in the room and suddenly all attention was directed at Detective-Sergeant Demosthenes H. de Goede who, with eyes rigidly fixed on a neutral corner, was apparently sustaining an emotional attack. His respiratory movements were deep and irregular, and he frequently had difficulty in getting his breath back after he had exhaled. Madam Ritchie jerked up straight in her chair, in tow of the emotional results of her innuendoes, deeply impressed by the sensitivity of this perceptive young man, the athletic young god who would protect them against . . . 'The Giant!' she said suddenly. 'Adam Kadmon Silberstein!'

Although it was a system specially devised by the police college for those who were prevented by their duties from taking part in athletics, it did look ever so much like a state of tension and encouraged her to further loud effusions. 'What's the good of concealing it? We all know! The monster! The idiot!'

Detective-Sergeant Demosthenes H. de Goede was busy with isometric exercises for the sake of his stomach muscles ... You draw in your breath for one count ... you exhale it for six counts ...

'There was a mark on Lila's neck!' screamed Madam Ritchie, carried away. 'I saw it myself! Two marks on her throat!'

... You force out your stomach when you inhale; you pull it in when you exhale ...

'A love bite!'

And two sharp little shrieks cut through the room, two shrieks from Hope and Prudence, which were repeated in a duet as they jumped up and looked out through the glass.

Because, for a few seconds, the Giant had appeared and passed the window with clumsy steps.

Chapter Six

Memento Mori

'Life is movement,' said Dr Johns as they wandered on. 'We are never at a standstill: we are continually on the go.' The earth was wet, the mud clung to their shoes. 'Nor is there any coherence. There are only those fragments that we encounter on our continual movement and which we wish to expand into a comprehensible whole.' The waters were noisy in the distant streams and confirmed the complete isolation of everyone who found himself at Welgevonden after rain. 'There is no beginning and no end,' said Dr Johns.

The blocks, endless blocks, of glass buildings with their visible residents had suddenly come to an end. The two men were now ascending a slight rise – a continuation of the lawn which apparently had no end. For a moment they were alone on the wide, monotonous landscape and then a group of figures appeared suddenly over the hump of the rise. They moved to and fro, like leaves in the wind, and then zigzagged straight down on Detective-Sergeant Demosthenes H. de Goede and Dr Johns: the uncle from Welkom, the uncle from the Karroo, the aunt with silver hair and the sobbing girl who looked like a little sow. A group of four, on enormous Welgevonden, looking for relatives.

They shuffled nearer questioningly and Dr Johns introduced Demosthenes H. de Goede to them. A doctor of medicine and a representative of the law! To them they represented the pillars of society and they pressed still nearer with an inundation of questions and reproaches. The uncle from Welkom raised a hand, subdued them and showed himself to be in future the leader of the family.

'No,' said Dr Johns. 'Lila's mother died at the birth of her child. Her grandfather, the gardener, and his wife passed away long ago. She lived by the grace of the owner and patron of the Foundation, Jock Silberstein. Lila was completely alone and had no living family on Welgevonden.' The uncle from the Karroo looked at the remnants of the relatives, the last of an unknown generation. He gathered them in his melancholy gaze as a desolate little group, raised them proudly to a Gideon's band, ranged them together for all time. On the great lawn of Welgevonden, on this particular wet day, a family tie was being forged that, in the future, would burden the post office with thick letters in blue envelopes, with white pages of unformed handwriting that bemoaned the weather and depicted syndromes with curled letters that aired grievances and laid claim to blood that was thicker than water.

'The house where she lived is over there . . .' said Dr Johns, and gestured in the direction of an invisible house in the distance with an asbestos roof.

The uncle from Welkom thanked him on behalf of the family and restrained himself in time from asking what it would cost. The thought was simply a matter of habit and a smile cleaved his lips. This story he simply *had* to tell to his relatives; perhaps in one of his later letters, when the hurt had passed. The feeling you had to ask what it cost when you saw a doctor. And then he suddenly became aware of the Sergeant.

He called the Sergeant aside and told him the rumour he had heard and, in strict confidence, his own suspicion : that Lila, his niece on his father's side, had been murdered by a giant.

One by one they took their leave of the influential pair and bowed themselves away, the proud citizenry; but not before the old man from Welkom had requested Dr Johns to thank Jock Silberstein for not having buried their niece in a pauper's coffin.

They moved over the hill as if blown by the slight wind, a group of four on their pilgrimage on behalf of the girl with the white face.

On their way they met the Giant, scattered and regrouped : a united body in silhouette, a corporate body against the horizon. Then they noticed the little house with the asbestos roof in the distance and raised their hands, cheered and disappeared abruptly over the hill.

'It's extraordinary,' said Dr Johns, as at last they left the lawn and wandered along a road, 'that all of us at Welgevonden knew Lila's mother. She was eighteen, the girl with the pale face.' In the distance they could see a row of cottages surrounded by trees. 'One of us was Lila's father, someone here is Lila's brother or sister.' Often they had to avoid puddles and turn off to find dry earth between the heather. 'And someone slept in unknowing incest with his daughter or sister.' Hooting and jeering interrupted his words. They looked around and hastily sought the safety of the heather. 'And does that not perhaps reflect a hidden degeneration in each of us? Lost love, secret sadism, the loved one who becomes hated, animal nature that is made synonymous with sexuality, the forbidden wish, the longing for revenge because we have lost paradise?'

Three trucks roared past them, splashed through the mud and cut deep double tracks in the wet earth. They were all green and yellow. 'Those were the trucks that transported the wine,' said Dr Johns, 'painted with the colours of Welgevonden.' At the back of the trucks sat a multitude of people, on benches and caged in by rails, in the manic-depressive condition of picnickers: a row of faces lifted in maniacal pleasure, with an occasional depressed face in between. 'The quarterly picnic at the trout lake,' said Dr Johns. 'Psychotherapeutic recreational joy.'

On the side of each of the trucks, in big yellow letters, was the following legend: THE WELGEVONDEN FOUNDATION; and on the other side, in bilingual resignation: DIE WELGEVONDEN FONDASIE.

The trucks disappeared over the hill with a lewd skip.

Dr Johns and Detective-Sergeant Demosthenes H. de Goede resumed their walk in silence. Detective-Sergeant Demosthenes H. de Goede was visibly upset by the ravage caused to his suede shoes by the mud. Presently he asked Dr Johns to wait: he removed his shoes, tied the laces together and hung them around his neck, rolled up his trousers and resumed his walk, visibly happier.

'Under such circumstances,' said Dr Johns, 'it's not at all surprising that werewolves, succubi, incubi and vampires haunted people.' A single walker appeared around a corner before them.

'But today the fear of our guilty love appears perhaps in other forms.' He nodded at the walker. 'Or, the worst of all, in ordinary forms.'

Reverend Williams greeted these two brothers, whom he had noticed at the funeral, cheerfully.

'Aaaah ...!' he said, his hand raised, waiting for them to supply their names.

'Doctor Johns ... Detective-Sergeant Demosthenes H. de Goede,' and Dr Johns gestured with a rapid movement of his hand.

Reverend Williams had been unprepared for the storm. His toilet requisites and clothes were in the city: as he had come, so he was still. The sweat that clung to his underclothing in the sticky heat, the collar that already showed black marks, the baggy trousers, the saturated shoes heavy with mud, the beard that grew unkempt, brought ruin to the image, based on Billy Graham, of himself as a parson. The approach in tatters belonged to another, folksy, popular, convivial type – and in that guise he felt himself strange. Therefore, and not without dignity, he fought the fight, true to himself, while circumstances entirely beyond his control were systematically stripping him.

Just like the uncle from Welkom, he was instantly tuned in to the wavelength of these quarters.

'A lamentable business,' he said and raised his face to a now cloudless heaven. 'An extremely unhappy state of affairs,' and he turned his gaze on a huge figure standing motionless in the distance. 'Such a lovable child, the victim of an evil world,' and he confined his observations to the two figures before him. 'I gather that the whole of Welgevonden is mourning for this unsullied girl.' And suddenly he changed over to a parsonic diction, in order to maintain his self-esteem in defiance of the collapse of his personal appearance. He rocked on his heels as he started his sentences; he rose on his toes as he reached a period. He hissed his *s*'s and crooned his *n*'s; he clicked his *c*'s and spat his *t*'s – he orchestrated his thoughts with the instruments of his words; he passed beyond the meaning of words, and by means of a combination of tone, pauses, dashes and resonance of empty rhetoric, he created Galatea from his hairy fist: a chaste Aphrodite with a white face, desired and reluctantly ravished; an evil desire of man aroused by the devil, the original sin in regard to the numen. The monster as the instrument of Belial !

And then he concluded with an enlightening call from the clouds for everyone to pass on to performing a glorious deed, while he sank down on the tips of his toes into the mud.

Entirely renewed, his apparel notwithstanding, he prepared to leave, but found this beyond the resources of his feeble physical strength. With the help of Detective-Sergeant Demosthenes H. de Goede he was freed from his shoes, which remained stuck in the mud, and wandered away on tender feet in resignation across the lovely, soft, yielding earth.

'Your task,' said Dr Johns as they themselves wandered on slowly in the direction of the cottages, 'is heroically great but not impossible. The Titans and Giants are only remembered because of the battles they lost.' He peered at the nearest cottage, which peered back from among a clump of trees. 'It's a legendary fact that evil has always been defeated by the son of a god from a human woman – Hercules, Christ, and . . .' and he nodded approvingly at Detective-Sergeant Demosthenes H. de Goede who, even as they walked, succeeded by means of isometric exercises in massaging his neck muscles, '. . . and also those who are destined by circumstances to become, like Hercules, the champions of the community.'

They saw a warning notice beside the road and stopped to look at it.

'Evil is actually impotent,' said Dr Johns. 'Satan is the great cuckold of the universe.'

It was clear that the notice had been painted by an amateur, although it was strikingly like the danger signals that the Provincial Administration had erected to warn against dangerous conditions which it, under compulsion of rock formation and highway futility, had itself created. Under a red triangle, this particular danger sign begged in shrill yellow letters: THE LORD HAVE MERCY UPON US.

Detective-Sergeant Demosthenes H. de Goede was particularly interested in this phenomenon and took out his notebook in which to write the words. His handwriting, as always, was exceptionally choice and neat.

'Funnily enough,' said Dr Johns as they resumed their walk, 'Satan is himself incorporeal. He needs a human being to become visible.' They stopped again before another sign. 'It's the human being that has become cunning and hidden himself in the struggle.'

This notice was coal black and square, with the legend in shining white: WEEPE, FASTE and PRAYE!

Detective-Sergeant Demosthenes H. de Goede, notebook in hand and pen at the ready, looked questioningly at Dr Johns.

'Seventeenth-century English,' said Dr Johns. 'Circa 1632.'

Detective-Sergeant Demosthenes H. de Goede wrote: 'Weepe, faste and praye,' and right next to that, in brackets, 'Weep, fast and pray.' He hesitated a moment, then added: 'Old E. 1623.'

'But perhaps,' said Dr Johns by way of afterthought, as they were drawing close to the cottage, 'it is the perfect cunning of Satan. Precisely by resigning himself to his invisibility, now that God is invisible too, he is more difficult to distinguish from God. He is a master planner in the sphere of formlessness, even if he is the ape of God.'

The cottage was surrounded by beech trees, narcissus, chincherinchee and daffodils. The road signs had reached a climax in a notice directly in front of the garden gate, where a *Memento Mori* had been placed precisely in the middle of a large board, beneath a wooden cross and a little Virgin figure.

Dr Johns and Detective-Sergeant Demosthenes H. de Goede stood nearer in order to study the *Memento Mori*.

The central feature was a vertical drawing of an open grave in which a skeleton lay. To left and right were two coffins with corpses in them, each wound in a shroud. In the top left-hand corner the figure of an old man with a long beard leaning on a scythe, with his other hand resting on an hourglass. In the top right-hand corner, a skeleton propped against a skull. Below, in an exact triangle, three death's-heads. Picks and shovels, crossed, balanced the drawing where necessary. From left to right, at the bottom, was written in black letters: AND AS I AM, SO MUST YOU BE. THEREFORE PREPARE TO FOLLOW ME.

To one side, at an angle in a corner, in cursive letters, the creator of the *Memento* (and, in fact, of the danger signs also) was given: 'O'Hara pinxit.'

Detective-Sergeant Demosthenes H. de Goede had already taken out his notebook and set aside a blank page when Dr Johns stopped him and drew his attention to a small shelf next to the notice where a whole pile of these pamphlets was available. Each took one and then went through the garden gate.

They admired the daffodils and the chincherinchee and the beds full of flowers that shone fresh and colourful in the sunlight. Then they noticed another small notice, hidden among the flora, hardly three inches above the ground: A WET SPRING RAISES FEAR OF FAMINE.

The door of the cottage was painted red and Dr Johns was about to knock when he saw an illuminated manuscript, beautifully designed in many colours, and fastened with drawing pins to the wall beside the door frame. He put on his glasses and studied the notice attentively.

'Amazing!' he said to Demosthenes H. de Goede. 'Something one seldom sees: a genuine Bill of Mortality.' He took off his glasses and returned them to his pocket. 'I think they first appeared in the days of Louis XIV, but this one is considerably different and shows a good deal of English influence.' He beckoned to Detective-Sergeant de Goede to come nearer. 'As you'll notice, there are three coloumns: the name in the first column, the day of death in the second, and the cause of death in the third.' He glanced fleetingly through the names. 'Very, very interesting,' he said. 'Here is the history of old residents and of regular visitors to Welgevonden.'

368 One for the Devil

Detective-Sergeant Demosthenes H. de Goede read the names and made brief notes on cause of death:

Name	Cause of Death
Old Mrs Silberstein ('The Duchess')	Liver growne
Sir Henry Mandrake	Plannett strucke
Miss Agatha Silberstein	Aged
Miss Florence Silberstein	Aged
The 'Gardener'	King's Evill
Giepie Ollenwaar	Gored by a bull
J. J. van Eeden	Infection by germ *Spirochaeta pallida*
Bebe Gulbenkian	Throwne by horse
20 Unknowne Blacks	In course of disturbances
One Albino Baby	Shot
Salome Silberstein	At birthe of monstrous childe

Detective-Sergeant Demosthenes H. de Goede found that his notebook was getting full and contented himself with looking quickly through the remaining names. He wrote the last name of all down, however.

Lila	Murthered by a Giant

Chapter Seven

How to Protect Oneself
Against Pamgri

After Dr Johns had knocked at the door, he stood back and looked closely at the window beside it. Meanwhile, Detective-Sergeant Demosthenes H. de Goede busied himself with putting on his shoes, combing his hair and tidying himself up in various ways after the exacting walk through the mud.

'He suffers from senile decay,' said Dr Johns, 'but during a *lucidum intervallum* he remains one of my best friends. If he scrabbles at the window pane in order to get out, we shall have to postpone the visit until later.'

They both now looked at the window. After a while they heard footsteps and the curtains were drawn aside. A small face, wizened with age, dwarfed by a broad-brimmed hat, peered sombrely through the pane. A staff was held in a bony white hand and a large toga hung overbearingly across meagre shoulders : the apparel of a funeral bearer at the time of the Great Plague. He was completely passive.

'Thank God, he's normal,' said Dr Johns. 'We can go in.'

He produced a key and unlocked the door. The sad little figure appeared full-length in the doorway and held out his hand to Dr Johns. Dr Johns handed over a key, and he seized it eagerly. The toga hung to his feet and swayed to and fro as he fumbled to find the pocket among all the folds. Only when he had pocketed the key, and placed the staff against a wall, did he come outside; and then he underwent a complete transformation. A toothless smile split his face, his small eyes narrowed and sparkled with alertness. He embraced Dr Johns and then turned to Detective-Sergeant Demosthenes H. de Goede, waiting courteously to be introduced to him.

'Judge O'Hara,' said Dr Johns. 'Detective-Sergeant Demosthenes H. de Goede.'

Judge O'Hara nodded amiably, and Detective-Sergeant Demosthenes H. de Goede, instantly adjusted to the demands of propriety of the jurisprudential hierarchy, saluted smartly : for the rest of the meeting, alert and in his proper place, he would observe protocol.

They were led into a small inside room which the sunlight, falling through barred windows, lighted and showed to contain leather-covered chairs and book-filled shelves which created the impression of an exclusive club in colonial days.

'I presume I may keep the key?' said Judge O'Hara to Dr Johns, as he poured them each a whisky and soda. The Sergeant was given a beer.

'But certainly, my good friend,' said Dr Johns.

'It's not that I find the isolation unwholesome,' said Judge O'Hara, and raised his glass to Demosthenes H. de Goede. 'It's simply the fact that I have a good deal of work to do and that my activities are not confined to the room.'

They drank in silence and Judge O'Hara folded the toga over his knees and settled the medieval hat more comfortably on his head.

'Detective-Sergeant Demosthenes H. de Goede is here in connection with the investigation into the death of Lila,' said Dr Johns.

For a moment the name meant nothing to Judge O'Hara, and Dr Johns explained who she was : the daughter of the white-faced girl, the granddaughter of the gardener who lived in the cottage with the asbestos roof, the white-faced girl who died at the birth of her daughter, Lila, who had just been murdered by an unknown sadist.

'Naturally,' said Judge O'Hara. 'The one who was raped by a Giant. I remember her well' – and he placed the tips of his fingers together in a judicial gesture. 'I assume you have already arrested the miscreant, Sergeant.' He turned to Demosthenes H. de Goede, who began to stutter diligently, but Dr Johns interrupted and explained that Detective-Sergeant Demosthenes H. de

Goede was, at this stage, merely getting acquainted with the residents of Welgevonden.

'The rape or dishonouring of a virgin has been one of the greatest sins since the earliest times,' said Judge O'Hara, and poured himself and Dr Johns another whisky and soda. 'Among the Jews the corrupter of the maiden had, for instance, to pay *zohar* to her father.' He nodded with approval when Detective-Sergeant Demosthenes H. de Goede refused a second beer. 'At the time of Moses, a man who deflowered a maiden was stoned.' The hat was too low over his eyes and he shifted it higher up, but a moment later it was back over his eyes. 'I have read,' said Judge O'Hara, 'that the basis for this singular retribution was the fear of demoniacal powers. Sexuality is the territory of evil, and the protected maidenly opening can only be made use of under the protection of a magical counter ritual.' He offered Dr Johns a third drink, which was not refused. He himself took a couple of long sips and relaxed, a genial medieval funeral bearer in his toga, which enclosed him in his chair like a big black blanket. 'The chief method of exorcism was to kick up a noise during coitus and thus to drive the evil spirits away. It is said that Rabbi Ben Huna rang a bell in such circumstances.'

Both he and Dr Johns shook peacefully in a fit of lively laughter while Detective-Sergeant Demosthenes H. de Goede kept his eyes high-mindedly, and his mind attentively, on the Judge.

'And then there are still the magical powers of purification of water,' Judge O'Hara continued. 'The Talmud calls fresh rain-water . . .'

'Adam Kadmon Silberstein, for instance, takes a regular bath near the masks, every morning,' said Dr Johns, and looked meaningfully at Detective-Sergeant Demosthenes H. de Goede.

'And fire,' said Judge O'Hara. 'The burning sconce . . .'

'And amulets,' added Dr Johns.

'Amulets,' said Judge O'Hara, 'in the form of sexual symbols. At the mysteries of Eleusis the pudenda was the vulva; the crown of the Emperor of Kafa was a phallic triangle.' He turned to Detective-Sergeant Demosthenes H. de Goede. 'Do you, for example, know the sign of the fig in Italy to protect oneself against the *malocchio*?'

Detective-Sergeant Demosthenes H. de Goede strained his memory to the utmost: his search covered the entire field of General Knowledge, Cultural Studies, Strange Customs to Some Aspects of Cosmology, as he had learned them in his final year at the police college, but he declared himself stutteringly defeated by the Judge's greater learning.

Judge O'Hara illustrated for him the sign of the vulva, and Detective-Sergeant Demosthenes H. de Goede went red to behind his ears when he recognized the indecent gesture of his childhood.

'But to return to serious matters,' said Judge O'Hara, after he had refilled the two glasses, 'the fury of the community is unleashed fully when the maiden, actually its protection against evil, is deflowered. And I imagine that you, in your perambulation of the estate, have been struck by this atmosphere of revenge . . .'

He looked questioningly at his two guests.

'We have still to determine if Lila was raped,' said Dr Johns carefully. 'Detective-Sergeant Demosthenes H. de Goede and I have even considered whether we shall perhaps not have to exhume the deceased.'

Suddenly Judge O'Hara sat up straight in his chair. The perpetual sparkle disappeared from his eyes, the depression of a while back returned to him.

'Exactly! Exactly . . .' he began, and stood up in confusion. The folds of the toga fell over his feet, the small figure became ominous in his strange apparel.

'And I know what you will find,' said Judge O'Hara in a sepulchral voice. 'Warm blood in her breasts and *in fundo ventricoli* . . . her face flushed, her limbs soft and supple . . . her hair and nails long and overgrown . . . her lips, cheeks and breasts swollen with fresh blood . . . new blood pulsing *in ventricolo cordis* . . .'

He walked tensely to and fro, obsessed by the image.

Dr Johns stood up and beckoned to Detective-Sergeant Demosthenes H. de Goede.

'Make a cross of tar on every door tonight!' said Judge O'Hara and seized Dr Johns by the arm. 'Invoke Saint Rochus, and Saint Sebastian and Saint Adrian to protect you.' He pulled Detective-Sergeant Demosthenes H. de Goede nearer, too, in the iron grip of his bony hands. 'Beware of the confidant who will come in false form!'

'We will disinter her,' said Dr Johns placatingly, 'simply to determine the true nature of her death, and Detective-Sergeant Demosthenes H. de Goede will do the necessary.'

'Destroy the bloodthirsty friend of Samchasai!' called Judge O'Hara and seized his staff.

Dr Johns pointed, unobserved, to the door and he and Detective-Sergeant Demosthenes H. de Goede began to move slowly towards it.

'Carry the sacred relics with you constantly! Never be without the Paschal wax! Write out the first fourteen verses of Saint John and never be without them! Wear the medal of Saint Benedict! Sing a requiem over the grave!' He opened his toga and revealed an undergarment which had scoured his sensitive skin until it was blood red. 'Chastise yourself with the hair of the Cilician goat!'

Dr Johns and the Detective were already at the door, but Judge O'Hara barred their way, his small eyes glowing with inner fire.

'I saw his sharp, long teeth! He assaults men, women and children! He uses the body to renew himself! He does not spare even his own sister!'

Dr Johns and Detective-Sergeant Demosthenes H. de Goede slipped through the door and looked back at Judge O'Hara standing with his staff aloft.

'Strew garlic on her grave! Destroy the pernicious incubus with the pale face and the red hair! They're the hallmarks of the Pamgri!'

He came toward them, flecks of foam at the corners of his mouth.

'Drive a wooden spike through her heart, because the curse is upon her! Transfix her with wood for the peace of her eternal soul!'

Dr Johns slammed the door on him, and when he tried to get out, locked it with another key.

'His key was a dummy,' said Dr Johns as they left. 'I make sure before I give him the right key,' and he looked sadly back at the little black figure who, scrabbling at the window, was trying vainly to get out.

Chapter Eight

The Descendants of Brutus the Bull

'Perhaps at this stage I should tell you more about the Foundation,' said Dr Johns as he and Detective-Sergeant Demosthenes H. de Goede walked away from the cottage in the direction of the farming area and the huge buildings in the distance known as the factory, the bottling plant and the cellars. They climbed a hill and wandered through paddocks in which sheep of various breeds were peacefully feeding on alfalfa and were so fat from little exercise and abundant food that they could hardly move. Around each paddock there was gathered a small group of people, where men in white were giving lectures.

'Around you,' said Dr Johns, 'you will see visitors, as well as residents and members of the family. Residents are allowed to have their families with them and it often happens that the residents, together with their families, decide to stay on even when they have received their discharge.' He smiled at Demosthenes H. de Goede, who kept looking back at the cottage they had just left. 'We are also often overwhelmed by visitors from outside and there are an unusual number of them now, because of a special occasion.' He listened to the waters thundering through the masks. 'At the moment, everyone has been trapped by the streams, and that naturally simplifies your task. I mean, it's like a detective story: the ideal seclusion, the broken communications, the castle in the forest, the disrupted paradise.'

Detective-Sergeant Demosthenes H. de Goede stammered a question and Dr Johns listened carefully.

'The special occasion?' His face cleared and he himself became excited. 'A particularly important event, and I trust that you will do everything in your power to prevent the unfortunate recent incident and the bitter task that lies ahead from harming the proceedings.' He waited until he had received Detective-Sergeant Demosthenes H. de Goede's gesture of promise. 'Good ! D'you see, the authorities concerned, which sanction the Foundation and contribute to it, rand for rand, have seen fit to make an award to Jock Silberstein and two others. The dignitaries, properly trapped . . .' He laughed delightedly at his own joke. 'The trapped dignitaries are already here, and the award will be made at a function tomorrow evening. We hope to have a full house and we hope that, by that time, the unpleasant task will have been accomplished.' He was silent for a while. 'Speed is therefore a necessity.'

Detective-Sergeant Demosthenes H. de Goede increased his pace impulsively and Dr Johns, with his short steps, had difficulty in keeping up. He was, however, remarkably athletic for someone of his advanced age.

'It is felt, however,' Dr Johns continued, 'that a doctorate cannot be dished out too lightly, especially because more than one person attached to the Foundation is concerned, so accordingly only Jock Silberstein will receive a doctor's degree, *honoris causa*, and the others suitable lesser degrees.'

They had already left the loafing yards and were on their way to a farther group of people gathered around cattle in a paddock.

'The second person is Henry Silberstein-van Eeden, Jock Silberstein's son-in-law ... And, may I add, certainly the hardest worker and the axis around which everything in this organization revolves. He deserves the degree of M.A. Admin., *honoris causa*.' Dr Johns was slightly winded in his attempt to keep up with Detective-Sergeant Demosthenes H. de Goede, who had unwittingly warmed up to racing speed.

Detective-Sergeant Demosthenes H. de Goede had often taken part in walking races at the police college and he unconsciously applied the necessary movements to attain the maximum speed : his elbows raised high, his shoulders hunched, his fists just grazing his chin, like pistons, and his legs moving in that singular movement that only the connoisseur can distinguish from a trot.

'The other person is Giepie Ollenwaar, the founder of the red-black Ollenwaar Stud Association.'

Dr Johns was now *trotting* unashamedly.

'M.Sc. Agric., *honoris causa,*' he gasped.

At that speed they approached the crowd around the cattle with unnecessary haste and then suddenly came to a halt, both breathing deeply.

'Uncle Giepie Ollenwaar, of blessed memory,' said Dr Johns, 'died eighteen years ago, however; but the authorities have seen fit to bestow the degree on him *in absentia,* because of his exceptional contribution.'

Detective-Sergeant Demosthenes H. de Goede had immediately made use of his faster breathing and employed it for isometric application. (You merely extend your stomach and then draw it in against the movement of normal breathing. It's also excellent for the lungs.)

They now walked more sedately towards the circle of people who, greeting him, made room for Dr Johns. A man in a white overall was about to speak.

'That's Dries van Schalkwyk,' whispered Dr Johns, 'the well-beloved secretary of the association and also a special field officer of the Foundation.'

A well-built, sunburned man with bristle-brush hair going grey in neat speckles at the temples, laughed at the crowd with a strong row of false teeth. A small, skinny bull with a curiously patterned skin colour was snuffling at him in a friendly way, and he repeatedly repulsed the shy muzzle with his elbow.

'Dear friends,' began Dries van Schalkwyk; and then he spotted Dr Johns. He rubbed his hands together. 'Dear friends, we have the special honour . . .' – and he came down from his dais – '. . . to have . . .' – he took Dr Johns by the arm and exhibited him – 'Doctor Johns in our midst.' He waited for the applause, which came only from the residents of Welgevonden; relatives and visitors stood aloof, watching.

Dr Johns whispered something in his ear.

'And, friends,' he said, 'an exceptional honour.' He took Demosthenes de Goede by the arm, too, and conducted both of them over the rope around the ring, up to the dais and the interested bull. 'Detective-Sergeant Demosthenes H. de Goede !'

There was a ripple through the audience and heads bumped together knowingly in whispers that presently changed to thunderous applause. It lasted a full minute, and Detective-Sergeant Demosthenes H. de Goede, encouraged by the well-beloved Dries, was obliged (against police regulations) to mount the dias. He was a magnificent man, and towered athletically above everyone : modest, mute and reassuring. He raised his fists in a boxer's gesture, dropped his head modestly to receive their adulation. At the right moment, with a sense of timing peculiar to the hero, he retired and allowed the speaker to continue with the proceedings.

'Dear friends,' said Dries van Schalkwyk, 'our time is limited,' and he looked down at his precious wristwatch, and then up again, with an unexpected change of emotion to seriousness and devotion which only the deceptive fool of understanding can handle. 'It is a habit I have followed without apology for eighteen years, and will repeat in the future.' He glared proudly and challengingly at the invisible scoffer on the horizon. 'Each year I ask those present to observe a moment's silence in honour of the death and memory of Uncle Giepie.'

It was the residents and their relations who first fell silent, and then the visitors who followed their example and made the silence moving. Even the wind lay still. It was an all-embracing silence that descended on the Foundation, and brought them nearer the earth and nature. Only the masks were noisy, and emphasized the inner conflict. Then the well-beloved Dries raised his hand and began his address.

'Dear friends, it isn't necessary for me to tell the residents and friends of Welgevonden who Uncle Giepie was and what he accomplished, but' – and he looked searchingly at the unknown faces – 'on account of the visitors and dignitaries in our midst, I should like to say a little about that remarkable man.' He cleared his throat, bared his teeth and rolled his eyes back, back into his thoughts where history was engraved.

'Thirty-six years ago a poor field-worker like myself ... (giggling) ... took a look at the whole of the breeding position and decided that he would, with the scanty means at his disposal, take the bull by the horns ... (appreciative laughter) ... and follow his own breeding principles. He began with one bull ... (he held up his forefinger) ... and with two cows ... (here he held up two fingers). Imagine to yourselves: one bull and two cows.' He paused for dramatic effect. 'That same poor son of the country-side, eighteen years later, left THREE HUNDRED THOUSAND RAND to the Welgevonden Foundation.' The anticipated mur-mur that, every year, ran through the audience, ran through it again now. The well-beloved Dries listened to it with a touch of nostalgia and the bitter cynicism of a priest who, later, would have to curb the enthusiastic abandon of new converts. He took a sip of water and looked at the dignitaries who were nodding approvingly at one another. (Someone began to clap hands, but stopped immediately, as the well-beloved Dries remained silent and smiled forgivingly.) 'That same Giepie Ollenwaar, who will be remembered not only for the three hundred thousand rand, but for a gift made one evening to a young couple, a gift that cannot be judged by money, a lovely event one summer evening at Welgevonden ...' He allowed a silence to establish itself, then broke it. 'A gift of the legendary bull, the mighty Brutus, to Henry and Salome Silberstein.'

He had complete control of his audience and looked at them with proud deprecation. The skinny little bull in the arena had come closer and was snuffling carefully at him with his wet muzzle. The well-beloved Dries stroked him absent-mindedly be-tween his ears and patted him away.

'Dear friends,' said Dries in rising tones and genuine abandon, 'Giepie Ollenwaar was eighteen years ahead of his time, but he was a man who at his death did not hesitate to say ... to me, that unforgettable evening ... "Improve on Brutus, Dries. Do not let the breeding policy die with me!"'

Beloved Dries had suddenly become white and calm and quiet – that dangerous calm of the dedicated, that silence in which lies power. He raised his face to the horizon where a giant-like figure appeared and then he lowered his unseeing gaze to the faces before him.

'And it was then, dear friends, that I realized that Uncle Giepie meant more than the indifferent, materialistic, conservative, right-wing reactionary would understand. I humbly, friends, accepted the mantle of Elia.'

The residents lived every moment, the ordinary visitors were in the dark and yet in a rapture, the eminent visitors inquired from their guide the name of the official.

The well-beloved Dries now spoke faster, more carelessly – almost self-deprecatingly.

'I accepted a task, friends, and carried on. Brutus was not the end. I kept pace with the times. I interpreted the prophetic thought of Uncle Giepie to the best of my ability. At the very outset I asked myself: does the world really want great and mighty stud bulls? Does it accord with the Will of our People? Do they not eat too much? Are they not uncontrollable? Do they meet the requirements of the Ordinary Breeder?' He was silent for a moment. 'Those, friends, were all questions that I asked myself in the silence of my room. And then' – he brought his hands together – 'and then, friends, I asked myself the following question: those great horns of Brutus ... does one sell horns to the abattoirs? Does the meat attain to the desired grade if the animals have bashed each other in the trucks with those great horns?' He raised his hands pensively to his head. 'And I asked myself, seeing Brutus there, with the black and the red, the two colours so strongly segregated ... so definitely and challengingly apart: what psychological effect would that have on the buyer?' He lowered his hands. 'It was very far from being my intention to yield ... but I asked myself: who is the buyer? How sensitively attuned is he, aesthetically, to the question of colour? And I immediately realized, friends, that adaptability was the answer. Not cunning in regard to the quality of your product, but to give as little offence as possible, to eliminate the petty, simply to feed the peoples and to satisfy the demands of a steadily increasing world population.'

There was applause from the eminent visitors; and the inhabitants, family and friends, although somewhat in the dark as far as this new trend in Dries' annual speech was concerned, joined in boisterously.

'Then I decided, friends . . .' (his shirt tail had come out of his trousers and he tucked it back) . . . 'my shirt's hanging out, friends . . . then I decided to shift the colours to a horizontal basis: the black above, the red below, except, and this is important, around the genitals, for manifestly scientific reasons.'

He took a sip of water and then saw for the first time the lumpish figure of the Giant slowly approaching the assembly. He frowned and took another sip.

'And now, friends, my time is limited – certain technical considerations.' He brought out a piece of paper and consulted it swiftly. He suppressed a smile and put the paper back in the pocket of his jacket. 'As you know, friends, breeding power comes above all. It's not what a bull looks like, but how he breeds. It is not *that* he breeds, but when he breeds.' He smiled audaciously at his audience. 'We are all scientists here; the ladies will excuse us.' He took from his pocket a hen's egg and looked attentively at it, then hid it in the hollow of his hand. 'You probably know about Pavlov's experiments, friends . . .' A single individual in the audience nodded. Dries pointed. '. . . a friend, there. But perhaps I should explain.' He closed his eyes. 'I took one of Brutus' children, a young bull, and brought him to the heifers. Once we had shown him a circular object, we allowed him to cover the heifers. Once we had shown him a square object, we gave him an electric shock.' He opened his eyes. 'By repetition, friends, the pattern was established and he covered the heifers only when he had seen the circular object. And then we progressed to the next step.' He looked at the egg in his hand, then folded it away again. 'Then, friends, then we showed the young bull an oval-shaped object – not a circle and not a square. And what was the result?' The solitary individual, who knew, leaned back comfortably and whispered something to his neighbour. 'Then, friends, this little bull had a real nervous breakdown because of his inability to come to a decision in the direction in which he had been conditioned.'

The well-beloved Dries descended suddenly from the dais and looked lovingly at the skinny little bull that had all the time been snuffling him. Then he looked at the gathering.

'The time has come, friends, to illustrate.'

He raised his hand, the fist balled. The little bull looked at it eagerly with its warm, soft eyes. He opened his fist and revealed the egg, held between thumb and forefinger. The bullock staggered back, its eyes became glazed, it lowed sonorously in pain, slowly its legs gave way and it collapsed. The well-beloved Dries mounted the rostrum again and waited smilingly for the tumult to die down. He offered the egg courteously to one of the women, wiped his hands on a handkerchief and took a sip of water. Meanwhile, the bullock lay peacefully on the ground, as if in a state of total hypnosis.

'Now, friends,' said the well-beloved Dries. 'You have probably seen the application long ago. Through a method of selection and mating we have determined these characteristics in the descendants of Brutus and have thereby managed, in the words of the amateur, to establish, as it were, a sort of built-in birth control.'

Apart from the residents and relations who understood the breeding policy, the rest of the audience seemed altogether mystified and the well-beloved Dries smiled forgivingly.

'Perhaps I should explain further,' he said and winked at one of the older residents who was bubbling with excitement and threatening to stand up and himself explain.

The well-beloved Dries raised his hand slightly, subdued the older inhabitant and resumed.

'One would like the heifers to be covered when conditions are ideal and when the heifers . . .' He looked questioningly at the audience.

'Are fat !' shouted the older resident.

'And,' said Dries, 'and when the heifers are fat, the genital periphery . . .'

He waited in vain.

'When the heifers are fat we say they are what from fatness . . .'

'Round,' shouted the older resident and suddenly the audience grasped Dries' thought process. Great excitement ensued and they could hardly wait for him to continue.

'And when it's been a dry year and the heifers are skinny and everything hangs, then the form is no longer round but . . .'

'Square,' said one of the eminent visitors inadvertently.

Dries shook his head benignly.

'That's impossible,' he said. 'When everything hangs the shape is . . .'

'Oval !' bawled the oldest resident and looked contemptuously at the eminent guest who tried in vain to conceal his discomfort.

'And when the shape is oval,' said Dries, 'then . . .' and he pointed significantly at the little bull, which still lay in schizophrenic inertia.

At that moment the Giant appeared among them and forced his way genially up to the bullock. He towered huge above the people, who unconsciously made way for him and looked at him apprehensively. The Giant kicked the animal gently and at this touch it began to show life at once, regained its legs and began snuffling the Giant.

Dries' smile had vanished, but he took no notice of the Giant. He ignored him as a speaker ignores a troublesome heckler at a meeting.

'At the slightest touch the bull recovered,' he said. 'In times of plenty the heifers are covered; in times of scarcity they are not covered. That, friends, was my breeding policy and on it I have built.'

The attention of the audience was clearly no longer entirely with the speaker. They were entranced by the spectacle of the Giant and the little bull, which looked a pet beside him. They were all discussing the sight with each other, except the older resident who had shifted up to the eminent visitor and was trying to gain his attention.

'Dear friends . . . order, friends ! Friends, that was therefore the breeding policy laid down, and it is my proud privilege hereby to announce that this year I can display Brutus III to you.'

It should have been a great moment, but something had gone wrong.

The older resident had managed to catch the attention of the eminent visitor, and snarled at him : 'Cobbler, stick to your last.' Then, satisfied, he shuffled back to his place.

The well-beloved Dries grimaced and raised his voice. (This was the breeder's lot; even Uncle Giepie had had, many a day, to tolerate the Philistinism of people.)

'Dear friends whereas Brutus was a colossal, clumsy animal, we have here a smaller animal, perfectly proportioned.' He paused and drank deeply from the glass of water. 'Whereas Brutus was voiceless, this animal has a beautiful deep voice : a sign of normal development.' He hesitated, for this was the moment at which he had intended to make his joke : one bull, one voice. He decided against it. 'Whereas Brutus had a fierce character and a wild nature, and killed even his creator . . .' Ah, he had their attention again. Their conversation ceased and they listened again. But he would punish them and not refer to the matter again. 'Whereas Brutus was destructive, this animal is by nature gentle and even-tempered.' He had once again lost the attention of the audience. 'Whereas this animal caused no losses at mating time, Brutus injured and overpowered the heifers.' He deliberately did not look at the Giant. He looked at his watch and decided suddenly to stop. He had retrieved their attention, but had lost his own enthusiasm. This year, the year of his triumph before so many eminent guests, something had gone awry. He suppressed with difficulty his fury toward the Giant.

'A few final announcements before we separate, friends,' he said. 'I remind you of tomorrow evening's proceedings, when certain awards will be made to Mr Jock Silberstein, Mr Henry Silberstein-van Eeden, and to Uncle Giepie Ollenwaar, *in absentia*. A full attendance will be appreciated. And lastly, I request you to pause for a moment in silent meditation in memory of our beloved Lila who was recently so brutally murdered.'

This time he looked straight at the Giant as the audience fell silent and the masks began to roar.

Thereafter the well-beloved Dries took up his satchel and walked rapidly towards his room, followed by the playfully gambling little bull without horns. Dries' figure had suddenly sagged, as if all the cares in the world were on his shoulders. He had been overcome with listlessness. He had lost his enthusiasm, and in the world of breeding that was fatal. Once you begin to doubt your calling, then the muse in you dies. The murderer had killed not only Lila, but something bigger. Tears began to trickle down his cheeks. This cried out to Heaven for retribution!

Chapter Nine

The Conversation on the Observation Tower

Residents, relations, guests and prominent visitors had left in groups the place where the universally-liked Dries had so unexpectedly concluded his address. African helpers had already removed the ring, the dais and the remaining cattle. The proceedings had been shortened by at least an hour and the entire programme had been spoiled. One of the guides tried to regroup everyone and fill out their hour with the last part of a lecture on German merino sheep. It would mean that this group's time would end with the first half of a lecture about something else – but that could not be helped.

'You'll notice,' said Dr Johns to Detective-Sergeant Demosthenes H. de Goede, as they went on, 'that here the emphasis is placed on farming and farming methods. But that was one of Jock Silberstein's conditions for the grant and the establishment of the Foundation.' He sniffed the fresh air and exhaled it pleasurably. 'It's a back-to-the-soil policy, a theory that there is a magical quality, a healing property, associated with everything to do with farming. It's a cult to which you expose yourself – so widespread that it reaches any group level of intelligence or development. It's actually the experience of a myth.'

He peered over his shoulder and pointed out to Detective-Sergeant Demosthenes H. de Goede that the Giant was following them.

'The theory is,' said Dr Johns, 'that in the cycles of nature all psychic material is realized, that the psychic processes are given form here. Welgevonden is teeming with primordial images – and the residents are encouraged to determine their spiritual coherence by personal experience.'

They now approached a shining aluminium tank, held in

position eighty feet into the air by four standards. A vertical ladder connected the ground with an observation tower up above. Dr Johns indicated to Detective-Sergeant Demosthenes H. de Goede that he should lead, and he did so dexterously, like a naval cadet. Halfway up he swung out into the thin air and waved his hat exuberantly. He did the rest of the distance in record time and relaxed in isometric repose while waiting for Dr Johns to follow him.

The little, bald-headed old man climbed considerably more slowly and laboriously. He turned first red then blue from exertion and reached the platform in a state of complete exhaustion. He recovered slowly and peacefully and then introduced Detective-Sergeant Demosthenes H. de Goede to someone who had watched their arrival from the farthermost point of the platform and who now came forward to meet them.

He was an attractive middle-aged man of steady, efficient appearance. He was dressed neatly in the livery of a rich farmer: suede shoes, a well-cut pair of khaki trousers, a Harris tweed jacket and a cravat which protruded just above his silk shirt. He was sunburned and his hair had been cut by an Italian barber. Sunglasses obscured his eyes, but the smile with which he greeted them was frank and sincere. He thrust out a farmer's hand to Detective-Sergeant Demosthenes H. de Goede, who reciprocated the iron grip with one of steel.

'Mr Silberstein-van Eeden . . . Detective-Sergeant Demosthenes H. de Goede,' said Dr Johns.

Shortly after this introduction, the platform jerked beneath the pressure of a further weight, and the Giant appeared. It was as if everything had suddenly become smaller: the tank, the platform, the entire structure. It seemed at times that the Giant would lose his balance at any moment and tumble down, but he came nearer, waveringly, and sat down next to Henry Silberstein-van Eeden. He fumbled along Henry's side until he found his hand and folded it firmly in his own. The parody of father and son on that swaying platform – the monster and the solid citizen, the expansive landscape, the isolation high in the thin blue air – was fixed for a moment like a photograph in Dr Johns' mind, and he cried out involuntarily: '*Riboinesjeloilom: kuk arop fun dem himl un kuk dir on dayn velt!*' (Dear Lord: look down from your heaven and see what is happening to your world.)

Beneath them the empty tank glowed in the sun and bounced beams of light against their eyes. The echo of every movement roared back. The evasive smells of grapes still clung to the sides; and below them, as far as they could see, stretched the Welgevonden estate, gleaming back from a thousand windows. The residents, relatives, visitors and distinguished guests moved like ants through the Foundation.

There was a clattering on the ladder: small metal sounds that announced a new arrival. Reverend Williams rose, tattered, up through the thin air and walked with burning feet across the hot iron to them, his jacket crumpled, his collar dirty, his beard misleadingly masculine. He nodded five times in a circle, breathed the air in and was transported by the landscape, nature all unspoiled. He saw the crude earth, the virgin, the Lila-image, and then he sharpened his gaze and noticed the glittering of glass and all the movement, and he called out a curse on all forms of violation.

'God forgive you,' he said to the Giant, who sought sanctuary beside his father.

The platform rang beneath the onslaught of many feet on rungs that made the ladder sound like a scale. Residents, relatives, guests and visitors poured up and across the platform and milled together ever more tightly in a circle that quickly became compressed into immobility. The distracted guide clung to the ladder and bellowed out his comment on the sights worth seeing to the clouds. He described all they could see in smooth-worn adjectives and encouraged them to spurt out a fountain of admiring Ooo's and Ah's. Then he invited them to spit, to see if they could reach the ground, until their saliva, carried on the wind, became a misty rain that never reached the ground but disintegrated in the air. He asked them to shout so that they could hear the echoes against the mountain, and their collective voices tore up the ravines, echoed from the cliffs and disappeared in a lament over the abysses. He asked them to be silent so that they could hear the masks and, in the silence, they heard them. Then he asked them to cheer and to express their delight in free nature. And beneath the cheering, as everyone cast his *doppelgänger* over the precipice, there rose into the sky an article of clothing, which filled with wind, stretched puffed-out arms in a gesture of benediction over the earth, and drifted slowly above the Foundation. Then the circle was complete and they were sucked back through the loudspeaker and chivied down again until only the Giant, his father, the Detective-Sergeant and Dr Johns remained with Reverend Williams who, after the ecstatic exuberance of a moment ago, found himself without his jacket.

He, too, departed: hopping across the hot metal, skipping lightly down the ladder until he appeared again down below, his hands before his eyes, his face raised to the drifting garment that, speck-like, disappeared over the horizon.

Henry Silberstein-van Eeden, his son hanging lovingly on his arm, turned to Dr Johns and Detective-Sergeant Demosthenes H. de Goede.

'Do you remember our conversations, Doctor Johns? How you and Judge O'Hara, eighteen years ago, patiently led me to a conception of the nature of chaos and order?'

He endured the fawning adulation of the Giant without any outward sign of feeling. He allowed the Giant to place his heavy arm around his shoulders and to press himself loutishly against him.

'Doctor Johns and Judge O'Hara were my mentors,' said Henry Silberstein-van Eeden to Detective-Sergeant Demosthenes H. de Goede. And then to Dr Johns: 'Aren't you proud of your product?' And a little later: 'And how's our friend getting on?'

'He was not allowed the key today,' said Dr Johns. 'The murder, alas, upset him.'

Henry Silberstein-van Eeden nodded understandingly. He sighed and shook the Giant's left arm from his shoulder.

'It's strange that no sooner did I see the beauty of order, than my mentor should have become involved in the struggle. Did order overwhelm him, Doctor Johns?'

'Chaos,' said Dr Johns.

Henry was powerless in the grip of a sentimental embrace. 'I am completely adapted,' said Henry, 'and I understand my emotions.' He tried in vain to wriggle free. 'I hate and I feel no guilt. You taught me everything ... love of order and for Salome, who was part of it. Do you remember her still after eighteen years, Doctor Johns? She was part of Welgevonden. When I married her I became part of it, too. She was the crown that you spread over everything.' Unexpectedly he wriggled free. 'I had truly not had enough of her, and just when I reached the stage of nearly understanding everything, she died. Have I not the right to hate?' – and once again he was smothered under another embrace.

Dr Johns placed his hand warningly on Demosthenes H. de Goede who, like a coiled spring, might come swiftly uncoiled at any moment. Detective-Sergeant Demosthenes H. de Goede relaxed gradually and moved to the edge of the platform from where he looked out over the Foundation and, with bulging abdominal muscles, combined countertension and isometric exercises almost motionlessly in his warming up for the struggle that lay certainly ahead.

'Why must I accept fate that determines everything blindly? Have I not the fullest right to revolt, although I can do nothing about it?'

Henry Silberstein-van Eeden, smothered by love, could hardly articulate his last sentence.

'She was dead before I understood everything,' said Henry. 'The struggle between chaos and order is the struggle between chaos and the Welgevonden in which Salome's spirit is embodied.' His voice was inaudible under the embrace. 'As a father I utter my curse ...' His words were muted, for in a moment of uncontrolled abandon the Giant kissed his father full on the mouth. '... Utter my curse,' repeated Henry, half stupefied, just before Dr Johns struck the Giant away and sent him stumbling to the edge of the platform. 'I expressed my curse,' said Henry, 'upon the one who threatens order, upon a brother who murdered his sister.'

Dumbfounded, the Giant walked around them to the ladder. He looked at them and began slowly to climb down. His feet struck deep sounds from each rung, his huge body disappeared gradually until only his white face and red hair protruded, disembodied, over the rim of the platform. His blue eyes remained sadly on Henry.

'Because, you know, Doctor Johns,' said Henry, 'she could have been the sister . . .'

'Or the daughter . . .' said Dr Johns.

'. . . of any one of us,' said Henry.

They both reflected deeply and then Henry said : 'Do you know, Doctor Johns, there is probably little that can be compared with one's guilt feeling. But there *is* something worse : the realization that everything is being destroyed without you or anyone else having any part in it.'

'The tendency today is away from the accusation,' said Dr Johns. 'It will become even more so. The whole tendency in psychiatry is to make man's propensity for sin less and less his own responsibility.'

They had taken off their jackets, for it was getting hot on the platform. Only the irregular breathing of the Detective-Sergeant broke the silence that had settled on their ruminations.

'And perhaps we now enter the terrain of the tragic,' said Dr Johns. 'Man is inclined to give free rein to his indignation and his sorrow only when there is blame that can be apportioned. When there is no blame, he submits . . .'

'Or he hates, as I do,' said Henry.

They looked at the face on the floor of the platform and the face laughed at them. The blue eyes looked from one to the other, but especially at Henry.

'No,' said Dr Johns. 'Sorrow and hate are pertinent only if there is blame. And therefore people always seek a scapegoat. Without a scapegoat, mankind cannot bring justice to his hate and sorrow. And . . .' He put on his jacket again as a breeze began to cool his sweaty body. 'And the less we are in the position to blame, the greater our need for a scapegoat.'

'I do not agree,' said Henry.

'It is not hate or grief that you feel,' said Dr Johns. 'It's something much deeper, more horrible, something that oppresses you deep within yourself and fills you with fear. Something that' – and he smiled at Henry – 'that brings you to seek your refuge in a place like the Foundation.'

Detective-Sergeant Demosthenes H. de Goede had finished his exercises and was wiping the sweat from his face and straightening the shoulders of his jacket. He had listened all the time to the conversation and, according to a Pelmanistic method, stored every thought in his memory.

'But it is a ghost that you cannot exorcise,' said Dr Johns. 'Therefore, to save yourself, even if you do not wish to know it, you look for a scapegoat.' He looked at the moving face of the Giant and the pathetic, never-ceasing smile. 'Therefore the tragic figure of our time is perhaps he who takes guilt upon himself to make valid for ourselves our hate or sorrow.'

Henry removed his dark glasses. But he replaced them immediately, as if by so doing he could conceal the signs of his vulnerability.

Dr Johns asked Henry why he dedicated himself with so much enthusiasm to the Foundation. Detective-Sergeant Demosthenes H. de Goede noted, Pelmanistically, Henry's answer that within the bounds of his talents (Dr Johns surprised at the word 'bounds') he did everything in his power to maintain order at Welgevonden, to fulfil order. If this did not come about, as now with the death of Lila, he bore no guilt. Disintegration under the parody of order, had already been there. He could only say that he had done his best. (That merely accentuated the tragedy of the disintegration – Dr Johns.) There was accordingly nothing else for him to do but to protect the order with renewed energy and dedication against further decay from within, by making the order as secure as possible externally. (But even if he, Henry, were blameless, and even if he lived according to the values of order and fought for the maintenance of order, if the rules of order were today a kind of mockery, if one found that values, sanctified by the years, were today becoming anachronistic, actually unpractical – what then?) Then you were still fighting to preserve everything – for the sake of eternal values. (And if those eternal values, tested in practice, were no longer so eternal and practical, was that morality any longer of any value?) No, he had to acknowledge: then you would have to renounce your values. (And then?) Then there was nothing left for you because you were formed by those values. (Unless?) Unless, of course, the fault lay not with the values, and the disintegration happened as a result of a culpability that could be attributed to someone and . . .

'. . . We can find a scapegoat,' said Dr Johns.

'And can prove that the primordial powers of chaos have taken over in the name of order,' said Henry.

Detective-Sergeant Demosthenes H. de Goede had now joined them and was threatening to take part in the conversation.

Dr Johns hastily proposed that they resume their stroll, since time was limited.

In the meantime, the Giant's head had disappeared and Henry declared that he preferred to remain on the platform and meditate further.

'My father-in-law, Jock Silberstein, and I often had conversations here,' he said.

They said good-bye and Detective-Sergeant Demosthenes H. de Goede stuttered to Dr Johns, as they slowly descended the ladder, his admiration for their host, Henry Silberstein-van Eeden.

'You should have known him eighteen years ago, when he had just come here,' said Dr Johns. 'He impressed us all with his erudition and his willingness to take part in controversy. These days he is quieter and works harder.'

Detective-Sergeant Demosthenes H. de Goede stuttered his last observation before they reached the ground.

'Precisely,' said Dr Johns. 'He is very kind to his son. Only a parent could tolerate everything so patiently.'

Chapter Ten

The African Quarter, Mon Repos

Dr Johns decided to take Detective-Sergeant Demosthenes H. de Goede by a roundabout way to the African quarter before showing him the factory, cellars and bottling plant. This necessitated their leaving the road and walking through fields and veld.

'Watch out for snakes,' said Dr Johns. 'There may still be a few here, although Henry Silberstein-van Eeden is trying systematically to extirpate them.'

They walked carefully through the long grass and looked attentively ahead of them.

'Mind !' screamed Dr Johns.

Detective-Sergeant Demosthenes H. de Goede leaped athletically into the air, and nimbly seized a stone as he landed on the ground again. Dr Johns was kneeling and studying something attentively in the trodden grass. He held up a small plant.

'How rare ! A real *ephialtion*.'

He nursed the plant in his hand as they proceeded.

'I sometimes wonder,' he said, 'if Henry and Salome actually found one another.' He took Detective-Sergeant Demosthenes H. de Goede by the arm. 'Now that we know one another better, I might as well tell you of my doubts.'

Detective-Sergeant Demosthenes H. de Goede looked happy.

'Imagine,' said Dr Johns, 'that Henry found after a time that Salome no longer loved him. While he could reproach, while he could blame himself, for instance, because he could not satisfy her in some respects, there was always hope. But if he suddenly realized that she no longer loved him and that there was no guilt on his part – he was left with a qualitative judgement of the situation, and so the situation became a thousand times more intolerable. Does that not, perhaps, explain his dedication to the Foundation?' He looked closely at Detective-Sergeant Demosthenes H. de Goede. 'If, one fine day, one finds incontrovertible evidence that something is vanishing and being reduced to nothing, what does one do then?' When Detective-Sergeant Demosthenes H. de Goede answered with difficulty, Dr Johns laughed. 'I see you have paid close attention. You are quite right: you do your best, you would move the earth to prevent the break-up, to prove to yourself that you can win back lost love. You would, like Henry, devote the whole of your life to something like the Foundation, in which you see the harmony that you associate with her. And if that harmony, too, is threatened and reminds you of her love which, inexplicably, has gone to ruin in a similar way, what are you to do then?'

Detective-Sergeant Demosthenes H. de Goede had his answer ready.

'Exactly,' said Dr Johns. 'Then you, like all of us, would be obliged to accept a scapegoat for the sake of your soul's peace.'

He walked on pensively.

'I do not envy you your task,' said Dr Johns, 'but I envy Henry still less his torment of soul when he presently discovers, on that platform, that he must admit the existence of the scapegoat.'

Detective-Sergeant Demosthenes H. de Goede's attention had wandered, because he had just seen something. In the middle of the field in which they were walking was an immense bronze statue of a gigantic animal. It gleamed in the sun like the observation tower and dominated the entire landscape.

'That's a statue of Brutus the bull,' said Dr Johns, 'erected by the Ollenwaar Stud Breeders' Association.' He pointed out words engraved in gold on a certain part of its anatomy. 'Ollenwaar tribute and Ollenwaar gratitude. Erected by the Red-Black Stud Breeders' Association.'

As they stood looking in admiration at the statue, they were unaware of a man who was lying on his back looking up into the sky in the shadow of the huge replica. It was the well-beloved Dries van Schalkwyk and he had just had a vision. He had, as was his habit when in doubt (and had he not begun to doubt when, a few moments before, he wondered if Brutus III was perchance not too small) taken refuge at the statue of Brutus – to admire Brutus' faults, to despise his brute strength, to belittle his dynamic spirit, to adjure the erotic nightmare by confrontation in the clear light of day. He had, in the past, always returned with renewed faith in his breeding policy and with the feeling that Uncle Giepie, in his prophetic vision, would understand. But today he found no help. There was even a moment when the feared Brutus aroused a forbidden longing in him. He was about to return to his room when he saw the vision. Dries van Schalkwyk, secretary of the R.B.S.B.A., had seen before his eyes the spirit of Uncle Giepie float, arms outstretched in blessing, over Welgevonden.

Suddenly he heard a voice and leaped up – after the vision ready for the annunciation – and then he saw Dr Johns and Detective-Sergeant Demosthenes H. de Goede. He gave them a friendly greeting but told them nothing of his visitation. That was a revelation for himself alone. He hurried off and met the Giant who had been following Dr Johns and Detective-Sergeant Demosthenes H. de Goede. Once again fury rose in him, but this time without that feeling of powerlessness. The sign was there! Retribution would follow! The moment was full of meaning!

'This is the African quarter, Mon Repos,' said Dr Johns as they drew nearer the symmetrical network of houses. 'It, too, is part of the Foundation.'

In the middle of a clump of trees, which were all dying simultaneously because their bark had been stripped off, was an arch, over the gate that gave admittance to the quarter, with the single word 'Welcome' painted on it. Next to the gate were a number of notices warning all visitors in choice English not to do certain things like spitting, committing acts of vandalism or loafing around. Directly before the gate a Blantyre, against a background of his own handiwork, was surrounded by an admiring crowd of intellectual visitors, eminent guests and several proud residents and relatives. A shining black guide and his white colleague were pointing out, describing and explaining every object.

Madam Ritchie, when she saw Dr Johns and Detective-Sergeant Demosthenes H. de Goede join the group, greeted the reunion exuberantly. Hope and Prudence, their hair in soft locks over their shoulders, looked shyly at Detective-Sergeant Demosthenes H. de Goede and lowered their eyes modestly. There was a blush on their cheeks and Detective-Sergeant Demosthenes H. de Goede stuttered a rapid question in Dr Johns' ear.

'It's difficult to say,' said Dr Johns as they followed the guides through the gate. 'I know that one is a resident and the other, of course, a relative – but I can't say offhand which.' He reflected for a moment. 'Perhaps Prudence . . . no, Hope . . .' He shook his head. 'I am sorry, but it's so difficult to remember.'

The guides drew attention to the walls of the entrance, on which numerous photographs of laughing Africans were displayed. Each African had been photographed with his arms full of rand notes, and below something was written in three languages: Xosa, Sotho and Venda.

The black guide translated: 'Bonamie Shekudu receives his award for services beyond the call of duty. Bonamie raised the alarm at the time of the beer hall fire. Bonamie distinguished himself at the extinguishment of the flames.'

'Benjamin M'Kodo refused to burn his identity card . . .'

'Nukunu Bubu planted three hundred and thirty-three trees . . .'

One of the intellectual visitors spotted other photographs hidden away behind screens and he approached one of the guides. White guide and black conferred together and then the black guide said that they had decided, perhaps contrary to regulations, to show the rest of the photographs, since it was a special occasion (indicating the eminent guests). Ladies were requested not to look. Madam Ritchie was the first to shriek as the screens were removed to show a series of photographs of Africans hanging rigid from sneezewood gallows.

'Shemane Babete, B.A., LL.B., paid the ultimate penalty for taking part in the rites of manducation.'

'Shikudu M'pane paid the ultimate penalty for decapitating his mother and using her eyes for *muti*.'

Both guides explained that the photographs served as deterrents.

An intellectual visitor asked the white guide to pose next to one of the photographs. A close-up was taken of only the faces without captions, for overseas distribution. Several of the visitors competed to be taken: as also Madam Ritchie, with many gestures and much chattering. She was rapidly becoming a 'personality' and had already exchanged addresses with one of the eminent visitors.

The Giant had also joined the group and was unexpectedly taken by one of the photographers, as he was grinning broadly, next to one of the gallows scenes.

After that they were all taken to the reception office to be shown the layout of the township on maps. The room filled from wall to wall and the guides had to stand on tables as they explained that there was a quartz mine under the terrain and that one of the big companies was mining it in conjunction with the Foundation. A photograph of the chairman of the directorate was pointed out: the open, unprejudiced, sensitive face of a great liberal, known for his progressive tendencies and political influence behind the scenes. Although he would have liked to remain anonymous, everyone recognized him at once as Julius Johnson.

Outside, the white guide was explaining a system of identification by which each African inhabitant or relative was known by a band around his head.

'The colour of the band,' said the white guide, 'indicates the individual's period of service in the mine and residence as an inhabitant of the township. It's quite simple: white, blue, green, yellow and red, respectively, for one to five years, with scarlet for ten years, after which the inhabitant concerned is discharged, with the right to stay on for a second decade as relative-inhabitant or relative-worker, with similar colour distinctions, namely, half-white, half-blue, half-green, half-yellow, half red to half-scarlet for the following service period of ten years.'

At this point several visitors asked questions.

Detective-Sergeant Demosthenes H. de Goede, instructed long ago, naturally, at the police college regarding the system, confined his attention to the shy Misses Hope and Prudence, who understood nothing and repeatedly asked him to explain, as they looked blindingly into his eyes.

The group was then taken to the community centre.

'The sports fields,' said the black guide and pointed to a group of black inhabitants kicking a soccer ball back and forth in clouds of dust (despite recent rains). They juggled cleverly with the ball, bouncing it from knee, shoulder, head, heel and side of foot, tapping it to and fro, shooting it between their own legs and stopping it with the tip of the boot. On the sidelines were a number of black inhabitants stretched out on benches and following the game with expressionless faces and who, at the appearance of the guides and their group, immediately directed their attention as expressionlessly at the new manifestation.

The game was stopped at a sign from the black guide, who occupied an important position in the hierarchy of the model township. The two captains, wearing blue and red bands respectively, were introduced to a few eminent visitors and photographed. Then one of the well-known guests was talked into kicking off, after Madam Ritchie had with great difficulty been balked in her intention of doing so herself. The eminent American guest kicked the heavy ball slap into the dust clouds, while everyone crowded around and slapped him heartily on the back.

The two guides smiled broadly at the singular success of their important visit. Things could so easily go wrong. There was, for instance, the murder two nights ago of the white girl Lila, which might have ruined everything – but all was going briskly and well.

In a moment of improvisation, the white guide invited Detective-Sergeant Demosthenes H. de Goede to take part in the game for a few minutes. He did so without hesitation. He bounced in among the black inhabitants, juggled the ball with them, bumped them away like rag dolls with his muscular shoulders and made a dead set for the goal. At the last moment, with the net open to

him, he passed the ball to one of the black players who, applaud-
ing himself thunderously, bounced it from foot to knee, and from
knee to head, into the net. It was a masterly handling of the
situation by the Detective-Sergeant who consummated the bon-
homie fittingly.

On the way to the medical quarters, with the two appealing
girls, Hope and Prudence, linked to each of his arms, Detective-
Sergeant Demosthenes H. de Goede as well as the rest of the party
was unaware of the Giant who had appeared on the field and
launched an attack on the ball. The players left the field and
gathered with the spectators, grumbling, under a tree, from
where they all watched the Giant with hostile faces. Alone on
the field, with the ball at his feet, he looked smilingly at the
group under the tree and then at the goal. Suddenly he kicked.
The ball glanced off the side of his shoe, rolled over the ground,
over the boundary, away in the midday sun.

'The pharmacy, hospital with fourteen beds and quarters of the
doctor,' said the white guide and introduced the female mission
doctor to them; against a background of coloured bottles along
the wall, she at once called upon them for funds. She revealed
certain statistics to them and mentioned a new wing that had to
be built. She led them through rooms tiled from side to side in
white. 'Easy to wash,' she explained. She showed them her patients
in the reception hall who, with coloured bands around their heads,
looked vaguely sick. She led them to an adjoining room where a
single bed in pure white isolation stood exactly in the middle of a
shining floor. 'This is where we handle emergency cases,' said
she, the mission doctor, and conjured up visions for them. (From
blood-warm Africa certain basic facts about life.) Her silent wish
was made a reality when a black inhabitant with a split skull
was at that very moment brought in; this gave her the opportunity to be photographed, for an international magazine, with
her finger in the wound. She took leave of the guests to pose for
more photos: exhausted beside a paraffin lamp, washing herself
in an earthenware bowl on a soapbox – the bags under her eyes
attributable to dedication, not dissipation.

She was about fifty years of age and not unattractive. Her skin was dull, her eyes soft and her figure masculine. Her predecessor had been devoured by Shemane Babete, B.A., LL.B. She had a secret wish that was indescribable. She ameliorated suffering and campaigned for a healthy body and universal suffrage. The cameras clicked continuously and the eminent visitors declared themselves proud to be photographed with her.

Both guides found it imperative to draw the attention of the group to passing time: it was already late, and a great deal lay ahead.

There followed fleeting impressions of a kitchen with cast-iron pots over fires and the sour smell of mealie porridge being warmed up. There were impressions of a recreation hall with a Ping-Pong table in the middle, darts on the walls, CNA periodicals on stands, photos of black women on the walls. Everywhere there were black inhabitants taking part in no game, who looked at no photo of black women and did not say a word.

One of the intellectual woman guests started a conversation. She asked a big black inhabitant in pidgin English where he came from and if he were married. He said something in his own language and a group around him burst out laughing. She saw that he wore a red band and asked him (proud of her knowledge) if he already had been with the Foundation for five years. He took no notice of her and she smiled at him. That was no good, so she asked him if he had children, pickaninnies. He simply looked at her. She told him that she was a visitor from Sweden, and that did not help, either. She offered him a cigarette and he put it behind his ear. She was still trying to establish contact with him when the guests left the hall and her friend plucked at her arm.

The Giant had come into the hall sometime after the others and walked right across the middle of it. The darts on the walls attracted his attention and he pocketed two of them. The black inhabitants at the door contemplated barring his way, but slowly gave way as the big figure loomed up.

A quick visit to the butchery (white tiles, meat in refrigerated rooms): 'They eat the same food as we do' (the white guide).

There was a longer pause at the Native shop, especially to give the eminent overseas guests an opportunity to make purchases. The coloured Bantu blankets, manufactured by a factory in Lady-brand, were first on the list. Hand-threaded bead objects second. (Especially the kind to which a story, supplied by the black guide, was attached: 'If she hasn't had a man yet; she's looking for a man. . .') Detective-Sergeant Demosthenes H. de Goede bought one of each of these for Hope and Prudence, to the great delight of everybody. Madam Ritchie pretended to be angry, and the black inhabitant-customers watched with expressionless faces.

Crossing the dusty square, loaded with purchases, the expedition began to tell on the visitors. The dust blew in their eyes, the trees in their dying hour gave scant shade. At a huge white screen ('Outdoor theatre,' said the black guide) they found a large crowd of black inhabitants. They walked past somewhat faster when the black guide began talking to one of the black inhabitants. He shot out his sentences like machine-gun bullets and ended the conversation with a rapid fusillade of words and raised his shoulders. After that he was noticeably quieter.

'There's something in the air,' said Dr Johns to Detective-Sergeant Demosthenes H. de Goede, who narrowed his eyes and sniffed the air. He moved his shoulders and thrust out his chin. He stuttered something to Dr Johns and looked here and there around him, as if scanning the whole area for exits, hiding places and entrenchments.

A shrill whistle sounded in the distance and then the ululation of women's voices. The crowd stirred and then everything was quiet again.

The guests now walked decidedly faster and closer together across the square to where a cafeteria sign welcomed them. They seemed visibly to relax when they saw the Coca-Cola advertisements and the chromium soda fountain inside. A laughing black inhabitant behind the counter quickly restored their spirits by asking cheerfully what they would like.

'With the compliments of the Foundation,' said the black guide, looking abstractly through the door at the black crowd in the distance.

The guests had recovered exuberantly: the women guests threw the Bantu blankets over their shoulders and paraded before the men; the men did all sorts of amusing things with the beads. The guides had some difficulty in moving the guests on to the next phase of the tour: the men had taken off their jackets and loosened their ties; the women had powdered their noses and found the toilet arrangements a problem – except the woman from Sweden, who went and returned without a scratch, to hold herself, in liberal self-sufficiency, aloof from the rest of the guests for the remainder of the expedition.

The next place was reassuringly near one of the big exit gates and they entered a room full of black inhabitants immersed in newspapers, encyclopedias and historical works.

'The library,' said the black guide, to the great excitement of the intellectual visitors. The woman from Sweden, in particular, was ecstatic when she leaned over shoulders and recognized the cover of a book by her beloved Bertrand Russell in the hands of one of the black inhabitants. She found a twin soul in laughing white teeth and black eyes which, more effectively even than aloofness, succeeded in setting her apart. The eminent visitors looked through the bookshelves and asked for more photographs. There was temporary disorganization when the black inhabitants were invited to join the groups to be photographed. Everyone had a jolly time there and left the library very happy, waving and allowing the inhabitants to return to their chairs and try to find the exact places in their books again.

On their way to the next room they were confronted by a couple of black tots who shoved a pamphlet into the hand of each of them. A little farther on they came across a row of children with white sashes across their bodies, placards held in front of their chests and black eyes fixed motionless on the centre of the square. The guides held aloof and lit cigarettes while the visitors read the pamphlets and placards.

'FREE JULIUS JOOL!'

'JULIUS JOOL MUST GO FREE!'

'FREEDOM FOR JULIUS JOOL!'

The eminent visitors wanted to know who Julius Jool was, but got no information from the children, who commanded no English or advanced ideas. The guides refrained from any comment. It was left to Dr Johns to explain and, of course, he began with that aspect of Julius Jool's nature which was of interest to him.

'Julius Jool is a hermaphrodite and a firebug,' Dr Johns told the visitors. He expatiated on the universal melody of masculine and feminine tonality, the product of Aphrodite and Hermes, the prehuman undifferentiated condition. He mentioned the bisexual creature born from an egg. He spoke of the Ganymede on a dolphin. He took them back to the birth of the primordial child from water and related it to the birth of Aphrodite, according to Hesiod.

As he spoke, the black children suddenly began to chant: 'FREE JULIUS JOOL!' 'FREE JULIUS JOOL!'

He referred to the birth of the doomed Titans from the intercourse of Heaven and Earth, Gaea and Uranus. He told about Cronus who emasculated his father with his left hand and flung the phallus in the sea. He looked in particular at Detective-Sergeant Demosthenes H. de Goede and told of the birth of Aphrodite from the foam – the end and beginning of ontogenesis, the incomprehensible conjunction of the phallus that became a child, the reconciliation of opposites. He referred also to the birth of the mythological Giants, and Detective-Sergeant Demosthenes H. de Goede nodded understandingly: and to the children of the phallus, the primitive phenomena born of the emasculation, blood brothers of the erotic spirit and the tormenting Erinyes.

He struggled to convey to the fascinated guests and eminent visitors an incomprehensible idea, while the black children, with staring eyes, renewed their refrain: 'JULIUS JOOL FOR FREEDOM! JULIUS JOOL FOR FREEDOM!'

At this stage, before he could expatiate on the incendiary inclinations of the hermaphroditic martyr, the guides intervened and drew attention again to the limited time available to the honoured guests. After a photograph had been taken of the Swedish woman with a child in her arms, the group moved on.

They came now to the last room, where a resident occupational guidance officer saw to it that every black inhabitant took a regular efficiency test. He explained one such test, which required the candidate to construct a cubic whole from asymmetrical blocks. Several of the guests were invited to have a try, but they all proved unwilling, except Madam Ritchie, who made a hopeless botch of the whole thing and, laughing cheerfully, fell back on feminine helplessness to save her face. One of the eminent visitors was pushed forward by a colleague, and he made a joke of the whole affair. After his first attempt one block remained. The whole process was repeated while everyone watched with interest and the eminent guest rapidly lost his temper as he realized that this time another spare block would remain over.

'The black inhabitants succeed about seventy per cent of the time,' said the black guide contentedly. 'Those who are not successful are confined to small jobs that don't require much competence or responsibility.'

The eminent visitor declared, when he was halfway through his third attempt, that he did not have time to complete it, but he described in the minutest detail by what principles it should be completed. He stepped back and looked longingly outside. Then he was saved by the entry of the Giant, who picked up the blocks and looked at them, while the guests nodded at each other and waited to see what would happen. The Giant's clumsy hands covered the blocks, shook them, fumbled with them and suddenly put down a completed cubic unit on the table. Everyone left the room while the Giant, captivated by the new toy, completed the cubic unit again and again in various ways.

Outside, they found the square filled with black inhabitants moving about restlessly. Every now and then they looked up into the sky and then, with clearly apparent hostility, at the guests. The two guides increased their pace and tried to take a circular course around the crowd, and the guests, encumbered by their heavy purchases, tried to keep up with them. They were quickly encircled by a stream of black inhabitants who had come from another quarter.

The black guide spoke again to one of the visitors and Hope and Prudence clung to Detective-Sergeant Demosthenes H. de Goede's arms. He drew the two girls more closely to him and looked around with calculation. One of the eminent visitors asked the white guide what was happening, and the guide repeated the question to the black guide in an African language.

'A short while ago they saw a human being floating through the air,' said the white guide. 'It was the spirit of their ancestors, with its arms spread out over the township.'

The white guide was undecided whether he should proceed and the eminent visitor took him aside.

'It's a sign,' whispered the white guide, 'that their ancestors are calling upon them to take over the land over which his spirit has floated. They must destroy everything his shadow fell upon and purify the land. They must destroy the evil spirits and purify the land with fire and blood.'

The leading phalanx of black inhabitants began stamping the ground rhythmically with their feet. The monotonous rhythm urged them on to more energetic movements and all of a sudden one of them leaped into the air with a blood-curdling cry. The ululation of women came from a distance and a shrill whistle tore the air.

The eminent guest who had had difficulty with the cubic unit regained considerable respect by helping the two guides with the removal of the women guests through the crowd, which gave way willingly. They had some difficulty with the woman from Sweden, who insisted on staying behind and taking part in the mass demonstration. They ignored the Giant, however, who joined the mob. He had begun to dance with those in the vanguard, his thundering feet sounding louder than theirs, his appearance more threatening, his abandon equal to theirs. He was blissfully unaware of the glowering eyes watching him with twofold hatred, with their primordial fear of the monster, of the aberrant mind that communicated with evil spirits, and with their hatred of the colour of his skin, upon which all their grievances were projected.

When everyone had passed through the gates, and were reminded of their recent adventure only by the shrill whistling and the ululation, they all sighed with wonderful relief. It had been an instructive visit. They were all full of praise for the Foundation and the officials. The guides were freely given tips and, in their turn, each visitor received a piece of coloured ribbon. (The Giant arrived in time to get a scarlet ribbon.)

At the gate everyone bought some of the Blantyre's wares: brightly polished *panga* blades of various designs. The guides had, however, a last request – just outside the township, on a hillock above a small lily-covered lake fed by water from the masks, an inter-denominational church for the black inhabitants had been built in typical style. It was safe there and worth a visit.

The guests, now guideless, followed a footpath paved with stone and reached the lake below the little church. They admired the lilies and the fish and then climbed the hillock to the church. Going around a corner, Madam Ritchie suddenly let out a stifled shriek and the guests ran forward. They saw a man with a long beard who had come out of the bushes beside Madam Ritchie. He was without shoes and shirt. They stared at him in astonishment but he maintained his dignity, in spite of his appearance. He explained that he was Reverend Williams, that he had bathed in the lake and on his return had found that someone had stolen his shirt. He hoped that everyone, considering the unusual circumstances, would excuse him. He looked at the church on the hill: the construction with the coloured windows and the roof like that on a huge rondavel, and he offered to explain to the visitors some interesting aspects of the building. He had often preached there in the past.

With Reverend Williams, shirtless, in the lead, they approached, ascending, the gigantic rondavel church on the hill. They were, however, just too late to see the interior, for as they reached the summit of the hill, the first flames leaped from the roof and smoke billowed up into the blue sky.

The conflagration, however, was something to see. It would

have satisfied the deepest urges of Julius Jool, absent, under house arrest. It was a conflagration which at that moment seemed to fill the heavens and offered many opportunities for the most beautiful colour photographs.

The Room of Confession

'I only hope that there is no repetition of eighteen years ago,' said Dr Johns as he looked back at the smoke column that hung over the hillock like a volcanic cloud. 'We have put up a good many new buildings, but living room is severely limited.'

They were now descending slightly and walking through a valley where arum lilies grew beside streams. Then they ascended a slight rise and could see the masks on the slopes.

'The trout lake is there, just around the bend,' said Dr Johns and pointed. On the crest of the hill the factory, cellars and bottling plant gleamed in the distance. In the meantime they wandered through wet heather and past pools of water.

They came across a herd of skinny heifers.

'They're not Welgevonden animals,' said Dr Johns. 'They were bought for experimental purposes.'

A little farther on they came across Brutus III, the bull, on his back, his legs erect as poles in the air. Dr Johns gave him a light kick behind the shoulder and the little bull struggled up, lowing with pain. He trotted a short distance with them and then spotted another group of heifers in the distance. He rushed through the heather, his voice raised to an awful bellow that dwindled into a plaintive cry of fear when, as so often before, he collapsed in the heather among them and died his particular temporary death.

'It is said,' remarked Dr Johns to Detective-Sergeant Demosthenes H. de Goede, 'that our well-beloved field worker got his inspiration for his fertilization formula from the cultivators of the bastard mealie seed, P.P.K. 64. The male is also a weak, sere, pathetic plant.'

They had now reached an entrance hall that led into the cellars.

Beside it was a small office in which an ancient, toothless resident wrote his name in a stylish, shaky hand on an admission form and handed it to them.

'Remember the function tomorrow night,' he said, mumbling his piece. 'A full attendance will be appreciated.'

They passed through dripping tunnels which imperceptibly descended to cellars. The walls were overgrown with moss and the sound of their footsteps rang dully against them. Everywhere in the vaults that followed were empty vats in which, once, wines had matured. The entire place was a museum in which was exhibited the complete process of grape juice – through fermentation – to wine. Names were neatly printed on placards; the history was indicated, step by step and from room to room, on labels; all the containers and the complete framework were there – only the contents were lacking. It was like one of those anthropological museums in which display cases contain skulls, artifacts and implements that span the centuries, and only life is absent.

In one of the vaults they came across Jock Silberstein. He was sitting in a chair beside a wooden table on which there were all sorts of goblets and pipettes that, in the old days, had been used by the wine tasters to determine the quality of the wine. His hands were clasped behind his head and he was peacefully snoozing, like someone who had a wearying day behind him. He was somewhat confused when he woke up and saw them.

'Have you by any chance seen Adam Kadmon?' he said immediately.

'He was with us a while ago,' said Dr Johns.

'What did he look like?' asked Jock Silberstein. 'I mean, there was nothing the matter with him?'

'There was nothing the matter,' said Dr Johns.

'They hate him,' said Jock Silberstein. 'I can feel it in the air.' Suddenly he heard something, listened attentively and then relaxed. 'There is something inviolate about him; something that embraces all nature, which has nothing to do with reason, that represents the natural forces. If only they would realize this.' The sounds now reached them more clearly and became identifiable as heavy footsteps. 'If they would only see him as a child, helpless and powerless in their world, but filled with all the primordial power of instinct and the untamableness of nature.'

At that moment the Giant arrived and seemed, although apparently innocent, monstrous in the cellar. Jock Silberstein jumped up hurriedly from the chair and went to meet him. The caressing words he spoke were inappropriate, the fondling of the clumsy creature banal, the childish gestures with which the fondling was rejected, grotesque.

'They hate him,' Jock grumbled fondly, 'they hate him, my poor child . . .'

Dr Johns and Detective-Sergeant Demosthenes H. de Goede left the cellar, embarrassed. They looked back and saw the Giant still brushing off the caresses.

Outside, Dr Johns took Detective-Sergeant Demosthenes H. de Goede to a small room next to the factory. Inside it, against the walls, were numerous copper pipes that intertwined and were connected to a steam boiler outside.

'It is an interesting place,' said Dr Johns. 'Henry Silberstein-van Eeden once told me that Jock Silberstein, when he was still actively engaged in farming, called it his room of confession.'

The Detective-Sergeant stuttered a question.

'At that time, I never really understood,' said Dr Johns and peered inquisitively around the room. 'I fancy he told me that Jock Silberstein opened the steam cock and then experienced a sort of spiritual release from what followed.' He indicated the various instruments. 'Shall we try?' He suddenly opened one of the taps and a deafening noise filled the room. They remained speechless, listening to the monotonous noise and said and stuttered something to one another that was inaudible. Only their mouths opened and shut. Dr Johns closed the tap and said: 'Extraordinary. Simply a noise.' He looked around the room again. 'Perhaps Henry did not tell the full story. Perhaps there is something else.' He opened the tap again, and then another; in the noise the room suddenly filled with steam so that they both gradually disappeared from one another in the mist.

At one moment they were still able to see one another, their mouths open to shout inaudible instructions to one another, the next they were frighteningly alone in an invisible world that made them feel more alone than people who had got lost in the mist on a mountain slope. The ceaseless noise grew louder, the mist glowed white as if it were itself a source of light. The noise came from all sides, their eyes were wide open in their attempt to see something through the moving white. There was a demoniac roaring in that ghastly solitude: a different hell from what one had imagined; it was unfamiliar to one's conception of darkness and the known images of fear. This was something indescribably new: a Hades without monsters, a bleak Hades without content, a Hades that kept one captive in a continuum of meaningless sound. It was not a room of confession and spiritual release, but a room of supernatural torment, and Detective-Sergeant Demosthenes H. de Goede felt himself flinging cry after cry of terror into nothingness.

And then, suddenly, he felt his tongue free; that pure, clear words which he could not hear were describing his solitude and fear. Detective-Sergeant Demosthenes H. de Goede – at the precise moment when he felt fear as he had never felt it at the police college and in his dangerous career, when he was fighting in this underworld against an enemy that he had never encountered before – rid himself temporarily of that defect which had burdened him throughout his life. His silver tongue articulated his fear in the most beautiful language; he was endowed suddenly with a power that had always been denied him: to give lucid expression to his deepest feelings. At that moment of unendurable suffering he experienced also his deepest wish fulfilment and greatest triumph. There was even a time when, in his cries of anguish, he welcomed suffering for the sake of his new freedom of speech. But it did not last long. Slowly but surely his fear grew greater and he became accustomed to that desired freedom. He was in the act of selling his soul to the evil spirits and he stumbled wildly around the room to destroy the contact. Screaming, groping and terrified, he fell and beat against the wall and the pipes until he reached the cocks and, with a last effort of strength, turned them off.

The mist cleared gradually and the noise stopped at once. And gradually the two figures in the room became visible. Dr Johns, small and shrunken, in a corner: an old man, wet with sweat, and with the aftermath of indescribable fear in his eyes; and Detective-Sergeant Demosthenes H. de Goede: sweat shining on his face, the powerful muscles of his arms swollen to bursting, his face lifted as he ejaculated a flood of mangled words that gradually subsided to a pathetic stutter.

In the silence that followed he tried to say something to Dr Johns, but when he failed to do so, he kept resignedly quiet and wiped the mist from his eyes.

They walked slowly away and did not see the Giant who had watched their every movement. The huge figure was about to enter the room when Jock Silberstein appeared, took him gently by the hand and led him away against his will.

They reached the hall known as the bottling plant, but had difficulty in getting in because of the crush caused by two streams of visitors who had arrived at the same time.

'I can't help it,' said one guide to the other, 'the well-beloved Dries' speech was cut short by an hour.'

Dr Johns showed Detective-Sergeant Demosthenes H. de Goede through a window a row of bottles that came sailing past on a conveyor belt, were filled and vanished through a monastic tunnel next door.

'Glutamic acid and thiamine,' said Dr Johns.

In the hall next door, labels were put on the bottles by an intricate machine. Against the wall was a huge accounting machine. Various residents were performing all sorts of tasks, clothed in the Welgevonden uniforms. Dr Johns had considerable difficulty in getting Detective-Sergeant Demosthenes H. de Goede away from the crowds.

'You've probably already wondered,' Dr Johns said to Detective-Sergeant Demosthenes H. de Goede, who looked back longingly at the crowds as they walked on, 'what Henry and I mean by order and chaos?' He repeated the question until he had his companion's full attention. 'I have often reflected on it and come to the following conclusion : it is the organized world of reason against the powers of the unconscious, the differentiated world of the civilized man against the undifferentiated primordial world from which he developed by the momentum of his will.'

He found it even more difficult to hold Detective-Sergeant Demosthenes H. de Goede's attention when they passed through a garden where red and yellow flowers were in the process of becoming bastardized and filling the courtyard of a square building with garish parti-colour.

'The development of reasoning was a great development,' said Dr Johns. 'Man acquired a soul and he must fight with all the powers at his disposal to protect that soul against the monster in his dark past.'

They were overwhelmed by the blaze of colours on their way to a small building at the side of the factory.

'It is the task of the hero to triumph over darkness,' said Dr Johns. 'The triumph of the rational over the great and dangerous unconscious. Society wishes to project its struggle in the struggle of its champion.'

He found it necessary first to stop Detective-Sergeant Demosthenes H. de Goede before they entered the room, where a small group was assembled.

'Society is helpless without its champion,' said Dr Johns. 'The more it itself employs its own will towards order, the more it is removed from the soil in which it roots; its freedom of will becomes a source of transgression against its deep-rooted instincts. In its dilemma it needs a crucifixion, someone to die in the name of chaos, a sacrifice of atonement to protect it against the primitive powers that threaten to falsify its order.'

Dr Johns observed that Detective-Sergeant Demosthenes H. de Goede was not listening and he was about to throw in the sponge when he saw the Giant walking through the flowers hand in hand with Jock.

'The Giant-child is the legendary personification of the powers of chaos,' he said slyly. 'It's a primordial child who in his inviolability embraces all nature.' He nodded encouragingly as Detective-Sergeant Demosthenes H. de Goede began now to take an interest. Something he had learned at the police college was dawning. 'It's a powerful being,' said Dr Johns, 'with the vulnerability of a child. It commands all the powers of free nature: primitive and unrestrained.'

He was satisfied when Detective-Sergeant Demosthenes H. de Goede narrowed his eyes to slits, began rolling his shoulders and disappeared purposefully through the crowd into the room.

The speaker, introduced by the guide, was Professor Dreyer – a man with wavy white hair, sunk motionless in thought on the platform by the window, his students leaning in rows against the wall on either side of him, their bored attention fixed on the visitors as they prepared to listen to him. The wall was covered with shelves full of test tubes and glass containers in which various coloured liquids shone in the sun. Professor Dreyer waited until the room was quite silent, so that only the noise of the masks in the distance could be heard, and then he began his talk.

He welcomed everyone on behalf of himself and his students. He disposed of his annual joke, while the students looked at each other, and then began with an explanation of his work. He would put it as simply and popularly as possible, so that everyone could understand. The eyes of the guests were soon glazed with concentration, and they left each other for a spiritual siesta as the voice and the masks droned on monotonously. The hypnotic text was perpetual fermentation: the complicated connection was the psychic implication of zymosis and libido. Schooled by church and community life, they suffered passively the particular didactic, as a variation of their thirst for knowledge. Once they were plucked back from the lassitude of their rumination to inspect a test tube, in which four layers of four different coloured liquids turned grey when moved and then reverted to motionless separation. Then the audience was allowed to subside into reverie, to the lullaby of abstruse explanation.

Half an hour passed in which beginning, middle and end were disposed of, and then they all returned with a shock to reality when Professor Dreyer, by way of a *coda*, suddenly changed his theme and began talking about a raped virgin called Lila.

The residents had known her as someone with a heart full of love. Was she not always willing to have a friendly little chat with everyone? A smile here, a little encouragement there. She often visited the laboratory (the students would corroborate) to ask how things were going there. (The students lowered their eyes to their hands.)

A layman, true; but not ashamed of her ignorance.

(There were tears in the old man's eyes.)

He called her friend, and now she was gone.

(During the funeral service he had embalmed her in his heart. He *was* the only one! Indescribable delight, like the ideal fermentation, indefinitely prolonged . . .)

He apologized for losing control of himself and for having had to end off, before the eminent visitors, with a reference to this tragic event. But it lay close to the heart of everybody at Welgevonden, and as he had been informed that the person in charge of the investigation was also in the audience, he wished simply to take advantage of this opportunity to wish him all success in his important task and, on behalf of everyone in the laboratory, to express his regret and, Dr Johns, to ask you to convey this to those concerned.

Professor Dreyer left the platform in silence, followed by his students. They resumed work (among the test tubes). The visitors recognized Detective-Sergeant Demosthenes H. de Goede and nodded amiably. Then they quietly followed the guide outside and allowed Dr Johns and the Detective-Sergeant to continue their important perambulation undisturbed.

Chapter Twelve

Dreyer the Oracle and the Cottage with the Asbestos Roof

There were all the signs that the day was drawing to an end: the sun lay low on the horizon, the clouds in the west had already been touched with the first rose and would later turn to a garish red, so typical of the country.

'The eminent visitors will enjoy the sunset,' said Dr Johns. 'I am glad that they will have the opportunity to see such a thing at Welgevonden. Our nature is one of our most valuable instruments of propaganda.'

Dr Johns walked slightly ahead and led Detective-Sergeant Demosthenes H. de Goede thus, unnoticed, towards another row of cottages. The one they were now approaching was certainly one of the gayest. It was surrounded by hollyhocks and carnations and there were so many flowers and creepers that the cottage could hardly be noticed. It looked like a piece of garden that was inhabited. Dr Johns opened the red garden gate and motioned Detective-Sergeant Demosthenes H. de Goede to enter.

He knocked at the green door and, as they waited, told him where they were and whom they were to meet.

'It's Mrs Dreyer, the wife of Professor Dreyer, to whom we have just listened.' He tilted his head to listen to a sound coming from the cottage. 'It is said that eighteen years ago she was Jock Silberstein's mistress. It is difficult to believe and is probably one of those malicious rumours so often circulated about the owner of a place like Welgevonden.' The sounds were now recognizable as footsteps. 'Mrs Dreyer is our Oracle of Delphi,' said Dr Johns hastily. 'She is the best fortune-teller in the whole Republic.'

The footsteps had come up to the door and stopped.

Detective-Sergeant Demosthenes H. de Goede took out his handkerchief and wiped his hands.

'No,' said Dr Johns, 'she uses teacups. Only Mazawattee tea is drunk, and remember to use your left hand because you are unmarried.'

The door opened and a plump little woman well in her fifties, dressed in a light, floral dress, invited them to enter without greeting them. She led them to a small sitting room, asked them to be seated and disappeared towards the kitchen.

Dr Johns and Detective-Sergeant Demosthenes H. de Goede sat upright in their chairs and listened to the sound of teacups clinking. They could clearly hear Mrs Dreyer's kettle begin to sing as she did various small domestic chores. Now and then the telephone rang and they listened to Mrs Dreyer making an appointment for this or that time. The sitting room was well polished and there were desert scenes on the walls and shepherdesses on the sideboard. Old Christmas decorations still hung in a corner and in another corner a model airplane was suspended from a string. The mats on the floor were colourful and had recently been dry-cleaned.

Detective-Sergeant Demosthenes H. de Goede asked Dr Johns' permission to light a cigarette and looked around the spotless room for a place to dispose of his match. Dr Johns showed him a glittering ashtray in the form of a gondola on the little table next to his chair. Beside it was a portrait of Jock Silberstein, and also one of the Queen of England.

'Remember it costs fifty cents,' said Dr Johns. 'Ten cents for the Foundation and forty for herself.'

Detective-Sergeant Demosthenes H. de Goede took out the money in anticipation and put it on the table.

Mrs Dreyer suddenly appeared in the room and with difficulty took a milk jug from a shelf above a cupboard on which water jugs, glasses and crockery were accurately arranged in a straight row. Her dress stretched to bursting point as she reached up to take the milk jug. Detective-Sergeant Demosthenes H. de Goede was just too late to help her, but she said nothing. She merely pulled her dress down and bowed her head like someone who has withdrawn from the world. Then she left them.

A little later there was a shuffling at the door and Dr Johns opened it. Mrs Dreyer brought in a tray with a single cup of tea on it. She offered it to Detective-Sergeant Demosthenes H. de Goede and went out again.

Detective-Sergeant Demosthenes H. de Goede took three spoonfuls of sugar, stirred and drank the cup at a single draught. A whole mouthful of tea-leaves remained on his tongue and he spat them carefully back. He had hardly shaken the cup three times with his left hand when Mrs Dreyer returned suddenly and sat down in front of him on a stool.

She looked attentively at the tea-leaves.

'You are unmarried,' she said.

The Detective-Sergeant looked in astonishment at Dr Johns.

She turned the cup around in her hand and peeped into it.

'I see a large H.'

She looked again.

'You do a considerable amount of inspection work in regard to your job.'

Something worried her. She held the cup up against the light and looked fleetingly at Detective-Sergeant Demosthenes H. de Goede.

'There's an unpleasant task ahead of you. I see a very big man in your future and you will have a lot to do with him. I see the letters A.K.S.'

She shook out some of the tea-leaves and turned the cup around and around.

'I see a crown. You are going to have considerable success in your work. Your health is good. You are shortly going overseas. There's a letter for you.'

She frowned.

'There's a lot of tea-leaves here widely dispersed. This is extremely unusual. You get around a good deal, don't you?'

She shook the cup and closed her eyes wearily.

'I have been very busy today,' she said to Dr Johns. 'Three

groups of visitors and eminent guests have been here today. I hardly knew where to turn.'

She looked into the cup again.

'There's a warning sign.' She showed Detective-Sergeant Demosthenes H. de Goede a thick pile of tea-leaves. 'But I can't quite make out what it means. Be careful. I see you do not easily allow yourself to be influenced, but be careful all the same before you come to a decision. There are many who look up to you.'

Suddenly she sniffed.

'I smell burning,' she said to Dr Johns.

She was about to jump up and go to the kitchen when she saw the column of smoke through the window. She became agitated all over again.

'Everything is in order,' Dr Johns comforted her. 'Everything is under control.'

'Eighteen years ago I was raped,' she said to Dr Johns. 'I thought things like that belonged to the past.'

'Everything is under control,' said Dr Johns.

She looked uneasily into the cup.

'Someone has died,' she said to Detective-Sergeant Demosthenes H. de Goede. 'But not a relation of yours. Nevertheless, the death of this person affects you. I see the letter L.'

She shook out more tea-leaves.

'I see a big reception with many people, in the near future. Important things will happen there. I see something that flies. It looks like a large bat. Be careful. I see a fight or a big conflict, but the right party will win. One day you will inherit a lot of money. Are there any questions?'

She looked at her watch.

'You have two questions and one wish,' said Dr Johns in a whisper to Detective-Sergeant Demosthenes H. de Goede.

Detective-Sergeant Demosthenes H. de Goede thought for a moment and then stuttered anxiously. 'Are his hands strong enough for karate or must he confine himself to judo?' asked Dr Johns.

Mrs Dreyer looked at him in amazement and then took refuge in the cup.

'Yes,' she said.

Detective-Sergeant Demosthenes H. de Goede was at once ready with his other question.

'Must he concentrate on the further development of the *latissimus dorsi*, or should he rather devote his attention to the regulation of the central abdominal belt?'

'No,' said Mrs Dreyer.

She put the cup back in the saucer and waited with closed eyes.

'The wish,' Dr Johns whispered.

Detective-Sergeant Demosthenes H. de Goede frowned with thought and then relaxed as he formulated his wish to himself.

'Your wish will be fulfilled,' said Mrs Dreyer and stood up. She peered out of the window and opened the curtains.

'I saw something remarkable this afternoon,' she said over her shoulder to Dr Johns and looked up into the sky. 'I could have sworn I saw a man flying through the air.' She turned her back to the window and walked back into the middle of the room. 'But perhaps it is because I am so overworked. Imagine: *three* groups of visitors in succession. I have not enough tea left for supper.' She shook hands with Detective-Sergeant Demosthenes H. de Goede when she saw the money on the table. 'Of course, it could have been a large bird,' she said pensively. She walked ahead of them down the passage to the front door and saw the smoke column from another angle.

'Are you sure, Doctor Johns, that we will not have a repetition of eighteen years ago?'

Dr Johns shook his head.

She went out of the door into the garden. She bent to pick a few dead flowers.

'When did you last see Jock Silberstein, Doctor Johns?'

'We have just seen him,' said Dr Johns. 'These days he has withdrawn from everything and actually is interested only in Adam Kadmon Silberstein.'

Mrs Dreyer turned on a tap and began to water the garden with a hose.

'You must tell him that he must not so easily forget his old friends, Doctor Johns.' She straightened her hair with her hand. 'It's months since I saw him.'

'That's true,' said Dr Johns. 'He ought to get around more. It doesn't do him any good to concern himself all the time with the Giant.'

Mrs Dreyer waved to them from the garden gate.

Detective-Sergeant Demosthenes H. de Goede was scarlet with excitement. He could hardly wait to be alone with Dr Johns. He stuttered so rapidly that even Dr Johns found it difficult to follow him.

'Yes,' said Dr Johns. 'Remarkable woman. She has a special gift.'

They walked considerably faster as the sun began to sink quickly and the clouds take on definite gradations of red.

The light fell, too, on Detective-Sergeant Demosthenes H. de Goede whose face, scarlet with excitement and reflected light, was painfully distorted in his effort to formulate to himself, once again, the events of the past half hour.

'You know,' said Dr Johns to Detective-Sergeant Demosthenes H. de Goede as they walked through the heather towards the next hill. 'I am thinking again of our earlier conversation today when we spoke about the mythological conflict between the gods and the Giants. The conflict was grotesquely comic. One knows with absolute certainty that the Olympian gods should win, but every time one of the gods wounds a Giant, Hercules has to finish him off.'

Dr Johns revelled in having found someone who had so intense an interest in this subject. It was remarkable how thoroughly young people were educated these days.

'As you know, there were twenty-four Giants,' said Dr Johns, 'but I know the names of only a few.' He reflected, the heather brushing damply against them, the herbal fragrance of the veld filling the surroundings. 'I know that Alcyoneus was the leader of the Giants. His nickname was The Mighty Ass. They say he was perhaps the soul of the sirocco. The burning breath of the wild ass that starts nightmares and incites man to murder and rape.'

A group of guests, eminent visitors, residents and relatives, led by a tired guide, struggled past them through the heather. Madam Ritchie and her two daughters were way behind, and they waved lustily to Detective-Sergeant Demosthenes H. de Goede, who was prevented by Dr Johns from joining them. Hope's and Prudence's hair hung in ragged strands around their shoulders and they looked like wild daughters of nature.

'And then, of course, there was Porphyrion,' said Dr Johns, 'who, at the moment of attacking Hera, was wounded by an arrow from Eros' bow. The terrible pain changed to lust, he wrenched her beautiful cloak from her and exposed her in glorious nakedness – and Hercules killed him.'

A second group of residents, guests and eminent visitors appeared from another direction. It seemed as if they were trying to catch up with the first group : proteas and harebells were trodden flat as they struggled through the mud. The guide, well ahead, repeatedly looked at his watch and encouraged them enthusiastically. A single, dejected figure was about to drop out.

'Pallas, the erotic, wished to dishonour his own daughter, Pallas Athena; she knocked him to the ground with a stone – and Hercules killed him.'

Dr Johns looked curiously at the dejected figure sitting alone among the heather.

'Ephialtes fought Aries, Apollo shot him in the left eye. Hercules passed and shot him in the right eye – and killed him.'

The dejected figure looked longingly at them. He plucked a protea hopelessly and threw it away. His torso was naked and he was blue with cold.

'Klutios was burned by Hecate with burning brands – and Hercules killed him.'

The dejected figure had his toes in the mud and messed around in it like an impatient child. His trousers were sopping and his beard full of pollen. He looked with tear-filled eyes at Dr Johns and Detective-Sergeant Demosthenes H. de Goede, who stopped close beside him.

'Eurytus was felled by Dionysus with his Bacchus-staff – and Hercules killed him.'

The dejected figure suddenly jumped up and took up a position, legs wide apart, right in their path, his arms on his hips, his body dripping with moisture from the heather.

'Where can I go?' he asked furiously. 'Is there no place where I can find shelter? And hot food and clothes?' He swung his arms. 'Every time I join up with people they take me to factories and lectures. Nobody concerns himself with me. Is that Christian?' He was so furious he could hardly speak.

Dr Johns and Detective-Sergeant Demosthenes H. de Goede looked with interest at the enraged figure.

'The place is very crowded with all the guests and eminent visitors,' said Dr Johns. 'The rain spoiled everything and the funeral was, of course, an unexpected event. One can actually not blame anyone. Tremendous organization is attached to all the proceedings.' He rubbed his chin and suddenly came to a decision. He pointed towards the cottages that he and Detective-Sergeant Demosthenes H. de Goede had just left. 'Go and ask at one of them. Someone will quite possibly have room for you.'

The furious figure had in the meantime calmed down and was doing his best to regain his dignity. Dripping, he bowed to Dr Johns and walked with sucking sounds through the mud towards a cottage in the distance.

'Hephaistos burned the giant Mimas with a red-hot iron,' said Dr Johns as he and Detective-Sergeant Demosthenes H. de Goede wandered on, '– and Hercules killed him.'

They moved faster, since the sun was low on the horizon and the first houses with asbestos roofs gleamed in the distance.

'It makes one feel sad,' said Dr Johns. 'Our little walk is fast coming to an end and,' he smiled at Detective-Sergeant Demosthenes H. de Goede. 'I can't thank you enough for your enlightened and pleasant company.'

Detective-Sergeant Demosthenes H. de Goede stuttered modestly.

Dr Johns blew his nose.

'It really was pleasant, and I hope that one day, when your

task is done, you will again visit us as a guest of the Foundation.'

They had now come right up to the little houses with asbestos roofs and stood for a moment to admire the scene. The spotless white houses stood in a row, each with a square of garden in front and a lavatory behind. The red of the sunset tinted the walls with all shades of red. It was a restful scene, a true evening scene.

'That little house in the middle,' said Dr Johns, 'belonged to the gardener, the grandfather of the white-faced girl, the great-grandfather of Lila who was murdered.'

They began to walk slowly toward the house.

'Eighteen years ago these were all houses of ill fame,' said Dr Johns and smiled at Detective-Sergeant Demosthenes H. de Goede who blushed. 'But they no longer fulfil that function. In fact, such places have become an anachronism, because that particular satisfaction is these days obtained in society itself, with the en-lightened co-operation of women of all classes.' He blew his nose again and fastened his jacket. He looked rather anxious and popped a little pill into his mouth. 'I think we can say with pride that we have deprived sex of its secretiveness and made it commonplace.'

They were now in front of the house and a gay little scene greeted them. The uncle from Welkom stood in the door, the uncle from the Karroo was working in the garden, the old woman with silver hair and the girl who looked like a little sow were each peeping out of a window.

'Welcome !' said the uncle from Welkom.

He had the dignity of one who is not only head of a family, but of an entire dynasty.

'Come in,' he said, 'and enjoy a cup of tea.'

All four of them had taken over the house and moved about as if they had been at home there for years. The old woman and the girl were both busy knitting with clicking needles and wool of a garish colour.

'We found them in one of the cupboards,' said the old woman with silver hair.

'We found the oddest articles of clothing,' said the girl who looked like a little sow. She named them, except the unmention-able, which she had herself put on. It was clear that the clothes of their only niece had already been divided among them.

The uncle from the Karroo wanted to know in whose name the house had been transferred. Had Lila perhaps inherited it from her grandfather?

'It belongs to the farm,' said Dr Johns as he blew his tea cool. 'It is part of the Foundation.'

The uncle from the Karroo knocked out his pipe on his shoe.

'Have you perhaps seen the will and the deed of transfer?' he asked Dr Johns.

The uncle from Welkom interrupted him.

'We won't bother Doctor Johns with such problems now,' he said. 'We can hold them over until a later and more appropriate time.'

'When the pain is past,' said the old woman with silver hair.

The girl who looked like a little sow began to cry softly.

A corn-cricket walked across the floor and disappeared toward the kitchen, as everyone watched it anxiously.

'*Eugaster longpipes,*' said Dr Johns.

'The place needs a thorough cleaning,' said the uncle from the Karroo.

'Tomorrow is another day,' said the uncle from Welkom.

They drank tea in silence and then the uncle from Welkom said with a sigh: 'So, it was here that our beloved niece, Lila, spent her last years. I hope everyone was kind to her.'

The uncle from the Karroo lit his pipe again.

'Tell me, Doctor Johns, is Mr Silberstein a Jew?'

Dr Johns put his empty cup down on the table and nodded.

The aunt nudged the girl, and the uncle from the Karroo drew deeply on his pipe.

'And the Giant, Adam Kadmon Silberstein,' asked the uncle from Welkom, 'is he a Jew, Doctor Johns?'

Dr Johns shrugged.

'Sort of half and half.'

The uncle from the Karroo and the uncle from Welkom looked meaningfully at one another. The old woman with silver hair and the girl who looked like a little sow kept their eyes fixed on their knitting.

'Our niece, Lila, was raped, was she not?' the uncle from Welkom asked in a soft voice.

'We are not quite sure,' began Dr Johns, but the uncle from Welkom stopped him and pointed to the old woman and the girl, who had stopped knitting and covered their faces with their hands. The girl who looked like a little sow suddenly got up and walked quickly from the room, her dress swaying and the last souvenir of Lila shining colourfully in the twilight.

The face of the uncle from the Karroo was hard.

'The unholy alliance!' he said suddenly. 'The foul conspiracy!' He turned to Detective-Sergeant Demosthenes H. de Goede. 'We trust in you, Sergeant,' he said hotly.

The uncle from Welkom whispered something to him. They both stood up. The aunt with silver hair made her farewells with a limp hand of grief and went to the kitchen to prepare the evening meal. A suppressed scream signified her second meeting with the corn-cricket and then they could all hear the scraping of a broom and the opening and closing of the back door.

At the garden gate the uncle from the Karroo said to Detective-Sergeant Demosthenes H. de Goede: 'There are rumours, Sergeant, about a giant, that our beloved Lila was . . .', but the uncle from Welkom stopped him.

'I think the Sergeant and I understand each other,' he said.

Detective-Sergeant Demosthenes H. de Goede and Dr Johns left the house with the asbestos roof, while the two uncles leaned over the hedge and looked fixedly up at the sky as if they espied the possibility of more rain.

'I tell you it was a vulture,' said the uncle from Welkom emphatically.

'It was an omen,' said the uncle from the Karroo equally emphatically. 'We often see them in the Karroo.'

The uncle from Welkom silenced him and gave a last wave

to Dr Johns and Detective-Sergeant Demosthenes H. de Goede. The last rays of the sun glowed on the house and painted the doors and blinds, which were being firmly bolted for the coming night.

Chapter Thirteen

Departure of a Meturgeman

They walked slowly through the heather and saw Welgevonden at its most beautiful. A single poplar was a burning monolith against the horizon.

'There is the trout lake,' said Dr Johns and pointed to a sheet of water that lay calm as a mirror under the slope of the mountain. A fleet of boats with their load of residents, guests and eminent visitors were congregating from far and wide at the wharf. The weeping masks drew a line of marble down to the fountain above the Welgevonden houses. The water moved in a shining stream, shot through the mouths like fountains and glittered with every imaginable colour. And all along the line of water the tired guests moved without their guides: a slow, lazy movement towards the buildings that waited among the trees.

'After tonight,' said Dr Johns with a touch of sadness in his voice, 'I shall have to leave you. My particular task will have been completed.'

They were moving down, past the trout lake, past the Corinthian columns reflected in the water, along the masks on the winding way of the stream.

'I am an old man,' said Dr Johns. 'I have passed the stage when I aspire to build up a definite personality. I am actually also past the stage of really taking an interest in individuals. I am curious only about the broad characteristics. If I die tomorrow, or the next day, I want the complete view only.' He was silent for a moment. 'But even that is no longer so important.'

Detective-Sergeant Demosthenes H. de Goede made a gesture of dissent.

Along the road they met Henry Silberstein-van Eeden. He

nodded briefly to Detective-Sergeant Demosthenes H. de Goede and turned to Dr Johns.

'I have thought about it,' he said, excited. 'I have realized that everywhere here I have freedom : in the Foundation, in the research offices, among the residents, in the laboratories.' He sought for the right words. 'The freedom of specialized niches : the small areas in which one can realize oneself.'

Dr Johns smiled and did his best to give his face an expression of venerable wisdom, but all he could achieve was a wrinkled look of cunning.

'It's a feeling of being alone that drives one to the Foundation,' said Henry. 'Yearning and loneliness. It is not *what* happens here, but the possibility that something revealing *will* happen, that here one will get away from the uncomprehensive abstraction of the world within one.' He still sought in vain for the right words in which to express his insight.

'And so the Foundation must be protected at all costs?' asked Dr Johns and winked at Detective-Sergeant Demosthenes H. de Goede.

But Henry walked on alone, unwilling at that stage to think about the most important consequences.

'They all come here,' said Dr Johns, 'in proportion as the Promethean guilt accumulates out there. Bomb-shocked victims of the explosions in themselves.'

Dr Johns and Detective-Sergeant Demosthenes H. de Goede greeted Madam Ritchie and her two daughters. They had brought their hair under control by tying it with red and blue ribbons from Mon Repos. Hope and Prudence ran to Detective-Sergeant Demosthenes H. de Goede like tall, slim daughters and embraced him. He looked with beaming face from one to the other and then his eyes grew serious as he tried, for the hundredth time, to decide on the particular status of each, resident or relative. Each felt equally soft, each was equally warm and the chatter of each was equally vapid. But Madam Ritchie was in a hurry : supper had still to be prepared, they had all to go to bed early because there was a long day and a great occasion ahead tomorrow. Mr de Goede was always welcome, however.

The two girls tore themselves away and waved gaily to him as they frisked off after their corpulent mother with ponytails and red and blue ribbons swaying.

'Everyone on Welgevonden,' said Dr Johns, 'follows his own illusions undisturbed. It is not that there is something here that the outside world hasn't got, it's just that everything happens more slowly, that it is a small order inside a big order.' He tried to think of an example. 'It's like an enormous theatre where everyone assembles – not to do anything, but to see a completed film.'

They greeted the universally-liked Dries, who walked hurriedly past them; he raised his hat. There was an ecstatic smile on his face. He looked frequently up into the air and his shining eyes reflected the aftermath of his vision. An improved breeding policy was already emergent, a sort of matriarchy with the bull's strain kept to a minimum, with the bull features broken down to the elemental, strictly controlled act of artificial insemination – that was the prophetic idea of Uncle Giepie, that was his triumph over the monster, that was the vision blessed by the figure in the clouds. He walked faster. Deep down inside him, half formed but genuine and true, the policy was growing – that he could feel, in his entire being.

'We can simply learn to live with what there is,' said Dr Johns. 'We can only hope that an empty ritual will again become meaningful.'

He bowed to one of the eminent guests.

'If only we could find something great,' sighed Dr Johns. 'But we are actually only a parody of the outside world. We differ only in that we provide a buffer for every resident. We protect fantasy when it clashes with reality, we protect the image of reality when it clashes with the fantasy of the time.'

They became aware of someone beside one of the masks: a shivering figure who hid himself behind the gushing maw until all the guests and visitors had passed. It was a shivering figure that made not the slightest attempt to attract attention or to ask for help. He simply sat with his back to the mask and his feet in the water that rushed noisily from the maw. His trousers were soaked, his torso was marked with red blotches, as if boiling water had fallen on him.

He did not at first answer when Dr Johns spoke to him. Then he said dolefully: 'She threw boiling tea over me. She said I was a barbarian who wished to rape her, and then she threw the boiling tea over me.'

He no longer tried to maintain his dignity. He had given up the struggle: he even felt strangely at home at Welgevonden, where he was treated so cavalierly.

'I was covered with tea-leaves,' said the shivering figure. 'And do you imagine that she tried to help me?' Indignation strove unsuccessfully to get the upper hand, then subsided beneath this peaceful fatalism. 'She stood before me, that fat little woman in her heathen dress, and she began telling my fortune. A witch of Endor!' He held his feet up to the stream of water and watched it spurt between his toes. 'She sees prison walls and the hand of justice. She sees the horsemen of the Apocalypse!' He paddled his feet in the stream. His chin was sunk on his chest and he seemed to be looking at his navel. He had already forgotten Dr Johns, in his shivering contemplation of the world.

'And this is the fountain,' said Dr Johns a moment later as they passed the last mask and looked between the statues at the lily-covered surface. 'It's particularly high, the water is boisterous, the cement pipes can't cope with carrying away the water to the industrial installations.'

The plastic swans swayed to and fro as if they had landed on a sea. Often the waves toppled a swan and then it reappeared a little way off, straight again.

'It's here that Jock Silberstein found Lila,' said Dr Johns.

All the visitors, eminent guests and residents had disappeared already in the direction of Welgevonden's houses. The sun was behind the mountain and the evening shadows were purple.

Detective-Sergeant Demosthenes H. de Goede looked at the grass around the fountain, but it was flattened by hundreds of feet. He was looking around for clues and found all sorts of garments and personal articles that had been lost. In the end he found a single line of unusual footprints. He knelt next to them and made notes busily in his notebook. According to their measurements, they must have been the footprints of a colossal person. When he did his calculations later that night, he would be able to determine the exact height and weight of the gigantic figure.

Entirely satisfied, he joined Dr Johns and they strolled lazily over the lawn to one of the glass houses that had been assigned him as his quaters for the duration of his visit. On the way they came across Jock Silberstein and Adam Kadmon Silberstein. The Giant was still being obstinate, but was firmly led by its hand.

'It's time for young boys to go home,' said Jock Silberstein and smiled at the Giant, who wore the scarlet ribbon of Mon Repos around his neck. 'Early to bed and early to rise, makes Adam Kadmon healthy and wise.'

At his own glass house, the nearest to the fountain, Dr Johns had to take his leave.

'And I, too, must go home,' said Jock Silberstein. 'Like Cronus, I am banished to the Golden Age and to the Blessed Island.' He pointed to the house of Welgevonden among the battling trees. The cumbersome figure of the Giant and the slighly crooked, tall man constituted an extraordinary pair as they walked away and for the last time left Dr Johns and Detective-Sergeant Demosthenes H. de Goede alone.

Dr Johns stood at the door of the glass house, a slight little man in the twilight.

'I hope I was helpful,' he said eagerly.

Detective-Sergeant Demosthenes H. de Goede stuttered a protest against the modesty of his conductor.

'I hope I did not influence you in any way,' Dr Johns folded his hands piously and looked after Jock Silberstein and the Giant on their way to the Big House. 'It would upset me very much if I were to discover that I exercised any influence in any way upon you and your detective work.'

Detective-Sergeant Demosthenes H. de Goede repeated his protest proudly.

Dr Johns' face brightened suddenly.

'One can say that I perhaps filled the role of a sort of present-day Meturgeman. I, too, merely formulated certain obscure aspects of the situation and summed them up in understandable language, not so?'

He unlocked the door and switched on the lights. Coincidentally, at that very moment, lights went on in many other glass rooms as well, as the guests, residents and dignitaries reached their rooms.

'I concede that I sometimes went so far as to play the role of exegete,' said Dr Johns reflectively.

Detective-Sergeant Demosthenes H. de Goede looked in amazement at the people who were undressing and, visible to one another, doing the most intimate things in their glass rooms.

'The rooms were specially designed for observation from outside,' said Dr Johns. 'The relatives, guests and eminent visitors must naturally adapt themselves to the Foundation, where everything is designed in the interests of the residents. You'd be surprised how quickly one becomes accustomed to it.'

Dr Johns suddenly stretched out his hand and greeted Detective-Sergeant Demosthenes H. de Goede ceremoniously. He still had the *ephialtion* in his other hand. Perhaps Detective-Sergeant Demosthenes H. de Goede would take it along? An exceptionally rare plant with certain magical properties, according to tradition.

Detective-Sergeant Demosthenes H. de Goede demonstrated, as so often before, his remarkable memory by stuttering a reminder to Dr Johns of his intention to ... well ... undertake certain ... excavations.

Dr Johns expressed his surprise at the Detective-Sergeant's retentive memory and reassured him that he, Dr Johns, still had every intention of carrying out his intention; but that the Detective-Sergeant could naturally have no official knowledge of this, in view of there being no warrant which, in the nature of the weather conditions, was unobtainable. The result of the investigation would, however, be made known to him in due course.

He greeted the Detective-Sergeant a second time and went into his room. His movements, although they could still see each other clearly, underwent the subtle transformation of someone alone and invisible to another.

Detective-Sergeant Demosthenes H. de Goede walked slowly

to his room, gaping as he went at the guests and eminent visitors who exposed themselves in the most intimate manner, apparently suffering from the same illusion as fish in an aquarium that the darkness outside, because of the light inside, enclosed them in a separate world. He lingered for a while at the Swedish lady's glass room and then entered his own room, where he at once became the victim of the same illusion when he switched on his light.

He undressed quickly, ate a few sandwiches that he took from his little tin trunk and got comfortably into bed. He took out his notebook, uncapped his fountain pen, and wrote: 'Just like fishes in an aquarium, mankind suffers from the illusion that he is invisible.' It would later form the nucleus of a poem in *The Police Officer*. Presently it occurred to him that he had not yet done his before-bed exercises, but he decided to forgo them, since he had been particularly active all day. He noticed the plant on the bedside table, smelled it, put it back and switched out the light. With hands folded behind his head, peaceful against the pillows, he could see clearly in the dark the lighted glass room next door, where the Swedish lady, under the general illusion of invisibility, was doing a striptease. It looked so genuine that after a while he even began to wonder whether, maybe, she were not enticing him in the most shameless manner. Later, he began worrying all over again because he had not done his bedtime exercises. Fortunately, there were also isometric exercises that one could do lying on one's back. His breathing grew more rapid and his body stiffened in the complicated process.

Thereafter he relaxed and drifted into a dreamless sleep with the *ephialtion* near his head.

Quibus Auxiliis?

Succubus

(It was shortly after midnight and all the wooden doors in the old section were tightly shut. The voices of the masks boomed out over the whole of Welgevonden. Only a single window was open to let in the light wind which stirred the curtain softly. A full moon made everything visible in its silver light and transformed the landscape, the castle-like buildings, the fountains, lakes and statues into a Gothic scene. In the light of the moon the rational diurnal statues had become the statues of the night; in sleep, the complicated network of reason had been transposed into the twilight world where Ephialtae and Hyphialtae awoke and floated with the wind over the Foundation to renew themselves.

The Giant-child lay on his gigantic bed in his room, enclosed by the cloud-grey walls. He dreamed with open eyes of his black-eyed mother; he waited as always for the appearance of his *lamia* with the great white breasts and the warm limbs; he waited with reluctant longing for the incestuous struggle that sapped his giant strength and then permitted him to sleep exhausted, until the following day with its promise of lustration by flowing water.

Something moved over at the waving curtain; his Lilaleman-larua would appear with her pallied face and bite him with her strong white teeth, while she groaned with pleasure.)

The curtains waved and the years stood still. There was heather and water and sunshine and pale moonlit nights. There were warm blood and swoons. There was something that was soft. There was the passion of abandonment. There was the very first night, the whisper of her dress and her pale face. She bent over him, her teeth gleamed and she slavered over him. There were games with someone with black eyes and suddenly it was dark.

There was something warm, soft against him. He fought back, winning and losing simultaneously. He drank from the white breasts. He caught a little bird and wrung its neck. The creature lay fluttering on the ground and expired in its own blood. Someone came from behind and he felt something soft. His hand was wet. The waters splashed over him. The masks roared and everything was cold. He felt strong again. Suddenly he was weak. His life was draining from him. He strangled her but his hands grew numb. He tried to strangle her but she bit him on the left side of his throat and he felt the warm blood. Once, he had lain in soft arms and soft hands had caressed him. He grew strong and wished to destroy the softness. On other days he longed for it. Where were the dark eyes? She appeared among the curtains and her breath smelled of blood. She asked him to kill her. She whispered something in his ear and he throttled her, but his hands grew slack. Where was she lying? She was everywhere. She rushed down on him and he struck her away from him. His hands sank into her body. And suddenly she was no longer there. He looked up into the black eyes and saw the enormous breasts. The breasts were big and the nipples black and pointed. He wept suddenly and was filled with longing for something that he could not understand. He could destroy everyone if he wished, but he suddenly felt weak. Someone must stroke him. He waited and saw something by the curtains. Sometimes he remembered the name Salome, but she said Lila! – Lila! she screamed, and then he faded away. The door was locked. The moon shone through the window. The fountain roared. Those faces roared. He wanted to sleep, but he could not sleep. The large man came and took his hand. His hand was rough and strong. And there, suddenly, was she! But they locked him in. The key grated in the lock and he lay straight on the bed. He stretched. His feet protruded from the blankets. He felt cold. There was something warm on him. A sharp pain. Her voice was soft and lovely. Do this! she said. Do this! she ordered. Why did nothing happen? He waited and waited and waited, and nothing happened. He called her name and nothing happened. He lay and waited, and watched the curtains. There were baubles in her hair. Her hair hung down on either side of her face. She laughed with sharp teeth. Come ! she said and the curtains waved. She always said Come ! and then she was gone. And suddenly she was there again. Something bit him and he felt exhausted. But then he felt strong again. Someone hurt him. He wept and someone comforted him. She was so small that one could bend her in two. Harder ! she screamed and was suddenly gone. He wished to sleep but he could not sleep. Where was she? The curtains moved but it was not she. Where is Lila? he asked and the man took his hand. His hand was rough and big. Nothing happened. The curtains swayed and swayed and there, suddenly, she was, but she was no longer there. He wanted to bite something but everything was tough and there was no blood. Bite ! she screamed. But there was nothing to bite. He felt her bite and something was sticky and viscous. And it was soft and everything melted away and the faces roared and the water was cool and all at once he was strong again. He waited and waited. The curtains swayed and the window was open. The waters were noisy and someone called. Someone called, everything called and called and called. The curtains were soft and melted in one's hands. The waters roared, but why was the sun not shining? The window frame was hard, everything was hard and suddenly there was nothing. But something hurt. One melted away and one's whole body was sticky. Something was wrong. There was something wrong and one was very tired. One's feet sank away and the waters roared. There was nothing soft and everything fled. One tried to call, but one had no voice. One called and nobody answered.

INCUBUS

(At the glass houses, the moonlight scene was different : it was a miniature city centre, asleep with other images of fear and other dreams : Ephialtae and Hyphialtae in other shapes; a jungle of glass and cement with its own bloodless monsters. The big glass windows were empty and shining, and shone emptily back to the pale moon.

Madam Ritchie was asleep on her foam-rubber mattress, her

face smeared with night cream, her scalp taut with curling pins, the acid in her stomach neutralized by fruit salts, her emotions calmed by tranquillizers, her body in the process of dehydration by means of a plastic sweatsuit which guaranteed so many liquid ounces in loss of weight. She lay motionless in a drugged semblance of death and dreamed dreams that she would not remember the next morning.

In the glass room next door Prudence slept surrounded by photographs of film stars. Her hair had been brushed three hundred times, her arms hung down on either side of the bed and the tips of her fingers touched the floor. Her young breasts swelled under the transparent nylon, a spider's web created under the trade name Vanity Fair; she needed no pills, her blood was warm and her skin soft. She lay relaxed on her back, exposed receptively in a condition of dreamless sleep.

In the third glass room Hope lay naked on a blanketless bed. Her hair, too, had been brushed three hundred times and lay in soft folds on either side of her face. Her body was full and young and exposed to the night. Her eyes were open and her lips moist: shameless wishful images thronged her distorted mind and became visible in the moonlight in the movements of her limbs, her restless hands and the erotic undulations of her whole body. This was the 'resting' image of the tormented resident; the pitiful nymphomaniac who suffered in solitude continual unsatisfaction; whose impotence was understood by nobody; who with frequent coitus would remain always sterile. All her movements in that half-sleep were a parody of provocation and satisfaction, a continual repetition of Satanic sterility, a witchdom between glass windows, and an eternal suffering on the pyre of the ceaseless fire in herself.)

The curtains moved and someone was in the room. There was a dark figure before the window. Chunky and dark against the moon. Black John with his cold sword. You lay still and nothing happened. You heard the movement and rolled towards it and you knew then in that taunting moment that nothing would happen. But it was the old thing: the ballet of hesitation. The moon shone through the window and still you could see nothing. But he was there. Black John was invisible in the shadows of the moon; there was no reflection of him in the mirror. You stretched out in sensual invitation, you spread yourself out in a position of maximum receptivity. You awaited the hated contact and you felt that you could wait no longer. You twisted your fingers through your hair and ran your fingers over your skin. It was a matter of time and then you heard the slight shuffle and waited for the ensuing silence. It was a creative urge that could never be stilled, but you obtained a limited satisfaction in the creative movement, although there was no satisfaction. Something very close to you moved and you answered with swelling breasts. There was a dragging sound and you stretched in thrilling suspense. Something touched the bed and you became soft with receptivity. You awaited first the hand that would touch here, there, everywhere – but you knew it would not happen at once. You awaited your lover in the dark with all the darkness in yourself.

You repeated the dark ritual mechanically and waited for the mechanical contact. There was no end to the unbearable repetition; there was no consummation of the aching wish. You found your substitute satisfaction in the act that had no end, in the repetition that would lead to nothing. You lived only for the movement without expectation that you would ever be carried to your destination.

And then you felt the hand assaulting your breasts. You heard and felt the presence that would destroy you. You felt the destruction as the heavy weight flattened your little mattress against the springs. You were compelled to play the part of a fugitive in the flight that *had* to satisfy you. (Even though you knew it could not happen.) You suffered the semblance of being overwhelmed, but you really felt overpowered. You felt the teeth in your throat and screamed with a pain you hated and welcomed. In the passion of your creativity you knew that creation would never be achieved. You clamoured yieldingly and fought compliantly. You were tortured by the welcome assault. You felt the hot blood that stirred your revulsion. You spurred destruction on; you whispered the death wish with a banality that came not from yourself.

You surrendered with murderous fury. And then you muttered
the name in imitation of the eventual satisfaction that you did
not feel.

You named your desire . . . Jock, Henry.

Named all the names of acquaintances and strangers and named
in vain the names that would exorcise evil by love, and would
save yourself. Named even Adam Kadmon with his clumsy body.
Called in vain to everyone you hated. Spoke the name of the
young hero. Named the athletic, half-godlike figure. Muttered
and called the name until all had passed and, wide awake, you
took your revenge and sent one shriek of dissatisfaction after the
other into the night. You screamed your fury in the moonlit
night and found your satisfaction in all the lights you caused to
spring up, in the glass houses that caught fire, and the noise in
the night.

You heard the monster, satiated, fleeing. You welcomed the
light in your room. You found your satisfaction in the anxious
faces of your dearest. You came nearest to complete satisfaction
through the anxiety and rage of those who loved you. You
burned, then, on the glorious pyre. You became suddenly visible
in the role of the holy virgin.

EXHUMATIO

(While the screams rent the night, the lights jerked on one after
another. Moonlight was replaced by electric light and the tableau
was continued in the numerous glass rooms. The residents, guests
and eminent visitors looked repeatedly at one another; they
jumped out of bed and exposed themselves to one another in all
the colourfulness of their intimate nightwear; the men in striped
pyjamas, the women in transparent pink and white material.

Madam Ritchie stumbled through to Prudence's room, she and
Prudence burst into Hope's room and fell on their knees next to
the bed from which the naked girl screamed lustily. They looked
at the open window and saw the moving curtains. Then they
joined her and screamed inordinately for help from the rest of the
Foundation.

In the glass rooms there was great activity. The residents, guests and eminent visitors hastily donned their dressing gowns and ran outside. In the bright light from the glass windows they met one another coming from all directions. There was such turmoil that the unknown miscreant could automatically disappear merely by standing still and becoming part of the crowd. They crowded around the blue glass house and saw Madam Ritchie throw a transparent gown over her naked daughter. Then she opened the door to them and they streamed in as if they had not seen enough. The two daughters became the object of their attention. They were quickly overwhelmed in the mass and, as more and more arrived, could scarcely move. Presently they filled the adjoining rooms and made the glass house hum with the force of their speculations. They no longer knew whether Hope or Prudence had been the victim and each of them had already arrived at his own decision and disseminated his own rumour. Hope and Prudence were both in tears; both, like the crowd, in dressing gowns; they were both sipping brandy that was being offered them. Most of the residents and guests could not get into the rooms and returned to their own rooms where they made coffee and continued their speculations, watching each other through the windows. The reappearance of the evildoer had completed the expected pattern. Lila's name was added to Hope's and Prudence's. The extent of the threat had increased – they all felt intimately concerned. Revenge and retribution were now really on campaign. The ranks of the community were closed.

The lights burned in all the glass houses except one : Detective-Sergeant Demosthenes H. de Goede's, who in dreamless sleep enjoyed his night's rest.

After an hour or two the noise and turmoil decreased – a point of satiety had been reached. The rooms emptied and Madam Ritchie, Hope and Prudence locked themselves securely in one room. One by one the lights went out and keys grated in locks. The moonlight regained its supremacy and shone softly silver in the shut glass.)

Somewhere on Welgevonden, in a cemetery beneath the moon,

as everyone slept again, a lively presentation of an old legend was revived. It was as if Dr John Dee and Edward Kelly stood again within the double circle amid the planetary symbols and the names of Raphael, Rael and Tarniel. Beside an open grave it was as if the two magicians were again in consultation with a ghostly apparition in a shroud, and were asking for an answer about the future.

In the moonlight everything was delusive. It could have been the recreation of an old Jewish custom, according to Rabbi Man-assah : that the dead would return for a year, that one could make an invocation to them, as the witch of Endor to the dead prophet Samuel, and that a light on the future could be obtained.

In that moonlight landscape it could also have been a scene from the Middle Ages where someone (dressed like that little figure in the dark cloak) wished to render evil harmless with a single stab of a holy aspen staff.

It could also have been of the modern time as, by way of distorting the past, the scientist brought the dead back to obtain, by means of investigation and dissection, an answer to his despair.

Those who had suffered a violent death were seldom left undisturbed if they bothered the community. By different incantations, alternating from age-old formulas of exorcism to the officialese of warrants, they were dissected for the sake of the peace of all.

In the moonlight, around the grave, by the light of a lantern, the process was repeated. And in the distance, beyond the light but visible nevertheless, was a giant figure that watched everything quietly.

Quomodo?

Quomodo?

When Detective-Sergeant Demosthenes H. de Goede awoke the next morning he found Judge O'Hara at his door. The old man in his black toga, grey with dust, nodded amiably, placed his staff in a corner of the room and sat down on a chair. With a movement of his hand he granted the Detective-Sergeant permission to do his physical exercises.

The curtains of the neighbouring glass rooms were drawn, since it was now daytime, and a good many residents, guests and eminent visitors were watching with interest the Detective-Sergeant who was warming up before doing more complicated movements. This compelled him to draw his own curtains, because of the small crowd that had gathered in front of his window.

'Greetings from Doctor Johns,' said Judge O'Hara. 'He can unfortunately not be here today.' He shook with a soundless fit of laughter. 'He asked me, however, to inform you that the necessary investigation was made last night.'

Detective-Sergeant Demosthenes H. de Goede, involved in freehand exercises, stuttered a question.

'I can't hear a word,' said Judge O'Hara.

Detective-Sergeant Demosthenes H. de Goede repeated his stuttered question.

Judge O'Hara found the repeated question equally incomprehensible.

'Write it down, man,' he said.

Detective-Sergeant Demosthenes H. de Goede wrote neatly on a piece of paper: 'What were Dr Johns' findings?'

'Exactly what he expected,' said Judge O'Hara impatiently. He looked around the room, saw the small plant beside the bed and nodded his satisfaction. 'I see you made provision for a good night's rest. Pity Hope and Prudence didn't have one too.'

Detective-Sergeant Demosthenes H. de Goede was completely in the dark and wished to write down another question, but Judge O'Hara ordered him to finish his exercises and to dress.

'I gather from Doctor Johns that, in the nature of things, he is interested in the mythological parallel to your mission. Early this morning I did some research and found something in Aristophanes that will certainly interest you. Verse 1039 of Rogers' translation of his well-known work, where the monster Typhon, against whom Hercules is fighting, is described: "And (it had) a *lamia*'s groin ..."' He looked triumphantly at Detective-Sergeant Demosthenes H. de Goede, who had just finished his exercises. He was, however, obviously disappointed at the Detective-Sergeant's lack of enthusiasm.

'*Lamia* ...' he repeated and watched with barely concealed dissatisfaction as the Detective-Sergeant dressed himself in brand new sports clothes which he had just taken from his little trunk. 'Perhaps you know the expression *empusa* better.' He looked expectantly up. 'It's a variant of the *lamia* and Rogers uses the word "vampires" in his translation of the *Ranae*.' He sat back cosily to enjoy the Detective-Sergeant's shock of interest. When there was still no reaction, he suddenly came under the influence of the policeman's iron self-discipline. 'It's at any rate interesting to know that Hercules also fought against a vampire,' he said forlornly.

Detective-Sergeant Demosthenes H. de Goede listened courteously, but he seemed to be confining his attention to a tie (in the colours of the police college) which he was tying in an Edwardian knot.

'Naturally I realize,' said Judge O'Hara, 'that a more complete understanding of vampires really came into being under Slavic influence, but all the same there are enough indications of their existence in the time of Hadrian. The case mentioned by Phlegon of Tralles, for instance.' He peeped expectantly at Detective-Sergeant Demosthenes H. de Goede, who had just put on an old boy's blazer. 'The case of Machates, who slept with the erotic vampire, Philinnion.'

The Detective-Sergeant was busy combing his hair and deepening the waves with the palm of his hand.

'I assume that it is unnecessary to refer to Menippos' bride, who united the arts of Aphrodite with her lust for blood.'

Judge O'Hara laughed heartily with Detective-Sergeant Demosthenes H. de Goede who, exquisitely dressed, was a paragon of youthful virility. There really *was* something attractive about this young man. Dr Johns was right. A pity though that he suffered from a speech defect. Judge O'Hara helpfully pushed the paper and pencil nearer.

'I hope you all had a good night's rest,' wrote Detective-Sergeant Demosthenes H. de Goede.

Judge O'Hara could hardly contain his feeling of amazement.

'Did you not hear? Hope or Prudence was violated last night by a gigantic vampire!'

Now he was pleasantly surprised by the Detective-Sergeant's unexpected reaction, as he wrenched open the door and ran outside in the direction of the blue glass house.

Judge O'Hara first took up his staff from beside the bed and then, slow and content, followed along the path to Hope's and Prudence's glass room.

2

They were welcomed by a melancholy Madam Ritchie. She had just received the condolences of one of the eminent visitors. There was a sombre air in the room and she led them to the room next door where Hope and Prudence, dressed in transparent nightgowns and similarly transparent dressing gowns, sat in soft armchairs – a picture of charming disconsolation. They wilted visibly when Detective-Sergeant Demosthenes H. de Goede entered and stood irresolutely between them.

He stuttered his questions excitedly, meaninglessly to everyone without the interpretation of his Meturgeman. Madam Ritchie was moved by the signs of consternation that she now noticed, for the second time, in the young man. She put her arm around his shoulder and led him to the third armchair. She nodded to her daughters to repeat the story for the umpteenth time. They told it in turn, supplementing one another continually, as they demonstrated the crime with eloquent movements of their bodies. Both Detective-Sergeant Demosthenes H. de Goede and Judge O'Hara were transported by the picture of the young girls illuminating the outrage with such discerning movements.

'That corresponds to the observations of Father R. from Santorini,' Judge O'Hara called out when they reached the end of their tale. 'That is eloquent witness to the fierce nature of the erotic vampire – the most lascivious of all *incubi*.'

'And there's a love bite on her neck,' whispered Madam Ritchie.

Detective-Sergeant Demosthenes H. de Goede stuttered his desire to see it, and thus to simplify for himself the task of distinguishing between the two, but Madam Ritchie put her hand calmingly on his shoulder and gave him a small, soft, affectionate squeeze.

She nodded to her daughters.

'It was a big man,' said Prudence.

'His power was terrible,' said Hope.

'One was powerless in his arms,' said Prudence longingly.

'He was bigger and stronger than an ordinary person,' said Hope carefully.

'Shortly after midnight,' said Judge O'Hara, 'the supernatural appearance and disappearance, the mark on the left side of the throat . . .' He suddenly stood up and pressed his aspen staff to him. 'It agrees perfectly with Slavonic traditions, and is of a characteristic pattern.'

Detective-Sergeant Demosthenes H. de Goede, too, stood up. He stuttered his intention to leave no stone unturned, he looked for the last time at the two pale girls with their plaited hair hanging over their shoulders, their femininity so vulnerably exposed. He repeated his intentions in a cold, measured stutter and left the room, purposeful in this final phase of his mission .

3

They reached the Welgevonden big house and rang the bell continuously until the Malay girl appeared, exposed her ruby smile
and then asked them softly to follow her. She led them through
all the rooms with all their treasures, which impeded their passage, to a small back room, on the door of which she knocked.
That morning she wore a Malay dress, her eyes were kindly and
friendly upon them.

Someone answered. She listened with an ear against the door,
expanded her smile to the second ruby, opened the door and
motioned to them to enter.

A moist heat beat up against Judge O'Hara and Detective-
Sergeant Demosthenes H. de Goede. They could hardly recognize
any objects for the mistiness that filled the room. But they gradually became accustomed to the dense atmosphere and then observed the 'slim' Mrs Silberstein naked in a *Lehmbad*, smeared up
to her eyes with healing *mousse*. A *Badearzt* was busy massaging
her body and was evidently dissatisfied over the compulsory in-
terruption of his manipulations.

Detective-Sergeant Demosthenes H. de Goede stuttered as
clearly as he could a single question: 'Pffffft ... ssssst ... wrrrrrs
... Adm ... Kdm ... Slbrsttttt?' and found, unexpectedly, understanding in the doctor who, with Teutonic thoroughness, described the exact position of the room.

They left the room before the 'slim' Mrs Silberstein could stop
the attractive Sergeant, and followed the instructions until they
reached a room that was locked. Judge O'Hara tapped on the door
with his staff and called the name of Adam Kadmon Silberstein
repeatedly, until Jock Silberstein appeared, unlocked the door and
went ahead of them into an empty room.

'He has gone again,' said Jock in amazement and looked anxiously out of the window.

4

They scoured all the well-known places on Welgevonden in their search. The inhabitants had not seen the Giant. One of the eminent visitors remembered clearly that he had seen the Giant but (thoughtfully with his finger to his temple) that had been the previous day at Mon Repos. Jock Silberstein left them to continue his search alone : he was already used to it; he spent most of his time these days looking for the Giant.

Now that Jock Silberstein was no longer present, the residents and relatives were much more outspoken. Everyone had heard of the second assault, on Hope ... or was it Prudence? Lucky she had not suffered the fate of poor Lila.

'We loved Lila very much,' said one of the residents, on his way to get a thiamine injection. 'We loved Lila very much. We loved Lila very much.'

An eminent visitor declared himself particularly interested in the methods of the Republic's C.I.D. and, with a bow to Judge O'Hara, the judiciary. Another visitor, attached to the press, was actively searching for the Giant, for an interview, and listened attentively to Judge O'Hara's dissertation on the erotic familiar or satyr that leeched onto his or her victim and drained his or her life force. He had his headline ready : VIRGINS OF WELGE-VONDEN VICTIMS OF VOLUPTUOUS FAMILIAR.

Judge O'Hara informed Detective-Sergeant Demosthenes H. de Goede that Azazel, in the form of a corpse-devouring serpent, also exhibited the characteristics of the vampire – according to well-known authorities such as Kornmannus in his *Miraculus Mortuorum* and Paulus Schalichius in his treatise *De Demonio Infernali*. He added, however, that that doctrine was disputed by others, according to information in Carzov's *Disputatio de Gigantibus*. This was the first time Judge O'Hara had been accorded such interested attention and he enjoyed every moment of the search for the 'pallid, blue-eyed, blood-sucking Giant,' as he frequently called Adam Kadmon.

As the day progressed, it was as if the pattern of the search-for-retribution had taken hold of all the residents, relatives and guests as an ordinary acceptable fact about which there was no further discussion. Everyone was, in the meantime, very busy with the preparations for the ceremony that evening, and the rape of Lila-Hope-or-Prudence was a sideshow that added spice to the dish. Lila, the beloved daughter of the earlier pale-faced girl became, as the day passed, an example to everyone of the maiden taunted by the evil figure in his demoniacal mimicry. Hunt-the-Giant became an interlude in the preparations for the important ceremony.

Detective-Sergeant Demosthenes H. de Goede and Judge O'Hara came across the well-beloved Dries and his gambolling little bull on their way to the heifers' camp. Dries did not know where the Giant was, but had no doubt of the Giant's ultimate fate. He was happy as never before. The moment of recompense had arrived, his breeding policy had been worked out, the monster was destroyed – he exulted in the future matriarchy that he would humbly serve.

Everywhere there were tracks of the Giant: they found them at the fountain, the Scene of the Disaster. They found them all over the wet earth. They found them even at the little house with the asbestos roof where the uncle from Welkom and his family had opened the doors and shutters to the sunny day. They encouraged the Detective-Sergeant on his important search and waved to him from doors and windows.

They found Henry Silberstein-van Eeden engrossed with his own particular problem, unaware of what was happening.

They came across Professor Dreyer with a test tube in his hand, sequestered and isolated in his research room.

They found goodwill and encouragement everywhere. There was no one with misgivings; only a few who stood aloof. Detective-Sergeant D. de Goede relentlessly pursued his sole objective: the destruction of the monster, for the moment inaccessible.

5

At the cottage with all the notices, they saw the scrabbling figure of Dr Johns behind the window. Detective-Sergeant Demosthenes H. de Goede took the key from Judge O'Hara and unlocked the door. The two decrepit old friends met and greeted one another in the passage as if nothing had happened. Detective-Sergeant Demosthenes H. de Goede locked them both in and resumed his search.

There are certain times in one's life when one must complete one's task alone and outsiders are simply in the way. Detective-Sergeant Demosthenes H. de Goede's patience was exhausted. He was tired of trying in vain to distinguish between resident, guest and relative. It demanded certain sacrifices: he was without his Meturgeman and without the judge. Perhaps, later, there would be questions from the top, but he was ready to take the responsibility. There are moments which require decisions that only one can take.

He walked rapidly through the Foundation, from side to side. He saw all the preparations for the evening, the throng of helpers who were getting the hall in order, erecting the loudspeakers and putting up outside extensions. This was a search that he knew and was used to. The object had been determined; the time had now come for the object to be located. It was the final phase, the last, unavailing flight. The end was unavertable – he knew the form so well. There were even times in this phase that he pitied the fugitive. But he had learned at the police college that one had to extirpate that pity, roots and all.

6

Comparatively late in the day, around twelve o'clock, Detective-Sergeant Demosthenes H. de Goede found a naked figure with a long beard stretched out happily on the grass having a sunbath.

He arrested him at once and locked him in one of the glass rooms.

Once again he felt that feeling of sympathy, which he so often felt, but a rule was a rule. If one relented in regard to minor infringements, one weakened the principle. The function of pardoning belonged to the judge; the official's job was confined to his duty.

'It's not the persecutor who is without feeling,' he wrote. 'It's the one who lays down the laws. There must be certitude for the protection of the guilty as well as the innocent. Prosecution, punishment and prevention must be clearly distinguished and limited to their relevant departments. The police officer, the judge and sociologist has each his own separate function.'

He picked up a fresh track of the Giant on the wet ground and looked attentively in the direction of the flat-trodden heather.

7

He came across a solitary girl at the fountain and recognized Hope. She wore her hair like a young girl, on either side of her shoulders. There was nobody else around. For a few wordless minutes they looked into each other's eyes and then she fell sobbing into his arms. She melted softly against his body and lifted her face to him. Her lips were moist and warm. She hung on his mouth, then pressed her face against his neck, and her teeth, in the fervent passion of her love, sank into his throat. He extricated himself with difficulty from her arms.

The Task had to be completed first. He stuttered a promise for later in her car. He would complete the Task for her – and for her sister, the unfortunate resident.

He gave a last look back at her and resumed his search, as the day passed and the preparations approached their completion.

8

He wrote: 'Welgevonden is a beautiful place. It's a true Paradise. Who am I, unworthy human being, that I presume to regain Paradise for them and for my loved one?'

He sat with his back to one of the masks and looked lazily in the midday sun at the sun's rays playing on the water. He stroked the place where she bit him and then he stood up languorously and resumed his wandering. The setter, Fido, appeared from behind a bush. Detective-Sergeant Demosthenes H. de Goede turned to stone. He looked around carefully.

The trees swayed in the wind, the lawn was empty and there was no sign of anyone.

9

The sun had set and Detective-Sergeant Demosthenes H. de Goede returned to his room to change for the evening. He shaved, bathed and dressed in a dinner suit. The lights had come on and residents, relatives and guests were already on their way to the hall; the noise they made came from all sides.

But there was still much time. His jacket hung over the chair and he lay stretched out on his bed, his hands folded behind his head, watching the woman from Sweden who was putting on the most beautiful lace underclothing and standing before the mirror doing her makeup, before getting into a golden evening dress.

He longed suddenly for Hope and then he began to dream of a little house in one of the suburbs. It was the night of the Police Ball, in aid of the Orphans' Fund. She, too, would make herself beautiful for him before a mirror: the attractive wife of Lieutenant Demosthenes H. de Goede.

He smiled all of a sudden and wrote, lying on his back: 'It's not dreams that estrange one from reality; it's reality that estranges one from one's dreams.'

Then he stood up. The time had come. First he took his weapon from the little trunk, turned it rapidly around his forefinger and placed it carefully in the holster strapped around his shoulder. Then he put on his jacket leisurely and stuck the *ephialtion* in his buttonhole.

The lights in the Swedish woman's glass house had gone out some time before, and she stood there, wide-eyed, in the dark watching him arming himself. Then he, too, switched out the

light and walked slowly past the house, in which she hid herself
in terror, towards the hall, to be in time for the ceremony.

10

The hall was crammed. The lights shone through the windows
and the glass doors onto the grass, and still the people came. On
the platform was a row of chairs on which the dignitaries would
sit and, slightly to one side, the chairs for the rector and for those
who would receive the honorary degrees. There were gladioli
in a vase on a little table and there were portraits of the Founders
on the walls. This was the hall in which the residents and their
families gathered every morning, for prayers and to receive their
instructions for the day. The front half was filled with residents
and their relatives, who turned around continually to stare at
the guests who occupied the back seats. Whenever one of the
dignitaries entered the hall and was led by a guide to the platform, a ripple of talk passed through the crowd and the identity
of the new arrival was excitedly discussed.

The other residents, relatives and guests, who could not find
seats inside, sat outside on the grass or stood around in groups.
It was a lovely evening: not too cold, not too hot, and the masks
droned monotonously in the distance.

At a certain time a small group of inhabitants mounted the
platform in single file and produced a violin, a saw and an accordion. They started off at once with 'Bootjie na Kammaland' and
followed that with 'Siembamba, Mamma se Kindjie.'

There was great applause when Jock Silberstein and 'slim'
Mrs Silberstein appeared and took their places on the platform.
The cheering was repeated when Henry Silberstein-van Eeden
followed soon afterwards. One chair still remained empty and
they all kept their eyes on that. The well-beloved Dries appeared
on the platform, a mourning band around his arm, and the audience rose to their feet as one man. They all sat down again with
a shuffling of chairs when Dries made a slight bow and took
his place on the empty chair. Then they renewed their cheering
when the rector of a well-known university appeared, followed

by other high dignitaries, and took up the remaining chairs. Here and there someone offered a chair to a lady, and one or two extra were passed from the back of the hall and placed on the platform.

The orchestra, composed of residents, ended the song with '... chuck him in the ditch, stamp on his head and he'll be dead', and left the platform in file, grinning broadly at the other residents, who whistled, stamped on the floor and bawled for an encore. A guide prevented the orchestra from returning to the platform.

Detective-Sergeant Demosthenes H. de Goede had just arrived and peeped into the hall. Then he disappeared unnoticed among the people on the grass and reconnoitred the surroundings.

The master of ceremonies, in a dinner jacket, had just begun speaking, welcoming the rector and introducing certain of the best-known dignitaries to the audience. An unpretentious little programme by residents and relatives would be completed before the actual performance started. Small locusts in black stockings streamed onto the platform, joined in a solid black mass and, their eyes fixed on landscapes by weekend painters on the walls, filled the hall with the ominous sounds of a children's voice choir: loudspeakers carried the sounds outside where the swelling crowd listened in dead silence to the disembodied little voices. The little white faces of the locusts whispered a last speculation on death and then the ranks disintegrated, to thunderous cheers, especially from their relatives.

The change was quick and testified to strict discipline. The heavy piano was swiftly moved by a crowd of tots and the next moment, the voices, with accompaniment, echoed through the hall to the outside, where the multitude sat back to back looking at the far horizon where a red glow from Mon Repos lit the landscape beautifully.

Occasionally someone sang a solo; occasionally there was a duet. Then the residents' orchestra was recalled for the finale: the lugubrious saw, the free-ranging violin, the ululating accordion, as the choir finally repeated: 'Siembamba, mama's pet, chuck him in the ditch; stamp on his head and he'll be d-e-a-d!'

11

And still they came, singly and in pairs, to find a place on the grass. Also a giant figure who had seen the lights from afar and heard the songs and who smiled like a child at the familiar tune.

He came soundlessly nearer through the trees and suddenly stopped at a small building. It was the place where the day before he had heard the drone and seen the mist. There was nobody around and he entered the little room. When he switched on the light he saw the coiled pipes against the wall and the two big taps. He opened both taps simultaneously and listened attentively to the increasing sound, as the steam enveloped him. The roaring grew louder, the light grew dim and he was alone in a white world. His mouth opened and shut and he was aware of himself screaming something in the ghostly mist. But he understood nothing. His mind groped in vain for the words that he could not hear. Something inside him was absolutely still, soundless. In the room of confession he had found words but, alas, no thoughts. It was only the sound that thundered on endlessly around him, and he accepted the sounds as he accepted all the sounds all around him every day. He felt wet and clammy and was invaded by lassitude. He leaned against the wall and felt the taps against his back. He felt for them and turned them off. Suddenly the noise stopped, and the mist dispersed gradually. He repeated the game until he was bored and then he left the little room – drawn like a moth to the lights and the other noise in the distance.

12

The master of ceremonies had just introduced a well-known professor, who would read Jock Silberstein's *curriculum vitae*.

He spoke of the achievements of that dynamic man, who had first made his mark in the farming-industrial sphere when, in the twilight of his life, he had used his material wealth to bring clarity into the shadowed lives of the multitude. In a community in which the formula had replaced the myth, he was perhaps in the process of transforming formula to myth. In this Foundation of his he was, for inhabitant and member of the family, clothing the commonplace in the raiment of fabulous significance. Perhaps his methods were unconventional; perhaps it was in conflict with present-day *procédé*, but in his attempt to restore continuity he brought, in his own manner, light into the darkness of troubled minds that needed light so much.

The speaker peered over the uplifted faces in the direction of the darkness outside.

Perhaps it had been granted him to restore the interlude on a plane where experience would replace decadent repetition; where the symbol would replace the sign; where logic would find coexistence in the boldest flight of the imagination . . .

As he spoke, Jock Silberstein looked, too, at the darkness outside. But his attention was far removed from the speaker. He had looked in vain among the faces in the hall and was searching now – where he could distinguish moving figures in the light on the grass – for a single, giant figure outside.

The Giant had appeared at the edge of the light. He heard the voice from the loudspeaker, he looked at the gathering and he was filled with an irresistible desire to join them, too. He tugged nervously at the scarlet ribbon around his neck and walked carefully nearer.

Jock Silberstein had just received cap and gown. He bowed to the guests as a Doctor, *honoris causa*, and he smiled acknowledgement of the thunderous applause with the aloof reserve of someone who has long since escaped from the clutches of self-assertion.

The master of ceremonies waited for him to take his seat next to the beaming Mrs Silberstein, and then he raised his hand for silence. Another eminent official of the university was called upon to read the *curriculum vitae* of Henry Silberstein-van Eeden. Soon after he started speaking the Giant appeared in the full light of the lawn.

The people in the hall, intent on the words of the speaker, were unaware of what was happening outside. They did not hear the stifled cries of the women, they did not see the men who, prompted by their strength in numbers, took up a threatening position. As the Giant, protected by that insensitivity born of his retarded mentality, reached the middle of the lawn, the crowd formed into a strong, growing circle around him. The gathering became as strong as the Giant himself; it became, as a mass, the equal of the Giant – a source of power that would measure power against power. The single rational cohesion disappeared; the single fear became the fear of everyone: reason disappeared in the throng; a primeval urge appeared to combat a primordial phenomenon. The huge figure carried the banner of evil, the scarlet ribbon of demoniacal powers; the dense throng carried the white banner of the crushed virgin. The troubled complexity of their lives was reduced to a simple truth. All the unintelligible conflicts within them suddenly assumed the appearance of understandable simplicity. By means of the alchemy of their mass thought-process the whore became a virgin and the nymphomaniac a threatened nymph. In their collective simplicity they knew only a dichotomy. The whole complexity of life became understandable through their mass action. They were filled with a sense of wonderful freedom, faced with the joy of an easy choice. The first stone that sailed through the air for the sake of Lila freed them from the bondage inherent in themselves. Every stone and every fling was a further step to liberation: the atavism that characterized the act was a progression that stimulated reason. Egged on by the promise, stupefied by their fury, they threw one stone after another at the easy target.

At first the Giant, thinking it a game, threw the stones back. One struck a woman on the mouth and she collapsed, blood flowing, which, appearing black in the electric light, left the impression of lungs crushed. The crowd droned nearer and threw the stones like hunters: the act was released from its greater meaning and brought down to a basis of maximum effectiveness. Many young men doubled themselves up to give a whiplash to their throws and to get, for the sake of the admiration of many young women, the stone into the target bull. It became a carnival

– with the masks roaring and under the coloured glare from Mon Repos. It was a Coney Island of the spirit – while the lecture continued over the loudspeaker. There were screams, there were lights and noise, there was a challenge of pretty eyes and the promise of reward for success. Even an eminent guest, from a lesser country, conscious of the ability of his forefathers and homesick for his native land, threw a stone at the target and struck the bull, to the loud applause of a female guest, relatives and residents.

And there, still, was the Giant, with no apprehension of the nature of events. The stones hurt him, but he was strong and his threshold of pain was high. There was on his face a smile of pure joy, he bared his sharp teeth as a wonderful feeling over-powered him : it was the first time he had been accepted by everyone, that they had wanted to play with him. Sometimes his smile changed to a grimace of pain when a stone struck him squarely on the body or the head, but then his face beamed again with pleasure. He was unaware of the blood that began flowing from his temples, and of the swollen bruises that began to form where the tissue was injured. He was unaware that with every injury, his appearance grew uglier and more grotesque. He returned stone for stone in this strange and interesting game.

When, here and there, a stone hit someone – even when the throwers missed the Giant and struck one another – it was as if the crowd's fury mounted to a new level. The uglier the Giant grew under systematic injury, the more passionate the crowd became. They had now reached the stage at which they had developed beyond their feelings of self-justification and beyond their hunter's instinct. When a chance stone struck a young girl, an extraordinary quavering sound rose from the mob. They approached murderously, but they did not yet dare to lay a hand on the Giant.

While all this was happening outside, the voice of the speaker came clear and strong over the microphone. The voice spoke of the zeal with which Henry Silberstein-van Eeden served the Foundation. He described the work done there. He dealt with the concept of moral responsibility and he warned against the confusion in our use of ethical concepts, the illogical use of words that did not distinguish between the attribution of blame and a qualitative judgement of a situation. On a place like the Foundation, where the basis of moral responsibility was restricted to the minimum, one came nearer to a tragic situation. And it was on this terrain that someone like Henry Silberstein-van Eeden performed his difficult work.

He too, like the previous speaker, looked to the darkness behind the lights outside, completely unaware, like everyone in the hall, of what was happening there. He described the unbearable feeling of disintegration without the possibility of casting blame; the fear in the wake of destruction by an object of destiny which is beyond one's reach. And perhaps it was Henry's task, in this work he was doing, to make clearer the meaning of the scapegoat; to enable everyone, indeed all the inhabitants of this weary planet, to conquer in the shrinking world of individual responsibility his solitude and defencelessness by means of an exalted accusation.

As he spoke, Henry looked outside. He, too, saw nothing, but deep within him he had a feeling that somewhere something infinitely important was happening. It was difficult to describe because it was a concept that he could not formulate. It was as if he were finding a sort of reconciliation with the Foundation and as if Salome were living again for him. There were tears in his eyes while the sacrifice outside was taking place – without his knowledge, but in an extraordinary way his own responsibility.

While cap and gown were being donned and the crowd cheered deafeningly, Detective-Sergeant Demosthenes H. de Goede appeared on the scene and prepared himself to defend the threatened people. The Giant had only now begun to detect the animosity of the crowd and he staggered around, stunned, as the stones, hitting him where they had struck before, really hurt him. He was no longer a big child joining in the game, but a lost child overwhelmed by an incomprehensible anxiety. And, like a child, he began crying softly. The tears rolled down his cheeks and he grimaced crookedly with grief. His hands were raised and he struggled around helplessly, moaning with that lowing sound peculiar to the mentally retarded. When one of the men dared to approach close to him and hit him on the head with a stick, he brushed him to the ground, unconscious, with a single movement of his hand.

Detective-Sergeant Demosthenes H. de Goede's duty was plain. He jumped forward athletically and chopped a karate blow on his neck, jerking his head up and making him grunt with pain. Then Detective-Sergeant Demosthenes H. de Goede leaped back, out of reach of the flailing arms.

The Giant now wept aloud like a wounded child, but the multitude heard it as a roar of fury. The soft figures of Hope and Prudence (their hair combed out over their shoulders) pressed for protection against Detective-Sergeant Demosthenes H. de Goede.

Taking advantage of the Giant's bewildered condition, someone gashed him with a stone over the eye. The Giant spun around and searched, half-blindly, with grasping hands, for his attacker. Detective-Sergeant Demosthenes H. de Goede was like lightning and struck him with a perfect bolo-hit in the other eye. He danced lightly away to where Hope and Prudence were waiting for him.

The Giant was now completely blinded by the blood in his eyes. The blood mingled with the tears, and dribbled on the corners of his mouth. He was sobbing so hard that he could scarcely breathe; he was so confused that he could not escape. The mob came carefully nearer. It was not so easy to finish off a Giant: it demanded time and determination. A courageous woman struck him on the body with a stick, but was hit by one of his arms. She rolled across the grass in a flowered line. Detective-Sergeant Demosthenes H. de Goede was, however, at hand, and delivered a swift and perfect ostrich kick straight to the Giant's stomach. He followed that up with a full nelson, but had to get out of the way quickly as even his muscular arms were wrenched loose. Two of the little darts the Giant had found at Mon Repos fell from his pocket, as well as a few marbles and a catapult. The crowd growled when it saw them. Someone jumped forward and picked up the two darts. He threw quickly. One missed and one struck the Giant near an eye. The Giant raised a hand to his face, withdrew the arrow and flung it away with a clumsy gesture. Detective-Sergeant Demosthenes H. de Goede deflected it with his arm, retrieved it and threw it skilfully back. The crowd cheered when it struck the Giant near his other eye.

And then, as if the possibility of flight had dawned on him, the Giant began to move slowly towards the darkness. Detective-Sergeant Demosthenes H. de Goede was quick to bar his way. He stood directly in the Giant's path, one foot forward, Hope's shawl in both hands. He waited until the stumbling Giant was upon him, and then executed a perfect veronica. As the Giant staggered past him, he punched him neatly behind the ear, giving the Giant momentum and making him fall over his feet.

Detective-Sergeant Demosthenes H. de Goede was dead calm. He stood waiting elegantly, a neat figure in his dress shirt and dinner jacket. With a suspicion of vanity, perhaps, he raised a hand to his lapel, bent it around and smelled the *ephialtion*. The crowd had fallen silent and was looking at the Giant lying on the ground. The sobs had abated, the big face was swollen, the red hair damp, tousled and caked. And then the big figure began to rise, grunting and groaning as if even those enormous, clumsy legs could no longer carry the body. The Giant's hands hung at his sides, his neck was crooked, his back bent. He had stopped crying. He turned his back slowly and painfully on the people and began, slowly at first and then more quickly, to stumble away towards the waters roaring in the dark.

Detective-Sergeant Demosthenes H. de Goede took his Beretta .35 slowly from its holster, while the crowd grew quite quiet again. In a loud voice he ordered Adam Kadmon Silberstein three times to stop and then he aimed with his right arm out straight and his left hand on his hip. He aimed low deliberately, to conform to police regulations, and then fired. The report was dulled by the renewed cheering as the well-beloved Dries rose to his

feet to expound the life, struggle and death of Uncle Giepie.
Everyone saw the Giant stumble for a moment, stop and then
disappear into the dark with a dragging foot.

It was all over. He would not get far. Detective-Sergeant Demosthenes H. de Goede replaced the weapon carefully and received
embraces from Hope and Prudence with calm self-control. He
was surrounded by the crowd and lifted on their shoulders, but
he remained a model of modesty. He gazed thoughtfully at the
jubilant residents, relatives and guests. It was as if a song of
praise were arising. He thought of the words of Dr Johns. Order
had been restored.

After everyone had calmed down and left him free to complete his task, he looked at Hope and Prudence, who were laughing with complete abandon, and then confirmed his choice. He
took the *ephialtion* from his buttonhole and offered it to Hope,
who blushed charmingly and received the pledge shyly from her
lover. The task was accomplished; the drama ended. In the distance, against the horizon, the fires of the Mon Repos churches
burned a fiery red. And he walked slowly towards the glow to
complete his assignment.

Quando?

Quando?

1

In the penumbra between the lights of the hall and the lights of Mon Repos the monster struggled with his shattered leg. He reached the first mask that roared, and clung to it with his mighty arms. In the twilight world of his thoughts there was no light. He was filled with an irresistible longing for the one he loved, but he did not know where to find him. From force of habit he lowered himself into the stream, but nothing warned him that his powers were exhausted. Even when the stream tore him away from the mask and the waters roared in his face, he was not aware of what was happening to him. As he floundered in vain and disappeared under the stream, he was still fighting against things he did not understand.

Deafening cheers came from the lighted hall and the Giant began his last journey upon the noisy stream. The crowd had risen to sing the song of the Foundation at the pitch of their voices, and the second mask spat the heavy object from its raging maw. The proceedings were concluded with three loud hurrahs for the alumni and the third mask rattled and struggled to rid itself of the object in its throat. The residents, relatives and eminent guests were amiably on their way to their glass houses when the fourth mask vomited the monster. The lights were already out when the so-manyeth mask fell dumb and then resumed all of a sudden its threnody. Only the isolated flashes from the searching detective shone like a lost firefly in the surroundings, as one mask after another wrestled with the object that grew larger and larger. The wind had already blown the plastic swan across the grass, laying as track a swollen counterpart. The Giant of Welgevonden was slowly but surely on his way to his final appointment, with a setter in a lily pond.

2

It was midnight and the moon shone over the Foundation. But many were not asleep. The windows were open and Dr Johns, Judge O'Hara, Jock Silberstein, Henry Silberstein-van Eeden and many guests and residents lay looking at the phosphorescent orb among the tattered clouds. The light shone down and was reflected from their faces: it brightened the countenance of a living-dead, the white incisors grinning in caves and towers. Hope and Prudence rolled around restlessly in their beds. The wind keened through the trees. But the monster was satisfied. There was peace at Welgevonden. The monster lay on his back, swollen and satisfied with live-giving blood, his eyes fixed blindly on the moon.

3

The cellar thundered under the destructive assault to drive out the evil spirits; the noise repeated the masks' cry of fear; it tried in vain to extirpate the question in the heart of the Founder; it was as meaningless as the stuttering sounds from the hero at the door. The Giant of Welgevonden lay on a table in the cellar with his hands folded to form the unmentionable Name of God. The scarlet ribbon around his neck had been washed pure white by the waters.

And then, when the first light of the rising sun shone on the windows, the noise suddenly ceased, and in the silence that followed a song rose in the morning air: the 'Adon 'Olam' in praise of God as the eternal Ruler of the incomprehensible Universe.

It was a song of praise, incomparably beautiful, for the dead, the goat of God and the goat of the wilderness.